SILVER SCREAM

SILVER SCREAM

Edited by David J. Schow
Introduction by Tobe Hooper

Stories by

John M. Ford
F. Paul Wilson
Robert Bloch
Ray Garton
Clive Barker
Steven R. Boyett
Joe R. Lansdale
Karl Edward Wagner
Craig Spector

Robert R. McCammon
Jay Sheckley
Chet Williamson
Richard Christian Matheson
Mick Garris
Douglas E. Winter
John Skipp
Edward Bryant
Ramsey Campbell
Mark Arnold

Illustrated by Kevin Davies

DARK HARVEST
Arlington Hts., Illinois ·1988

Limited Edition: ISBN-0-913165-28-X
Trade Edition: ISBN-0-913165-27-1

Manufactured in the United States of America
FIRST EDITION
Dark Harvest / P.O. Box 941 / Arlington Heights, IL / 60006

TABLE OF CONTENTS

The Publishers would like to express their gratitude to the following people. Thank you: Dawn Austin, Kathy Jo Camacho, Tony Camacho, Stanley Mikol, Phyllis Mikol, Wayne Sommers, Dr. Stan Gurnick PhD, Tony Hodes, Bertha Curl, Kurt Scharrer, Ken Morris, Luis Trevino, Raymond, Teresa and Mark Stadalsky, Tom Pas, and Ann Cameron Williams.

INTRODUCTION

Starring Tobe Hooper

FADE IN: HOLLYWOOD MANSION - NIGHT

The home of a famous HORROR FILM DIRECTOR. It is the infamous
"dark and stormy night." CAMERA TRACKS ominously up to the
PARLOR WINDOW.

DISSOLVE THRU TO: THE HORROR FILM DIRECTOR

Bearded, bemused, composed, devilish, seated in a wingback chair.
He's been waiting for us. Impish humor dances in his eyes like
firelight. His name is TOBE.

                    TOBE
        I am often asked, what scares me?

He looks around as CAMERA PUSHES IN to MEDIUM CLOSE SHOT as he
CONFIDES in the audience.

                    TOBE
        I can quite frankly respond that in this
        particular instance, being sandwiched
        between the covers of this book, in the
        company of these writers, scares me.

CUT TO: GRAINY BLACK-AND-WHITE FLASHBACK FOOTAGE

    Tobe Hooper was very nearly born in a movie theatre. His
parents owned a number of hotels throughout Texas, and on the
day of his birth his mother was in attendance at a theatre next
door to one of the hotels, in Austin, when she determined it was
time to report to the delivery room. Thus it can be said that
the cinema's influence on Hooper was pre-natal, and the theatre
frequently functioned as his babysitter during his early youth.
He later realized his eye had become trained, "as though I was
seeing the world through a viewfinder." He never really allowed
for any other career choice after that. Upon graduation from
the University of Texas film school he directed documentaries,
short films and commercials, amassing many awards from film
festivals in Australia, France, San Francisco, Atlanta and New

York. He completed an independent feature, EGGSHELLS (An American
Freak Illumination), followed by his first assault on the world of
commercial film: THE TEXAS CHAINSAW MASSACRE, which critic Rex Reed
deemed "the most horrifying film I have ever seen" ... and which
became the highest-grossing independent film ever made.

RESUME TOBE

                              TOBE
                        (steepling fingers)

> The sheer force and intensity of the written
> word has always had the unique feature of
> stimulating the reader to image their own
> visions of an author's intended reality --
> a "mind's eye movie," if you will. Horror
> and fantasy stories have the additional
> quality of stimulating images that are
> surreal.

LIGHTNING STRIKES visibly through the window. CAMERA begins to
TRACK AROUND TOBE'S POSITION, relentlessly MOVING, constantly
changing the ANGLE and thus, our PERSPECTIVE on Tobe.

                              TOBE
                         (continuing)

> The commonality of the tales in SILVER
> SCREAM is that they all touch, in some
> way, on an aspect of that specific
> nether-world of moving light and shadow:
> cinema.

RESUME FLASHBACK simultaneously with the next LIGHTNING STRIKE.

Originally titled LEATHERFACE by Hooper, THE TEXAS CHAINSAW
MASSACRE was derived from the exploits of Plainfield, Wisconsin
mass killer Ed Gein, and set a new standard of intensity for all
horror films to follow. For more than a dozen years, Gein kept
busy with the pursuits of multiple murder, grave robbing, dismem-
berment, fratricide and cannibalism, while living in a town of less
than 700 people. He stored severed heads in his fridge and mounted
skulls on his bedposts. A heart was found simmering in a pot on his
stove, its waiting bowl a skullcap. He stitched together a belt of
human nipples and a lampshade from flesh. He executed rituals intended to raise his mother from the dead, while wearing the faces,
hair and hides of his victims. Hooper broadened Gein's

psychopathy to encompass an entire homicidal family: the Hitchiker, Grandfather, the Old Man and that chainsaw-wielding superstar, Leatherface. Hooper's visual approach to such exploitational material was astonishing. His artful use of lighting, complex tracking shots, constantly varying camera angles and subtle use of color not only amplified the film's sheer visceral impact, but also established Hooper's wide-ranging cinematic vocabulary.

RESUME TOBE

An unflinching FULL SHOT. It's him and us.

> TOBE
>
> Just as frequently, I'm asked what movies scare me. Many films have influenced me in profound or elemental ways.
> (pause)
> A PLACE IN THE SUN, for instance.
> (snaps fingers)

ON FINGER-SNAP, COMMENCE FULL-FRAME EXCERPTS

As though we are staring dead ahead into a movie screen filled with one film clip after another. Tobe's VOICE continues OVER as Raymond Burr, playing a D.A., declaims like a tent revivalist.

> TOBE (V.O.)
>
> It had a marked effect on me as a child: That dark windup to a guy who's not really guilty -- except in his heart -- as he goes to the electric chair. I then found that dreams of being executed were pretty common for second graders, once we discovered the idea of capital punishment.

CLIP B: Elizabeth Taylor in all her southern belle beauty.

> TOBE (V.O.)
>
> When I saw RAINTREE COUNTY, for some reason at that moment I decided I wanted to make films for a living. I think it might have been the first film I ever saw in 70-millimeter, with a stereo magnetic sound track.
> (beat)
> Or NIGHT OF THE HUNTER. When you look at it now, it doesn't seem made that well ... but when I saw it, I was the same age as Pearl and her brother, and there are a few shots in that movie I'll never forget.

CLIP C: EXTREME CLOSEUP of the words <u>love</u> and <u>hate</u> on Robert Mitchum's knuckles.

> TOBE (V.O.)
>
> Hammer monster movies caused me to pull out an 8mm movie camera for the first time -- THE CURSE OF FRANKENSTEIN and HORROR OF DRACULA.

CLIPS D & E: Christopher Lee drops violently into the acid bath ... then rots to dust in a spray of sunlight.

> TOBE (V.O.)
>
> I promptly shot my own Frankenstein film, and my own Dracula film.
> (beat)
> I think the first film that really <u>scared</u> me was Howard Hawks' THE THING

CLIP F: James Arness bursts into flames, howling.

> TOBE (V.O.)
>
> VERTIGO I could watch over and over; its <u>mood</u> really got to me. It was ...

CLIP G: Jimmy Stewart suffers a blast of acrophobia.

> TOBE (V.O.)
>
> ... a <u>tonal</u> thing, a <u>cloak</u> that Hitchcock draped over me. PSYCHO is probably my favorite.

As Janet Leigh eats the bread knife of doom (CLIP H), we SHOCK CUT back to the FLASHBACK FOOTAGE:

"CHAINSAW was not really based on PSYCHO," Hooper asserts. "All I knew about Ed Gein was from relatives who lived twenty miles from Plainfield, who used to spook me with stories about Gein's house." Robert Bloch had based his novel, Psycho, on other aspects of the Gein case. "Later," said Hooper, "our family doctor told me that when he was a pre-med student, he once skinned a cadaver's face and wore it as a mask to a Hallowe'en party of med school guys. That's where Leatherface came from; we weren't consciously 'doing' Gein and had done no Gein research. In fact, we found out most of the real information after CHAINSAW was finished."

RESUME FILMCLIP MONTAGE

Picking up speed like a jet on a runway. GRADUALLY DISSOLVE
THRU to Tobe speaking so he appears BEYOND the images, ghostly
at first, then attaining solidity. At the close of the FINAL
CLIP, we have returned to the original MEDIUM SHOT.

> TOBE
>
> I'm quite fond of FREAKS, THE MANCHURIAN
> CANDIDATE and SECONDS, by Frankenheimer,
> PORTRAIT OF JENNIE, THE HAUNTING, and the
> original INVASION OF THE BODY SNATCHERS.
> CURSE OF THE DEMON just stuck in my head.
> And THE EXORCIST. Friedkin, of course.

(MONTAGE: The armless/legless man squirms through the rain with
a knife in his teeth; Frank Sinatra sees blood and brains splatter
a photo of Stalin in a nightmare fugue; Rock Hudson, screaming, is
dragged off to be recycled; Joseph Cotten watches Jennifer Jones
age before his eyes; Julie Harris gets stranded on the spiral
iron staircase; Kevin McCarthy and Dana Wynter hide from the
Pod People in a Bronson Caverns "mineshaft;" and a skyscraper-
tall gargoyle makes short work of demonologist Niall MacGinnis.
Then Linda Blair lets fly with a pea soup attack.)

Just as Tobe comes into FULL FOCUS we CUT SHARP to the FLASHBACK
FOOTAGE. It should be startling.

> Hooper completed editing on CHAINSAW just prior to seeing
> THE EXORCIST for the first time. As the first step in his future
> association with William Friedkin, he arranged with Todd-AO to
> utilize some of the sound effects tracks in CHAINSAW. The sound
> of Regan's bedsprings, for example, is also the sound of the
> chicken cage that attracts the attention of the Terry character
> in CHAINSAW ... right before she bites the big one.

RESUME TOBE - NEW ANGLE

He hefts the book in his lap and thumbs through the pages.

> TOBE
>
> SILVER SCREAM presents an equally varied
> array of cinema horrors. What is unique
> to this anthology is a sort of tail-chasing-
> the-dog effect. It is with a cinematic
> consciousness that these authors spin their
> stories; in turn, each tale becomes a
> catalyst for the reader to project the

           images that interpret the story's concepts
           onto their own "mind's eye screen."

The rain outside is coming down HARD now, and it is clear that
Tobe is alone inside the house.

WRACK FOCUS to reveal a TV SET as it POPS ON BY ITSELF. The
static melts through to a music video in mid-play. It is
Billy Idol's "Dancing With Myself." Visible around the singer
are props from FUNHOUSE and POLTERGEIST. There is NO SOUND.

TRUCK BACK to settle on an EXTREME CLOSEUP of Tobe. His
attention is still focused TOWARD FRAME, toward us. He is
used to TVs coming on by themselves.

                         TOBE

           A wide range of that cinematic mindset and
           imagery is represented here.
                (indicates BOOK, he begins
                flipping the pages, scanning)
           There are the harsh realities of film-as-
           business, as observed by Mick Garris in
           "A Life in the Cinema" -- a tale that moves
           from sardonic wit to an absolutely bizarre
           conclusion infused with deranged eroticism.
                (flip)
           And "Son of Celluloid," featuring Clive
           Barker's film-gobbling cancer mutating itself
           into John Wayne.
                (grins, flips again)
           Here we have the perverse indoctrination of
           a young boy into becoming a kind of film
           "director," in Ray Garton's "Sinema."

The BOOK seems to cast a faint PHOSPHORESCENCE. We can SEE the
turning pages, reflected in Tobe's glasses.

                         TOBE

           Could sexual fantasies actualize themselves?
           Richard Christian Matheson asks, "what if?"
                (flip)
           Or an exotic blend of movie serial fantasy,
           adventure and suspense -- in actual serial
           chapters -- found in Robert R. McCammon's
           "Night Calls the Green Falcon."

CAMERA PUSHES IN TIGHT on the TV during the above dialogue.
Now the TV screen FILLS THE FRAME. The video is interrupted
by a FAST MONTAGE in BLACK-AND-WHITE, emulating the style of
the flashbacks:

The man who began with an anti-war Vietnam film and, for PBS, a film protesting the destruction of architechtural landmarks and a documentary on Peter, Paul & Mary, now continued to mine the mother lode of fright with all of his subsequent films: EATEN ALIVE, the 4-hour TV miniseries SALEM'S LOT, FUNHOUSE, the blockbuster hit POLTERGEIST, LIFEFORCE (based on the Colin Wilson book Space Vampires), the big-budget remake of the cult classic INVADERS FROM MARS, and then the nerve-shattering sequel to THE TEXAS CHAINSAW MASSACRE. Even as you read, Tobe Hooper is out there ... somewhere ... making movies, fabricating fresh terrors. And it's too late for you to escape.

RESUME TOBE

He rises from his chair, in his host mode. The TV is blank, black. The rain continues its chainsaw razzing against the windowpanes.

                         TOBE
          I invite you to draw open the curtain on
          your own mind's eye screen, let the house
          lights dim, and allow the shadow plays to
          form.

We DIM DOWN as per above until only Tobe's face is visible within a dwindling circle of candleflame light.

                         TOBE
          Um ... 70-millimeter Super Panavision and
          THX Dolby stereo sound optional, of course.

                                        FADE TO BLACK

                                        CUT SHARP TO:

PREFLASH

by

John M. Ford

Exterior, hospital, day. Fischetti pushes Griffin's wheelchair out the door and to the street. Pietra Malaryk is at the curb, leaning against her Chevy wagon, a brand new Arriflex under her arm. Malaryk smiles as Griffin looks up; she hands him the camera. "Welcome back, A.D.," she says.

Griffin checks the Arri. It is a double to the one he lost in the accident. There is a 400-foot magazine of Ektachrome Commercial already loaded; the battery belt is in Malaryk's hand.

Griffin stands up, aware that Fish and Malaryk are both waiting for him to fall down again. He doesn't. He says goodbye to Fischetti, and Fish nods and wheels the chair back.

Griffin shoulders the camera. The balance is strange: it has been eight months since he has had a camera on his shoulder, since the accident. That is a long time not to be whole.

His vision is still blurry, with flashes of phosphene light, but he frames Fischetti pushing the chair, small against the face of stone and little windows, and he presses the trigger.

"How is it, A.D.?" Malaryk asks. Malaryk is as good a cameraman as Griffin ever was and will know that he is lying when he says it's perfect, but that's what he says anyway.

They get into Malaryk's car. Grifin shoots through the window until the magazine is gone. People on the street see the lens, and smile, and wave, and make obscene gestures. The sun makes darting afterimages in Griffin's eyes.

It was explained to Griffin that his skull has splintered internally, spalled like concrete, and the bone chips in his brain cannot be removed without either killing him or turning him into a vegetable, probably a cabbage. Griffin,

15

not wanting to be either dead or dead-and-breathing, therefore agreed to sign the malpractice waiver. They did not operate, he would not sue. There is no one to collect the money anyway.

As they drive through the sunlight, a good place for cabbages, Griffin puts the Arri down and turns to look at Malaryk. She is wearing the standard issue bush jacket with pockets full of photo goodies, over a deep-cut cotton blouse.

That is what she is wearing down the right side of Griffin's vision. Down the left she appears in grainy black and white, lying on a bed, wearing a bathrobe over underwear. There are dark stains on her skin and clothing, and something blurred. Griffin thinks that if he were editing this film he would slow it down for a better look, and it slows down. The blurred object is a crowbar. A man dark against vertical strips of light is swinging it. There is a barely discernible line between the color frame and the monochrome, that wobbles when Griffin tries to focus on it.

Griffin puts a hand to his temple. There is brilliant light like a lens flare, and then the black-and-white film is gone.

"Are you okay, A.D.?" Malaryk says.

He demounts the Arri magazine and labels it, so she will know he's all right.

"So what'cha going to do?" Malaryk says. "Been awful quiet in the pool without you and Carrick."

"Got some offers to do music videos."

"Music videos. You?"

"I can't go into the bush anymore, Pia. Who'd buy me a ticket?"

"Music vidiocy. You. The whole thing's dying."

"Everything dies," Griffin says.

When Griffin was nineteen years old and independently wealthy, he was sitting in a Miami bar chain-smoking Russian cigarettes. The TV was showing a half-hour news special on the Salvador war. Nobody was watching it.

A guy came into the bar. He looked like a street bum: dust all over army-surplus clothes, week's beard. There was a still camera around his neck: as he pushed up to the bar, Griffin saw it was a Leica. Thousand-buck camera with a thousand-buck lens around this bum's dirty neck. Griffin had only paid eight hundred cash for the suit he was wearing.

The guy with the camera ordered a Black Bush with water on the side. He looked at Griffin. "So what do you do, kid?"

Just like that.

"Oh, a buncha shit," Griffin said. "This is one of the things I do." He lit a fresh cigarette with a five-dollar bill. "So what do you do, man?"

PREFLASH

The grubby guy pointed at the television set. The camera was bouncing through the jungle, following a squad of soldiers. One of the grunts got hit, went down. The camera spun, paused over him — just a glance at the soldier, but enough to tell you he was dead.

No. More. Enough to be a little ceremony, an amen over his death.

Griffin felt a pain in his hand. The cigarette had dropped from his lips and burned him. He looked around, saw that everybody in the bar was staring at the TV.

"Shot that two days ago," the guy said. "Film beat me here."

This guy had done that with fifteen seconds of film? On a fucking television set?

'My name's Carrick," he said. "If you're Griffin, somebody told me you were good."

"I — yeah," Griffin said. "Yeah, I'm good."

"Fair enough. How'd you like to be good at something?"

Griffin was in the hospital four weeks before he was conscious. For another four after that he couldn't move, couldn't feed himself, couldn't do any of the stuff that adults are supposed to do for themselves. He could think, naturally. And he could talk. He could scream, too, but no one listened to that so he didn't do it for very long.

"So how come you guys go down to wars and get shot at?" Fischetti said, easing a bite of mashed potatoes into Griffin's mouth. "I mean, it ain't like somebody was givin' you orders."

Griffin chewed and swallowed as if he were thinking hard, which he wasn't. He said "It is, though, at least at first. You start out by following somebody."

"A.D., this is Suzy Lodi."

Griffin is being introduced to a tall, thin woman in a straight-mesh dress. He braces himself for the sight of her death, as he has learned to do since leaving the hospital, rehearsing the possibilities. Suicide, he supposes, or a fast car full of hamburger, or the ever-popular cocaine heartburst. Can he really be the only one who sees this? He has imagined cutting people open, looking for the hidden cameras.

Griffin looks up, at large eyes, a pointed chin, a look of vulnerability. There is no film.

17

SILVER SCREAM

After a moment Griffin catches himself straining to see, and pulls back from the edge in an almost physical sense. No film. It is as if a terrible beating has suddenly stopped.

"I've been looking forward to meeting you," Suzy Lodi says. Somehow her voice retains most of its recorded quality: the depth, the energy. She is like a clean mountain waterfall rushing through the coked-out, juiced-out, smacked-out people in this five-thousand-dollar suite overlooking . . . Griffin cannot remember what city they are in. Maybe Paris. Jesus Christ in Panavision, she is beautiful. Is she straight? Her first album had a single called "Preference Me" that was Number Eleven until someone decided it was obscene, which drove it to Number Three with a bullet.

"So," Lodi says, "you know what they say the A.D. stands for?"

He knows. In movies it means Assistant Director, in print Art Director, in history books the godless are trying to replace it with C.E.

But when people talk about Griffin it means Already Dead.

The A.D. actually stands for Absalom David, because Griffin's mother was an illiterate who couldn't keep her Bible stories straight. There were no books in Griffin's house. There was no newspaper. There were magazines, if they had enough pictures. And there was television, most of the hours of the day. Dody Griffin's entire print vocabulary was of products whose names were writ large on the glass while an announcer spoke them. She could read Dial and Oreo and every major brand of beer.

When A.D. Griffin was fifteen, he came home to find that his mother had mistaken a bottle of ant poison for cough syrup. She was sitting half-upright, her lap full of vomit, in front of the cartoon adventures of Rambo.

Griffin found the car keys, loaded the old Buick with what he thought he could hock, and drove off.

Suzy Lodi leads Griffin into another room of the suite and points to a man all in black, five feet and a couple of inches tall.

"Jesse Rain. My lyricist. Also my manager."

Rain has black hair just to his collar, and his clothes are entirely black: denim jeans, silk shirt, boots and hard-worn leather jacket. A black scarf wraps his throat. He is drinking Perrier from the bottle.

Rain's face is hard and planar, like a cliff, his cheeks hollow and gray with beard stubble. He wears black Wayfarers and a ring carved entirely from

PREFLASH

some smooth black stone. Griffin thinks of a Karsh photograph; he expects the film of Rain's death to look like double vision, monochrome both sides. But there is no film.

The relief is lesser than with Suzy, but it is still there, and cool, and pleasant.

Rain sips his mineral water, looks shade-eyed at Griffin. "Hello, A.D. You're interested in shooting some tape of Suzy." His voice is very measured, like an actor speaking blank verse.

"I don't work in tape," Griffin says. "Only film."

"Film, then."

"Aren't you going to ask why?" Griffin is aware that he is staring, but there is no film. Not of Lodi, not of Rain. He looks at another partygoer, just to make sure, and indeed there it is, perforated ulcer, hemorrhage until Griffin's fingers against his temple break the frame with light. But not of Lodi. Not of Rain.

Jesse Rain says "Do you ask why Suzy sings with words?"

"You got me."

"I think I might," Rain says seriously, and Griffin doesn't know what the hell he means by it. "But I'll want to see a sample first. One of the songs from Suzy's first album, *Middle Distance*. At our expense."

"If you're going to pay for it anyway, why don't we just —"

"It isn't that I don't trust you," Rain says. "It's that not everyone can shoot Suzy Lodi."

"See these?" Carrick said to Griffin, holding up a yard of sixteen-milli-meter in a cotton-gloved hand. "Edge numbers. That's what it's all about. We're all doing edge numbers, dancing right on the sprocket-holed brink."

"I know how to edit, for chrissake."

"Sure. Bet you've read every word Comrade Eisenstein ever wrote, all about how it don't mean a thing if it ain't got that montage. *Look here*, A.D. me lad." He swept his hand across two dozen lengths of film hanging in a cloth-lined editing bin. "You can pick up a piece of film and look at it and say 'yeah, here's where this one fits.' You can put it together with your *hands*, understand? On tape, well, there's a time code in there somewhere, say the magic word SMPTE and it all fits, but you can't see time codes. You can't see *anything* on tape, because there *isn't* anything on tape but some oxide particles with a religious orientation. Tape is attitudinal, A.D., but film grabs that hot raw light coming through the gate and makes something out of it."

"That's bullshit."

"It sure is, A.D. . . . but it's *my* bullshit."

19

SILVER SCREAM

* * *

The space between the accident and four weeks later in the hospital is dark. Not totally dark, and not empty. There are half-lit shapes there. Griffin thinks — believes — that he could enter the darkness, see the things close, touch them, know them.

The thought terrifies him. The faith is worse.

Suzy Lodi wears black, against an overexposed white background. Her tight leather dress is an inkblot, her bare arms enveloped by light like fog.

> *Put the wires into my nerves and brain*
> *Wash my body down with novocaine*
> *If the treatment doesn't ease the pain*
> *Pull the plug and start again*
>
> *You've got to cut wide open, rub salt in your soul*
> *You've got to crawl through fire, naked on the coal*
> *You've got to breathe deep water, draw until you drown*
> *You've got to reach for heaven, pull the temple down*

As she moves in front of the front-projection screen, the light absorbs her limbs, gives them back. She is dancing, but dancing with nothing.

> *Drive the nails into my hands and feet*
> *Daily paper for my winding sheet*
> *If the hammer doesn't wake the street*
> *Draw the stake, resume the beat*
>
> *You've got to cut . . .*

Jesse Rain stops the projector, turns up the room lights, taps his black ring on the black tabletop. He takes a sip from the glass of Cold Spring at his elbow, and smiles. Without the sunglasses his eyes are colorless, like spring water. "I like it, A.D.," he tells Griffin. "I like it very much. There are nine songs on the new album. What do you feel like committing to?"

There is something in the way Rain says "committing" that makes Griffin think of distance.

* * *

20

PREFLASH

Griffin and Carrick and one of the BBC guys were out in the Guate-
malan bush when a bunch of Green Berets stumbled over them: no officers,
just a couple of shot-up fireteams looking for home and mother. They said
there were Cubans behind them, at least eighty thousand reinforced with
tanks and planes and Erwin Rommel and Genghis Khan.

There were some shots. The grunts, not all that paralyzed, shot back.
Finally Carrick said to Griffin, "Enough of this shit, I am not getting killed
by these wieners," and he picked up his camera just exactly like Duke Wayne
hefting a maching gun, yelled "Okay, men, *let's make movies!*"

They all got up and followed him, the grunts shouting and shooting,
until they crashed into five Cubans with a disassembled mortar. The Berets
killed them all. One of the soldiers got the Bronze Star.

"Remember," Carrick said to Griffin when all the noise was over, "use
this power only for good."

"I hear you've got a contract," Malaryk says. They are sitting in the
TWA private lounge at Kennedy, over margaritas and bowls of little pretzels.
In half an hour Malaryk will take off for the Persian Gulf. Another ship has
been sunk, what goes around comes around.

The lounge is a long curved room with a cathedral ceiling and ruffled
white curtains hiding its windows, since the people here pay two hundred
bucks a year to forget that this is an airport. Griffin keeps looking past
Malaryk at the high drapes, because when he looks at her he sees a crowbar
crushing her skull, over and over in coarse monochrome, lit by high thin
windows.

"We're going to do three off the new record, *Windwriting*. If those work,
Jesse Rain wants to do a full video album."

"That's nice," Malaryk says, and Griffin can hear that it isn't quite a lie.

"Beats staring at the ceiling."

"Doug Lelbnecht said that any time you want a field job — "

"Tell Doug I said thanks."

"You tell him," Malaryk says, bitterness on the soundtrack. "I've got
work to do."

They have another drink on Malaryk's network and then her plane is
called. Griffin puts a hand behind his head and pinches, and through light,
light, light, kisses Malaryk. How does he tell her to frisk guys for crowbars
before letting them into her bedroom?

He aches for her himself, eight months is a long time not to be whole,
but the face of the man with the iron is blurred.

There is the usual American pantomime of security. One of the toy soldiers at the checkpoint will die in a hit-and-run in Washington Square Park. The other has her respirator switched off by a man who is not wearing a doctor's coat and is grinning as he pulls the plug. Who knows, maybe both the killers are international terrorists.

Griffin watches the plane go, comforted in knowing it cannot crash.

"Some days I think it's all going to come back to us," Griffin said to Carrick once between firefights. "The detachment, I mean. Keeping distance has to have a price."

"Molto wrongo," Carrick said. "Nobody ever paid for keeping a distance. Nobody ever got shot who wasn't in the line of fire."

"But you've always been as close as anybody."

"So I'll get shot," Carrick said.

Griffin's crew has responded to the decline in the promoclip market. They have met the challenge of spiraling costs, of the American drive to find a better way. They have come to Toronto to shoot.

> Once you played with line and color
> Threw the paint against the wall
> And your scribbled name was hanging
> Under hot lights in the hall
> But now the studio's empty
> And the gallery's closed
> And you can hear the doors are slamming
> No matter where you go
> Fashions you thought you were in
> Gone before they quite begin
> Tell me how long have you been
> Alone

There is something in Suzy Lodi that does not want to be filmed. It is easy to ignore this because she is beautiful; there is enough for the camera there, and all the directors before Griffin have been satisfied with it, to dance with her image.

Griffin has instead used long lenses and tight apertures to stretch the field, to go deep. For a softly bitter ballad someone else would have shot in

PREFLASH

black and white, with smooth slow camera movements, Griffin has used a series of jumping still frames in hypersaturated color.

> *Once you drew and cast the numbers*
> *Dealt the red upon the black*
> *And no matter how you lost it*
> *One more play would win it back*
> *But now the pot of gold's empty*
> *And the banks are all closed*
> *And no one's got a dime to lend you*
> *Just look how much you owe*
> *Take your chips and cash them in*
> *Leave the table, you can't win*
> *Tell me how long have you been*
> *Alone*

Red paint and green felt and empty blue skies tear holes in the retinas; blacks and whites are slabs applied with a palette knife; there is no relief anywhere. Not even in Suzy Lodi's voice, calm as it is. The reviewer for *Rolling Stone* says, "When she asks 'how long have you been alone,' there isn't any doubt who left the guy."

> *There was a time for conversation*
> *In your educated way*
> *There was an audience just waiting*
> *For whatever you would say*
> *But now the words are so empty*
> *And your mind is so closed*
> *And you believe there's someone listening*
> *But you don't really know*
> *Razor wit can cut too thin*
> *Voices fading in the din*
> *Tell me how long have you been*
> *Alone*

The single goes platinum in eleven days. The following week there is a rumor that returns of engagement rings are up thirty percent.

But there are always rumors.

In the seconds before darkness, Griffin was looking through his viewfinder at four Iowa Nazis in brown shirts with stars 'n' stripes armbands.

23

SILVER SCREAM

Griffin was behind what was being called a safety line: the Iowa Nazis agreed that they would not cross the line if the counterdemonstrators and the press and the cops did not cross it.

What the Nazis were doing today in the public eye was killing pigs with spears. A boar hunt, they called it, and issued a statement with some crap about the bold traditions of the Teutonic Knights. One of the counter-marchers had a sign reading ALEXANDER NEVSKY HAD THE RIGHT IDEA. It also seemed to be related to a manhood ritual from South Africa, another land of Right Ideas. Griffin felt flashed back to the good old days: he was shooting *Mondo Cane* in the Corn Belt.

The four he was watching had rifles. This was supposed to be all right too. As the film wound out, one raised his gun.

Griffin's Arriflex exploded next to his temple, into it. He plunged into shadow.

Griffin's clip for Suzy Lodi's "Paper Corridors" has been blamed for an increase in draft evasion, despite that the song has nothing to do with the draft. Griffin has been accused of using subliminals. His reply is that "subliminals are bullshit," which is quoted — at least, all but the last four letters — in most of the national journals.

"Have you ever thought . . ." Griffin says to Jesse Rain one quiet after-noon, not really knowing how to say it, ". . . of writing Suzy something political?"

"Do you mean something polemical?" Rain picks up a guitar, begins knocking out the bouncing chords of Sixties beach rock. He sings:

> So keep your eye on the Russians
> 'Cause I think that they're gonna invade now
> You've got to hide in your shelter
> 'Til the fallout has gone and decayed now
> Now every girl loves a soldier
> So I sure hope we're gonna get laid now
> And we'll have guns guns guns
> 'Til atomics blow the Commies away-y-y!

"On Suzy's first EP," Rain says as the ringing dies, "I gave her a song called 'An East Wind Coming,' all about Chernobyl. I put everything I had into it. It bored people blind."

"Did that make it not worth doing?"

"Yeah," Rain says. "It did."

PREFLASH

*   *   *

After the accident Griffin was comatose for four weeks. The first face he saw was Fischetti's. The second was Malaryk's. He had expected to see Carrick, but Carrick was dead. He had been blown out of the sky leaving Yemen. Yemen, for God's sake.

Griffin did not weep until Malaryk had kissed him and gone, and then he began to cry uncontrollably. His arms would not respond properly, his hands were no goddamn use at all. Fish came in and dried his face without saying a word. Griffin understood that none of this was new to Fischetti. He wondered how Fish kept distance. How far the distance was.

The line of those waiting to enter Club Glare is half a block long in cold Manhattan drizzle. Jesse Rain, Suzy Lodi, and Griffin walk past the line to another door, and are admitted instantly.

The Club's sound system is loud enough to ignite paper. Its lighting carries enough wattage to give a small African nation all the blessings of civilization.

The dj in the glass booth overhead goes by the name of Wrack Focus. She reminds Griffin of Ming the Merciless in red leather. She is tipped to Suzy's presence, makes the announcement — the applause almost drowns the music — and puts on Griffin's clip of "Paper Corridors." It was shot in darkened Government buildings in Ottawa, using preflashed film: the raw stock had been briefly exposed to light, making it more sensitive. There is a cost in haziness, but they can shoot in darker corners.

Griffin and Lodi and Rain get a table with a good view of the crowd and vice versa. Griffin and Lodi order Veuve Clicquot. Rain gets straight Perrier, without even a twist.

Griffin looks at the giant video screen. But he's seen that. He looks at the crowd. Film flips by, death death death. He looks at Suzy, and that is calming at first, and then —

"I'm going upstairs," Jesse Rain says. "See you when."

"'night, Jess," says Suzy.

"He's going to sleep up there?"

"No. Talk to somebody, I think. But that's the last we'll see of him tonight."

Griffin cannot think of a stranger place to do business than inside this jukebox, and he has seen business done where revolutions per minute referred to the transfer of power.

"Is everything all right, Miz Lodi?" says the voice of a BBC announcer. Griffin looks up. There is a seven-foot Haitian in a Club Galre T-shirt looking back at him.

"Just fine, Robert. A.D., this is Rather Rotten Robert. Robert's job is to break the arms of anybody who hassles us, right, Robert?"

Robert smiles, showing more gold than teeth, and says in the perfect Oxbridge purr, "That's quite correct, Miz Lodi."

Through his left eye Griffin sees the huge man kick a .44 out of a zipunk's hand and then throw the zipunk out the door one-handed; as Robert turns, a bald girl with fishhooks in her lips picks up the big pistol and fires it twice, punching Robert's heart out of his body, taking off a corner of his skull. Rather Rotten Robert says "Oh, now, why, lady," and then there is blue light, neon through a beer bottle.

"May I bring you another bottle, sir, madam?" Robert says.

"I think we're going early tonight," Suzy says. "Would you call the car?"

"Certainly, Miz Lodi."

Griffin looks at Suzy Lodi, and there is no film. It has been a long time not to be whole. They go out past the line of those who cannot enter, and for once what they're thinking is right.

It's never like one expects, but even moreso tonight. No torn or thrown clothing. No dominance or submission beyond a little friendly no-I'm-on-top. No kinks and very little perspiration; as clean as a really good porn film. Just the sweet uncomplicated joy of an exchange of tenderness between two people who don't give a damn for each other.

Griffin goes home early the next afternoon to find a message on his answering machine from Malaryk, in town again and wanting to talk to him, and he doesn't even feel guilty.

There is a knock at Griffin's door. Standing in the hall is a man in a bulky coat, a hat half across his face. He looks straight at Griffin, and the face is empty of anything like expression. The medium, in this case, is the message. Griffin turns away before he looks any closer.

"Are you fully recovered from your injury, Mr. Griffin?" the man says, and again it is not the words but the tone.

"I'm doing all right."

"Very glad to hear that, Mr. Griffin. Glad to see you've found productive work. You are enjoying your work?"

"Sure."

"No desire to return to your former job?"

"This pays better."

"Yes," the man says. "I'd keep that in mind. Should anyone make any sort of counteroffer to you — do remember the difference in pay."

Griffin stares. He can't help it, perhaps. The film rolls. Griffin sees the man being knifed in a narrow street, buildings with an East European look. The camera looks down on him as he lurches, holding his stomach in his hands, bumps against a street sign.

"Be careful on Kalininstrasse," Griffin says.

"I hope you're listening to me, Mr. Griffin," the man says in color right frame, while in left frame he falls and makes a splash in his own blood. The man is puzzled. He is used to people being afraid of him, and to their standing up bravely to him, but Griffin's response has him stymied.

"You too," Griffin says, and looks, and looks, until the man turns around and goes.

Griffin shuts the door, and manages not to vomit until he reaches the bathroom.

One look away
One voice that won't stop screaming
One wish that keeps on coming true
One lonely day
One night of lucid dreaming
One coded message coming through
Breaking through to blue

Malaryk keeps looking at the bar television during the Suzy Lodi clip. She is fascinated, so much so she keeps not telling Griffin what it is that was so important this morning.

One barren place
One scent that always lingers
One introspective point of view
One hidden face
One hand with seven fingers
One wired instruction what to do
Breaking through to blue

"— but I think I got tape of somebody's missiles in somebody else's cargo holds," Malaryk says suddenly. "I held the camera on the stenciling, and the bills of lading, and if they're all readable —"

"Pia," Griffin says slowly, "has a man —"

SILVER SCREAM

The crowbar falls and falls and falls before the thin windows.
"A man what?"
"Be careful," Griffin says, and leaves her, no doubt wondering.

Griffin knows he must have film of Carrick somewhere. He knows that he shot it, as tests, as jokes, as remembrance, for any reason except the one he has in mind now. Tape will not do. Tape is attitudinal, a cool medium at a safe distance.

He finds a reel, jams it onto the editor spools, slaps off the lights and begins to crank.

There is Carrick, moving, living in the light. This is Guatemala film.

And down the left side of Griffin's vision, Yemeni film. The crew is getting out, a Hercules is waiting to take them all home.

They crowd aboard the Hercules, it takes off, there is a round of gallows jokes and straight shots of whiskey, the plane reaches altitude.

There is a bright light as if the film has broken, the lamp unconfined through the gate. And then nothing.

Griffin runs the film back, slows it down. The light contracts to a sphere, to a point. It goes out, leaving a knapsack in a seat. It was all over in three frames, one-eighth of a second. No one felt a thing.

Griffin stops the projection again, counts the passengers. There are twelve. He runs back to the boarding, counts again. Thirteen. The one with the knapsack in his hand does not take a seat. He drops the bag, turns as if going after more gear.

Griffin stops the film. The man's face is blurred with motion, but Griffin has seen it that way before. In Kalininstrasse. And behind a swinging crowbar.

In the next-to-last frame before the fogged footage, the Iowa Nazi raised his automatic rifle. Bits of film camera crumpled into Griffin's head. But the man with the rifle did not fire it. Griffin has filmed men shooting rifles on four continents, including directly at him, and this one did not.

Griffin wonders who was standing next to him, behind the safety line. But he has no film of that.

He looks at the telephone. He knows the digits that in the right sequence will connect him with Malaryk. But what after that?

The phone rings.

Griffin picks it up.

"A.D.?" Jesse Rain says. "Couple of things I'd like to discuss with you."

* * *

28

PREFLASH

"Get the hell out of here, Griffin," the high-school principal told the fifteen-year-old. "I don't know what you bother to come to school for."

"Because I run your audio-visual department better than that drunk Haley ever did, and you don't have to pay me."

The principal swung the yardstick in his hand at Griffin. Griffin grabbed it and snapped it in half. He ran. He'd been told to get out, after all.

He ran home, because that was the only place he had to run. When he got there, he paused, and thought, and gathered, and kept on running.

Rain takes Griffin to the Club Glare, and upstairs. Here the floor hums with the sound for those below, and sometimes the light flashes through the windows like lightning, but they are isolated. Rain looks down at the dance floor, the keystoned video screen. They are above even Wrack the dj.

When they sit down, Griffin has a pint glass of Guinness at the proper temperature, Rain one of Vichy water.

Rain says "What do you see when you look at me, A.D.?" The words rhyme so that for a moment Griffin thinks it is a new lyric for Suzy. Then he hears them properly. After a moment, he says "What am I supposed to see?"

"You're an artist. I'd hoped you could tell me."

"I make movies."

"You know it's more than that," Rain says. "You work with light. While some of us . . ."

Rain's lips are moving. Griffin cannot hear the words, if they are words; only a soft whistling. Rain dips two fingers into the straight-sided glass. There is a flare of light from his ring, with star-filter points.

The water glass is empty, and a black-furred mouse clutches the back of Rain's hand. It runs up his sleeve, perches on his shoulder.

"Look hard at the mouse," Jesse Rain says. "See anything?"

Griffin looks. The mouse looks back, curious little eyes. There is no film.

"I'm going to throw him under a truck when we're done here," Rain says. "Anything yet?"

No. The mouse licks Rain's ear.

Rain says "I know your work. You know mine. Technique."

Griffin looks Rain straight in the colorless eyes. Rain feeds a peanut to the mouse, says "A.D. can you see me?" to the beat of the Who song.

No. Lightning strikes in Griffin's brain, and he pulls at his drink. So this isn't how Carrick did it after all. Griffin had thought — but no, this is different.

Rain says "It doesn't have to hurt. It can be more fun than anything.

29

Anything. You just need to work on your technique." His face is a test card and his voice is a click track. The mouse snuggles down on Rain's shoulder. Surely a mouse has to die. Everything dies.

Rain says "Did she act like a puppet? Was there any lack of spontaneity?" No. Griffin's crotch tightens at the thought.

"Technique." Rain stands up, the mouse crawling into his jacket. He says "Let's go. I can only stand so much of this place."

They descend into the noise, and go out. Rather Rotten Robert clears a way for them. Every time Griffin looks up he sees the bullet opening Robert's skull, so he looks mostly down. On the street there is a line of people waiting to be approved for entry; a glance shows Griffin clips of stopped hearts and fried brains and overturned cars and a bent propellor taking hungry bites. Griffin touches his jaw joint and the film breaks, white light through the gate, painful but clean.

Rain says "This way. Easy now — you get thrown in the drunk tank and you're in for a long and visionary night."

The neon blurs and goes out: Griffin realizes he is being bundled into a stretch limo. Plush and leather caress him, dark glass soothes his eyes. Rain puts a cold beer into Griffin's hand and he suckles it.

"Where are we going?" Griffin says finally.

"Where do you want to go? Remember we have a clip to shoot in the morning. Want to do it in Paris? We'll pick up Suzy, be on the jet by two. Suzy likes Paris. That's where she met you, remember?"

"Take me up to East 92nd."

Rain twists the cap off a bottle of Evian. They drive north.

Griffin sold the family car, which he wasn't licensed to drive anyway, and pawned the household goods. The hockshop had a sixteen-millimeter movie camera, a Canon Scoopic. Griffin bought it, and a reel-to-reel tape recorder. "Nobody uses this stuff no more, they all make videotape," the pawnbroker said. "What you gonna be, Cecil B. de Mille?"

"Herschell Gordon Lewis," Griffin said, but the pawnbroker didn't get it.

Four years later A.D. Griffin was producing, directing, scripting and lensing hardcore for the inner-city markets and the occasional softcore splatter for the drive-ins. He had a before-tax income of thirty thousand dollars, and an after-tax income of thirty thousand dollars. He had neither a credit card nor a checking account, and had never written a ledger entry in his life. Most of the people he dealt with thought he was just a runner for the real A.D. Griffin. He didn't care. He had everything.

He thought he had everything, until Carrick showed up. What goes around comes around.

PREFLASH

* * *

Fischetti's fingers dug deep into Griffin's back, working out the pain, putting Griffin's mind back in touch with his vacationing limbs. Griffin thought about things in order, said "You know who Eisenstein was, Fish?"

"Sure. He was a Jew that built atom bombs."

Rain's limousine lets Griffin off at the steps to Malaryk's brownstone. It has begun to rain. Rain says nothing as Griffin leaves the car. When Griffin turns back for a moment, the limo is gone.

He climbs the stairs to a high double door, wire in its glass panes. To his right is a column of glowing doorbell buttons. Malaryk's is the third up. Griffin glances up, through the rain.

The building has high, narrow windows.

Griffin stops. Either he can change what is happening up there, or he cannot. Either he has been seeing the truth or he has not.

If a man cannot trust himself, trusting God is a small consolation. Griffin looks away from the door, high crane shot of the sidewalk below.

There is a young couple, teens, walking past, drenched, nuzzling, not feeling the rain. In Griffin's left eye, the boy kills the girl with a potato peeler. The state electrocutes him. What goes around comes around. She is wearing an oversized T-shirt, plastered to her breasts with rain. It reads CHOOSE LIFE.

Griffin spins around, panning over the lighted doorbells. He stumbles down the steps. Water splashes into his shoes.

A man comes out from between the buildings, coat turned up against the rain. He is whistling to himself. He might be on his way to the corner for a paper. But he isn't. Griffin stares at him, and stares, watching the film of his death over and over.

It isn't enough.

The man has a chalk mark on his shoulder now, a broad white M. All around him are scrapings and thuds and footsteps. Hands reach up from sewer gratings. The underworld pursues the murderer, for if the police cannot, who else is left?

Griffin tilts up. The sign on the lamppost no longer reads Kalininstrasse. Beneath it the man is just as dead.

So.

Griffin takes a few squelching steps. He sees a little man in a long black coat, just ahead. The man snaps his arm out straight: Griffin barely sees the blur of black fur before it disappears beneath a passing truck. He can hear the crunch of tiny bones.

The man in black walks away. Griffin turns another way. So much water.

He will bind Suzy Lodi in black cloth and soak her with water, so that her movements are struggling and slow. Filters and lighting will show each drop in high contrast as it rolls down her face, her body, to the pool that rises past her hips, black as oil. In the last bars of the song it will reach her chin, and still rise, until there is only a silver ripple on darkness. Jesse Rain will write a lyric, and it will sell a million pressings. Kids will drown and not be missed. Double platinum.

A siren shrieks. The cars pull up, the cops pile out. So someone did hear something, say something. Down left frame, one of them is shotgunned in the face by a stocking-masked bandit, another hangs himself dressed in women's lingerie. Fog and darkness make the right frame seem as colorless as the left, except for the red and blue flares of light. Griffin saves the image for a future video. There will be music.

Griffin turns his back.

A little further on, Griffin's transportation is waiting, calmly pawing the pavement with its eight-inch claws. It turns its head, and dips it, clicking the eagle beak, as submissive as such a creature might ever appear.

Griffin climbs on his namesake's back, running a hand over the feathers of the head, the stiff but smooth fur on the huge shoulders. He is taken into the night sky, they bank over the city smoother than a gyrostabilized helicopter mount. It's more fun than anything.

The street where they are clustering round death is only one square of an endless dark grid, and at every point of the grid there are police, firemen, ambulances, lights sparking hopelessly against the night.

So he doesn't have Carrick's gift, so what. He has his own, and Rain has shown him what it's good for. Griffin will go back now, to the people he can stand to look at, because they have nothing inside them.

Regret dies last. But everything dies.

CUTS

by

F. Paul Wilson

It started in Milo's right foot. He awoke in the dark of his bedroom with a pins-and-needles sensation from the lower part of his calf to the tips of his toes. He sat up, massaged it, walked around the bedroom. Nothing helped. Finally, he took a Darvocet and went back to bed. He managed to get to sleep but was awake again by dawn, this time with both feet tingling. In the wan light, he inspected his lower legs.

A thin, faintly red line around each leg about three inches up from the ankle. Milo snapped on the night table light for a closer look. He touched the line. It was more than a line — an indentation, actually, like something left after wearing a pair of socks too tight at the top. But it felt as if the constricting band were still there.

He got up and walked around. It felt a little funny to stand on partially numb feet but he couldn't worry about it now. In just a couple of hours he was doing a power breakfast at the Polo with Regenstein from TriStar and he had to be sharp. He padded into the kitchen to put on the coffee.

As he wove through L.A.'s morning commuter traffic, Milo envied the drivers with their tops down. He would have loved to have his 380 SL opened up to the bright early morning sun. Truthfully, he would have been glad for an open window. But for the sake of his hair he stayed bottled up with the AC on. He couldn't afford to let the breeze blow his toupee around. It had been especially stubborn about blending in with his natural hair this morning and he didn't have any more time to fuss with it. And this was his good piece.

33

SILVER SCREAM

His back-up had been stolen during a robbery of his house last week, an occurrence that still baffled the hell out of him. He wished he didn't have to worry about wearing a rug. He had heard about a new experimental lotion that was supposed to start hair growing again. If that ever panned out, he'd be first on line to —

His right hand started tingling. He removed it from the wheel and fluttered it in the air. Still it tingled. The sleeve of his sports coat slipped back and he saw a faint indentation running around his forearm, just above the wrist. For a few heartbeats he studied it in horrid fascination.

What's happening to me?

Then he glanced up and saw the looming rear of a truck rushing toward his windshield. He slammed on the brakes and slowed to a screeching stop inches from the tailgate. Gasping and sweating, Milo slumped in the seat and tried to get a grip. Bad enough he was developing mysterious little constricting bands on his legs and now his arm, he had almost wrecked the new Mercedes. This sucker cost more than his first house back in the seventies.

When traffic started up again, he drove cautiously, keeping his eyes on the road and working the fingers of his right hand. He had some weirdshit disease, he just knew it, but he couldn't let anything get between him and this breakfast with Regenstein.

"Look, Milo," Howard Regenstein said through the smoke from his third cigarette in the last twenty minutes. "You know that if it was up to me the picture would be all yours. You know that, man."

Milo nodded, not knowing that at all. He had used that same line himself a million times — maybe *two* million times. *If it was up to me . . .* Yeah, right. The great cop-out: I'm a nice guy and I have all the faith in the world in you but those money guys, those faithless, faceless Philistines who hold the pursestrings won't let guys with vision like you and me get together and make a great film.

"Well, what's the problem, Howie? I mean, give it to me straight."

"All right," Howie said, showing his chicklet caps between his thin lips. He was deeply tanned, wore thick horn-rimmed glasses; his close cropped curly hair was sandy-colored and lightly bleached. "Despite my strong — and, Milo, I do mean *strong* — recommendation, the money boys looked at the grosses for *The Hut* and got scared away."

Well. That explained a lot of things, especially this crummy table half hidden in an inside corner. The real power players, the ones who wanted everybody else in the place to see who they were doing breakfast with, were out in the middle or along the windows. Regenstein probably had three breakfasts scheduled for this morning. Milo was wondering what tables had been reserved for the others when a sharp pain stabbed his right leg. He winced and reached down.

"Something wrong?" Regenstein said.

"No. Just a muscle cramp." He lifted his trouser leg and saw that the indentation above his ankle was deeper. It was actually a cut now. Blood oozed slowly, seeping into his sock. He straightened up and forced a smile at Regenstein.

"*The Hut,* Howie? Is *that* all?" Milo said with a laugh. "Don't they know that project was a loser from the start? The book was a bad property, a piece of cliched garbage. Don't they know that?"

Howie smiled, too. "Afraid not, Milo. You know their kind. They look at the bottom line and see that Universal's going to be twenty mill in the hole on *The Hut,* and in their world that means something. And maybe they remember those PR pieces you did a month or so before it opened. You never even mentioned that the film was based on a book. Had me convinced the story was all yours, whole cloth."

Milo clenched his teeth. That had been when he had thought the movie was going to be a smash.

"I had a *concept,* Howie, one that cut through the bounds and limitations of the novel. I wanted to raise the level of the material but the producers stymied me at every level."

Actually, he had been pretty much on his own down there in Haiti. He had changed the book a lot, made loads of cuts and condensations. He had made it "A Milo Gherl Film" but somewhere along the way he had lost it. Unanimously hostile one-star reviews with leads like, "Shut 'The Hut'" and "New Gherl Pix the Pits" hadn't helped. Twentieth had been pushing an offer in its television division and he had been holding them off — who wanted to do tv when you could do theatricals? But as the bad reviews piled up and the daily grosses plummeted, he grabbed the tv offer. It was good money, had plenty of prestige, but it was still television.

Milo wanted to do films, and very badly wanted in on the new package Regenstein was putting together for TriStar. Howie had Jack Nicholson, Bobby DeNiro, and Kathy Turner firm, and was looking for a director. But he wasn't going to be. He knew that now.

Well, at least he could use the tv job to pay the bills and keep his name before the public until *The Hut* was forgotten. That wouldn't be long. A year or two at most and he'd be back directing another theatrical. Not a package like Regenstein's, but something with a decent budget where he could do the screenplay and direct. That was the way he liked it — full control on paper and on film.

He shrugged at Regenstein and put on his best good-natured smile. "What can I say, Howie? The world wasn't ready for *The Hut.* Someday, they'll appreciate it."

35

Yeah, right, he thought as Regenstein nodded noncommittally. At least Howie was letting him down easy, letting him keep his dignity here. That was important. All he had to do now was —

Milo screamed as pain tore into his left eye like a bolt of lightning. He lurched to his feet, upsetting the table as he clamped his hands over his eye in a vain attempt to stop the agony. *Pain!* Oh Christ, pain as he had never known it was shooting from his eye straight into his brain. This had to be a stroke! What else could hurt like this?

Through his good eye he had a whirling glimpse of everybody in the dining room standing and staring at him as he staggered around. He pulled one hand away from his eye and reached out to steady himself. He saw a smear of blood on his fingers. He took the other hand away. His left eye was blind, but with his right he saw the dripping red on his palm. A woman screamed.

"My God, Milo!" Regenstein said, his chalky face swimming into view. "Your eye! What did you do to your *eye?*" He turned to a gaping waiter. "Get a doctor! Get a fucking ambulance!"

Milo was groggy from the Demerol they had given him. In the blur of hours since breakfast he'd been wheeled in and out of the emergency room so many times, poked with so many needles, examined by so many doctors, X-rayed so many times, his head was spinning.

At least the pain had eased off.

"I'm admitting you onto the vascular surgery service, Mr. Gherl," said the bearded doctor as he pushed back one of the white curtains that shielded Milo's gurney from the rest of the emergency room. His badge said, *Edward Jansen, M.D.,* and he looked tired and irritable.

Milo struggled up the Demerol downgrade. "Vascular surgery? But my eye — !"

"As Dr. Burch told you, Mr. Gherl, your eye can't be saved. It's ruined beyond repair. But maybe we can save your feet and your hand if it's not too late already.

"*Save* them?"

"If we're lucky. I don't know what kind of games you've been into, but getting yourself tied up with piano wire is about the dumbest thing I've ever heard of."

Milo was growing more alert by the second now. Over Dr. Jansen's shoulder he saw the bustle of the emergency room personnel, saw an old black mopping the floor in slow, rhythmic strokes. But he was only seeing it with his right eye. He reached up to the bandage over his left. *Ruined?* He

36

CUTS

wanted to cry, but Dr. Jansen's piano wire remark suddenly filtered through to his consciousness.

"Piano wire? What are you talking about?"

"Don't play dumb. Look at your feet." Dr. Edwards pulled the sheet free from the far end of the gurney.

Milo looked. The nail beds were white and the skin below the indentations were a dusky blue. And the indentations had all become clean, straight, bloody cuts right through the skin and into the meat below. His right hand was the same.

"See that color?" Jansen was saying. "That means the tissues below the wire cuts aren't getting enough blood. You're going to have gangrene for sure if we don't restore circulation soon."

Gangrene! Milo levered up on the gurney and felt his toes with his good hand. *Cold!* "No! That's impossible!"

"I'd almost agree with you," Dr. Jansen said, his voice softening for a moment as he seemed to be talking to himself. Behind him, Milo noticed the old black moving closer with his mop. "When we did X-rays, I thought we'd see the wire imbedded in the flesh there, but there was nothing. Tried Xero soft-tissue technique in case you had used fishing line or something, but that came up negative, too. Even probed the cuts myself but there's nothing in there. Yet the arteriograms clearly show that the arteries in your lower legs and right forearm are compressed to the point where very little blood is getting through. The tissues are starving. The vascular boys may have to do bypasses."

"I'm getting out of here!" Milo said. "I'll see my own doctor!"

"I'm afraid I can't allow that."

"You can't stop me! I can walk out of here anytime I want!"

"I can keep you seventy-two hours for purposes of emergency psychiatric intervention."

"Psychiatric!"

"Yeah. Self-mutilation. Your mind worries me almost as much as your arteries, Mr. Gherl. I'd like to make sure you don't poke out your other eye before you get treatment."

"But I didn't —!"

"Please, Mr. Gherl. There were witnesses. Your breakfast companion said he had just finished giving you some disappointing news when you screamed and rammed something into your eye."

Milo touched the bandage over his eye again. How could they think he had done this to himself?

"My God, I swear I didn't do this!"

"That kind of trauma doesn't happen spontaneously, Mr. Gherl, and according to your companion, no one was within reach of you. So one way or the other, you're staying. Make it easy on both of us and do it voluntarily."

37

Milo didn't see that he had a choice. "I'll stay," he said. "Just answer me one thing: You ever seen anything like this before?"

Jansen shook his head. "Never. Never *heard* of anything like it either." He took a sudden deep breath and smiled through his beard with what Milo guessed was supposed to be doctorly reassurance. "But, hey. I'm only an ER doc. The vascular boys will know what to do."

With that, he turned and left, leaving Milo staring into the wide-eyed black face of the janitor.

"What are you staring at?" Milo said.

"A man in *big* trouble," the janitor said in a deep, faintly accented voice. He was pudgy with a round face, watery eyes, and two days' worth of silvery growth on his jowls. With a front tooth missing on the top, he looked like Leon Spinks gone to seed for thirty years. "These doctors can't be helpin' what you got. You got a *Bocor* mad at you and only a *Houngon* can fix you."

"Get lost!" Milo said.

He lay back on the gurney and closed his good eye to shut out the old man and the emergency room. He hunted for sleep as an escape from the pain and the gut-roiling terror, praying he'd wake up and learn that this was all just a horrible dream. But those words wouldn't go away. *Bocor* and *Houngon* . . . he knew them somehow. Where?

And then it hit him like a blow — *The Hut!* They were voodoo terms from the novel, *The Hut!* He hadn't used them in the film — he'd scoured all mention of voodoo from his screenplay — but the author had used them in the book. If Milo remembered correctly, a *Bocor* was an evil voodoo priest and a *Houngon* was a good one. Or was it the other way around? Didn't matter. They were all part of Bill Franklin's bullshit novel.

Franklin! Wouldn't he like to see me now! Milo thought. Their last meeting had been anything but pleasant. Unforgettable, yes. His mind did a slow dissolve to his new office at Twentieth two weeks ago . . .

"Some conference!"

The angry voice startled Milo and he spilled hot coffee down the front of his shirt. He leaped up from behind his desk and bent forward, pulling the steaming fabric away from his chest. "Jesus H. —"

But then he looked up and saw Bill Franklin standing there and his anger cooled like fresh blood in an arctic breeze. Maggie's anxious face peered over Franklin's narrow shoulder.

"I tried to stop him, Mr. Gherl, honest I did, but he wouldn't listen!"

"You've been ducking me for a month, Gherl!" Franklin said in his nasal voice. "No more tricks!"

CUTS

Maggie said, "Shall I call security?"

"I don't think that will be necessary, Maggs," he said quickly, grabbing a Kleenex from the oak tissue holder on his desk and blotting at his stained shirt front. Milo had moved into this office only a few weeks ago, and the last thing he needed today was an ugly scene with an irate writer. He could tell from Franklin's expression that he was ready to cause a doozy. Better to bite the bullet and get this over with. "I'll talk to Mr. Franklin. You can leave him here." She hesitated and he waved her toward the door. "Go ahead. It's all right."

When she had closed the door behind her, he picked up the insulated brass coffee urn and looked at Franklin. "Coffee, Billy-boy?"

"I don't want coffee, Gherl! I want to know why you've been ducking me!"

"But I haven't been ducking you, Billy!" he said, refreshing his own cup. He would have to change this shirt before he did lunch later. "I'm not with Universal anymore. I'm with Twentieth now, so naturally my offices are here." He swept an arm around him. "Not bad, ay?"

Milo sat down and tried his best to look confident, at ease. Inside, he was anything but. Right now he was a little afraid of the writer stalking back and forth before the desk like a caged tiger. Nothing about Franklin's physical appearance was the least bit intimidating. He was fair-haired and tall with big hands and feet attached to a slight, gangly frame. He had a big nose, a small chin, and a big adam's apple — Milo had noticed on their first meeting two years ago that he could slant a perfectly straight line along the tips of those three protuberances. A moderate overbite did not help the picture. Milo's impression of Franklin had always been that of a patient, retiring, rational man who never raised his voice.

But today he was barging about with a wild look in his eyes, shouting, gesticulating, accusing. Milo remembered an old saying his father used to quote to him when he was a boy: *Beware the wrath of a patient man.*

Franklin had paused and was looking around the spacious room with its indirect lighting, its silver-gray floor-to-ceiling louvered blinds and matching carpet, the chrome and onyx wet bar, the free-form couches, the abstract sculptures on the lucite coffee table and on Milo's oversized desk.

"How did you ever rate this after perpetrating a turkey like *The Hut?*"

"Twentieth recognizes talent when it sees it, Billy."

"My question stands," Franklin said.

Milo ignored the remark. "Sit down, Billy-boy. What's got you so upset?"

Franklin didn't sit. He resumed his stalking. "You know damn well what! My book!"

"You've got a new one?" Milo said, perfectly aware of which book he meant.

39

SILVER SCREAM

"No! I mean the only book I've ever written — *The Hut!* — and the mess you made out of it!"

Milo had heard quite enough nasty criticism of that particular film to last him a lifetime. He felt his anger flare but supressed it. Why get into a shouting match?

"I'm sorry you feel that way, Billy, but let's face facts." He spread his hands in a consoling gesture. "It's a dead issue. There's nothing more to be done. The film has been shot, edited, released, and — "

"— and withdrawn!" Franklin shouted. "Two weeks in general release and the theatre owners sent it back! It's not just a flop, it's a catastrophe!"

"The critics killed it."

"Bullshit! The critics blasted it, just like they blasted other 'flops' like *Flashdance* and *Top Gun* and *Ernest Goes to Camp*. What killed it, Gherl, was word of mouth. Now I know why you wouldn't screen it until a week before it opened: You knew you'd botched it!"

"I had trouble with the final cut. I couldn't — "

"You couldn't get it to make sense! As I walked out of that screening I kept telling myself that my negative feelings were due to all the things you'd cut out of my book, that maybe I was too close to it all and that the public would somehow find my story in your mass of pretentions. Then I heard a guy in his early twenties say, 'What a boring waste of time!' and I knew it wasn't just me." Franklin's long bony finger stabbed through the air. "It was you! You raped my book!"

Milo had had just about enough of this. "You novelists are all alike!" he said with genuine disdain. "You do fine on the printed page so you think you're experts at writing for the screen. But you're not. You don't know the first goddam thing about visual writing!"

"You cut the heart out of my story! *The Hut's* was about the nature of evil and how it can seduce even the strongest among us. The plot was like a house of cards, Gherl, built with my sweat. Your windbag script blew it all down! And after I saw the first draft of the script, you were suddenly unavailable for conference!"

Milo recalled Franklin's endless stream of nit-picking letters, his deluge of time-wasting phone calls. "I was busy, dammit! I was writer-director! The whole thing was on my shoulders!"

"I warned you that the house of cards was falling due to the cuts you made. I mean, why did you remove all mention of voodoo and zombiism from the script? They were the two red herrings that held the plot together."

"Voodoo! Zombies! That's old hat! Nobody would pay to see a voodoo movie!"

"Then why set the movie in Haiti, f'Christsake? Might as well have been in Pasadena! And that monster you threw in at the end? Where in hell did you come up with that? It looked like the Incredible Hulk in drag! I spent years in research. I slaved to fill that book with terror and dread — all you brought to the screen were cheap shocks!"

"If that's your true opinion — and I disagree with it absolutely — you should be glad the film was a flop. No one will see it!"

Franklin nodded slowly. "That gave me comfort for a while, until I realized that the movie isn't dead. When it reaches the video stores and the cable services, tens of millions of people will see it — not because it's good, but simply because it's there and it's something they've never heard of before and certainly have never seen. And they'll be directing their rapt attention at your corruption of my story, and they'll see 'Based on the Novel by William Franklin' and think that the pretentious, incomprehensible mishmash they're watching represents my work. And that makes me *mad*, Gherl! Fucking-ay crazy *mad!*"

The ferocity that flashed across Franklin's face was truly frightening. Milo rushed to calm him. "Billy, look: Despite our artistic differences and despite the fact that *The Hut* will never turn a profit, you were paid well into six figures for the screen rights. What's your beef?"

Franklin seemed to shrink a little. His shoulders slumped and his voice softened. "I didn't write it for money. I live off a trust fund that provides me with more than I can spend. *The Hut* was my first novel — maybe my only novel ever. I gave it everything. I don't think I have any more in me."

"Of course you do!" Milo said, rising and moving around the desk toward the subdued writer. Here was his chance to ease Franklin out of here. "It's just that you've never had to suffer for your art! You've had it too soft, too cushy for too long. Things came too easy on that first book. First time at bat you got a major studio film offer that actually made it to the screen. That hardly ever happens. Now you've got to prove it wasn't just a fluke. You've got to get out there and slog away on that new book! Deprive yourself a little! *Suffer!*"

"Suffer?" Franklin said, a weird light starting to glow in his eyes. "I should suffer?"

"Yes!" Milo said, guiding him toward the office door. "All great artists suffer."

"You ever suffer, Milo Gherl?"

"Of course." *Especially this morning, listening to you!*

"Look at this office. You don't look like you're suffering for what you did to *The Hut*."

"I did my suffering years ago. The anger you feel about *The Hut* is small change compared to the dues I've had to pay." He finally had Franklin across the threshhold. "I'm through suffering," he said as he slammed the door and locked it.

From the other side of the thick oak door he thought he heard Franklin say, "No, you're not."

SILVER SCREAM

* * *

"Missing any personal items lately, mister?" said a voice.

Milo opened his good eye and saw the big black guy standing over him, leaning on his mop handle. What was *wrong* with this old fart? What was his angle?

"If you don't leave me alone I'm gonna call —" He paused. "What do you mean, 'personal items?'"

"You know — clothing, nail clippings, a brush or comb that might hold some of your hair. That kinda stuff."

A chill swept over Milo's skin like an icy breeze in July. *The robbery!* Such a bizarre thing — a pried-open window, a few cheap rings gone, his drawers and closets ransacked, an old pair of pajamas missing. And his toupee, the second-string hairpiece . . . gone. Who could figure it? But he had been shaken up enough to go out and buy a .38 for his night table.

Milo laughed. This was so ludicrous. "You're talking about a voodoo doll, aren't you?"

The old guy nodded. "It got other names, but that'll do."

"Who the hell *are* you?"

"Name's Andre but folks call me Andy. I got connections you gonna need."

"*You* need your head examined!"

"Maybe. But that doctor said he was lookin' for the wires that was cuttin' into your legs and your arm but he couldn't find them. That's because the wires are somewheres else. They around the legs and arm of a doll somebody made of you."

Milo tried to laugh again but found he couldn't. He managed a weak, "Bullshit."

"You'll believe me soon enough. And when you do, I'll take you to a *Houngon* who can help you out."

"Yeah," Milo said. "Like you really care about me."

The old black showed his gap-tooth smile. "Oh, I won't be doin' you a favor, and neither will the *Houngon*. He'll be wantin' money for pullin' your fat out the fire."

"And you'll get a finder's fee."

The smile broadened. "Thas right."

That made a little more sense to Milo, but still he wasn't buying. "Forget it!"

"I be around till three. I'll keep checkin' up on you case you change you mind. I can get you out here when you want to go."

"Don't hold your breath."

Milo rolled on his side and closed his eyes. The old fart had some nerve

42

trying to run that corny scam on him, and in a hospital yet! He'd report him, have him fired. This was no joke. He'd lost his eye already. He could be losing his feet, his hand! He needed top medical-center level care, not some voodoo mumbo-jumbo . . .

. . . but no one seemed to know what was going on, and everyone seemed to think he'd put his own eye out. God, who could do something like that to himself? And his hand and his feet — the doc had said they were going to start rotting off if blood didn't get flowing back into them. What on earth was happening to him?

And what about that weird robbery last week? Only personal articles had been stolen. All the high ticket stereo and video stuff had been left untouched.

God, it couldn't be voodoo, could it? Who'd even —

Shit! Bill Franklin! He was an expert on it after all those years of research for *The Hut.* But he wouldn't . . . he couldn't . . .

Franklin's faintly heard words echoed in Milo's brain: *No, you're not.*

Agony suddenly lanced through Milo's groin, doubling him over on the gurney. Gasping with the pain, he tore at the clumsy stupid nightshirt they'd dressed him in and pulled it up to his waist. He held back the scream that rose in his throat when he saw the thin red line running around the base of his penis. Instead, he called out a name.

"Andy! *Andy!*"

Milo coughed and peered through the dim little room. It smelled of dust and sweat and charcoal smoke and something else — something rancid. He wondered what the hell he was doing here. He knew if he had any sense he'd get out now, but he didn't know where to go from here. He wasn't even sure he could find his way home.

The setting sun had been a bloody blob in Milo's rearview mirror as he'd hunched over the steering wheel of his Mercedes and followed Andy's rusty red pick-up into one of L.A.'s seamier districts. Andy had been true to his word: He'd spirited Milo out of the hospital, back to the house for some cash and some real clothes, then down to the garage near the Polo where his car was parked. After that it was on to Andy's *Houngon* and maybe end this agony.

It *had* to end soon. Milo's feet were so swollen he was wearing old slippers. He had barely been able to turn the ignition key with his right hand. And his dick — God, his dick felt like it was going to explode!

After what seemed like a ten-mile succession of left and right turns during which he saw not a single white face, they had pulled to a stop before a

SILVER SCREAM

dilapidated storefront office. On the cracked glass was painted:

M. Trieste
Houngon

Andy had stayed outside with the car while Milo went in.

"Mr. Gherl?"

Milo started at the sound and turned toward the voice. A balding, wizened old black, six-two at least, stood next to him. His face was a mass of wrinkles. He was dressed in a black suit, white shirt, and thin black tie.

Milo heard his own voice quaver: "Yes. That's me."

"You are the victim of the *Bocor?*" His voice was cultured, and accented in some strange way.

Milo pushed back the sleeve of his shirt to expose his right wrist. "I don't know what I'm the victim of, but Andy says you can help me. You've *got* to help me!"

He stared at the patch over Milo's eye. "May I see?"

Milo leaned away from him. "Don't touch that!" It had finally stopped hurting. He held his arm higher.

M. Trieste examined Milo's hand, tracing a cool dry finger around the clotted circumferential cut at the wrist. "This is all?"

Milo showed him his legs, then reluctantly, opened his fly.

"You have a powerful enemy in this *Bocor,*" M. Trieste said, finally. "But I can reverse the effects of his doll. It will cost you five hundred dollars. Do you have it with you?"

Milo hesitated. "Let's not be too hasty here. I want to see some results before I fork over any money." He was hurting, but he wasn't going to be a sucker for this clown.

M. Trieste smiled. He had all his teeth. "I have no wish to steal from you, Mr. Gherl. I shall accept no money from you unless I can effect a cure. However, I do not wish to be cheated either. Do you have the money with you?"

Milo nodded. "Yes."

"Very well." M. Trieste struck a match and lit a candle on a table Milo hadn't realized was there. "Please be seated," he said and disappeared into the darkness.

Milo complied and looked around. The wan candlelight picked up an odd assortment of objects around the room: African ceremonial masks hung side by side with crucifixes on the wall; a long conga drum sat in a corner to the right while a statue of the Virgin Mary, her small plaster foot trodding a writhing snake, occupied the one on his left. He wondered when the drums would start and the dancers appear. When would they begin chanting and daubing him with paint and splattering him with chicken blood? God, he

44

must have been crazy to come here. Maybe the pain was affecting his mind. If he had any smarts he'd —

"Hold out your wrist," M. Trieste said, suddenly appearing in the candle-light opposite him. He held what looked like a plaster coffee mug in his hand. He was stirring its contents with a wooden stick.

Milo held back. "What are you going to do?"

"Help you, Mr. Gherl. You are the victim of a very traditional and particularly nasty form of voodoo. You have greatly angered a *Bocor* and he is using a powerful *loa*, via a doll, to lop off your hands and your feet and your manhood."

"My left hand's okay," Milo said, gratefully working the fingers in the air.

"So I have noticed," M. Trieste said with a frown. "It is odd for one extremity to be spared, but perhaps there is a certain symbolism at work here that we do not understand. No matter. The remedy is the same. Hold your arm out on the table."

Milo did as he was told. His swollen hand looked black in the candle-light. "Is . . . is this going to hurt?"

"When the pressure is released, there will be considerable pain as the fresh blood rushes into the starved tissues."

That kind of pain Milo could handle. "Do it."

M. Trieste stirred the contents of the cup and lifted the wooden handle. Instead of the spoon he had expected, Milo saw that the man was holding a brush. It gleamed red'y.

Here comes the blood, he thought. But he didn't care what was in the cup as long as it worked.

"Andre told me about your problem before he brought you here. I made this up in advance. I will paint it on the constrictions and it will nullify the influence of the *loa* of the doll. After that, it will be up to you to make peace with this *Bocor* before he visits other afflictions on on you."

"Sure, sure," Milo said, thrusting his wrist toward M. Trieste. "Let's just get on with it!"

M. Trieste daubed the bloody solution onto the incision line. It beaded up like water on a freshly waxed car and slid off onto the table. Milo glanced up and saw a look of consternation flit across the wrinkled black face towering above him. He watched as the red stuff was applied again, only to run off as before.

"Most unusual," M. Trieste muttered as he tried a third time with no better luck. "I've never . . . ." He put the cup down and began painting his own right hand with the solution. "This will do it. Hold up your hand."

As Milo raised his arm, M. Trieste encircled the wrist with his long dripping fingers and squeezed. There was an instant of heat, and then M. Trieste cried out. He released Milo's wrist and dropped to his knees cradling his right hand against his breast.

"The poisons!" he cried. "Oh, the poisons!"

Milo trembled as he looked at his dusky hand. The bloody solution had run off as before. "What poisons?"

"Between you and this *Bocor*! Get out of here!"

"But the doll! You said you could —!"

"There is no doll!" M. Trieste said. He turned away and retched. "There *is* no doll!"

With his heart clattering against his chest wall, Milo pushed himself away from the table and staggered to the door. Andy was leaning on his truck at the curb.

"Wassamatter?" he said, straightening off the fender as he saw Milo. "Didn't he —?"

"He's a phoney, just like you!" Milo screamed, letting his rage and fear focus on the old black. "Just another goddam phoney!"

As Andy hurried into the store, Milo started up his Mercedes and roared down the street. He'd drive until he found a sign for one of the freeways. From there he could get home.

And from home, he knew where he wanted to go . . . where he *had* to go.

"Franklin! Where are you, Franklin?"

Milo had finally found Bill Franklin's home in the Hollywood Hills. Even though he knew the neighborhood fairly well, Milo had never been on this particular street, and so it had taken him a while to track it down. The lights had been on inside and the door had been unlocked. No one had answered his knocking, so he'd let himself in.

"*Franklin*, goddamit!" he called, standing in the middle of the cathedral-ceilinged living room. His voice echoed off the stucco walls and hardwood floor. "Where are you?"

In the ensuing silence, he heard a faint voice say, "Milo? Is that you?"

Milo tensed. Where had that come from? "Yeah, it's me! Where are you?"

Again, ever so faintly: "Down here . . . in the basement!"

Milo searched for the cellar door, found it, saw the lights ablaze from below, and began his descent. His slippered feet were completely numb now and he had to watch where he put them. It was as if his feet had been removed and replaced with giant sponges.

"That you, Milo?" said a voice from somewhere around the corner from the stairwell. It was Franklin's voice, but it sounded slurred, strained.

"Yeah, it's me."

46

CUTS

As he neared the last step, he pulled the .38 from his pocket. He had picked it up at the house along with a pair of wirecutters on his way here. He had never fired it, and he didn't expect to have to tonight. But it was good to know it was loaded and ready if he needed it. He tried to transfer it to his right hand but his numb, swollen fingers couldn't keep hold of the grip. He kept it in his left and stepped onto the cellar floor —

— and felt his foot start to roll away from him. Only by throwing himself against the wall and hugging it did he save himself from falling. He looked around the unfinished cellar. Bright, reflective objects were scattered all along the naked concrete floor. He sucked in a breath as he saw the hundreds of sharp curved angles of green glass poking up at the exposed ceiling beams. They looked like shattered wine bottles — big, green, four-liter wine bottles smashed all over the place. And in among the shards were scattered thousands of marbles.

"Be careful," said Franklin's voice. "The basement's mined." The voice was there, but Franklin was nowhere in sight.

"Where the hell are you, Franklin?"

"Back here in the bathroom. I thought you'd never get here."

Milo began to move toward the rear of the cellar where brighter light poured from an open door. He slid his slippered feet slowly along the floor, pushing the green glass spears ahead of him, rolling the marbles out of the way.

"I've come for the doll, Franklin."

Milo heard a hollow laugh. "Doll? What doll, Milo? There's just me and you, ol' buddy."

Milo shuffled around the corner into view of the bathroom. And froze. The gun dropped from his fingers and further shattered some of the glass at his feet. "Oh, my God, Franklin! Oh, my *God!*"

William Franklin sat on the toilet wearing Milo's rings, his old slippers, his stolen pajamas, and his other hairpiece. His left eye was patched and his feet and his right hand were as black and swollen as Milo's There was a maniacal look in his remaining eye as he grinned drunkenly and sipped from a four-liter green-glass bottle of white wine. The cuts in his flesh were identical to Milo's except that a short length of twisted copper wire protruded from each. A screwdriver and a pair of pliers lay in his lap.

M. Trieste's parting words screamed through his brain: *There is no doll!*

"See?" Franklin said in a slurred voice. "You said I had to suffer."

Milo wanted to be sick. "Christ! What have you done?"

"I decided to suffer. But I didn't think I should suffer alone. So I brought you along for company. Sure took you long enough to figure it out."

Milo bent and picked up the pistol. His left hand wavered and trembled as he pointed it at Franklin. "You . . . you . . ." He couldn't think of anything to say.

47

SILVER SCREAM

Franklin casually tossed the wine bottle out onto the floor where it shattered and added to the spikes of glass. Then he pulled open the pajama top. "Right here, Milo, old buddy!" he said, pointing to his heart. "Do you really think you want to put a slug into me?"

Milo Thought about that. It might be like putting a bullet into his own heart. He felt his arm drop. "Why . . . how . . . I don't deserve . . ."

Franklin closed his eye and grimaced. He looked as if he were about to cry. "I know," he said. "It's gone too far. Maybe you really don't deserve all this. I've always known I was a little bit crazy, but maybe I'm a lot crazier than I ever thought I was."

"Then for God's sake, man, loosen the wires!"

"No!" Franklin's eye snapped open. The madness was still there. "I entrusted my work to you. That's a sacred trust. You were responsible for *The Hut's* integrity when you took on the job of adapting it to the screen."

"But I'm an artist, too!" Why was he arguing with this nut? He slipped the pistol into his front pocket and reached around back for the wire cutters.

"All the more reason to respect another man's work! You didn't own it — it was only on loan to you!"

"The contract —"

"*Means nothing!* You had a moral obligation to protect my work, one artist to another."

"You're overreacting!"

"Am I? Imagine yourself a parent who has sent his only child to a reputable nursery school only to learn that the child has been raped by the faculty — then you will understand *some* of what I feel! I've come to see it as my sacred duty to see to it that you don't molest anyone else's work!"

Enough of this bullshit! If Franklin wouldn't loosen the wires, Milo would cut them off! He pulled the wire cutters from his rear pocket and began to shuffle toward Franklin, sweeping the marbles and daggers of glass ahead of him.

"Stay back!" Franklin cried, He grabbed the pliers and pushed them down toward his lap, grinning maliciously. "Didn't know I was left-handed, did you?" He twisted something.

Searing pain knifed into Milo's groin. He doubled over but kept moving toward Franklin. Less than a dozen feet to go. If he could just —

He saw Franklin drop the pliers and pick up the screwdriver, saw him raise it toward his right eye, the good eye. Milo screamed,

"NOOOOO!"

And then agony exploded in his eye, in his head, robbing him of the light, sending him reeling back in sudden impenetrable blackness. As he felt his feet roll across the marbles, he reached out wildly. His legs slid from under under him and despite the most desperate flailings and contortions, there was nothing to grasp on the way down but empty air.

THE MOVIE PEOPLE

by

Robert Bloch

Two thousand stars.

Two thousand stars, maybe more, set in the sidewalks along Hollywood Boulevard, each metal slab inscribed with the name of someone in the movie industry. They go way back, those names; from Broncho Billy Anderson to Adolph Zukor, everybody's there.

Everybody but Jimmy Rogers.

You won't find Jimmy's name because he wasn't a star, not even a bit player — just an extra.

"But I deserve it," he told me. "I'm entitled, if anybody is. Started out here in 1920 when I was just a punk kid. You look close, you'll spot me in the crowd shots in *The Mark of Zorro*. Been in over 450 pictures since, and still going strong. Ain't many left who can beat that record. You'd think it would entitle a fella to something."

Maybe it did, but there was no star for Jimmy Rogers, and that bit about still going strong was just a crock. Nowadays Jimmy was lucky if he got a casting call once or twice a year; there just isn't any spot for an old-timer with a white muff except in a western barroom scene.

Most of the time Jimmy just strolled the boulevard; a tall, soldierly-erect incongruity in the crowd of tourists, fags and freakouts. His home address was on Las Palmas, somewhere south of Sunset. I'd never been there but I could guess what it was — one of those old frame bungalow-court sweatboxes put up about the time he crashed the movies and still standing somehow by the grace of God and the disgrace of the housing authorities. That's the sort of place Jimmy stayed at, but he didn't really *live* there.

Jimmy Rogers lived at the Silent Movie.

The Silent Movie is over on Fairfax, and it's the only place in town where you can still go and see *The Mark of Zorro*. There's always a Chaplin

49

comedy, and usually Laurel and Hardy, along with a serial starring Pearl White, Elmo Lincoln, or Houdini. And the features are great — early Griffith and DeMille, Barrymore in *Dr. Jekyll and Mr. Hyde*, Lon Chaney in *The Hunchback of Notre Dame*, Valentino in *Blood and Sand*, and a hundred more.

The bill changes every Wednesday, and every Wednesday night Jimmy Rogers was there, plunking down his ninety cents at the box office to watch *The Black Pirate* or *Son of the Sheik* or *Orphans of the Storm*.

To live again.

Because Jimmy didn't go there to see Doug and Mary or Rudy or Clara or Gloria or the Gish sisters. He went there to see himself, in the crowd shots.

At least that's the way I figured it, the first time I met him. They were playing *The Phantom of the Opera* that night, and afterward I spent the intermission with a cigarette outside the theatre, studying the display of stills.

If you asked me under oath, I couldn't tell you how our conversation started, but that's where I first heard Jimmy's routine about the 450 pictures and still going strong.

"Did you see me in there tonight?" he asked.

I stared at him and shook my head; even with the shabby hand-me-down suit and the white beard, Jimmy Rogers wasn't the kind you'd spot in an audience.

"Guess it was too dark for me to notice," I said.

"But there were torches," Jimmy told me. "I carried one."

Then I got the message. He was in the picture.

Jimmy smiled and shrugged. "Hell, I keep forgetting. You wouldn't recognize me. We did *The Phantom* way back in 'twenty-five. I looked so young they slapped a mustache on me in Make-up and a black wig. Hard to spot me in the catacombs scenes — all long shots. But there at the end, where Chaney is holding back the mob, I show up pretty good in the background, just left of Charley Zimmer. He's the one shaking his fist. I'm waving my torch. Had a lot of trouble with that picture, but we did this shot in one take."

In weeks to come I saw more of Jimmy Rogers. Sometimes he was up there on the screen, though truth to tell, I never did recognize him; he was a young man in those films of the twenties, and his appearances were limited to a flickering flash, a blurred face glimpsed in a crowd.

But always Jimmy was in the audience, even though he hadn't played in the picture. And one night I found out why.

Again it was intermission time and we were standing outside. By now Jimmy had gotten into the habit of talking to me and tonight we'd been seated together during the showing of *The Covered Wagon*.

We stood outside and Jimmy blinked at me. "Wasn't she beautiful?" he asked. "They don't look like that any more."

THE MOVIE PEOPLE

I nodded. "Lois Wilson? Very attractive."

"I'm talking about June."

I stared at Jimmy and then I realized he wasn't blinking. He was crying. "June Logan. My girl. This was her first bit, the Indian attack scene. Must have been seventeen — I didn't know her then, it was two years later we met over at First National. But you must have noticed her. She was the one with the long blond curls."

"Oh, *that* one." I nodded again. "You're right. She was lovely."

And I was a liar, because I didn't remember seeing her at all, but I wanted to make the old man feel good.

"Junie's in a lot of the pictures they show here. And from 'twenty-five on, we played in a flock of 'em together. For a while we talked about getting hitched, but she started working her way up, doing bits — maids and such — and I never broke out of extra work. Both of us had been in the business long enough to know it was no go, not when one of you stays small and the other is headed for a big career."

Jimmy managed a grin as he wiped his eyes with something which might once have been a handkerchief. "You think I'm kidding, don't you? About the career, I mean. But she was going great, she would have been playing second leads pretty soon."

"What happened?" I asked.

The grin dissolved and the blinking returned. "Sound killed her."

"She didn't have a voice for talkies?"

Jimmy shook his head. "She had a great voice. I told you she was all set for second leads — by nineteen thirty she'd been in a dozen talkies. Then sound killed her."

I'd heard the expression a thousand times, but never like this. Because the way Jimmy told the story, that's exactly what had happened. June Logan, his girl Junie, was on the set during the shooting of one of those early ALL TALKING—ALL SINGING—ALL DANCING epics. The director and camera crew, seeking to break away from the tyranny of the stationary microphone, rigged up one of the first traveling mikes on a boom. Such items weren't standard equipment yet, and this was an experiment. Somehow, during a take, it broke loose and the boom crashed, crushing June Logan's skull.

It never made the papers, not even the trades; the studio hushed it up and June Logan had a quiet funeral.

"Damn near forty years ago," Jimmy said. "And here I am, crying like it was yesterday. But she was my girl —"

And that was the other reason why Jimmy Rogers went to the Silent Movie. To visit his girl.

"Don't you see?" he told me. "She's still alive up there on the screen, in all those pictures. Just the way she was when we were together. Five years we had, the best years for me."

51

SILVER SCREAM

I could see that. The two of them in love, with each other and with the movies. Because in those days, people *did* love the movies. And to actually be *in* them, even in tiny roles, was the average person's idea of seventh heaven.

Seventh Heaven, that's another film we saw with June Logan playing a crowd scene. In the following weeks, with Jimmy's help, I got so I could spot his girl. And he'd told the truth — she was a beauty. Once you noticed her, really saw her, you wouldn't forget. Those blond ringlets, that smile, identified her immediately.

One Wednesday night Jimmy and I were sitting together watching *The Birth of a Nation*. During a street shot Jimmy nudged my shoulder. "Look, there's June."

I peered up at the screen, then shook my head. "I don't see her."

"Wait a second — there she is again. See, off to the left, behind Walthall's shoulder?"

There was a blurred image and then the camera followed Henry B. Walthall as he moved away.

I glanced at Jimmy. He was rising from his seat.

"Where you going?"

He didn't answer me, just marched outside.

When I followed I found him leaning against the wall under the marquee and breathing hard; his skin was the color of his whiskers.

"Junie," he murmured. "I saw her —"

I took a deep breath. "Listen to me. You told me her first picture was *The Covered Wagon*. That was made in 1923. And Griffith shot *The Birth of a Nation* in 1914."

Jimmy didn't say anything. There was nothing to say. We both knew what we were going to do — march back into the theatre and see the second show.

When the scene screened again we were watching and waiting. I looked at the screen, then glanced at Jimmy.

"She's gone," he whispered. "She's not in the picture."

"She never was," I told him. "You know that."

"Yeah." Jimmy got up and drifted out into the night, and I didn't see him again until the following week.

That's when they showed the short feature with Charles Ray — I've forgotten the title, but he played his usual country-boy role, and there was a baseball game in the climax with Ray coming through to win.

The camera panned across the crowd sitting in the bleachers and I caught a momentary glimpse of a smiling girl with long blond curls.

"Did you see her?" Jimmy grabbed my arm.

"That girl —"

"It was Junie. She winked at me!"

THE MOVIE PEOPLE

This time I was the one who got up and walked out. He followed, and I was waiting in front of the theatre, right next to the display poster.

"See for yourself." I nodded at the poster. "This picture was made in 1917." I forced a smile. "You forget, there were thousands of pretty blond extras in pictures and most of them wore curls."

He stood there shaking, not listening to me at all, and I put my hand on his shoulder. "Now look here —"

"I *been* looking here," Jimmy said. "Week after week, year after year. And you might as well know the truth. This ain't the first time it's happened. Junie keeps turning up in picture after picture I know she never made. Not just the early ones, before her time, but later, during the twenties when I knew her, when I knew exactly what she was playing in. Sometimes it's only a quick flash, but I see her — then she's gone again. And the next running, she doesn't come back.

"It got so that for a while I was almost afraid to go see a show — figured I was cracking up. But now you've seen her too —"

I shook my head slowly. "Sorry, Jimmy. I never said that." I glanced at him, then gestured toward my car at the curb. "You look tired. Come on, I'll drive you home."

He looked worse than tired; he looked lost and lonely and infinitely old. But there was a stubborn glint in his eyes, and he stood his ground.

"No thanks. I'm gonna stick around for the second show."

As I slid behind the wheel I saw him turn and move into the theatre, into the place when the present becomes the past and the past becomes the present. Up above in the booth they call it a projection machine, but it's really a time machine; it can take you back, play tricks with your imagination and your memory. A girl dead forty years comes alive again, and an old man relives his vanished youth —

But I belonged in the real world, and that's where I stayed. I didn't go to the Silent Movie the next week or the week following.

And the next time I saw Jimmy was almost a month later, on the set.

They were shooting a western, one of my scripts, and the director wanted some additional dialogue to stretch a sequence. So they called me in, and I drove all the way out to location, at the ranch.

Most of the studios have a ranch spread for western action sequences, and this was one of the oldest; it had been in use since the silent days. What fascinated me was the wooden fort where they were doing the crowd scene — I could swear I remembered it from one of the first Tim McCoy pictures. So after I huddled with the director and scribbled a few extra lines for the principals, I began nosing around behind the fort, just out of curiosity, while they set up for the new shots.

Out front was the usual organized confusion; cast and crew milling around the trailers, extras sprawled on the grass drinking coffee. But here in the back I was all alone, prowling around in musty, log-lined rooms built for use in forgotten features. Hoot Gibson had stood at this bar, and Jack Hoxie had swung from this dance-hall chandelier. Here was a dust-covered table where Fred Thomson sat, and around the corner, in the cut-away bunkhouse —

Around the corner, in the cut-away bunkhouse, Jimmy Rogers sat on the edge of a mildewed mattress and stared up at me, startled, as I moved forward.

"You —?"

Quickly I explained my presence. There was no need for him to explain his; casting had called and given him a day's work here in the crowd shots.

"They been stalling all day, and it's hot out there. I figured maybe I could sneak back here and catch me a little nap in the shade."

"How'd you know where to go?" I asked. "Ever been here before?"

"Sure. Forty years ago in this very bunkhouse. Junie and I, we used to come here during lunch break and —"

He stopped.

"What's wrong?"

Something *was* wrong. On the pan make-up face of it, Jimmy Rogers was the perfect picture of the grizzled western old-timer; buckskin britches, fringed shirt, white whiskers and all. But under the make-up was pallor, and the hands holding the envelope were trembling.

The envelope —

He held it out to me. "Here. Mebbe you better read this."

The envelope was unsealed, unstamped, unaddressed. It contained four folded pages covered with fine handwriting. I removed them slowly. Jimmy stared at me.

"Found it lying here on the mattress when I came in," he murmured. "Just waiting for me."

"But what is it? Where'd it come from?"

"Read it and see."

As I started to unfold the pages the whistle blew. We both knew the signal; the scene was set up, they were ready to roll, principals and extras were wanted out there before the cameras.

Jimmy Rogers stood up and moved off, a tired old man shuffling out into the hot sun. I waved at him, then sat down on the moldering mattress and opened the letter. The handwriting was faded, and there was a thin film of dust on the pages. But I could still read it, every word . . .

Darling:

I've been trying to reach you so long and in so many ways. Of course I've seen you, but it's so dark out there I can't always be sure, and then too you've changed a lot through the years.

THE MOVIE PEOPLE

But I *do* see you, quite often, even though it's only for a moment. And I hope you've seen me, because I always try to wink or make some kind of motion to attract your attention.

The only thing is, I can't do too much or show myself too long or it would make trouble. That's the big secret — keeping in the background, so the others won't notice me. It wouldn't do to frighten anybody, or even to get anyone wondering why there are more people in the background of a shot than there should be.

That's something for you to remember, darling, just in case. You're always safe, as long as you stay clear of closeups. Costume pictures are the best — about all you have to do is wave your arms once in a while and shout, "On to the Bastille," or something like that. It really doesn't matter except to lip-readers, because it's silent, of course.

Oh, there's a lot to watch out for. Being a dress extra has its points, but not in ballroom sequences — too much dancing. That goes for parties, too, particularly in a DeMille production where they're "making whoopee" or one of von Stroheim's orgies. Besides, von Stroheim's scenes are always cut.

It doesn't hurt to be cut, don't misunderstand about that. It's no different than an ordinary fadeout at the end of a scene, and then you're free to go into another picture. Anything that was ever made, as long as there's still a print available for running somewhere. It's like falling asleep and then having one dream after another. The dreams are the scenes, of course, but while the scenes are playing, they're real.

I'm not the only one, either. There's no telling how many others do the same thing; maybe hundreds for all I know, but I've recognized a few I'm sure of and I think some of them have recognized *me*. We never let on to each other that we know, because it wouldn't do to make anybody suspicious.

Somtimes I think that if we could talk it over, we might come up with a better understanding of just how it happens, and why. But the point is, you *can't* talk, everything is silent; all you do is move your lips and if you tried to communicate such a difficult thing in pantomime you'd surely attract attention.

I guess the closest I can come to explaining it is to say it's like reincarnation — you can play a thousand roles, take or reject any part you want, as long as you don't make yourself conspicuous or do something that would change the plot.

Naturally you get used to certain things. The silence, of course. And if you're in a bad print there's flickering; sometimes even the air seems grainy, and for a few frames you may be faded or out of focus.

SILVER SCREAM

Which reminds me — another thing to stay away from, the slapstick comedies. Sennett's early stuff is the worst, but Larry Semon and some of the others are just as bad; all that speeded-up camera action makes you dizzy.

Once you can learn to adjust, it's all right, even when you're looking off the screen into the audience. At first the darkness is a little frightening — you have to remind yourself it's only a theatre and there are just people out there, ordinary people watching a show. They don't know you can see them. They don't know that as long as your scene runs, you're just as real as they are, only in a different way. You walk, run, smile, frown, drink, eat —

That's another thing to remember, about the eating. Stay out of those Poverty Row quickies where everything is cheap and faked. Go where there's real set-dressing, big productions with banquet scenes and real food. If you work fast you can grab enough in a few minutes, while you're off-camera, to last you.

The big rule is, always be careful. Don't get caught. There's so little time, and you seldom get an opportunity to do anything on your own, even in a long sequence. It's taken me forever to get this chance to write you — I've planned it for so long, my darling, but it just wasn't possible until now.

This scene is playing outside the fort, but there's quite a large crowd of settlers and wagon-train people, and I had a chance to slip away inside here to the rooms in back — they're on camera in the background all during the action. I found this stationery and a pen, and I'm scribbling just as fast as I can. Hope you can read it. That is, if you ever get the chance!

Naturally, I can't mail it — but I have a funny hunch. You see, I noticed that standing set back here, the bunkhouse, where you and I used to come in the old days. I'm going to leave this letter under the mattress, and pray.

Yes, darling, I pray. Someone or something *knows* about us, and about how we feel. How we felt about being in the movies. That's why I'm here, I'm sure of that; because I've always loved pictures so. Someone who knows *that* must also know how I loved you. And still do.

I think there must be many heavens and many hells, each of us making his own, and —

The letter broke off there.

No signature, but of course it didn't need one. And it wouldn't have proved anything. A lonely old man, nursing his love for forty years, keeping her alive inside himself somewhere until she broke out in the form of a visual

56

THE MOVIE PEOPLE

hallucination up there on the screen — such a man could conceivably go all the way into a schizoid split, even to the point where he could imitate a woman's handwriting as he set down the rationalization of his obsession.

I started to fold the letter, then dropped it on the mattress as the shrill scream of an ambulance siren startled me into sudden movement.

Even as I ran out the doorway I seemed to know what I'd find; the crowd huddling around the figure sprawled in the dust under the hot sun. Old men tire easily in such heat, and once the heart goes —

Jimmy Rogers looked very much as though he were smiling in his sleep as they lifted him into the ambulance. And I was glad of that; at least he'd died with his illusions intact.

"Just keeled over during the scene — one minute he was standing there, and the next —"

They were still chattering and gabbling when I walked away, walked back behind the fort and into the bunkhouse.

The letter was gone.

I'd dropped it on the mattress, and it was gone. That's all I can say about it. Maybe somebody else happened by while I was out front, watching them take Jimmy away. Maybe a gust of wind carried it through the doorway, blew it across the desert in a hot Santa Ana gust. Maybe there *was* no letter. You can take your choice — all I can do is state the facts.

And there aren't very many more facts to state.

I didn't go to Jimmy Rogers' funeral, if indeed he had one. I don't even know where he was buried; probably the Motion Picture Fund took care of him. Whatever *those* facts may be, they aren't important.

For a few days I wasn't too interested in facts. I was trying to answer a few abstract questions about metaphysics — reincarnation, heaven and hell, the difference between real life and reel life. I kept thinking about those images you see up there on the screen in those old movies; images of actual people indulging in make-believe. But even after they die, the make-believe goes on, and that's a form of reality too. I mean, where's the borderline? And if there *is* a borderline — is it possible to cross over? *Life's but a walking shadow —*

Shakespeare said that, but I wasn't sure what he meant.

I'm still not sure, but there's just one more fact I must state.

The other night, for the first time in all the months since Jimmy Rogers died, I went back to the Silent Movie.

They were playing *Intolerance*, one of Griffith's greatest. Way back in 1916 he built the biggest set ever shown on the screen — the huge temple in the Babylonian sequence.

One shot never fails to impress me, and it did so now; a wide angle on the towering temple, with thousands of people moving antlike amid the gigantic carvings and colossal statues. In the distance, beyond the steps guarded by rows of stone elephants, looms a mighty wall, its top covered with tiny figures. You really have to look closely to make them out. But I did look closely, and this time I can swear to what I saw.

One of the extras, way up there on the wall in the background, was a smiling girl with long blond curls. And standing right beside her, one arm around her shoulder, was a tall old man with white whiskers. I wouldn't have noticed either of them, except for one thing.

They were waving at me . . .

SINEMA

by

Ray Garton

Brett Deever had been looking for his dog, Gabby, for half an hour when he found, instead, a hand.

It lay a couple of yards below him, at the edge of Vintner Creek, which rushed with muddy waters left over from unexpectedly heavy summer rains. A tangle of tree branches were jammed between two large rocks, resisting the flow, and stuck along with other netted detritus was the hand. From Brett's vantage atop the creek's three-foot-high embankment, it could have been a dark, tattered glove, clinging to the branches as if for life.

Brett's typical nine-year-old curiosity took him down the embankment and carefully through the mud until he was within reach of the glove, or doll hand, or —

He stopped when he saw the jut of bone sticking from the purple mush of wrist.

It did not look like a doll's hand now.

"Gabby?" he called softly, nervously, backing up the bank. A clump of bushes began to rustle, and when Brett finally turned his head he saw Gabby's German Shepherd rump half-out of the brush, tail sweeping back and forth enthusiastically. The dog was grumbling contentedly, making moist chewing sounds. As Brett drew closer, his stomach began to roil like a cluster of worms.

Gabby was flat on his belly, eyes bright. He lifted his head to smile at Brett around dark, meat-flecked teeth, pink tongue dangling. He had been worrying what looked like the stripped branch of a sapling.

Except it still had a foot.

There was more, and after a sharp, happy bark, Gabby flopped on his back and rolled in it. Flies took to the air in clouds, like specks of soot on a breeze.

59

SILVER SCREAM

Brett stared.

He knew he should be reacting strongly, somehow — screaming or running or vomiting, something like that. The awful smell made him a bit queasy, of course, but what he could see — some stubby fingers and toes, the swollen, blackened half of the face that was visible — elicited no emotions in him.

The walls were up.

He felt numb, detached.

He felt nothing.

Just like in church.

In a town as small as Manning, any death, even one by natural causes, remains the topic of conversation for weeks. A murder is talked about for months on end. When it is one in a series of murders, however, as this was, it is not talked about so much as *felt*. It is conspicuous by the silence it leaves behind.

But Manning is not just *any* small town. It is located in California's Napa Valley on the St. Helena Highway between St. Helena and Calistoga. It is actually a village more than a town, with a population of only 1,750. Most people in the Valley, however, think of it not as a town or a village, but as a sort of commune.

It is inhabited almost exclusively by Seventh-day Adventists.

Manning was founded in 1897 when the Seventh-day Adventists, led by their "prophet," Ellen G. White, settled in the Napa Valley. Another village, Angwin, rose up around the college built by the Adventists atop a hill just above Manning.

Seventh-day Adventists worship on Saturday, the seventh day, rather than Sunday; as with the Jewish faith, their Sabbath begins at sunset on Friday and ends at sunset on Saturday. During that time, the only place in town that is open is the church. Weekend mail is delivered on Sunday instead of Saturday (Manning has its own little post office which, of course, employs only Seventh-day Adventist residents). Sometimes Delbert Mundy, manager of the Manning Food Market — which sells no alcoholic beverages, no cigarettes, no meat, and nothing containing caffeine, all of which are condemned in the writings of Ellen White — can be seen on Saturday evenings standing just inside the market's front doors, keys in hand, staring at his wristwatch, waiting for the sun to go down so he can open up.

The thing about Manning that Brett Deever hated most — despised, in fact — was that, unlike its neighboring towns St. Helena and Calistoga, both of which are larger but still quite small, Manning had no movie theater.

It would have done Brett no good if it had.

Along with drinking alcohol and coffee, eating pork and seafood, reading fiction, wearing make-up or jewelry, dancing and playing cards, the Seventh-day Adventist Church's list of condemned activities also includes going to movies.

The summer rains that had hit the Valley with such a vengeance earlier in the month had caused Vintner Creek to disgorge all kinds of garbage onto its muddy banks, none of which was as horrible as the chewy treat Gabby had discovered.

While Brett had found a hand, and Gabby, a foot, the police and their dogs had uncovered a lot more, all of it identifiable with the help of lab techs from San Francisco. Despite massive decay, the body parts were identified as belonging to Jimmy Greenlaw. He was the third such victim in two years.

All three boys had been approximately the same age. The first had been a resident of St. Helena, the second from Angwin, and Jimmy had spent his eight years of life in Manning. All three had been Seventh-day Adventists.

The boys had been sodomized, then dismembered, and their remains cast into the waters of Vintner Creek to find their way into the digestive tracts of various fish and forest animals.

The bone scoring suggested the killer used dull kitchen implements, and that he'd done a sloppy, amateurish job of it. The cut patterns on the bones were a near match; the semen tracks were an *exact* match.

The police claimed there was other linking evidence proving the killings to be the work of a single person or group. They refused, however, to discuss such niceties as chemical proof and tissue damage with the press.

That was just fine with Brett's grandma.

"They'll be back, those reporters," she said a few days after Brett's discovery, seating him at the kitchen table. Grandma was a large gray woman who dressed colorlessly and seldom smiled. She was especially unsmiling now; she'd just chased two more reporters from the front door. As she poured Brett a glass of soy milk, she said sternly, "And you'll not talk to them. Always sticking their microphones into people's faces after something awful's happened. The more awful the *better*, far as they're concerned. That's why I'll not have any newspapers in this house. Rags, all of them." She lowered herself into a chair across from Brett. "No television, either. All those reporters *smiling* while they tell about murders and rapes and homo-seck-shuls spreading AIDS. Course, the television *shows* are just as bad. Nothing but sex and killing . . ."

61

SILVER SCREAM

Brett sipped the thick sweet milk, wiped off his creamy white mustache and said, "Larry Jackson says *they* have a television, but his parents only let him watch *good* shows. He says —"

"I don't care. A television is Satan's doorway into the home. I know *some* say they can handle it, but if Sister White were still alive, *she'd* tell them differently. Maybe they're watching good shows now —" She spat *good shows* with bitter skepticism. "— but you just *wait*. You watch enough of that stuff and it . . . it *affects* you." She searched Brett's face for a moment and her eyes clouded with worry. She reached across the table and closed her puffy liver-spotted hand over Brett's small one. "You haven't been thinking about that boy, have you? About those . . . what you found?"

Brett shook his head, resisting the urge to roll his eyes. "No, Grandma."

"Good. Good. It's not healthy to dwell on that sort of thing. It can . . . affect you." She watched him a moment longer, as if waiting for a reaction of some sort, then said, "Go study your Sabbath school lesson, Brett, honey. And say a prayer for that poor boy's family. After dinner, you can give me a back rub."

He polished off his milk and Grandma stroked his hair gently, sympathy glistening in her eyes.

The policemen had been the same way. All of a sudden, everyone was treating him as if he were breakable just because he'd found a dead boy. Brett didn't understand what the big deal was. It wasn't as if Jimmy had been a friend of his; Brett had no friends to speak of. They'd had a passing acquaintance in Sabbath school, but that was all. Sure, it was a bad thing that happened and Jimmy's parents were probably crushed, but Brett wouldn't let *his* feelings get involved.

On his way through the living room, Brett glimpsed his Grandpa. Brett seldom got more than a glimpse of him, usually rounding a corner or going through a doorway in his wheelchair, the two stumps of his legs — souvenirs from the Big War — hidden beneath a brown wool blanket. He had his own bedroom downstairs where he ate all of his meals and spent most of his time listening to gospel music on his record player. Brett never heard Grandma talking to him, and he couldn't remember the last time he'd heard Grandpa speak; the only sound he made was the muffled rumble of his chair wheeling over the old wooden floor.

In his room upstairs, Brett locked his door — something Grandma strongly disapproved of — and pulled a fat three-ring binder from under his bed. He flopped onto the mattress and opened the book, searching through the heavy construction paper pages. Pasted to each page were movie advertisements cut out of newspapers. He looked for one in particular and when he found it, he folded his arms beneath his chest, tucked the tip of his tongue into the corner of his mouth, and stared at it, relished it.

The ad took up a quarter of the page and written at the top in letters that appeared to be carved in flesh was the title:

SINEMA

BEDSIDE MANNERS

Below that:

If you sleep in the dark,
he'll find you . . .
If you sleep with a light on,
he'll find you faster . . .

Below the words was a picture of a man's bluejeaned legs from behind; a bloodied axe hung at his side. Between his spread legs, facing him, a woman lay in bed clutching the blankets to her breasts, mouth open in a horrified scream.

The woman was Brett's mother.

The book held nearly sixty ads for all kinds of movies ranging from Academy Award winners complete with quotes of praise from the critics to grade-Z horror films promising lots of bosoms and blood; Brett collected them all. Because Grandma would not allow newspapers into the house, Brett had to fish discarded editions from garbage cans and trash bins, always careful that no one was watching. Once he'd found the entertainment section, he folded the paper up and stuffed it into his book bag, then sneaked it to his room, where it was subjected to scissors and paste. Risky business for a Seventh-day Adventist boy, but even more risky with Grandma around.

Grandma had a nervous tic that wriggled her lower lip now and then, especially when she was upset. At the very mention of movies or theaters, Grandma's lip began to twitch so fast it seemed about to wriggle off her face. "If you ever go into such a place," she'd say firmly, "your guardian angel does not go with you. It puts a distance between you and the Lord and can be dangerous. Bad things can happen. Your soul is unprotected and if you should die within those walls, you're lost forever."

Brett never understood exactly why it was wrong to go to movies. There were certainly no rules against having a television or watching movies at home on a VCR. There were approved and unapproved movies, of course. The Adventists Brett knew who owned televisions all claimed to use discretion in choosing programs and movies, but they still *watched* them. Sometimes the church held a "Family Film Night" when they would show *The Wilderness Family* or some Disney movie that was on the Approved List and charge admission to raise money for new carpet in the sanctuary, or something. But going to see a movie in a theater was absolutely forbidden.

Brett had been given several explanations for this law such as, "In a theater you're with a bad crowd, the wrong element," and, "Movies contain unchristian and immoral themes and are a powerful negative influence." None of them satisfied him. *Lost forever* was a pretty strong consequence to pay, but it did not dampen his desire to go to a theater. Brett dreamed of going to movies the way most boys his age dreamed of being a fireman, a secret agent, or an astronaut.

63

SILVER SCREAM

He sometimes met other children his age who were not Seventh-day Adventists and asked them what it was like to go to movies. Puzzled by his urgent questioning, they told him of the warm smell of popcorn in the lobby, the posters on the walls, the way the voices hushed in the auditorium as the lights slowly died, of the coming attractions shown before the movie started, and the *movies* . . .

He asked them again and again about the movies they saw, wanting to know every detail from beginning to end.

"How come bad things don't happen to the other kids who go to movies?" he asked Grandma once.

"They haven't been shown the truth yet. You *have*. They don't know they're doing wrong, so the Lord won't hold it against them. But someday He'll show them."

There was always a shadow of worry on her face when he asked about movies; Brett suspected she feared he would turn out like his mother.

It had been so long since Brett had seen his mother that he'd forgotten what her voice sounded like. She called him every Christmas and birthday (although she'd forgotten his ninth), but the calls were brief and her voice was fuzzy with distance. He remembered her face only because he had a picture of her tucked in the back of the binder with her letter and postcards.

And now he had a new one: BEDSIDE MANNERS.

A little more than three years ago, Mom had left Brett with Grandma and Grandpa so she could go to Hollywood to become an actress. That's what she'd been doing before he came along, she'd claimed; she hadn't quite made it then, so she wanted to give it another try.

Grandma spoke of Mom only when Brett got a phonecall from her. After the call, she would hug Brett to her enormous breasts — she always smelled of mothballs and Ben-Gay — and mutter, "Imagine your own mother running off like that. And to *that* town to work with those, those *people*. At least she had the good sense to leave you with me so I could raise you in Christ."

Sometimes it was easy to hate Mom for leaving him with Grandma and Grandpa; he hated Manning, the church, and everything that came with it. But he wouldn't let himself hate her because he always knew she'd come back for him someday. Now he knew he was right.

Brett took his mother's most recent letter from the back of the book. He only got her letters during the summer when he could get to the mailbox first. When he was in school, Grandma burned the letters before he could find them.

> Brett honey,
> Got my first movie role! It's a cheapie hor-
> ror flick called *Bedside Manners* and the part

64

is small — I play a "victim" in the first ten
minutes — but they're using me on the
poster, so it's good exposure . . .

Brett skipped down to the last paragraph.

I've got a little money now and hope to
come up north and get you soon. Would you
like to live in LA with me? There are good
schools here and lots of things to do . . .

Brett's chest swelled with the very thought of going away with Mom.
. . . *hope to come up north and get you soon* . . .
. . . *get you soon* . . .
. . . *soon* . . .
He heard Grandma in the hall and quickly put the book away, unlocking
the door before she tried the knob, then he lay back on his bed again.

Brett was so happy that even the thought of having to give Grandma
another of those smelly Ben-Gay backrubs after dinner could not depress
him . . .

Mr. Moser was the only person in the small Manning church with
whom Brett felt comfortable. The rest of the people there seemed to be
stiff, emotionless machines, programmed to smile at certain times, frown or
look sympathetic at others, set to shed a tear or say "A-*men!*" during the ser-
mon, and to sing the designated hymn when the organ began to play. On
Friday afternoons, they washed their cars, cleaned and pressed their finest
clothes; they came to church looking their best but seemed to leave their
souls at home.

As Brett sat with his grandparents (Grandpa always parked his wheelchair at the end of a pew) and looked at the empty staring faces around him
— some nodding off, others watching the droning pastor but apparently
seeing something else — he felt a sadness that was hard to shake. So he
didn't watch them anymore. He shut them out along with the whiney organ
music and the pastor's level, reverent voice that went on and on. Brett
learned how to shut himself off during the hour or so that the service lasted;
he heard nothing, saw nothing, and felt nothing. Afterward, instead of feeling agitated and depressed as he normally would, he felt relaxed, as if he'd
taken a nap.

He didn't have to do that in Sabbath school, though, because the teacher, Mr. Moser was different than the others. Brett wasn't the only one fond of him; all the kids liked Mr. Moser. There was nothing forced or artificial about him. When he laughed, it was real; his round little belly bounced like a ball and his darkly bearded moon face split into a broad grin.

When he was concerned, as he was that Sabbath after Brett's discovery, his heavy eyebrows lowered over his eyes and his forehead became creased with lines of genuine worry.

He took Brett aside after Sabbath school.

"How are you, Brett?"

"Fine."

"You're sure?"

"Oh. You mean after finding that . . . boy. Sheesh, everybody's worried about me now."

"Well, that's a pretty awful thing to find."

Brett shrugged.

"A pretty hard thing to forget, too, I'd think," Mr. Moser added.

"I'm okay. Really."

Mr. Moser studied Brett's face thoughtfully for a moment, then smiled.

"How would you like to come out to my place after church, Brett? We could have lunch, then go for a walk and look for lizards."

Brett was thrilled at the opportunity to get out of his grandparents' house for the day and even happier to spend the afternoon with Mr. Moser.

"I'll have to ask Grandma," he said, "She's kinda careful about letting me out of the house because of this . . . well, you know, the killer. But I'm sure she won't mind if she knows I'm with you . . ."

Mr. Moser lived at the end of a dirt road about a mile and a half off Glass Mountain Road. His house was small and homey, nestled in the shade of several tall trees. He had no neighbors within sight of his house and plenty of rocky, hilly land around on which to hunt lizards and snakes.

They had a lunch of taco salad and strawberry shortcake for dessert, then went outside for a long walk in the summer sun.

It made Brett feel important to be alone with his teacher; he had Mr. Moser's undivided attention *and* his interest. As they walked, they didn't talk about Sabbath school or church — in fact, Brett completely forgot it was the Sabbath, which would have been impossible had he been with Grandma. Mr. Moser wanted only to talk about Brett.

"What would you like to do, Brett, more than anything in the world?"

"Do? What do you mean?"

"Go to Disneyland? Fly a plane? Ride a rocket to the moon?"

66

They were walking along a dusty trail and Brett began to thoughtfully kick a rock along ahead of him, wondering if he could confide in Mr. Moser. He decided it was safe to be honest.

"I'd like to go to a movie," he said quietly.

"Pardon?"

"A movie. You know, in a theater."

"Ah. The forbidden fruit." Mr. Moser smiled knowingly.

"Huh?"

"Nothing. Never been to a movie, huh?"

"I've never even *seen* a movie. Not a *real* one, anyway, like *Raiders of the Lost Ark* or *Alien.* Just those stupid movies they show on Family Nights. And sometimes Grandma won't even let me go to *those.*"

Mr. Moser stopped and sat on a fat tree stump, chuckling quietly.

Brett frowned, thinking perhaps he'd said something wrong.

"What's funny?" he asked.

"Well, it's just that . . . see, I'm chairman of the Entertainment Committee. I'm one of the people who *chooses* those stupid movies."

"Oh." Brett could feel his face growing hot with embarrassment. "I'm sorry."

"No, no, don't apologize, Brett," Mr. Moser laughed. "I know most of those movies aren't very good, but we're kind of limited. It *is* a church function, after all. There aren't many good family-oriented films to choose from. We're always looking for new ones to put on the Approved List, but the committee's standards are pretty rigid. No swearing, no drinking, no smoking. I know what you mean, though; if I have to sit through *Zebra in the Kitchen* one more time, I may be sick." He rubbed his palms up and down his blue-jeaned thighs thoughtfully for a moment, then asked, "If you haven't seen any real movies, then how do you know about *Raiders of the Lost Ark* and *Alien?*"

Hesitantly, Brett told him about his collection of movie ads.

Mr. Moser listened intently, watching Brett with great interest. When he was finished, Mr. Moser said, "Have you ever seen a VCR, Brett?"

"We don't even have a TV."

Mr. Moser winked. "Then let's go back to the house. I've got something to show you."

Back in the house, Mr. Moser opened a tall cabinet in the living room. On the middle shelf was a large television set. Below was a black machine with the time glowing in green numbers on the side. Rows of what appeared to be books filled the top shelf.

"This is a video cassette recorder," Mr. Moser said, "and these —" He gestured at the book-like objects. "— are video cassettes."

Brett stared into the cabinet with awe, his lips parted.

"When a movie is submitted for approval," Mr. Moser said, "I sometimes invite the committee over here and, if it's available on video cassette, we watch it here, then vote on it."

"So you get to see unapproved movies, too?" Brett whispered. "Not just the kid stuff?"

"Well, it's not likely that anyone is going to submit a movie like *Body Heat* or *Tootsie* for approval, but, yes, I get to see all the movies."

"Wow," he breathed, leaning forward to reverently inspect the VCR. "How many videos do you have up there?"

"About sixty movies or so on tape."

"*Sixty?* Sheeesh . . ."

"All kinds of movies. You name it, and I've probably got it."

Brett stared up at the rows of tapes, imagining what it would be like to sit down and watch all of them — each one, back to back. He glanced at Mr. Moser, thinking there was probably little chance of seeing any of those movies.

But Mr. Moser had a broad grin on his face.

"Would you like to see one, Brett?" he asked.

"But . . . it's the Sabbath."

"Would that bother you?"

"Wouldn't it bother *you?*"

"Well . . . why don't we make this our little secret. Just between the two of us. Okay?"

Brett held his breath a moment, expecting him to say he was just joking. It was too much to ask for.

"Okay, Brett?"

Slowly, disbelievingly, Brett nodded, then smiled as he realized Mr. Moser was serious. *Really serious!*

Mr. Moser scanned the tapes and pulled one down, took it from its box, and slipped it into the machine.

"This is a good one," he said. "It's a Disney movie, but don't let that fool you. It's called *Never Cry Wolf*. It wasn't approved because there are a few swear words in it and a shot of Charles Martin Smith in the buff from behind. It's great, though. Sit down. You want some chips?"

Within minutes, Brett was seated wide-eyed in front of the television munching on potato chips and drinking a Crush.

For two hours, he was far away from Manning.

In the following weeks, Brett spent a good deal of his time over at Mr. Moser's watching one movie after another.

Grandma was pleased because Brett had told her he was working with

68

Mr. Moser on some Sabbath school projects. No further explanation was needed; she was glad to know he was investing his time in wholesome activities.

The day after he watched *Never Cry Wolf*, Brett saw *Starman*, a movie that would never even be *considered* for approval; Seventh-day Adventists frown bitterly upon science fiction and fantasy. At the end of the movie, the alien, played by Jeff Bridges, made love with Karen Allen. It was a gentle, tasteful love scene (the movie was only rated PG) with no frantic grunting or moaning, but it was nevertheless startling to Brett. He had neither seen nor imagined people touching each other, with their hands *and* their mouths, the way Jeff Bridges and Karen Allen were on the screen.

He squinted curiously, straightened his posture, and said, "What are they doing?"

Mr. Moser sniffed and fidgeted on the sofa.

"They're, um, making love."

"What?"

"Making love."

"What's that?"

"Well . . . when a man and woman care very much for one another, they, um . . . they share their bodies with each other. They kiss and hold each other. Like that." He gestured toward the screen.

"You mean *sex?*"

Mr. Moser nodded slightly, his eyes on the television; he looked embarrassed and uncomfortable.

So that's what Grandma's always complaining about, Brett thought, turning his attention back to the movie.

Nothing but sex and killing . . .

He could see nothing bad about what the man and woman were doing. In fact, it was pleasant; they seemed to be enjoying themselves.

As the tape was rewinding, Brett turned to Mr. Moser and said, "That didn't look like a bad thing. The sex, I mean. People are always talking about it like it's a bad thing."

"Well, it can be . . . misused," Mr. Moser said, clearing his throat nervously. "But if it's between a man and woman who love one another and who are married, it's perfectly natural and . . . healthy."

"But *they* weren't married," Brett pointed out with a nod toward the television.

"*That* is why the Church doesn't want you to watch movies unless they're approved by a committee."

Brett returned the following day for a showing of *The Color Purple*.

"I think you'll like this, Brett," Mr. Moser said enthusiastically as he put the tape in the VCR. "It's a great movie. In fact, it just barely missed the Approved List."

SILVER SCREAM

"How come?"

"Oh, some swearing and drinking. But what really did it was the lesbian relationship."

"The what?"

Mr. Moser glanced at Brett with a startled expression and Brett realized that, for a moment, Mr. Moser had forgotten he wasn't talking to another adult.

"We'll talk about it after the movie."

It *was* a great movie, although very sad. Brett was surprised at how much the film moved him. By the time it was over, his eyes were puffy and sticky with tears. He didn't want to talk for a while and was silent as the tape rewound. Mr. Moser watched him, waiting for him to speak.

"So what's a . . . lez-bean?" he finally asked.

"Well, what did you think of the movie?"

"It was good. But I didn't see anything that looked like it might be a lez-bean relationship. Whatever that is. So what is it?"

"It was pretty subtle; I guess you'd have to be looking for it. Remember when Shug and Celie went home after the big fight in the bar?"

Brett nodded.

"And they were alone together? And they started . . . well, touching each other?"

Another nod.

"That's were, um —" He was fidgeting again. "— where their lesbian relationship began."

Brett waited for him to go on; when he didn't, Brett said, "I still don't know what it is."

Mr. Moser sighed. "A lesbian is . . . well, it's a woman who would rather make love with . . . with another woman that with a man."

Brett frowned as he thought that over.

"You mean . . . *sex?* The women do *sex* together?"

Mr. Moser nodded and said, "Have sex, not do."

Brett pondered the new information, chewing his lip. Something about it bothered him; it didn't fit into his rapidly growing view of things.

"Are there men lesbians, too?" he asked.

Mr. Moser nodded as he turned away from Brett and ejected the tape. "Homosexuals," he muttered, putting the tape in its box.

. . . *and the homo-seck-shuls spreading the AIDS,* Grandma had grumbled.

There was another of her mysterious complaints explained.

"Why would anyone want to —" Brett began, but Mr. Moser interrupted him.

"How would you like a popcorn ball? I made some this morning."

Taking that as a hint to change the subject, Brett said, "Okay."

70

SINEMA

* * *

Brett waited for the mail carrier each day, but heard nothing more from his mother. After each disappointing delivery, he would play with Gabby until he knew Mr. Moser was home from work — Mr. Moser was an X-ray technician at the Seventh-day Adventist hospital in Deer Park and got off at three p.m. — then hop on his bike and head for his Sabbath school teacher's house.

A day did not pass without a few warnings from Grandma.

"Don't talk to any strangers," she'd say. "And stay away from those Mexican hitch-hikers, you hear? Probably one of them who's killing all those poor little boys. Always drinking their beer and smoking their dope . . . Course, if you keep saying your prayers, Jesus'll watch over you and nothing will happen."

In Brett, Mr. Moser had found a protege; in Moser, Brett had gained a mentor, and he watched one movie after another, so many that he would have lost count if he did not list them in a spiral-bound pocket pad — a new kind of scrapbook. Beneath the title of each film were notes; Brett learned something new from each film whether he enjoyed the movie or not.

Sometimes, while sitting on the sofa in front of the TV, munching snacks, drinking a soda, Brett would glance up and see Mr. Moser watching him peripherally, usually chewing a nail or passing a hand up and down his thigh nervously, as if wiping sweat from his palm. His eyes darted away the moment Brett spotted him watching, and he always returned his attention to the movie.

Gremlins, The Terminator and *Cujo* defined Brett's next week, followed by all three *Star Wars* movies in a row. Of the trilogy, Brett's favorite was the first; he nearly jumped to his feet and cheered during the final scene in which the heroes were rewarded for their valor.

At first, Brett found it a bit disconcerting to watch unapproved movies with the chairman of the entertainment committee. But Mr. Moser reassured him.

"Remember, Brett," he said, "it's our secret."

One day, Mr. Moser said, "Brett, I think it's time you left behind the little kid stuff." He took down a tape and removed it from its box. "I think you should start learning a little about movies and the people who make them, seeing how you love them so much. Do you know who Alfred Hitchcock was?"

Brett shook his head. He knew Mr. Moser's "teacher voice" by heart; it was the same tone he used in Sabbath school when imparting lessons. Brett was infinitely more interested in the lessons Mr. Moser reserved for him personally, and so paid rapt attention, eager to please. He enjoyed what he

71

SILVER SCREAM

was learning, savoring the taste of what Moser had called the forbidden fruit.

Mr. Moser slid a new tape into the VCR. "Hitchcock was a very famous movie director, maybe the most imitated director ever." He saw the puzzlement on Brett's face, and because he was good at teaching, he explained. "The director is the one in charge on a movie set. He tells people what to do, where to stand, how to act. He makes changes in the story; decides how each scene is going to be filmed. He orchestrates everything. Anyway, this movie is Hitchcock's first sound film. The first sound film to come out of England, in fact. It's old — 1929 — but it's good. I just got it and thought you might like to see it. It's called *Blackmail.*"

The title conjured images of letters written on black stationery in Brett's mind. He'd never heard the word "blackmail" before and had no idea what it meant.

As he watched, he learned.

For three weeks, Brett kept their secret and his list of movies grew a little longer each day. From Mr. Moser he learned about movies; from the movies he learned about life.

It was the Friday night of the third week of their secret that things changed.

Friday nights were always gloomy. Grandma never smiled — not that she did much smiling anyway — and was grumpier than usual. The darkness seemed a little darker and the scratchy music from Grandpa's room seemed more mournful than the rest of the week. Grandpa usually sat in the living room on Friday nights, his grave, shiny-bald head hanging heavily from his neck, for which it seemed much too big. He drummed his thick fingers on the armrests of his wheelchair, his eyes blackened by shadow, as Grandma rocked in the squeaky rocking chair, reading Sister White and humming off-key to the music.

Brett was more than eager to get out for the evening.

On that Friday night, Brett arrived to find Mr. Moser on the phone.

"I'm sorry, Jim," he was saying. "I completely forgot about it. I can be there in five minutes . . . No, no, I have nothing planned. I'll be right there."

When he hung up, Mr. Moser paced before the phone for a moment, chewing a thumbnail, almost as if Brett wasn't there. His eyes finally darted to Brett and his lips curled into a forced smile that was little more than a flash of teeth.

"A Sabbath school committee meeting," he muttered. "Forgot all about it."

"Oh. Do you want me to go?"

72

"No, no," he replied quickly, turning fully to Brett, holding out his arms and waggling his hands. "No, sit down, have a soda, put in a movie. I shouldn't be gone more than twenty-thirty minutes. I have —" He lowered his voice secretively and smiled. "— I have a surprise for you, Brett. It'll just have to wait a few minutes now, that's all." He took his wallet and keys from the coffee table. "Don't answer the phone, just let the machine get it. Be back in a few."

After he was gone, Brett opened the cabinet and, with the help of a chair from the kitchen, pulled *Ghostbusters* down from the shelf. Mr. Moser had showed him how to operate the VCR so he slipped in the tape, turned on the television, and pushed PLAY.

The empty house rang with Brett's laughter as he watched the movie and drank a root beer from the refrigerator. Ten minutes into the tape, he pushed the pause button and headed for the bathroom.

Mr. Moser had given Brett a tour of the house during his first visit. Pointing to the door beyond the bathroom, Mr. Moser had said, "That's my bedroom, and that," he'd added, pointing across the hall, "is the linen closet. If you ever spend the night, there are extra blankets and pillows in there."

"What's this?" Brett had gone to a closed door at the end of the hall.

"Laundry room." He'd taken Brett's arm then and led him back into the living room, saying, "It's a mess."

After he finished in the bathroom, Brett stood at the bedroom door a moment and decided Mr. Moser wouldn't mind if he just took a peek inside to see what his bedroom looked like.

It was dark in the bedroom and Brett reached for a light switch, found it, and flipped it up.

The first thing he saw was the huge screen across the room. He thought it was probably a big-screen TV; he'd heard about them, but had no idea they were *this* big.

Bret stepped over to the television to get a better look and saw that there was another VCR hooked up to it, just like the one in the living room.

He brushed his fingertips lightly around the labeled controls — ON-OFF, VOLUME, COLOR, TINT . . .

Watching a movie on that big screen would almost be like watching it in a theater . . .

Maybe this *is the surprise,* he thought.

Brett hurried into the living room, ejected *Ghostbusters,* returned to the bedroom and turned on the television. When he tried to insert the tape into the VCR, he found another already in the slot. He pushed EJECT and the tape eased out like a tongue from a mouth.

The top of the tape was black as night and the white spools in the casing stared at him like dead eyes.

Looking around, Brett found no box for the tape, but a white label was attached to the tape's edge. In block letters written with a felt-tip marker was written WARNER BROS. CARTOONS #2.

He glanced at the clock beside the bed. Mr. Moser had been gone only fifteen minutes. That left another fifteen; he'd probably be a little longer than he'd said if it was a meeting.

Slipping the tape back into the slot, he pressed PLAY, and sat back against the foot of the bed.

Cheerful music began to play and the words LOONEY TOONS appeared on the large screen.

"Bugs Bunny!" Brett exclaimed happily when the rabbit appeared, munching a carrot. He'd seen pictures of Bugs in a coloring book his mother had sent him. Grandma had taken the book away from him and, in its place, given him a book called *Uncle Arthur's Bible Stories*. No rabbits in *that* book.

After the credits, a short bald man appeared holding a rifle. He was walking through the woods on tiptoe looking right and left.

"Shhh!" he hissed to Brett, looking right out of the screen at him, "I'm hunting wabbits. Heh-heh-heh-heh!"

Bugs suddenly poked his head out of a hole in the ground, took a bite of carrot, smacked his lips a few times, and said, "Aaaaahh, what's up, D—"

The cartoon was gone.

The screen danced with black and white speckles; Mr. Moser called them "ant races".

For a moment, Brett chilled with the fear that he'd done something wrong, something that had perhaps broken the VCR.

He sighed with quiet relief when the picture returned.

But it was not the cartoon of a moment before.

Garbled music played over the television speakers and the screen filled with a square platform surrounded by a fence of ropes. Two huge, sweaty men stood in opposite corners of the square.

"And in *this* corner!" a faceless voice shouted. "Measuring in at ten and three-quarter inches! *Mickey* . . . "the *Bone*" . . . Semen*inski!*"

The men stepped out of their corners as an invisible crowd cheered them on. Their arms were held slightly outward, fingers crooked into threatening claws.

Both men wore tight masks over their faces, one black and one red. Hugging their massive bodies were leather outfits that criss-crossed and zig-zagged; silver spikes and zippers shined all over the costumes.

That was not, however, what shocked Brett.

What made Brett's mouth fall open loosely, what made his breath catch in his throat, was the large triangular opening below each man's waist and the stiff fleshy rod that jutted from thick dark patches of curly hair.

Brett closed his eyes a moment, certain he was not seeing what he *thought* he was seeing. Surely he'd come in on the middle of something —

74

perhaps a recording mistake on Mr. Moser's part — and had missed an important scene that would explain what he thought he'd seen.

But when he opened his eyes again . . .

The men were circling one another menacingly, eyeing the exposed sections between their legs.

An odd memory suddenly flashed behind Brett's eyes, vivid in detail. He was sitting in a tub of soapy water bathing on the third night after moving in with his grandparents. The bathroom door opened and Grandma came in — he remembered how overwhelming the smell of Ben-Gay had been — wearing her bathrobe.

"Wash good," she'd said with a smile. Then her eyes had darkened and she'd leaned over the tub. "But when you wash *there*," she'd whispered, pointing to his private area (that's what Mom had called it) hidden beneath the suds, "wash *quickly*. Don't touch it anymore than you have to."

"What?" he'd said, puzzled.

Her lower lip had begun to twitch as she said, 'Your pee-pee. Your *penis*. It's . . . bad. *Dirty*. If you touch it too much, it . . . wakes *up*. Makes you think bad thoughts. So wash it *quickly*." She'd smiled then and left him to his bath.

Never quite sure what she'd meant, Brett remembered what she'd said each time he bathed and did as he'd been told, not wanting to awaken his penis.

The men on the screen, however, were apparently *trying* to awaken theirs. They were handling themselves, *pulling* on themselves, making their penises grow even larger as they circled one another again and again.

The red man suddenly lunged for his opponent, grabbing unsuccessfully for his penis.

He was not unsuccessful the second time.

The crowd roared.

The garbled music continued, rambling almost tunelessly.

"And the Bone is *down!*" the faceless voice cried.

The red man straddled the Bone, holding his penis in a fist. Reaching up to his masked face, the red man opened a zipper over his mouth, rounded his lips into a large O, and leaned forward.

The invisible crowd went wild.

Brett buried his shock in a forced, familiar numbness until he could watch the film without reacting.

He felt nothing.

Just like in church.

*   *   *

75

SILVER SCREAM

The Sabbath school committee meeting was over in twenty minutes, just as Mr. Moser had suspected it would be. The entire committee was present — eight people in all — and, as usual, they sat around the conference table and socialized after the official business was out of the way.

Mr. Moser excused himself from the chatter, left the room, and headed down the main corridor of the church for the front entrance, walking at a brisk pace, thinking of Brett . . .

"Ed! What's your hurry?"

He stopped and turned to see Pastor Alexander coming out of his study.

"Well," he began, pushing a smile onto his face, "I'm, uh . . . I'm in no hurry, really."

"Then step in here for a minute. I want you to meet someone."

Mr. Moser followed the little man with the big walrus mustache into his study where a man, woman, and little boy were seated on a brown leather-upholstered sofa.

"Ed Moser," Pastor Alexander said formally, "I'd like you to meet the Rileys, Jack, Betty, and their son Jason."

Mr. Moser smiled, shook Jack Riley's hand, and said, "Pleased to meet you."

"The Rileys have just moved to Manning," the pastor said. "This is going to be their first Sabbath with us."

"Oh. Well. Welcome. Glad to have you." He glanced at his watch and made note of the time; he'd been gone almost half an hour.

Pastor Alexander moved behind his desk and seated himself in his squeaky chair. "Have a seat, Ed."

Still smiling, Mr. Moser thought of Brett back at the house, sitting in front of the television set watching a movie. What would it be tonight? *Jaws? Stripes?* Maybe *The Wizard of Oz*. He seated himself in a chair facing the Rileys.

"Ed is one of our Sabbath school teachers," Pastor Alexander said. "He works in X-ray at our hospital up the hill — has quite a reputation up there — but I'm happy to say he's very generous with his time. Ed's devoted to our children here at the church." The pastor winked at Jason and said, "You'll be in his class tomorrow, Jason."

The boy smiled hesitantly at Mr. Moser.

"We'll be glad to have you, Jason," Mr. Moser said. "I've got a great bunch of boys in my class. Boys *and* girls, of course."

Jason blushed beneath his freckles and looked away bashfully.

"Fine looking boy you have there," Mr. Moser said to the proudly beaming Rileys. "Fine looking boy."

*   *   *

SINEMA

There was a second movie on the tape and it began as soon as the Bone and the man in red milked one another's penises. That's what it looked like to Brett — milk. Thick, like soy milk.

More of the same.

Brett hit FAST FORWARD, waited a moment, then pushed PLAY. Still more.

He pushed REWIND and sat watching the ant races, his mind buzzing with questions.

Did Mr. Moser *watch* these movies? He must, or else why would he own them?

But did he *enjoy* them?

He must, or else why would he *watch* them?

Then was Mr. Moser a man lesbian? A —

. . . and the homo-seck-shuls spreading the AIDS . . .

— homosexual?

If he liked to *watch* men doing sex together (if that was what those men had been doing, and Brett suspected it was), then . . .

. . . then he must like to do *it, too*, Brett thought.

The tape finished rewinding with a solid *thunk*.

Maybe he was just curious, Brett suggested to himself as he ejected the tape.

Surely Mr. Moser didn't have any *more* of those movies.

Then again, he *had* been very uncomfortable talking about sex.

Maybe even guilty.

Brett stood and dashed down the hall to the living room where he cupped his hands to the pane of the front window and looked for Mr. Moser's headlights in the night.

Nothing.

He hurried back to the bedroom and began his search.

Brett looked through drawers — careful not to disturb anything — under the bed, in the closet.

He found nothing but underwear and clothes, shoes and some dusty boxes and books.

Disappointed, Brett sat on the edge of the bed and slowly looked around him for a place he might have missed.

To his left, at the head of the bed, there were two rectangular sliding doors, each with a round brass knob in the center. Brett slid one aside, then the other.

Boxed video tapes were neatly stored on the headboard shelf, labels facing out.

From left to right were WARNER BROS. CARTOONS — #1-#7, with #2 missing. There were three more tapes labeled LITTLE RASCALS — #1-#3.

SILVER SCREAM

Brett removed the fourth cartoon tape and put it in the VCR.

After about two minutes of a Daffy Duck cartoon and a few seconds of ant races, Brett saw two young men stroking their penises beside a swimming pool. When one of them gasped, "Okay, *suck* me, *now!*" Brett rewound the tape, ejected it, and replaced it in the headboard.

Mr. Moser was not just curious.

Wondering why they were labeled differently, Brett couldn't resist taking a look at one of the LITTLE RASCALS tapes. He chose #3.

The film — "Our Gang" in *The He-Man Woman-Haters Club* — was old with fuzzy black-and-white images and music and voices that seemed to be coming through a wall of gauze.

A fat little boy and a tall skinny one with funny hair were entering a makeshift clubhouse.

The fat one said, "Well, Alfalfa, this is the headquarters of the He-Man Woman-Haters Club."

There were some other boys in the clubhouse and they all waved at Alfalfa, who waved back and said, "Gee, Spanky, I'd sure like to join. What do I have to —"

Ant races.

The ant races were replaced by blackness; Brett slowly realized that the blackness was a room, unlit and unoccupied.

A light came on with a distant *click*, and Brett saw what looked like a doctor's examination table. It was covered with a sheet of heavy plastic. Tied to the table was a naked little boy. Brett squinted at the boy's still face.

It was Jimmy Greenlaw.

A naked man stepped into the picture, his back to the camera. His skin was white and flabby. When he finally spoke —

"Okay," he breathed with anticipation. "Ooo*okay.*"

— Brett recognized the voice.

It belonged to Mr. Moser.

It was only a matter of minutes before Jason Riley lost his bashfulness and was chatting with Mr. Moser as if they were old buddies.

"Do you like Bible stories, Jason?" Mr. Moser asked.

"Sure do," the boy said with an enthusiastic nod.

"They're my specialty. Tomorrow I'm telling the story of Daniel in the lion's den."

"Oh, that's his *favorite*," Mrs. Riley chimed, putting an arm around her son.

"Good," Mr. Moser grinned. "It's my favorite story to tell."

78

SINEMA

Mr. Riley politely said it was time to go home and they all stood at once. Pastor Alexander suggested that he and Mr. Moser walk them to their car and they headed down the corridor at a leisurely pace, Jason walking beside Mr. Moser, who rested a hand on the boy's shoulder.

"Looking forward to having you in my class, Jason," Mr. Moser said through a smile.

Brett's fingers dug into the carpet beneath him and he felt something uncoil in his gut as he watched.

His back still turned, Mr. Moser ran his hands over Jimmy's small, still body, his breaths heavy and moist. He turned so Brett could see him in profile, reached under the table, and produced a white, blue-labeled bottle. Brett recognized it as the stuff that Grandma used to remove ring around the collar. As Mr. Moser poured some of the thick liquid soap in his hand and began rubbing it on his rigid penis, Brett sang under his breath, "Ring-around-the-collar, ring-around-the-collar," then closed his eyes for a moment. He opened them again when he heard Mr. Moser sigh, then moan, then pant.

The Sabbath school teacher was holding Jimmy's legs up and apart and lying between them, his dimpled buttocks jutting up and down spastically.

At the Riley's car in the front parking lot, Pastor Alexander suggested Mr. Moser say a prayer and the five people joined hands in a small circle.

"Dear Heavenly Father," he began, "we thank You for bringing these good people to our town and our church. We ask that you watch over them as they settle into their new home . . ."

Brett sucked in a sharp, sickened breath and diverted his eyes, looking at the room on the screen.

It looked like a garage only smaller, with lots of dusty shelves on the walls. Behind Mr. Moser and Jimmy was a large rusty metal sink; next to that were a washer and dryer. Below the table was a drain centered on the concrete floor surrounded by a large dark stain.

Laundry room . . . it's a mess in there . . .

SILVER SCREAM

Jimmy screamed and Brett turned back to the television in time to see Mr. Moser lift a hatchet over his head and bring it down with a heavy, wet *crunch*.

". . . We especially ask that you watch over young Jason. Guide him in Your Way, oh Lord, and protect him from the snares and temptations of the Evil One . . ."

Blood shot upward in a crimson spray.
Jimmy's scream became a shrill, piercing wail.

". . . Guide them safely home now, Father, and rest them well so that we can all gather tomorrow in Your name. We ask these favors in the Name of Your Son Jesus . . . amen."
"Amen," they repeated in unison.
Mr. Moser gave Jason a friendly hug and said, "You'll have to come over to my place real soon and we'll go lizard hunting."
"Okay," Jason said happily. "I'd like that."
Mr. Moser bid them goodnight and walked to his car.

Another chop.
. . . *a mess* . . .
Brett's fists unclenched and the tight knot in his stomach relaxed as he began to distance himself from what he was seeing.
Just like in church.

Driving down the road in his car, Mr. Moser slipped a cassette into his stereo. It was a tape he often played for his children in Sabbath school, an album of Anita Bryant singing some children's gospel favorites. The first song began and he sang along.

"Jesus loves the little chillllldren . . . all the children of the worrrllld . . ."

He smiled, knowing that in just a few minutes, he would be able to give Brett his surprise.

After Mr. Moser had taken Jimmy apart and milked his penis over the armless, legless, lifeless trunk of the boy's body, the ant races came back on.

Brett watched them for several seconds, his mouth dry. He thought of Mr. Moser teaching Sabbath school, acting out Bible stories, making the kids — Brett included — laugh.

And he thought of what he'd just seen.

I have a surprise for you, Brett . . .

. . . a surprise . . .

Brett stood, left the room, went to the door at the end of the hall, and opened it.

The sink was across the room.

The table was covered with canvas and boxes were stacked on it, making it look like a sort of workbench.

The drain in the floor looked clogged with black soggy lumps.

To the right of the doorway was a tall wooden cupboard. Brett opened it and stared for a while at the tripod and the black and gray camera case beneath it.

He hurried down the hall to the front window and looked out again. He still saw no headlights, but knew he probably didn't have much time to cover his traces.

Back in the bedroom, he felt vaguely ill, like he might throw up, but he started to hum a church hymn and the feeling went away; he didn't want to make a mess he couldn't conceal.

He ejected the LITTLE RASCALS tape and returned it to the headboard, then picked up *Ghostbusters* from the floor, wishing he had time to finish watching it; wishing even more that he could see it in a *real* theater on a *real* movie screen . . .

The idea that came from that thought made his hands tremble.

Hurried by a gnawing feeling of urgency — he *knew* Mr. Moser could not be gone much longer — Brett returned to the living room, rewound *Ghostbusters*, and put it away. He found a brown paper bag in the kitchen, took it to the bedroom, removed LITTLE RASCALS - #3 from the headboard, and stuffed it in the bag. He turned all the lights off on his way out of the house, locked the door, and put the tape in the basket between his handlebars.

81

SILVER SCREAM

Less than a minute after he turned onto Glass Mountain Road, Brett heard a car up ahead. The glow of headlights illuminated the upcoming curve in the road and Brett drove his bike into the ditch, tumbled into the weeds and remained perfectly still, hoping he was out of sight.

The car passed, slowed, turned into the driveway.

It was Mr. Moser.

Brett waited until the crunch of the tires on the gravel road began to fade, then pulled his bike onto the pavement again. Before getting back on, he leaned over and vomited until his eyes burned.

He wiped his mouth on the back of his hand and rode home, already thinking about tomorrow morning.

Mr. Moser came to Sabbath school late the following morning. He rushed in looking rumpled and winded; his hair was mussed and his brow glowed with perspiration. The moment he entered, his eyes locked with Brett's and narrowed briefly to dark bloodless cuts.

He seemed preoccupied as he led the class through song service, kept tugging his tie as he quizzed them on the weekly Sabbath school lesson, and wiped his brow again and again as he stuttered through a retelling of Daniel's stay in the lion's den. He cut the story short and excused himself, asking Mrs. Juarez, the pianist, to take over. Before leaving the room, Mr. Moser looked at Brett and nodded toward the door.

Brett followed him.

In the main corridor, Brett could hear the sanctuary organ playing a hymn; voices sang along glumly, blending and garbling until they seemed to be singing in some ancient long-dead tongue.

Mr. Moser took a handkerchief from his pocket and mopped his face and neck; when he was through, the white cloth looked drenched.

"I don't seem to be feeling too well, Brett," he said nervously. "What do you suppose might be wrong?"

"I don't know. The flu, maybe?"

"I don't think so." He dabbed the underside of his chin with the handkerchief. "Enjoy the movie last night?"

"Uh-huh."

"You, uh . . . you left before I could give you your surprise. That wasn't very nice. I thought maybe —"

"I took it, Mr. Moser."

He froze, still as a snapshot, his eyes searching Brett's face, his mouth open slightly, tongue darting around inside.

"Don't worry," Brett whispered. "It's in a safe place. And I won't tell anyone. *If . . .*"

82

SINEMA

"If?" Mr. Moser breathed. "If *what?*"

"If you do what I ask."

A moment later, Mr. Moser chuckled; his nostrils flared and what might have been a tear glistened in his eye.

"Blackmailed," he muttered, shaking his head in wonderment. "I'm being blackmailed."

"If anything happens to me," Brett said, "someone will find the tape. There's a note attached that explains everything." It was a lie, of course, but Mr. Moser could never know that.

Mr. Moser wiped an eye and scrubbed his shiny face.

"I don't want much," Brett said.

"And what . . . is that?"

"I want you to take me to the movies. Whenever I want to go."

The music and singing stopped and somewhere in the church a chorus of voices exclaimed, "A-*men!*"

The next day, Brett called Mr. Moser and said he wanted to see the new Clint Eastwood movie. He *really* wanted to see *Bedside Manners* more than anything but it was only playing in San Francisco, which was too far away, and he wanted to see it with Mom; that would make it special. He and Mr. Moser agreed to go to a theater in Santa Rosa so no one they knew would see them.

After hanging up, Brett went to the kitchen and told Grandma he was going for a bike ride and would be back in time for supper.

"You stick close to the house," she ordered. "Don't go riding off someplace where you're all alone. And say your *prayers.*"

On his way through the dark living room, Brett saw Grandpa sitting in the far corner by the phonetable. His big gnarled hands were joined on his lap and his head turned slowly, following Brett as he passed.

"See you later," he said, his voice sounding like gravel being crushed. Grandpa did something then that Brett had never seen him do before and he didn't know quite what to make of it at first. The old man's lips pulled back around his scraggly teeth; the corners of his mouth twitched into slight curls. He was *smiling!* "Have a good time," he said.

In the car, Brett and Mr. Moser were silent for the first half of the forty-five minute drive.

SILVER SCREAM

Mr. Moser fidgeted at the wheel, drumming his fingers and cracking his knuckles as he drove. He acted as if he was alone in the car.

Brett finally spoke: "Was I going to be next?"

Mr. Moser blinked, wiped his mouth, shifted his buttocks in the seat, but kept his eyes on the road and said nothing.

"That was the surprise, wasn't it?"

No reply.

"Why do you do it?"

Still nothing.

"Because you enjoy it?"

Silence.

"It doesn't bother you that it's wrong?"

Mr. Moser sniffed and ran a hand through his hair; he was crying silently.

It bothers him, Brett thought, deciding not to ask anymore questions.

The theater they went to held six screens. Brett stood in the lobby, breathed in the smell of popcorn, and looked at the rows of posters on the walls. He took in each and every detail around him — even the feeling of the carpet beneath his shoes — as if he were in the last hour of his life and wanted to miss nothing.

He looked up at Mr. Moser and said, "I'd like some popcorn."

Without meeting Brett's eyes, Mr. Moser got in line, bought a carton of popcorn, then they went into the auditorium and found seats.

Moments later, the lights dimmed and the screen came alive.

The back of Brett's neck prickled with excitement and he stuffed a fistfull of popcorn into his mouth.

The next two hours were everything Brett had hoped they would be.

Two days later, Brett called Mr. Moser again from the upstairs phone and said he wanted to go see the new James Bond movie that evening. Grandma was gone shopping and Brett wanted to hurry out before she returned; the less explaining he had to do, the better. He raced downstairs and through the living room, stumbling to a halt when he heard his name called.

Grandpa was sitting in the corner again by the phonetable. He was holding something out to Brett.

SINEMA

"Here," he said.

Brett stepped forward and saw two one dollar bills held between Grandpa's beefy fingers.

"For Milk Duds," Grandpa whispered conspiratorially with a crooked smile.

Brett chilled for a moment, realizing he'd been found out, but Grandpa's smile was reassuring. He seemed to be saying, *Just between us.*

As Brett took the money, Grandpa said, "Have fun."

Riding his bike to Mr. Moser's house, Brett wondered how often Grandpa listened in on telephone conversations, and how much he'd heard.

Over the following two weeks, Brett had Mr. Moser take him to seven movies; one day they even saw two, back to back.

At first, they said little, but began to talk a bit more each time, until it seemed they were nothing more than two friends going to the movies together.

They did not mention Jimmy Greenlaw or the tape or Mr. Moser's laundry room.

Sometimes Brett spotted Mr. Moser staring at him, like he used to when Brett watched movies on his VCR. But now he stared with tense eyes and chewed his lip nervously; he would look away immediately, but Brett always knew — felt, anyway — that he'd been staring at him for a while. Brett tried not to wonder what Mr. Moser thought about while he stared at him because that reminded him of what he'd seen on that video tape, and that conjured thoughts too frightening to entertain.

During the first week, Brett worried about Grandpa. How much did he know? Most importantly, would he tell Grandma?

By the second week, Brett felt better. Grandma knew nothing yet, and when they passed in the house, Grandpa always gave him a silent secret smile and a wink, something he'd never done before.

For the time being, he seemed to be safe.

It was turning out to be a fun and interesting summer.

Until he came home after his seventh movie — a Steve Martin comedy — and found his mom seated on the sofa talking with Grandpa.

When he walked in, she dashed across the room and greeted him with a laughing, perfumed embrace.

85

SILVER SCREAM

She was beautiful. Her hair fell around her head in a golden mane; tiny stones sparkled in her earlobes and bracelets clicked together on her wrists. She looked like a movie star.

"How *are* you, baby?" she breathed. "*Look* at you, you're such a *big* boy! Oh, give your mom another hug!" She covered his face with kisses and ran her fingers through his hair.

Brett could hear Grandma washing dishes and humming a hymn in the kitchen; naturally she wouldn't be visiting with Mom. Apparently there was no love lost there.

"How about a sundae?" Mom exclaimed. "A big one with *everything!* C'mon, let's go. I've got some surprises for you in the car." She kissed Grandpa's forehead and said, "Be back in a while, Pop."

As Brett followed her out of the house, he heard Grandma's voice behind him.

"*Brett!*" she hissed.

When he turned, she hunkered down in front of him and whispered, "Now, I don't want you eating *any* of that ice cream stuff. Jesus doesn't like you to pour all that bad sugar in your body — it's His temple." She tossed a glance over his shoulder in the direction Mom had gone and her face darkened with intense bitterness. "And I don't care *what* your *mother* says."

Brett went out the front door behind Mom and Grandpa's quiet throaty laughter faded behind them.

On the way to St. Helena, Brett trembled with anticipation, unable to stop smiling; he knew his days in Manning were numbered now and he'd be going to live with Mom in Los Angeles soon. He'd be able to go to movies anytime he wanted without fear of being caught or punished; there would be no more dreary Sabbaths, no more long church services with long church faces, and — best of *all* — no more Grandma.

"The stuff in the back seat's all yours," Mom said breathlessly. She was bouncing in her seat like a little girl.

Brett put the two boxes in his lap and opened them; one held shirts and pants, another held a blazer and tie.

"Brand new, all designer, expensive stuff," Mom said. "See that blazer? Roll up the sleeves a little and you'll look just like Don Johnson on *Miami Vice.*"

Brett had never seen *Miami Vice.* Didn't she know that? Didn't she know what it was like living with Grandma? Sure she did; Grandma was her *mother.*

"You'll be the best dressed guy in church, kiddo!" she laughed.

SINEMA

Church? Brett thought.

"There's more."

He found a bag full of school supplies; paper, pens and binders with pictures of the Hollywood sign on them, and a drinking mug that read on the side, HOORAY FOR HOLLYWOOD!

"Now you're all set for school in the fall," Mom said.

Something wasn't right.

Brett said, "But I thought I was gonna —"

"Where shall we go for ice cream?" Mom asked quickly.

Brett felt himself sinking into the seat of the rented car as some of his excitement drifted away like a thin mist.

"I thought I was gonna come live with you," Brett said over his hot fudge sundae.

"Well, honey . . . we'll see."

"But you said —"

"I know, and I *meant* it, sweety. It's just that . . . well, things are a little different now." She stirred her milkshake thoughtfully, frowning. "I met this man. He's a producer, a very *successful* producer, I should add. Four big hits in two years. He's . . . I've . . . well, I moved in with him last week. He's got this *incredible* place, you should *see* it! A pool, a theater in the back. Clark *Gable* used to live there!"

Brett didn't know who Clark Gable was and didn't care.

"Anyway, my producer friend — his name is Jeff — he wants to use me. He thinks I'd be good for a lead. Can you imagine that, baby, a *lead*! A starring role! But . . . well, for now, there's just no way I could take you back with me. Not now. Maybe later, after I've done a couple pictures. But not now."

Brett suddenly lost all interest in his sundae. His stomach ached and his head felt bloated with thoughts of staying in Manning, trapped in Grandma's house, listening to those skin-crawling hymns and having to give Grandma more Ben-Gay back rubs.

He had to concentrate hard to steady his voice as he said, "But Mom, you said —"

"I know, honey, but I *can't*. Not *now*. But . . . that's okay, isn't it? I mean, you're doing well here, aren't you? Grandpa says your grades are good, and he says you've made friends with your Sabbath school teacher. That's *great*. I mean, Lord knows, I'm not much of a Bible reader these days, but I suppose it's good for you. C'mon, sweety-pie. You've waited this long, can't you wait a little longer?"

He put his spoon down and stared at the table.

87

SILVER SCREAM

"Hey, how about a movie tonight?" Mom asked, taking his hand. "I'll go back to my hotel and change and we can go to dinner, then catch a movie. Whatever you want to see. Tonight's your night. Can't be out too late, though. I've got an early plane to catch."

She was leaving *tomorrow*!

Without him!

Panic began to rise in his throat. He wanted to cry, scream, kick something, but he remained silent, thinking of church, trying to shut the feelings off.

They would go to dinner and a movie that night and maybe he could change her mind. At least he got to pick the movie. And he knew exactly which one he wanted to see.

After he showered and changed, Brett went downstairs to wait for Mom to come back from her hotel and get him. He slumped on the sofa and stared out the window.

Grandpa's chair rumbled into the living room and his gravelly voice said, "You don't look too happy, boy."

Brett didn't reply.

Grandpa stopped in front of him and began drumming his fingers on the wheelchair's armrests.

"Your mom's not gonna take you with her, eh?"

Brett shook his head.

"Well. Guess you'll just have to make the best of things here, eh?"

Brett shrugged.

"Not so bad, is it? You got your friend Mr. Moser to keep you company." He winked and added, "Don't worry, boy, your secret's safe with me. You got Gabby. And, in her own way, I suppose, Grandma . . . well, she thinks the world of you." Then, with a frown, he muttered, "Hell of a lot more'n she thinks of me." His eyes suddenly snapped open wide and he looked around cautiously as if he might have been overheard. In a moment, his face relaxed and he smiled as if he'd just remembered something. "Grocery shopping," he mumbled.

Brett sat up straight, surprised; this was the most Grandpa had ever said to him. In fact, it was the most Brett had ever heard him say, *period*.

"Course, now, if I had a pair of those," Grandpa said, pointing at Brett's legs, "you and me, we would have a good old time."

Brett chuckled. "Grandma wouldn't let us."

Grandpa's head fell back and his wheelchair squeaked beneath the weight of his laughter.

SINEMA

"I suppose not. Fact, I just might be better off *without her* than I would be *with legs*. But . . ." He waved a hand with resignation. "You going to the movies with your mom tonight?"

Brett nodded. "Have you ever been to the movies, Grandpa?"

"Used to go a lot. Before I met your grandma. I often wish we had a TV in here so I could watch some of them old movies late at night. Don't sleep like I used to. We got enough money saved up to get a good one, you know. Color. Remote control. I look at 'em in the catalogs sometimes. But . . ." Another wave.

Brett looked at Grandpa for a long moment, seeing a different person in that wheelchair, much different from the silent, empty old man who wheeled around in the dark. He wondered what it would be like to live there with Grandpa, just the two of them. Maybe they'd stay up late at night and watch old movies. Grandpa could tell him about the movies he'd seen when *he* was a boy, about his days in the Army and how it felt to fight in a war. And they could listen to *real* music instead of those depressing hymns, music like he'd heard in the movies.

A car rolled to a stop out front and honked.

"There's your mom," Grandpa said. "You better git. And don't worry. Things won't be so bad."

Brett stood and gave Grandpa a long hug so unexpectedly that it surprised them both, then he rushed out to meet his mom.

Over dinner, Mom asked, "So what movie would you like to see?"

Brett smiled with anticipation and said, "*Bedside Manners*."

Mom's fork stopped half way to her mouth and she slowly lowered it to her plate with a frown.

"Well . . ." she said, drawing the word out to a troubled sigh. "I don't think so, honey."

Brett's smile disappeared and his spirits dropped even further.

"How *come?*"

"Well, it's not such a good movie. *Really*. I mean, it's low budget and, and . . . well, there's one scene where you can see the boom hanging about two feet into the frame, and . . ."

"What's a boom?"

"Never mind. It's just a bad movie, that's all."

"I don't care, Mom. I just wanna see *you*."

"Look, sweetie, my part is really small and I'm . . . well, I get . . ." She sniffed and straightened her posture. "I just don't think you should see it. It's not a movie for kids."

89

SILVER SCREAM

"But *Mom,* I wanted to see it with *you!*"

"Lower your voice!" she hissed, glanced around to see if anyone had heard. "Now that's *it,* okay? There's a lot of sex and violence in the movie and I don't want you to see it. Maybe when you're older . . . Hey, how about the new Benji movie, huh? I hear it's pretty good."

Brett clenched his fist around his fork and turned his eyes away from Mom; he knew he could not conceal his anger and disappointment if he looked at her. His appetite was gone.

Mom continued eating, apparently unaware that he was upset.

"Are you really gonna leave me tomorrow?" he whispered.

"I have to, honey. Good grief, you sound like you'll never see me again."

"For how long?"

"I don't know. Until . . . well, for a while. It's not so bad, babe." She reached for his hand, but he pulled it away. "Don't do this, now. You've got friends here."

No I don't, he thought.

"Grandma takes good care of you."

No she doesn't.

"I know she's a little weird. God knows *I* don't get along with her, but that's different. We've *never* gotten along. Grandma loves you. So does Grandpa. You'll be okay."

No I won't.

"Until you get more movie roles?" he muttered.

"What? Oh, yeah. A couple leads under Jeff and I'll be able to take good care of you."

"A lead? You mean, like a star?"

"Yeah, a starring role. In a good movie, none of this low budget horror crap."

"Is that what you really want? To star in a movie?"

"More than anything, sweetie. More than *anything.* Now eat your dinner."

"I'm not hungry."

"Not hun . . . well, why didn't you *say* so?" she snapped. "This is an expensive dinner. Now *eat.*"

He stared at the plate silently for a while.

"I have to go to the bathroom," he lied.

"Okay. But when you come back, you'll eat, right?"

He nodded, then left the table and crossed the restaurant. As he rounded the tables and chairs, he thought of a scene from one of the movies he'd watched at Mr. Moser's. *Prime Cut.* Lee Marvin played a gangster who was sent to Kansas City to find and punish Gene Hackman. Not only had Hackman gone back on a few promises made to old friends and business partners and cheated them out of a lot of money, he'd even killed some of

90

them — and had one ground up into hot dogs at his meat packing plant. When Marvin was through with him, Hackman ended up full of bullets and fed to some pigs.

Brett liked that. Hackman had deserved it; it had been a fitting punishment.

Some people simply deserved to be punished.

On the other hand, some deserved to be rewarded, like Luke, the Princess, Han, and Chewbacca at the end of *Star Wars*.

Brett thought about rewards and punishments as he walked toward the RESTROOMS sign in the back and passed by the men's room.

He went on to a bank of payphones, fishing in his pocket for some change.

Mom tapped her fingernails on the steering wheel as she drove out of St. Helena.

"You're just upset with me, that's all," she said stiffly. "I wanted us to have a nice evening together, but . . ." She shook her head and sighed.

Brett gazed straight ahead, barely hearing her. His mind was intentionally blank, his body relaxed.

"I'm just tired," he said quietly.

"Then why don't you let me take you home instead of to your friend's?"

"I have to pick up something I left there. Then I'll go home."

She sighed again. "I came a long way to see you, you know. And my friend *paid* for it. What's he going to think when I tell him you didn't even want to be *with* me?"

He pressed his lips together over the sharp reply that came to mind.

Brett watched the road ahead for several minutes, then said, "Turn right here. Then take the first left."

When the car started down the dirt road, Mom said, "Jesus, this is a rented car, you know! *Gawd!*"

Lighted windows at the end of the road drew nearer.

"Is this the house?"

Brett nodded.

She stopped in the drive and Brett said, "Come in. He'd like to meet you."

Mom sighed but turned off the ignition and got out, following him to the door.

"Aren't you going to *knock*?" she asked when Brett walked into the house.

"He doesn't mind." He let her in and closed the door. "He said he was —"

91

He swallowed a dry knot in his throat. "— was going to do some laundry tonight. He's probably in the laundry room."

Brett led her to the end of the hall, opened the door — he wouldn't let his hands tremble — and stepped aside so she could go ahead.

The light beyond the door was so dim the room seemed gray. As soon as Mom stepped down into the room, her heels clicking on the dirty concrete floor, Brett swung the door shut. It hit with a slam like gunfire.

"Brett!" she called. "What the hell are you —"

She stopped, there was a scuffle, then Mom screamed.

Brett stared at the door for a moment, listening to the screaming and the awful, thick hacking noises, the retching and coughing. Then he began to back away, trying to shut the sounds from his ears, realizing that Mom wasn't the only one screaming.

In the living room, he turned and crossed to the front door. Mom stopped screaming, but Mr. Moser continued; his cries of, "I'm sorry, I'm so sorry, my God, I'm sorry!" died in the wet sounds of vomiting.

Brett went outside and stood on the porch, thinking of nothing.

It could have been a minute or an hour later when Mr. Moser came out of the house and into the dim yellow glow of the porch light; Brett wasn't sure.

Mr. Moser held his hands out before him, palms up, fingers clawed, staring at them as if they weren't his own. Blood speckled his twisted face and his sleeveless arms were black with it to his elbows. He was gulping sobs and his eyes sparkled with tears.

"Dear Jesus," he breathed over and over, "dear Jesus . . ."

"Did you get it?" Brett asked. "On video tape?"

"I . . . if I'd known earlier, I . . . I was so upset, so scared . . . I didn't have time to . . ."

"You didn't get it?" Brett snapped, anger flaring in his head for a moment.

"I couldn't, I was too . . . too . . . Why, Brett? Why did you make me do this, *why?*"

"I thought you enjoyed it," Brett replied flatly, still preoccupied with the fact that his mother's murder had not been videotaped.

"Not this, not an adult, a . . . a *woman.*"

"Oh. Well. I think it's time you left behind the little kid stuff, Mr. Moser." He turned and stared silently at his mom's rented car.

Mr. Moser paced behind him, muttering, "Oh, God, oh Jesus-God . . ." He stopped abruptly and snapped in a hoarse, pained voice, "And what am I gonna do about the *car*, huh?"

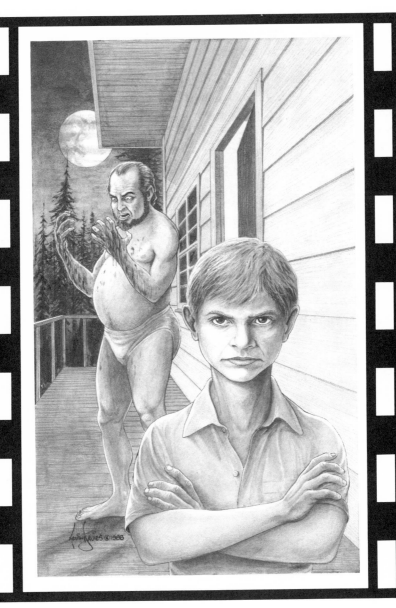

"It's rented."

"Rented? Oh God, that's just . . . that's . . . *rented!*"

Brett stepped off the porch.

"If I get caught, you're in just as much trouble as I am, you know. You helped! You're an *accomplice!*"

Brett turned to him and, genuinely worried for a moment, said, "You think anybody'd believe that? I mean, I'm just a *kid,* and . . . and you killed all those boys. I've got that tape . . ." He thought about it a while, then shook his head, feeling better, and muttered, "No. I don't think so, Mr. Moser. I really don't." He started across the drive toward the dirt road. "I think I'm gonna walk home. They don't expect me for a couple hours."

"What will you tell them?"

"I don't know. I'll think of something."

"But . . . what if they notice she doesn't bring you home?"

"They go to bed real early. Especially Grandma."

Grandma. Brett thought of her stern gaze and the smell of those messy Ben-Gay back rubs.

He turned to Mr. Moser again and said, "Get rid of the car by tomorrow afternoon. I want to go into San Francisco."

"What? *Why?*"

"There's a movie I want to see. *Bedside Manners.*" Then, to himself, Brett muttered, "*You* saw her die, now *I* need to."

But Grandma . . . she was still around to make Brett's life miserable. And Grandpa's.

Mr. Moser bellowed, "Are you out of your —"

"And keep that video camera loaded and ready. Later in the week, I'm gonna bring my grandma over."

Brett watched as Mr. Moser slowly turned his back, then began to kick the side of his house, pulling his hair and screaming like a toddler throwing a tantrum.

Mr. Moser's screams faded as Brett started down the road, looking forward to getting to know Grandpa.

SON OF CELLULOID

by

Clive Barker

ONE: TRAILER

Barberio felt fine, despite the bullet. Sure, there was a catch in his chest if he breathed too hard, and the wound in his thigh wasn't too pretty to look at, but he'd been holed before and come up smiling. At least he was free: that was the main thing. Nobody, he swore, nobody would ever lock him up again, he'd kill himself rather than be taken back into custody. If he was unlucky and they cornered him, he'd stick the gun in his mouth and blow off the top of his head. No way would they drag him back to that cell alive.

Life was too long if you were locked away and counting it in seconds. It had only taken him a couple of months to learn that lesson. Life was long, and repetitive and debilitating, and if you weren't careful you were soon thinking it would be better to die than go on existing in the shit-hole they'd put you in. Better to string yourself up by your belt in the middle of the night rather than face the tedium of another twenty-four hours, all eighty-six thousand four hundred seconds of it.

So he went for broke.

First he bought a gun on the prison black market. It cost him every-thing he had and a handful of IOUs he'd have to make good on the outside if he wanted to stay alive. Then he made the most obvious move in the book: he climbed the wall. And whatever god looked after the liquor-store muggers of this world was looking after him that night, because hot damn if he didn't scoot right over that wall and away without so much as a dog sniffing at his heels.

And the cops? Why they screwed it up every which way from Sunday, looking for him where he'd never gone, pulling in his brother and his sister-in-law on suspicion of harbouring him when they didn't even know he'd escaped, putting out an All-Points Bulletin with a description of his pre-prison self, twenty pounds heavier than he was now. All this he'd heard from

95

SILVER SCREAM

Geraldine, a lady he'd courted in the good old days, who'd given him a dressing for his leg and the bottle of Southern Comfort that was now almost empty in his pocket. He'd taken the booze and sympathy and gone on his way, trusting to the legendary idiocy of the law and the god who'd got him so far already.

Sing-Sing he called this god. Pictured him as a fat guy with a grin that hooked from one ear to the other, a prime salami in one hand, and a cup of dark coffee in the other. In Barberio's mind Sing-Sing smelt like a full belly at Mama's house, back in the days when Mama was still well in the head, and he'd been her pride and joy.

Unfortunately Sing-Sing had been looking the other way when the one eagle-eye cop in the whole city saw Barberio draining his snake in a back alley, and recognized him from that obsolete APB. Young cop, couldn't have been more than twenty-five, out to be a hero. He was too dumb to learn the lesson of Barberio's warning shot. Instead of taking cover, and letting Barberio make a break, he'd forced the issue by coming straight down the alley at him.

Barberio had no choice. He fired.

The cop fired back. Sing-Sing must have stepped in there somewhere, spoiling the cop's aim so that the bullet that should have found Barberio's heart hit his leg, and guiding the returning shot straight into the cop's nose. Eagle-eye went down as if he'd just remembered an appointment with the ground, and Barberio was away, cursing, bleeding and scared. He'd never shot a man before, and he'd started with a cop. Quite an introduction to the craft.

Sing-Sing was still with him though. The bullet in his leg ached, but Geraldine's ministrations had stopped the blood, the liquor had done wonders for the pain, and here he was half a day later, tired but alive, having hopped half-way across a city so thick with vengeful cops it was like a psycho's parade at the Policemen's Ball. Now all he asked of his protector was a place to rest up awhile. Not for long, just enough time to catch his breath and plan his future movements. An hour or two of shut-eye wouldn't go amiss either.

Thing was, he'd got that belly-ache, the deep, gnawing pain he got more and more these days. Maybe he'd find a phone, when he'd rested for a time, and call Geraldine again, get her to sweet-talk a doctor into seeing him. He'd been planning to get out of the city before midnight, but that didn't look like a plausible option now. Dangerous as it was, he would have to stay in the locality a night and maybe the best part of the next day; make his break for the open country when he'd recouped a little energy and had the bullet taken out of his leg.

Jeez, but that belly griped. His guess was it was an ulcer, brought on by the filthy slop they called food at the penitentiary. Lots of guys had belly and

96

shit-chute problems in there. He'd be better after a few days of pizzas and beers, he was damn sure of that.

The word *cancer* wasn't in Barberio's vocabulary. He never thought about terminal disease, especially in reference to himself. That'd be like a piece of slaughterhouse beef fretting about an ingrowing hoof as it stepped up to meet the gun. A man in his trade, surrounded by lethal tools, doesn't expect to perish from a malignancy in his belly. But that's what that ache was.

The lot at the back of the Movie Palace cinema had been a restaurant, but a fire had gutted it three years back, and the ground had never been cleared.

It wasn't a good spec for rebuilding, and no-one had shown much interest in the site. The neighborhood had once been buzzing, but that was in the sixties, early seventies. For a heady decade places of entertainment — restaurants, bars, cinemas — had flourished. Then came the inevitable slump. Fewer and fewer kids came this way to spend their money: there were new spots to hit, new places to be seen in. The bars closed up, the restaurants followed. Only the Movie Palace remained as a token reminder of more innocent days in a district that was becoming tackier and more dangerous every year.

The jungle of convolvulus and rotted timbers that throttled the vacant lot suited Barberio just fine. His leg was giving him jip, he was stumbling from sheer fatigue, and the pain in his belly was worsening. A spot to lay down his clammy head was needed, and damn quick. Finish off the Southern Comfort, and think about Geraldine.

It was one-thirty am; the lot was trysting-ground for cats. They ran, startled, through the man-high weeds as he pushed aside some of the fencing timbers and slid into the shadows. The refuge stank of piss, human and cat, of garbage, of old fires, but it felt like a sanctuary.

Seeking the support of the back wall of the Movie Palace, Barberio leaned on his forearm and threw up a bellyful of Southern Comfort and acid. Along the wall a little way some kids had built a makeshift den of girders, fire-blackened planks and corrugated iron. Ideal, he thought, a sanctuary within a sanctuary. Sing-Sing was smiling at him, all greasy chops. Groaning a little (the belly was really bad tonight) he staggered along the wall to the lean-to den, and ducked through the door.

Somebody else had used this place to sleep in: he could feel damp sacking under his hand as he sat down, and a bottle clinked against a brick somewhere to his left. There was a smell close by he didn't want to think too much about, like the sewers were backing up. All in all, it was squalid: but it was safer than the street. He sat with his back against the wall of the Movie Palace and exhaled his fears in a long, slow breath.

No more than a block away, perhaps half a block, the babe-in-the-night wail of a cop-car began, and his newly acquired sense of security sank without a trace. They were closing in for the kill, he knew it. They'd just been playing him along, letting him think he was away, all the time cruising him like sharks, sleek and silent, until he was too tired to put up any resistance. Jeez: he'd killed a cop, what they wouldn't do to him once they had him alone. They'd crucify him.

OK Sing-Sing, what now? Take that surprised look off your face, and get me out of this.

For a moment, nothing. Then the god smiled in his mind's eye, and quite coincidentally he felt the hinges pressing into his back.

Shit! A door. He was leaning against a door.

Grunting with pain he turned and ran his fingers around this escape hatch at his back. To judge by touch it was a small ventilation grille no more than three feet square. Maybe it let on to a crawlspace or maybe into someone's kitchen — what the hell? It was safer inside than out: that was the first lesson any newborn kid got slapped into him.

The siren-song wailed on, making Barberio's skin creep. Foul sound. It quickened his heart hearing it.

His thick fingers fumbled down the side of the grille feeling for a lock of some kind, and sure as shit there was a padlock, as gritty with rust as the rest of the metalwork.

Come on Sing-Sing, he prayed, one more break is all I'm asking, let me in, and I swear I'm yours forever.

He pulled at the lock, but damn it, it wasn't about to give so easily. Either it was stronger than it felt, or he was weaker. Maybe a little of both.

The car was slinking closer with every second. The wail drowned out the sound of his own panicking breath.

He pulled the gun, the cop-killer, out of his jacket-pocket and pressed it into service as a snub-nosed crowbar. He couldn't get much leverage on the thing, it was too short, but a couple of cursing heaves did the trick. The lock gave, a shower of rust scales peppered his face. He only just silenced a whoop of triumph.

Now to open the grille, to get out of this wretched world into the dark.

He insinuated his fingers through the lattice and pulled. Pain, a continuum of pain that ran from his belly to his bowel to his leg, made his head spin. Open, damn you, he said to the grille, open sesame.

The door conceded.

It opened suddenly, and he fell back on to the sodden sacking. A moment and he was up again, peering into the darkness within this darkness that was the interior of the Movie Palace.

SON OF CELLULOID

Let the cop-car come, he thought buoyantly, I've got my hidey-hole to keep me warm. And warm it was: almost hot in fact. The air out of the hole smelt like it had been simmering in there for a good long while.

His leg had gone into a cramp and it hurt like fuck as he dragged himself through the door and into the solid black beyond. Even as he did so the siren turned a corner nearby and the baby wail died. Wasn't that the patter of lawlike feet he could hear on the sidewalk?

He turned clumsily in the blackness, his leg a dead-weight, his foot feeling about the size of a watermelon, and pulled the grille-door to after him. The satisfaction was that of pulling up a drawbridge and leaving the enemy on the other side of the moat, somehow it didn't matter that they could open the door just as easily as he had, and follow him in. Childlike, he felt sure nobody could possibly find him here. As long as he couldn't see his pursuers, his pursuers couldn't see him.

If the cops did indeed duck into the lot to look for him, he didn't hear them. Maybe he'd been mistaken, maybe they were after some other poor punk on the street, and not him. Well OK, whatever. He had found himself a nice niche to rest up awhile, and that was fine and dandy.

Funny, the air wasn't so bad in here after all. It wasn't the stagnant air of a crawlspace or an attic, the atmosphere in the hidey-hole was alive. Not fresh air, no it wasn't that, it smelt old and trapped sure enough, but it was buzzing nevertheless. It fairly sang in his ears, it made his skin tingle like a cold shower, it wormed its way up his nose and put the weirdest things in his head. It was like being high on something: he felt that good. His leg didn't hurt anymore, or if it did he was too distracted by the pictures in his head. He was filling up to overflowing with pictures: dancing girls and kissing couples, farewells at stations, old dark houses, comedians, cowboys, undersea adventures — scenes he'd never lived in a million years, but that moved him now like raw experience, true and incontestable. He wanted to cry at the farewells, except that he wanted to laugh at the comedians, except that the girls needed ogling, the cowboys needed hollering for.

What kind of place was this anyhow? He peered through the glamour of the pictures which were damn close to getting the better of his eyes. He was in a space no more than four feet wide, but tall, and lit by a flickering light that chanced through cracks in the inner wall. Barberio was too befuddled to recognise the origins of the light, and his murmuring ears couldn't make sense of the dialogue from the screen on the other side of the wall. It was 'Satyricon', the second of the two Fellini movies the Palace was showing as their late-night double feature that Saturday.

Barberio had never seen the movie, never even heard of Fellini. It would have disgusted him (faggot film, Italian crap). He preferred undersea adventures, war movies. Oh, and dancing girls. Anything with dancing girls.

Funny, though he was all alone in his hidey-hole, he had the weird sensation of being watched. Through the kaleidoscope of Busby Berkeley

99

routines that was playing on the inside of his skull he felt eyes, not a few —
thousands — watching him. The feeling wasn't so bad you'd want to take a
drink for it, but they were always there, staring away at him like he was
something worth looking at, laughing at him sometimes, crying sometimes,
but mostly just gawping with hungry eyes.

Truth was, there was nothing he could do about them anyhow. His
limbs had given up the ghost; he couldn't feel his hands or feet at all. He
didn't know, and it was probably better that he didn't, that he'd torn open his
wound getting into this place, and he was bleeding to death.

About two-fify-five am, as Fellini's 'Satyricon' came to its ambiguous
end, Barberio died in the space between the back of the building proper and
the back wall of the cinema.

The Movie Palace had once been a Mission Hall, and if he'd looked up
as he died he might have glimpsed the inept fresco depicting an Angelic
Host that was still to be seen through the grime, and assumed his own
Assumption. But he died watching the dancing girls, and that was fine by
him.

The false wall, the one that let through the light from the back of the
screen, had been erected as a makeshift partition to cover the fresco of the
Host. It had seemed more respectful to do that than paint the Angels out
permanently, and besides the man who had ordered the alterations half-
suspected that the movie house bubble would burst sooner or later. If so, he
could simply demolish the wall, and he'd be back in business for the worship
of God instead of Garbo.

It never happened. The bubble, though fragile, never burst, and the
movies carried on. The Doubting Thomas (his name was Harry Cleveland)
died, and the space was forgotten. Nobody now living even knew it existed.
If he'd searched the city from top to bottom Barberio couldn't have found a
more secret place to perish.

The space however, the air itself, had lived a life of its own in that fifty
years. Like a reservoir, it had received the electric stares of thousands of
eyes, of tens of thousands of eyes. Half a century of movie-goers had lived
vicariously through the screen of the Movie Palace, pressing their sym-
pathies and their passions on to the flickering illusion, the energy of their
emotions gathering strength like a neglected cognac in that hidden passage
of air. Sooner or later, it must discharge itself. All it lacked was a catalyst.

Until Barberio's cancer.

TWO: THE MAIN FEATURE

After loitering in the cramped foyer of the Movie Palace for twenty
minutes or so, the young girl in the cerise and lemon print dress began to

100

look distinctly agitated. It was almost three in the morning, and the late-night movies were well over.

Eight months had passed since Barberio had died in the back of the cinema, eight slow months in which business had been at best patchy. Still, the late-night double bill on Fridays and Saturdays always packed in the punters. Tonight it had been two Eastwood movies: spaghetti westerns. The girl in the cerise dress didn't look like much of a western fan to Birdy; it wasn't really a women's genre. Maybe she'd come for Eastwood rather than the violence, though Birdy had never seen the attraction of that eternally squinting face.

'Can I help you?' Birdy asked.

The girl looked nervously at Birdy.

'I'm waiting for my boyfriend,' she said. 'Dean.'

'Have you lost him?'

'He went to the rest-room at the end of the movie and he hasn't come out yet.'

'Was he feeling . . . er . . . ill?'

'Oh no,' said the girl quickly, protecting her date from this slight on his sobriety.

'I'll get someone to go and look for him,' said Birdy. It was late, she was tired, and the speed was wearing off. The idea of spending any more time than she strictly needed to in this fleapit was not particularly appealing. She wanted home; bed and sleep. Just sleep. At thirty-four, she'd decided she'd grown out of sex. Bed was for sleep, especially for fat girls.

She pushed the swing door, and poked her head into the cinema. A ripe smell of cigarettes, popcorn and people enveloped her; it was a few degrees hotter in here than in the foyer.

'Ricky?'

Ricky was locking up the back exit, at the far end of the cinema.

'That smell's completely gone,' he called to her.

'Good.' A few months back there'd been a hell of a stench at the screen-end of the cinema.

'Something dead in the lot next door,' he said.

'Can you help me a minute?' she called back.

'What'd you want?'

He sauntered up the red-carpeted aisle towards her, keys jangling at his belt. His tee-shirt proclaimed 'Only the Young Die Good'.

'Problem?' he said, blowing his nose.

'There's a girl out here. She says she lost her boyfriend in the john.'

Ricky looked pained.

'In the john?'

'Right. Will you take a look? You don't mind, do you?'

And she could cut out the wisecracks for a start, he thought, giving her

101

a sickly smile. They were hardly on speaking terms these days. Too many high times together: it always dealt a crippling blow to a friendship in the long run. Besides, Birdy'd made some very uncharitable (accurate) remarks about his associates and he'd returned the salvo with all guns blazing. They hadn't spoken for three and a half weeks after that. Now there was an uncomfortable truce, more for sanity's sake than anything. It was not meticulously observed.

He about turned, wandered back down the aisle, and took row E across the cinema to the john, pushing up seats as he went. They'd seen better days, those seats: sometime around 'Now Voyager'. Now they looked thoroughly shot at: in need of refurbishing, or replacing altogether. In row E alone four of the seats had been slashed beyond repair, now he counted a fifth mutilation which was new tonight. Some mindless kid bored with the movie and/or his girlfried, and too stoned to leave. Time was he'd done that kind of thing himself: and counted it a blow for freedom against the capitalists who ran these joints. Time was he'd done a lot of damn-fool things.

Birdy watched him duck into the Men's Room. He'll get a kick out of that, she thought with a sly smile, just his sort of occupation. And to think, she'd once had the hots for him, back in the old days (six months ago) when razor-thin men with noses like Durante and an encyclopaedic knowledge of De Niro movies had really been her style. Now she saw him for what he was, flotsam from a lost ship of hope. Still a pill-freak, still a theoretical bisexual, still devoted to early Polanski movies and symbolic pacifism. What kind of dope did he have between his ears anyhow? The same as she'd had, she chided herself, thinking there was something sexy about the bum.

She waited for a few seconds, watching the door. When he failed to re-emerge she went back into the foyer for a moment, to see how the girl was going on. She was smoking a cigarette like an amateur actress who's failed to get the knack of it, leaning against the rail, her skirt hitched up as she scratched her leg.

'Tights,' she explained.

'The Manager's gone to find Dean.'

'Thanks,' she scratched on. 'They bring me out in a rash, I'm allergic to them.'

There were blotches on the girl's pretty legs, which rather spoiled the effect.

'It's because I'm hot and bothered,' she ventured. 'Whenever I get hot and bothered, I get allergic.'

'Oh.'

'Dean's probably run off, you know, when I had my back turned. He'd do that. He doesn't give a f—. He doesn't care.'

Birdy could see she was on her way to tears, which was a drag. She was bad with tears. Shouting matches, even fights, OK. Tears, no go.

'It'll be OK' was all she could find to say to keep the tears from coming. 'No it's not,' said the girl. 'It won't be OK, because he's a bastard. He treats everyone like dirt.' She ground out the half-smoked cigarette with the pointed toe of her cerise shoes, taking particular care to extinguish every glowing fragment of tobacco.

'Men don't care, do they?' she said looking up at Birdy with heart-melting directness. Under the expert make-up, she was perhaps seventeen, certainly not much more. Her mascara was a little smeared, and there were arcs of tiredness under her eyes.

'No,' replied Birdy, speaking from painful experience. 'No they don't.'

Birdy thought ruefully that she'd never looked as attractive as this tired nymphet. Her eyes were too small, and her arms were her worst feature, she'd convinced herself of that. There were men, a lot of them, who got off on big breasts, on a sizeable ass, but no man she'd ever known liked fat arms. They always wanted to be able to encircle the wrist of their girlfriend between thumb and index finger, it was a primitive way to measure attach-ment. Her wrists, however, if she was brutal with herself, were practically undiscernible. Her fat hands became her fat fore-arms, which became, after a podgy time, her fat upper arms. Men couldn't encircle her wrists because she had no wrists, and that alienated them. Well, that was one of the reasons anyhow. She was also very bright: and that was always a drawback if you wanted men at your feet. But of the options as to why she'd never been successful in love, she plumped for the fat arms as the likeliest explanation.

Whereas this girl had arms as slender as a Balinese dancer's, her wrists looked thin as glass; and about as fragile.

Sickening, really. she was probably a lousy conversationalist to boot. God, the girl had all the advantages.

'What's your name?' she asked.

'Lindi Lee,' the girl replied.

It would be.

Ricky thought he'd made a mistake. This can't be the toilet, he said to himself.

He was standing in what appeared to be the main street of a frontier town he'd seen in two hundred westerns. A dust storm seemed to be raging, forcing him to narrow his eyes against the stinging sand. Through the swirl of the ochre-grey air he could pick out, he thought, the General Stores, the Sheriff's Office and the Saloon. They stood in lieu of the toilet cubicles. Optional tumble-weed danced by him on the hot desert wind. The ground beneath his feet was impacted sand: no sign of tiles. No sign of anything that was faintly toilet-like.

103

SILVER SCREAM

Ricky looked to his right, down the street. Where the far wall of the john should have been the street receded, in forced perspective, towards a painted distance. It was a lie, of course, the whole thing was a lie. Surely if he concentrated he'd begin to see through the mirage to find out how it had been achieved; the projections, the concealed lighting effects, the backcloths, the miniatures; all the tricks of the trade. But though he concentrated as hard as his slightly spaced-out condition would allow, he just couldn't seem to get his fingers under the edge of the illusion to strip it back.

The wind just went on blowing, the tumble-weed tumbled on. Somewhere in the storm a barn-door was slamming, opening and slamming again in the gusts. He could even smell horse-shit. The effect was so damn perfect, he was breathless with admiration.

But whoever had created this extraordinary set had proved their point. He was impressed: now it was time to stop the game.

He turned back to the toilet door. It was gone. A wall of dust erased it, and suddenly he was lost and alone.

The barn-door kept slamming. Voices called to each other in the worsening storm. Where was the Saloon and the Sheriff's office? They too had been obscured. Ricky tasted something he hadn't experienced since childhood: the panic of losing the hand of a guardian. In this case the lost parent was his sanity.

Somewhere to his left a shot sounded in the depths of the storm, and he heard something whistle in his ear, then felt a sharp pain. Gingerly he raised his hand to his ear-lobe and touched the place that hurt. Part of his ear had been shot away, a neat nick in his lobe. His ear-stud was gone, and there was blood, real blood, on his fingers. Someone had either just missed blowing off his head or was really playing silly fuckers.

'Hey, man,' he appealed into the teeth of this wretched fiction, whirling around on his heel to see if he could locate the aggressor. But he could see no one. The dust had totally enclosed him: he couldn't move backwards or forwards with any safety. The gunman might be very close, waiting for him to step in his direction.

'I don't like this,' he said aloud, hoping the real world would hear him somehow, and step in to salvage his tattered mind. He rummaged in his jeans pocket for a pill or two, anything to improve the situation, but he was all out of instant sunshine, not even a lowly Valium was to be found lurking in the seam of his pocket. He felt naked. What a time to be lost in the middle of Zane Grey's nightmares.

A second shot sounded, but this time there was no whistling. Ricky was certain this meant he'd been shot, but as there was neither pain nor blood it was difficult to be sure.

Then he heard the unmistakable flap of the saloon door, and the groan of another human being somewhere near. A tear opened up in the storm for

104

a moment. Did he see the saloon through it, and a young man stumbling out, leaving behind him a painted world of tables, mirrors, and gunslingers? Before he could focus properly the tear was sewn up with sand, and he doubted the sight. Then, shockingly, the young man he'd come looking for was there, a foot away, blue-lipped with death, and falling forward into Ricky's arms. He wasn't dressed for a part in this movie anymore than Ricky was. His bomber jacket was a fair copy of a fifties style, his tee-shirt bore the smiling face of Mickey Mouse.

Mickey's left eye was bloodshot, and still bleeding. The bullet had unerringly found the young man's heart.

He used his last breath to ask: 'What the fuck is going on?' and died.

As last words went, it lacked style, but it was deeply felt. Ricky stared into the young man's frozen face for a moment, then the dead weight in his arms became too much, and he had no choice but to drop him. As the body hit the ground the dust seemed to turn into piss-stained tiling for an instant. Then the fiction took precedence again, and the dust swirled, and the tumble-weed tumbled, and he was standing in the middle of Main Street, Deadwood Gulch, with a body at his feet.

Ricky felt something very like cold turkey in his system. His limbs began a St. Vitus' dance, and the urge to piss came on him, very strong. Another half-minute, he'd wet his pants.

Somewhere, he thought, somewhere in this wild world, there is a urinal. There is a graffiti-covered wall, with numbers for the sex-crazed to call, with 'This is not a fallout shelter' scrawled on the tiles, and a cluster of obscene drawings. There are water-tanks and paperless toilet-roll holders and broken seats. There is the squalid smell of piss and old farts. Find it! God's name find the real thing before the fiction does you some permanent damage.

If, for the sake of argument, the Saloon and the General Stores are the toilet cubicles, then the urinal must be behind me, he reasoned. So step back. It can't do you any more harm than staying here in the middle of the street while someone takes pot-shots at you.

Two steps, two cautious steps, and he found only air. But on the third — well, well, what have we here? — his hand touched a cold tile surface.

'Whoo-ee! he said. It was the urinal: and touching it was like finding gold in a pan of trash. Wasn't that the sickly smell of disinfectant wafting up from the gutter? It was, oh boy, it was.

Still whooping, he unzipped and started to relieve the ache in his blad-der, splashing his feet in his haste. What the hell: he had this illusion beat. If he turned round now he'd find the fantasy dispersed, surely. The saloon, the dead boy, the storm, all would be gone. It was some chemical throw-back, bad dope lingering in his system and playing dumb-ass games with his im-agination. As he shook the last drops on to his blue suedes, he heard the hero of this movie speak.

SILVER SCREAM

'What you doin' pissin' in mah street, boy?'

It was John Wayne's voice, accurate to the last slurred syllable, and it was just behind him. Ricky couldn't even contemplate turning round. The guy would blow off his head for sure. It was in the voice, that threatful ease that warned: I'm ready to draw, so do your worst. The cowboy was armed, and all Ricky had in his hand was his dick, which was no match for a gun even if he'd been better hung.

Very cautiously he tucked his weapon away and zipped himself up, then raised his hands. In front of him the wavering image of the toilet wall had disappeared again. The storm howled: his ear bled down his neck.

'OK boy, I want you to take off that gunbelt and drop it to the ground. You hear me?' said Wayne.

'Yes.'

'Take it nice and slow, and keep those hands where I can see them.'

Boy, this guy was really into it.

Nice and slow, like the man said, Ricky unbuckled his belt, pulled it through the loops in his jeans and dropped it to the floor. The keys should have jangled as they hit the tiles, he hoped to God they would. No such luck. There was a clinking thud that was the sound of metal on sand.

'OK,' said Wayne. 'Now you're beginning to behave. What have you got to say for yourself?'

'I'm sorry?' said Ricky lamely.

'Sorry?'

'For pissing in the street.'

'I don't reckon sorry is sufficient penitence,' said Wayne.

'But really I am. It was all a mistake.'

'We've had about enough of you strangers around these parts. Found that kid with his trousers round his ankles takin' a dump in the middle of the saloon. Well I call that uncouth! Where's you sons of bitches been educated anyhow? Is that what they're teaching you in them fancy schools out East?'

'I can't apologise enough.'

'Damn right you can't' Wayne drawled. 'You with the kid?'

'In a manner of speaking'

'What kind of fancy-talk is that?' he jabbed his gun in Rick's back: it felt very real indeed. 'Are you with him or not?'

'I just meant —'

'You don't mean nothing in this territory, mister, you take that from me.'

He cocked the gun, audibly.

'Why don't you turn round, son and let's us see what you're made of?'

Ricky had seen this routine before. The man turns, he goes for a concealed gun, and Wayne shoots him. No debate, no time to discuss the ethics of it, a bullet would do the job better than words.

SON OF CELLULOID

'Turn round I said.'

Very slowly, Ricky turned to face the survivor of a thousand shootouts, and there was the man himself, or rather a brilliant impersonation of him. A middle period Wayne, before he'd grown fat and sick-looking. A Rio Grande Wayne, dusty from the long trail and squinting from a lifetime of looking at the horizon. Ricky had never had a taste for Westerns. He hated all the forced machoism, the glorification of dirt and cheap heroism. His generation had put flowers in the rifle-barrels, and he'd thought that was a nice thing to do at the time; still did, in fact.

This face, so mock-manly, so uncompromising, personified a handful of lethal lies — about the glory of America's frontier origins, the morality of swift justice, the tenderness in the heart of brutes. Ricky hated the face. His hands just itched to hit it.

Fuck it, if the actor, whoever he was, was going to shoot him anyway, what was to be lost by putting his fist in the bastard's face? The thought became the act: Ricky made a fist, swung and his knuckles connected with Wayne's chin. The actor was slower than his screen image. He failed to dodge the blow, and Ricky took the opportunity to knock the gun out of Wayne's hand. He then followed through with a barrage of punches to the body, just as he'd seen in the movies. It was a spectacular display.

The bigger man reeled backwards under the blows, and tripped, his spur catching in the dead boy's hair. He lost his balance and fell in the dust, bested.

The bastard was down! Ricky felt a thrill he'd never tasted before; the exhilaration of physical triumph. My God! he'd brought down the greatest cowboy in the world. His critical faculties were overwhelmed by the victory.

The dust-storm suddenly thickened. Wayne was still on the floor, splattered with blood from a smashed nose and a broken lip. The sand was already obscuring him, a curtain drawn across the shame of his defeat.

'Get up,' Ricky demanded, trying to capitalise on the situation before the opportunity was lost entirely.

Wayne seemed to grin as the storm covered him.

'Well boy,' he leered, rubbing his chin, 'we'll make a man of you yet . . .'

Then his body was eroded by the driving dust, and momentarily something else was there in its place, a form Ricky could make no real sense of. A shape that was and was not Wayne, which deteriorated rapidly towards inhumanity.

The dust was already a furious bombardment, filling ears and eyes. Ricky stumbled away from the scene of the fight, choking, and miraculously he found a wall, a door, and before he could make sense of where he was the roaring storm had spat him out into the silence of the Movie Palace.

There, though he'd promised himself to butch it up since he'd grown a moustache, he gave a small cry that would not have shamed Fay Wray, and collapsed.

107

SILVER SCREAM

* * *

In the foyer Lindi Lee was telling Birdy why she didn't like films very much.

'I mean, Dean likes cowboy movies. I don't really like any of that stuff. I guess I shouldn't say that to you —'

'No, that's OK.'

'— But I mean you must really love movies, I guess. 'Cause you work here.'

'I like some movies. Not everything.'

'Oh.' She seemed surprised. A lot of things seemed to surprise her. 'I like wild-life movies, you know.'

'Yes . . .'

'You know? Animals . . . and stuff.'

'Yes . . .' Birdy remembered her guess about Lindi Lee, that she wasn't much of a conversationalist. Got it in one.

'I wonder what's keeping them?' said Lindi.

The lifetime Ricky had been living in the dust-storm had lasted no more than two minutes in real time. But then in the movies time was elastic.

'I'll go look,' Birdy ventured.

'He's probably left without me,' Lindi said again.

'We'll find out.'

'Thanks.'

'Don't fret,' said Birdy, lightly putting her hand on the girl's thin arm as she passed. 'I'm sure everything's OK.'

She disappeared through the swing doors into the cinema, leaving Lindi Lee alone in the foyer. Lindi sighed. Dean wasn't the first boy who'd run out on her, just because she wouldn't produce the goods. Lindi had her own ideas about when and how she'd go all the way with a boy; this wasn't the time and Dean wasn't the boy. He was too slick, too shifty, and his hair smelt of diesel oil. If he had run out on her, she wasn't going to weep buckets over the loss. As her mother always said, there were plenty more fish in the sea.

She was staring at the poster for next week's attraction when she heard a thump behind her, and there was a pie-bald rabbit, a fat, dozy sweetheart of a thing, sitting in the middle of the foyer staring up at her.

'Hello,' she said to the rabbit.

The rabbit licked itself adorably.

Lindi Lee loved animals; she loved True Life Adventure Movies in which creatures were filmed in their native habitat to tunes from Rossini, and scorpions did square-dances while mating, and every bear-cub was lovingly called a little scamp. She lapped up that stuff. But most of all she loved rabbits.

108

SON OF CELLULOID

The rabbit took a couple of hops towards her. She knelt to stroke it. It was warm and its eyes were round and pink. It hopped past her up the stairs.

'Oh I don't think you should go up there,' she said.

For one thing it was dark at the top of the stairs. For another there was a sign that read 'Private. Staff only' on the wall. But the rabbit seemed determined, and the clever mite kept well ahead of her as she followed it up the stairs.

At the top it was pitch black, and the rabbit had gone.

Something else was sitting there in the rabbit's place, its eyes burning bright.

With Lindi Lee illusions could be simple. No need to seduce her into a complete fiction like the boy, this one was already dreaming. Easy meat.

'Hello,' Lindi Lee said, scared a little by the presence ahead of her. She looked into the dark, trying to sort out some outline, a hint of a face. But there was none. Not even a breath.

She took one step back down the stairs but it reached for her suddenly, and caught her before she toppled, silencing her quickly, intimately.

This one might not have much passion to steal, but it sensed another use here. The tender body was still budding: the orifices unused to invasions. It took Lindi up the few remaining stairs and sealed her away for future investigation.

'Ricky? Oh God, Ricky!'

Birdy knelt beside Ricky's body and shook him. At least he was still breathing, that was something, and though at first sight there seemed to be a great deal of blood, in fact the wound was merely a nick in his ear.

She shook him again, more roughly, but there was no response. After a frantic search she found his pulse: it was strong and regular. Obviously he'd been attacked by somebody, possibly Lindi Lee's absent boyfriend. In which case, where was he? Still in the john perhaps, armed and dangerous. There was no way she was going to be damn fool enough to step in there and have a look, she'd seen that routine too many times. Woman in Peril: standard stuff. The darkened room, the stalking beast. Well, instead of walking bang into that cliché she was going to do what she silently exhorted heroines to do time and again: defy her curiosity and call the cops.

Leaving Ricky where he lay, she walked up the aisle, and back into the foyer.

It was empty. Lindi Lee had either given up on her boyfriend altogether, or found somebody else on the street outside to take her home. Whichever, she'd closed the front door behind her as she left, leaving only a hint of

Johnson's Baby Powder on the air behind her. OK, that certainly made things easier, Birdy thought, as she stepped into the Ticket Office to dial the cops. She was rather pleased to think that the girl had found the common-sense to give up on her lousy date.

She picked up the receiver, and immediately somebody spoke.

'Hello there,' said the voice, nasal and ingratiating, 'it's a little late at night to be using the phone, isn't it?'

It wasn't the operator, she was sure. She hadn't even punched a number. Besides, it sounded like Peter Lorre.

'Who is this?'

'Don't you recognise me?'

'I want to speak to the police.'

'I'd like to oblige, really I would.'

'Get off the line, will you? This is an emergency! I need the police.'

'I heard you first time,' the whine went on.

'Who are you?'

'You already played that line.'

'There's somebody hurt in here. Will you *please* —'

'Poor Rick.'

He knew the name. Poor Rick, he said, as though he was a loving friend.

She felt the sweat begin in her brow: felt it sprout out of her pores. He knew Ricky's name.

'Poor, poor Rick,' the voice said again. 'Still I'm sure we'll have a happy ending. Aren't you?'

'This is a matter of life and death,' Birdy insisted, impressed by how controlled she felt sure she was sounding.

'I know.' said Lorre. 'Isn't it exciting?'

'Damn you! Get off this phone! Or so help me —'

'So help you what? What can a fat girl like you hope to do in a situation like this, except blubber?'

'You fucking creep.'

'My pleasure.'

'Do I know you?'

'Yes and no,' the tone of the voice was wavering.

'You're a friend of Ricky's, is that it?' One of the dope-fiends he used to hang out with. Kind of idiot-game they'd get up to. 'All right, you've had your stupid little joke,' she said, 'now get off the line before you do some serious harm.'

'You're harassed,' the voice said, softening. 'I understand . . .' it was changing magically, sliding up an octave, 'you're trying to help the man you love . . .' its tone was feminine now, the accent altering, the slime becoming a purr. And suddenly it was Garbo.

'Poor Richard,' she said to Birdy. 'He's tried so hard, hasn't he?' She was gentle as a lamb.

SON OF CELLULOID

Birdy was speechless: the impersonation was as faultless as that of Lorre, as female as the first had been male.

'All right, I'm impressed,' said Birdy, 'now let me speak to the cops.'

'Wouldn't this be a fine and lovely night to go out walking, Birdy? Just we two girls together.'

'You know my name.'

'Of course I know your name. I'm very close to you.'

'What do you mean, close to me?'

The reply was throaty laughter, Garbo's lovely laughter.

Birdy couldn't take it any more. The trick was too clever; she could feel herself succumbing to the impersonation, as though she were speaking to the star herself.

'No,' she said down the phone, 'you don't convince me, you hear?' Then her temper snapped. She yelled: 'You're a fake!' into the mouthpiece of the phone so loudly she felt the receiver tremble, and then slammed it down. She opened the Office and went to the outer door. Lindi Lee had not simply slammed the door behind her. It was locked and bolted from the inside.

'Shit,' Birdy said quietly.

Suddenly the foyer seemed smaller than she'd previously thought it, and so did her reserve of cool. She mentally slapped herself across the face, the standard response for a heroine verging on hysteria. Think this through, she instructed herself. One: the door was locked. Lindi Lee hadn't done it, Ricky couldn't have done it, she certainly hadn't done it. Which implied —

Two: There was a weirdo in here. Maybe the same he, she or it that was on the phone. Which implied —

Three: He, she or it must have access to another line, somewhere in the building. The only one she knew of was upstairs, in the storeroom. But there was no way she was going up there. For reasons see Heroine in Peril. Which implied —

Four: She had to open this door with Ricky's keys.

Right, there was the imperative: get the keys from Ricky.

She stepped back into the cinema. For some reason the houselights were jumpy, or was that just panic in her optic nerve? No, they were flickering slightly; the whole interior seemed to be fluctuating, as though it were breathing.

Ignore it: fetch the keys.

She raced down the aisle, aware, as she always was when she ran, that her breasts were doing a jig, her buttocks too. A right sight I look, she thought for anyone with the eyes to see. Ricky, was moaning in his faint. Birdy looked for the keys, but his belt had disappeared.

'Ricky . . .' she said close to his face. The moans multiplied.

'Ricky, can you hear me? It's Birdy, Rick. *Birdy.*'

111

'Birdy?'

'We're locked in, Ricky. Where are the keys?'

'. . . keys?'

'You're not wearing your belt, Ricky,' she spoke slowly, as if to an idiot, 'where-are-your-keys?'

The jigsaw Ricky was doing in his aching head was suddenly solved, and he sat up.

'Boy!' he said.

'What boy?'

'In the john. Dead in the john.'

'Dead? Oh Christ. Dead? Are you sure?'

Ricky was in some sort of trance, it seemed. He didn't look at her, he just stared into middle-distance, seeing something she couldn't.

'Where are the keys?' she asked again. 'Ricky. It's important. Concentrate.'

'Keys?'

She wanted to slap him now, but his face was already bloody and it seemed sadistic.

'On the floor,' he said after a time.

'In the john? On the floor in the john?'

Ricky nodded. The movement of his head seemed to dislodge some terrible thoughts: suddenly he looked as though he was going to cry.

'It's all going to be all right,' said Birdy.

Ricky's hands had found his face, and he was feeling his features, a ritual of reassurance.

'Am I here?' he inquired quietly. Birdy didn't hear him, she was steeling herself for the john. She had to go in there, no doubt about that, body or no body. Get in, fetch the keys, get out again. Do it *now*.

She stepped through the door. It occurred to her as she did so that she'd never been in a men's toilet before, and she sincerely hoped this would be the first and only occasion.

The toilet was almost in darkness. The light was flickering in the same fitful way as the lights in the cinema, but at a lower level. She stood at the door, letting her eyes accommodate the gloom, and scanned the place.

The toilet was empty. There was no boy on the floor, dead or alive.

The keys were there though. Ricky's belt was lying in the gutter of the urinal. She fished it out, the oppressive smell of the disinfectant block making her sinuses ache. Disengaging the keys from their ring she stepped out of the toilet into the comparative freshness of the cinema. And it was all over, simple as that.

Ricky had hoisted himself on to one of the seats, and was slumped in it, looking sicker and sorrier for himself than ever. He looked up as he heard Birdy emerge.

'I've got the keys,' she said.

He grunted: God, he looked ill, she thought. Some of her sympathy had evaporated however. He was obviously having hallucinations, and they probably had chemical origins. It was his own damn fault.

'There's no boy in there, Ricky.'

'What?'

'There's no body in the john; nobody at all. What are you on anyhow?'

Ricky looked down at his shaking hands.

'I'm not on anything. Honestly.'

'Damn stupid,' she said. She half-suspected that he'd set her up for this somehow, except that practical jokes weren't his style. Ricky was quite a puritan in his way: that had been one of his attractions.

'Do you need a doctor?'

He shook his head sulkily.

'Are you sure?'

'I said no,' he snapped.

'OK, I offered.' She was already marching up the rake of the aisle, muttering something under her breath. At the foyer door she stopped and called across to him.

'I think we've got an intruder. There was somebody on the extension line. Do you want to stand watch by the front door while I fetch a cop?'

'In a minute.'

Ricky sat in the flickering light and examined his sanity. If Birdy said the boy wasn't in there, then presumably she was telling the truth. The best way to verify that was to see for himself. Then he'd be certain he'd suffered a minor reality crisis brought on by some bad dope, and he'd go home, lay his head down to sleep and wake tomorrow afternoon healed. Except that he didn't want to put his head in that evil-smelling room. Suppose she was wrong, and *she* was the one having the crisis? Weren't there such things as hallucinations of normality?

Shakily, he hauled himself up, crossed the aisle and pushed open the door. It was murky inside, but he could see enough to know that there were no sand-storms, or dead boy, no gun-toting cowboys, nor even a solitary tumble-weed. It's quite a thing, he thought, this mind of mine. To have created an alternative world so eerily well. It was a wonderful trick. Pity it couldn't be turned to better use than scaring him shitless. You win some, you lose some.

And then he saw the blood. On the tiles. A smear of blood that hadn't come from his nicked ear, there was too much of it. Ha! He didn't imagine it

113

at all. There was blood, heel marks, every sign that what he thought he'd seen, he'd seen. But Jesus in Heaven, which was worse? To see, or not to see? Wouldn't it have been better to be wrong, and just a little spaced-out tonight, than right, and in the hands of a power that could literally change the world?

Ricky stared at the trail of blood, and followed it across the floor of the toilet to the cubicle on the left of his vision. Its door was closed: it had been open before. The murderer, whoever he was, had put the boy in there, Ricky knew it without looking.

'OK,' he said, 'now I've got you.'

He pushed on the door. It swung open and there was the boy, propped up on the toilet seat, legs spread, arms hanging.

His eyes had been scooped out of his head. Not neatly: no surgeon's job. They'd been wrenched out, leaving a trail of mechanics down his cheek.

Ricky put his hand over his mouth and told himself he wasn't going to throw up. His stomach churned, but obeyed, and he ran to the toilet door as though any moment the body was going to get up and demand its ticket-money back.

'Birdy . . . Birdy . . .'

The fat bitch had been wrong, all wrong. There was death here, and worse.

Ricky flung himself out of the john into the body of the cinema.

The wall-lights were fairly dancing behind their Deco shades, guttering like candles on the verge of extinction. Darkness would be too much; he'd lose his mind.

There was, it occurred to him, something familiar about the way the lights flickered, something he couldn't quite put his finger on. He stood in the aisle for a moment, hopelessly lost.

Then the voice came; and though he guessed it was death this time, he looked up.

'Hello Ricky,' she was saying as she came along Row E towards him. Not Birdy. No, Birdy never wore a white gossamer dress, never had bruise-full lips, or hair so fine, or eyes so sweetly promising. It was Monroe who was walking towards him, the blasted rose of America.

'Aren't you going to say hello?' she gently chided.

'. . . er . . .'

'Ricky. Ricky. Ricky. After all this time.'

All this time? What did she mean: all this time?

'Who are you?'

She smiled radiantly at him.

'As if you didn't know.'

'You're not Marilyn. Marilyn's dead.'

'Nobody dies in the movies, Ricky. You know that as well as I do. You can always thread the celluloid up again —'

114

— that was what the flickering reminded him of, the flicker of celluloid through the gate of a projector, one image hot on the next, the illusion of life created from a perfect sequence of little deaths.

'— and we're there again, all-talking, all-singing.' She laughed: ice-in-a-glass laughter, 'We never fluff our lines, never age, never lose our timing —'

'You're not real,' said Ricky.

She looked faintly bored by the observation, as if he was being pedantic.

By now she'd come to the end of the row and was standing no more than three feet away from him. At this distance the illusion was as ravishing and as complete as ever. He suddenly wanted to take her, there, in the aisle. What the hell if she was just a fiction: fictions are fuckable if you don't want marriage.

'I want you,' he said, surprised by his own bluntness.

'I want *you*,' she replied, which surprised him even more. 'In fact I need you. I'm very weak.'

'Weak?'

'It's not easy, being the centre of attraction, you know. You find you need it, more and more. Need people to look at you. All the night, all the day.'

'I'm looking.'

'Am I beautiful?'

'You're a goddess: whoever you are.'

'I'm yours: that's who I am.'

It was a perfect answer. She was defining herself through him. I am a function of you; made for you out of you. The perfect fantasy.

'Keep looking at me; looking *forever*, Ricky. I need your loving looks. I can't live without them.'

The more he stared at her the stronger her image seemed to become. The flickering had almost stopped; a calm had settled over the place.

'Do you want to touch me?'

He thought she'd never ask.

'Yes,' he said.

'Good.' She smiled coaxingly at him, and he reached to make contact. She elegantly avoided his fingertips at the last possible moment, and ran, laughing, down the aisle towards the screen. He followed, eager. She wanted a game: that was fine by him.

She'd run into a cul-de-sac. There was no way out from this end of the cinema, and judging by the come-ons she was giving him, she knew it. She turned and flattened herself against the wall, feet spread a little.

He was within a couple of yards of her when a breeze out of nowhere billowed her skirt up around her waist. She laughed, half-closing her eyes, as the surf of silk rose and exposed her. She was naked underneath.

Ricky reached for her again and this time she didn't avoid his touch. The dress billowed up a little higher and he stared, fixated, at the part of Marilyn he had never seen, the fur divide that had been the dream of millions.

There was blood there. Not much, a few fingermarks on her inner thighs. The faultless gloss of her flesh was spoiled slightly. Still he stared; and the lips parted a little as she moved her hips, and he realised the glint of wetness in her interior was not the juice of her body, but something else altogether. As her muscles moved the bloody eyes she'd buried in her body shifted, and came to rest on him.

She knew by the look on his face that she hadn't hidden them deep enough, but where was a girl with barely a veil of cloth covering her nakedness to hide the fruits of her labour?

'You killed him,' said Ricky, still looking at the lips, and the eyes that peeked out between. The image was so engrossing, so pristine, it all but cancelled out the horror in his belly. Perversely, his disgust fed his lust instead of killing it. So what if she *was* a murderer: she was legend.

'Love me,' she said. 'Love me forever.'

He came to her, knowing now full well that it was death to do so. But death was a relative matter, wasn't it? Marilyn was dead in the flesh, but alive here, either in his brain, or in the buzzing matrix of the air or both; and he could be with her.

He embraced her, and she him. They kissed. It was easy. Her lips were softer than he'd imagined, and he felt something close to pain at his crotch he wanted to be in her so much.

The willow-thin arms slipped around his waist, and he was in the lap of luxury.

'You make me strong,' she said. 'Looking at me that way. I need to be looked at, or I die. It's the natural state of illusions.'

Her embrace was tightening; the arms at his back no longer seemed quite so willow-like. He struggled a little against the discomfort.

'No use,' she cooed in his ear. 'You're mine.'

He wrenched his head around to look at her grip and to his amazement the arms weren't arms any longer, just a loop of something round his back, without hands or fingers or wrists.

'Jesus Christ!' he said.

'Look at me, boy,' she said. The words had lost their delicacy. It wasn't Marilyn that had him in its arms any more: nothing like her. The embrace tightened again, and the breath was forced from Ricky's body, breath the tightness of the hold prevented him from recapturing. His spine creaked under the pressure, and pain shot through his body like flares, exploding in his eyes, all colours.

'You should have got out of town,' said Marilyn, as Wayne's face blossomed under the sweep of her perfect cheek-bones. His look was contemptuous, but Ricky had only a moment to register it before that image cracked too, and something else came into focus behind this facade of famous faces. For the last time in his life, Ricky asked the question:

'Who are you?'

His captor didn't answer. It was feeding on his fascination; even as he stared twin organs erupted out of its body like the horns of a slug, antennae perhaps, forming themselves into probes and crossing the space between its head and Ricky's.

'I need you,' it said, its voice now neither Wayne nor Monroe, but a crude, uncultivated voice, a thug's voice. 'I'm so fucking weak; it uses me up, being in the world.'

It was mainlining on him, feeding itself, whatever it was, on his stares, once adoring — now horrified. He could feel it draining out his life through his eyes, luxuriating in the soul-looks he was giving it as he perished.

He knew he must be nearly dead, because he hadn't taken a breath in a long while. It seemed like minutes, but he couldn't be sure.

Just as he was listening for the sound of his heart, the horns divided around his head and pressed themselves into his ears. Even in this reverie, the sensation was disgusting, and he wanted to cry out for it to stop. But the fingers were working their way into his head, bursting his ear-drums, and passing on like inquisitive tapeworms through brain and skull. He was alive, even now, still staring at his tormentor, and he knew that the fingers were finding his eyeballs, and pressing on them now from behind.

His eyes bulged suddenly and broke from their housing, splashing from his sockets. Momentarily he saw the world from a different angle as his sense of sight cascaded down his cheek. There was his lip, his chin —

It was an appalling experience, and mercifully short. Then the feature Ricky'd lived for thirty-seven years snapped in mid-reel, and he slumped in the arms of fiction.

Ricky's seduction and death had occupied less than three minutes. In that time Birdy had tried every key on Ricky's ring, and could get none of the damn things to open the door. Had she not persisted she might have gone back into the cinema and asked for some help. But things mechanical, even locks and keys, were a challenge to her womanhood. She despised the way men felt some instinctive superiority over her sex when it came to engines, systems and logical processes, and she was damned if she was going to go whining back to Ricky to tell him she couldn't open the damn door.

By the time she'd given up the job, so had Ricky. He was dead and gone. She swore, colourfully, at the keys, and admitted defeat. Ricky clearly had a knack with these wretched things that she'd never quite grasp. Good

luck to him. All she wanted now was out of this place. It was getting claustro-
phobic. She didn't like being locked in, not knowing who was lurking around
upstairs.

And now to cap it all, the lights in the foyer were on the blink, dying
away flicker by flicker.

What the hell was going on in this place anyhow?

Without warning the lights went out altogether, and beyond the doors
into the cinema she was sure she heard movement. A light spilled through
from the other side, stronger than torchlight, twitching, colourful.

'Ricky?' she chanced into the dark. It seemed to swallow her words.
Either that or she didn't believe it was Ricky at all, and something was telling
her to make her appeal, if she had to, in a whisper.

'Ricky . . .?'

The lips of the swing-doors smacked together gently as something
pressed on them from the other side.

'. . . is that you?'

The air was electric: static was crackling off her shoes as she walked
towards the door, the hairs on her arms were rigid. The light on the other
side was growing brighter with every step.

She stopped advancing, thinking better of her enquiries. It wasn't
Ricky, she knew that. Maybe it was the man or woman on the phone, some
pebble-eyed lunatic who got off on stalking fat women.

She took two steps back toward the Ticket Office, her feet sparking,
and reached under the counter for the Motherfucker, an iron bar which
she'd kept there since she'd been trapped in the Office by three would-be
thieves with shaved heads and electric drills. She'd screamed blue murder
and they'd fled, but next time she swore she'd beat one (or all of them) senseless rather than be terrorised. And the Motherfucker, all three feet of it, was
her chosen weapon.

Armed now, she faced the doors.

They blew open suddenly, and a roar of white noise filled her head, and
a voice through the roar said:

'Here's looking at you, kid.'

An eye, a single vast eye, was filling the doorway. The noise deafened
her; the eye blinked, huge and wet and lazy, scanning the doll in front of it
with the insolence of the One True God, the maker of celluloid Earth and
celluloid Heaven.

Birdy was terrified, no other word for it. This wasn't a look-behind-you
thrill, there was no delicious anticipation, no pleasurable fright. It was real
fear, bowel-fear, unadorned and ugly as shit.

She could hear herself whimpering under the relentless gaze of the
eye, her legs were weakening. Soon she'd fall on the carpet in front of the
door, and that would be the end of her, surely.

SON OF CELLULOID

Then she remembered Motherfucker. Dear Motherfucker, bless his phallic heart. She raised the bar in a two-handed grip and ran at the eye, swinging.

Before she made contact the eye closed, the light went out, and she was in darkness again, her retina burning from the sight.

In the darkness, somebody said: 'Ricky's dead.'

Just that. It was worse than the eye, worse than all the dead voices of Hollywood, because she knew somehow it was true. The cinema had become a slaughterhouse. Lindi Lee's Dean had died as Ricky had said he had, and now Ricky was dead as well. The doors were all locked, the game was down to two. Her and it.

She made a dash for the stairs, not sure of her plan of action, but certain that remaining in the foyer was suicidal. As her foot touched the bottom stair the swing-doors sighed open again behind her and something came after her, fast and flickering. It was a step or two behind her as she breathlessly mounted the stairs, cursing her bulk. Spasms of brilliant light shot by her from its body like the first igniting flashes of a Roman Candle. It was preparing another trick, she was certain of it.

She reached the top of the stairs with her admirer still on her heels. Ahead, the corridor, lit by a single greasy bulb, promised very little comfort. It ran the full length of the cinema, and there were a few storerooms off it, piled with crap: posters, 3-D spectacles, mildewed stills. In one of the storerooms there was a fire-door, she was sure. But which? She'd only been up here once, and that was two years ago.

'Shit. Shit. Shit,' she said. She ran to the first storeroom. The door was locked. She beat on it, protesting. It stayed locked. The next the same. The third the same. Even if she could remember which storeroom contained the escape route the doors were too heavy to break down. Given ten minutes and Motherfucker's help she might do it. But the Eye was at her back: she didn't have ten seconds, never mind ten minutes.

There was nothing for it but confrontation. She spun on her heel, a prayer on her lips, to face the staircase and her pursuer. The landing was empty.

She stared at the forlorn arrangement of dead bulbs and peeling paint as if to discover the invisible, but the thing wasn't in front of her at all, it was behind. The brightness flared again at her back, and this time the Roman Candle caught, fire became light, light became image, and glories she'd almost forgotten were spilling down the corridor towards her. Unleashed scenes from a thousand movies: each with its unique association. She began, for the first time, to understand the origins of this remarkable species. It was a ghost in the machine of the cinema: a son of celluloid.

'Give your soul to me,' a thousand stars said.

'I don't believe in souls,' she replied truthfully.

119

SILVER SCREAM

'Then give me what you give to the screen, what everybody gives. *Give me some love.*'

That's why all those scenes were playing, and replaying, and playing again, in front of her. They were all moments when an audience was magically united with the screen, bleeding through its eyes, looking and looking and looking. She'd done it herself, often. Seen a film and felt it move her so deeply it was almost a physical pain when the end credits rolled and the illusion was broken, because she felt she'd left something of herself behind, a part of her inner being lost up there amongst her heroes and her heroines. Maybe she had. Maybe the air carried the cargo of her desires and deposited them somewhere, intermingled with the cargo of other hearts, all gathering together in some niche, until —

Until this. This child of their collective passions: this technicolour seducer; trite, crass and utterly bewitching.

Very well, she thought, it's one thing to understand your executioner: another thing altogether to talk it out of its professional obligations.

Even as she sorted the enigma out she was lapping up the pictures in the thing: she couldn't help herself. Teasing glimpses of lives she'd lived, faces she'd loved. Mickey Mouse, dancing with a broom, Gish in 'Broken Blossoms', Garland (with Toto at her side) watching the twister lowering over Kansas, Astaire in 'Top Hat', Welles in 'Kane', Brando and Crawford, Tracy and Hepburn — people so engraved on our hearts they need no Christian names. And so much better to be teased by these moments, to be shown only the pre-kiss melt, not the kiss itself; the slap, not the reconciliation; the shadow, not the monster; the wound, not death.

It had her in thrall, no doubt of it. She was held by her eyes as surely as if it had them out on their stalks, and chained.

'Am I beautiful?' it said.

Yes it was beautiful.

'Why don't you give yourself to me?'

She wasn't thinking any more, her powers of analysis had drained from her, until something appeared in the muddle of images that slapped her back into herself. 'Dumbo'. The fat elephant. *Her* fat elephant: no more than that, the fat elephant she'd thought *was* her.

The spell broke. She looked away from the creature. For a moment, out of the corner of her eye, she saw something sickly and fly-blown beneath the glamour. They'd called her Dumbo as a child, all the kids on her block. She'd lived with that ridiculous grey horror for twenty years, never able to shake it off. She thought of it cradled in the trunk of its mother, condemned as a Mad Elephant, and she wanted to beat the sentimental thing senseless.

'It's a fucking lie!' she spat at it.

'I don't know what you mean,' it protested.

'What's under all the pizzazz then? Something very nasty I think.'

SON OF CELLULOID

The light began to flicker, the parade of trailers faltering. She could see another shape, small and dark, lurking behind the curtains of light. Doubt was in it. Doubt and fear of dying. She was sure she could smell the fear off it, at ten paces.

'What are you, under there?'

She took a step towards it.

'What are you hiding? Eh?'

It found a voice. A frightened, human voice. 'You've no business with me.'

'You tried to kill me.'

'I want to live.'

'So do I.'

It was getting dark this end of the corridor, and there was an old, bad smell here, of rot. She knew rot, and this was something animal. Only last spring, when the snow had melted, she'd found something very dead in the yard behind her apartment. Small dog, large cat, it was difficult to be sure. Something domestic that had died of cold in the sudden snows the December before. Now it was besieged with maggots: yellowish, greyish, pinkish: a pastel fly-machine with a thousand moving parts.

It had around it the same stink that lingered here. Maybe that was somehow the flesh behind the fantasy.

Taking courage, her eyes still stinging with 'Dumbo', she advanced on the wavering mirage, Motherfucker raised in case the thing tried any funny business.

The boards beneath her feet were creaking, but she was too interested in her quarry to listen to their warnings. It was time she got a hold of this killer, shook it and made it spit its secret.

They'd almost gone the length of the corridor now, her advancing, it retreating. There was nowhere left for the thing to go.

Suddenly the floorboards folded up into dusty fragments under her weight and she was falling through the floor in a cloud of dust. She dropped Motherfucker as she threw out her hands to catch hold of something, but it was all worm-ridden, and crumbled in her grasp.

She fell awkwardly and landed hard on something soft. Here the smell of rot was incalculably stronger, it coaxed the stomach into the throat. She reached out her hand to right herself in the darkness, and on every side there was slime and cold. She felt as though she'd been dumped in a case of partially-gutted fish. Above her, the anxious light shone through the boards as it fell on her bed. She looked, though God knows she didn't want to, and she was lying in the remains of a man, his body spread by his devourers over quite an area. She wanted to howl. Her instinct was to tear off her skirt and blouse, both of which were gluey with matter; but she couldn't go naked, not in front of the son of celluloid.

SILVER SCREAM

It still looked down at her.

'Now you know,' it said, lost.

'This is you —'

'This is the body I once occupied, yes. His name was Barberio. A criminal; nothing spectacular. He never aspired to greatness.'

'And you?'

'His cancer. I'm the piece of him which did aspire, that did long to be more than a humble cell. I am a dreaming disease. No wonder I love the movies.'

The son of celluloid was weeping over the edge of the broken floor, its true body exposed now it had no reason to fabricate a glory.

It was a filthy thing, a tumour grown fat on wasted passion. A parasite with the shape of a slug, and the texture of raw liver. For a moment a toothless mouth, badly moulded, formed at its head-end and said: 'I'm going to have a find a new way to eat your soul.'

It flopped down into the crawlspace beside Birdy. Without its shimmering coat of many technicolours it was the size of a small child. She backed away as it stretched a sensor to touch her, but avoidance was a limited option. The crawlspace was narrow, and further along it was blocked with what looked to be broken chairs and discarded prayer-books. There was no way out but the way she'd come, and that was fifteen feet above her head.

Tentatively, the cancer touched her foot, and she was sick. She couldn't help it, even though she was ashamed to be giving in to such primitive responses. It revolted her as nothing ever had before; brought to mind something aborted, a bucket-case.

'Go to hell,' she said to it, kicking at its head, but it kept coming, its diarrhoeal mass trapping her legs. She could feel the churning motion of its innards as it rose up to her.

Its bulk on her belly and groin was almost sexual, and revolted as she was by her own train of thought she wondered dimly if such a thing aspired to sex. Something about the insistence of its forming and reforming feelers against her skin, probing tenderly beneath her blouse, stretching to touch her lips, only made sense as desire. Let it come then, she thought, let it come if it has to.

She let it crawl up her until it was entirely perched on her body, fighting every moment the urge to throw it off — and then she sprang her trap.

She rolled over.

She'd weighed 225 pounds at the last count, and she was probably more now. The thing was beneath her before it could work out how or why this had happened, and its pores were oozing the sick sap of tumours.

It fought, but it couldn't get out from under, however much it squirmed. Birdy dug her nails into it and began to tear at its sides, taking cobs out of it, spongey cobs that set more fluids gushing. Its howls of anger turned into

122

howls of pain. After a short while, the dreaming disease stopped fighting. Birdy lay still for a moment. Underneath her, nothing moved.

At last, she got up. It was impossible to know if the tumour was dead. It hadn't, by any standards that she understood, lived. Besides, she wasn't touching it again. She'd wrestle the Devil himself rather than embrace Barberio's cancer a second time.

She looked up at the corridor above her and despaired. Was she not to die in here, like Barberio before her? Then, as she glanced down at her adversary, she noticed the grille. It hadn't been visible while it was still night outside. Now dawn was breaking, and columns of dishwater light were creeping through the lattice.

She bent to the grille, pushed it hard, and suddenly the day was in the crawlspace with her, all around her. It was a squeeze to get through the small door, and she kept thinking every moment that she felt the thing crawling across her legs, but she hauled herself into the world with only bruised breasts to complain of.

The abandoned lot hadn't changed substantially since Barberio's visit there. It was merely more nettle-thronged. She stood for a while breathing in draughts of fresh air, then made for the fence and the street beyond it.

The fat woman with the haggard look and the stinking clothes was given a wide berth by newsboys and dogs alike as she made her way home.

THREE: CENSORED SCENES

It wasn't the end.

The police went to the Movie Palace just after nine-thirty. Birdy went with them. The search revealed the mutilated bodies of Dean and Ricky, as well as the remains of 'Sonny' Barberio. Upstairs, in the corner of the corridor, they found a cerise shoe.

Birdy said nothing, but she knew. Lindi Lee had never left.

She was put on trial for a double murder nobody really thought she'd committed, and acquitted for lack of evidence. It was the order of the court that she be put under psychiatric observation for a period of not less than two years. The woman might not have committed murder, but it was clear she was a raving lunatic. Tales of walking cancers do nobody's reputation much good.

In the early summer of the following year Birdy gave up eating for a week. Most of the weight-loss in that time was water, but it was sufficient to

123

encourage her friends that she was at last going to tackle the Big Problem. That weekend, she went missing for twenty-four hours.

Birdy found Lindi Lee in a deserted house in Seattle. She hadn't been so difficult to trace: it was hard for poor Lindi to keep control of herself these days, never mind avoid would-be pursuers. As it happened her parents had given up on her several months previous. Only Birdy had continued to look, paying for an investigator to trace the girl, and finally her patience was rewarded with the sight of the frail beauty, frailer than ever but still beautiful sitting in this bare room. Flies roamed the air. A turd, perhaps human, sat in the middle of the floor.

Birdy had a gun out before she opened the door. Lindi Lee looked up from her thoughts, or maybe *its* thoughts, and smiled at her. The greeting lasted a moment only before the parasite in Lindi Lee recognised Birdy's face, saw the gun in her hand and knew exactly what she'd come to do.

'Well,' it said, getting up to meet its visitor.

Lindi Lee's eyes burst, her mouth burst, her cunt and ass, her ears and nose all burst, and the tumour poured out of her in shocking pink rivers. It came worming out of her milkless breasts, out of a cut in her thumb, from an abrasion on her thigh. Wherever Lindi Lee was open, it came.

Birdy raised the gun and fired three times. The cancer stretched once towards her, fell back, staggered and collapsed. Once it was still, Birdy calmly took the acid-bottle out of her pocket, unscrewed the top and emptied the scalding contents on human limb and tumour alike. It made no shout as it dissolved, and she left it there, in a patch of sun, a pungent smoke rising from the confusion.

She stepped out into the street, her duty done, and went her way, confidently planning to live long after the credits for this particular comedy had rolled.

THE ANSWER TREE

by

Steven R. Boyett

He hated waiting in lines. A line was a bunch of people between him and something he wanted to do, a symptom of a crowded world. What this city needed was one good plague.

He thrust his hands into the pockets of his tweed jacket. His right hand fingered the ticket for which he had paid fifty dollars.

This certainly did not look like the sort of line you expected to see outside a porn theater. First off, you never saw a line in front of a porn theater anyway, because people who liked to see dirty movies didn't like being seen going to watch dirty movies. And the crowd was depressingly young, disturbingly clean-cut, and competitively fashionable, with that ROTC-candidate look all college boys seemed to favor nowadays. UCLA film school, he guessed.

He shook his head. What had happened to kids? Why had they given in? They sat slack-jawed in his lecture classes, looking hypnotized and awaiting programming, taking notes only when he wrote something on the board. They looked, now that he thought about it, like people watching television — a medium he despised and could never sell to. It certainly wasn't because of *him* that his students were apathetic; his lectures were dynamic and interesting, and film criticism was an involving subject even when taken up by amateurs, which he most certainly was not.

What this line did have in common with a porn-movie crowd, he realized, was that they carefully avoided looking at one another. They were a group engaging in an illicit activity, but they were not collaborators. They were isolated individuals who knew exactly why they had been drawn here, and had enough social conscience to feel vaguely reluctant about mingling with others who shared their peculiar taste in entertainment.

127

SILVER SCREAM

The line began to move. He pulled the ticket from his pocket and glanced at it. ADMIT ONE, it read in that dot-matrix print he despised, and that was all. Twenty-five bucks a word.

The acne-riddled teenager at the door tore his ticket and said "Enjoy the show" in a monotone, not even glancing at him.

The theater was clean and modern, not at all the seedy box he'd expected to find in a porn theater on Hollywood Boulevard. He found a seat as close to the exact center of the theater as he could get, removed his coat, opened his notepad, and checked to see that his penlight was working.

Bienvido, was scrawled on the top margin of the blue-ruled pad. **Answer Tree.**

He left notepad and coat to mark his seat and went to the concession stand to get a Coke.

Very little indeed is known about Jorge Luis Armando Bienvido. He was born in the Iberian peninsula circa 1920. He was an orphan whose childhood was marked by peer rejection, violence, and emotional and financial instability. His foster parents beat and sexually abused him, and he often ran away from home. His earliest memory, he said in one of the two interviews he granted in his life, was of watching his mother perform fellatio upon his father. "He had a bottle in one hand, I remember it was green. In his other hand was my mother's hair. He kept pulling. I was not spying; our house had only one room. He pulled. Her eyes were closed tight, I remember thinking as if she were eating something that tasted bad. He pulled and she coughed, and I remember that I thought he poured wine upon her face. Many years later I realized, of course, that that was not at all what he had done."

When he was twelve, young Luis ran away from home for the last time. His travels during the ensuing two years are undocumented. It was in the city of Sagunto on the Mediterranean coast, that fourteen-year-old Luis — minus his left eye and right index finger, and plus a scar across his throat — surfaced again.

In Sagunto a small production crew from Germany were filming scenes for a propaganda movie. There were horses and German men wearing swords and odd hats and looking most un-Spanish. Spain was in the throes of an economic despair that America had only tasted; opportunity in the form of a German film crew that needed to employ locals was a gift from God.

128

THE ANSWER TREE

Young Luis was hired on as a gofer. He delivered messages, props, food, script pages, lightbulbs (the Germans had brought their own), and anything else that needed delivering. And he watched. And he learned.

— *The Tyranny of Flesh:*
The Films of Luis Bienvido,
Introduction, by Howard Grange
(University of California Press, 1984)

"— and, like, this guy Grange is telling us all this shit, you know? About Jung and Freud and all. And I'm like, whoa! — this is supposed to be a *film* class, right? I already *got* a C in psychology. I mean —"

In the line for refreshments he listened to two students in front of him. He felt conspicuous with his tweed jacket and leather elbow patches, his salt-and-pepper beard. He stood directly behind them so that their reflections in the mirror behind the concession stand obscured him.

"What kind of stuff did you watch?" the student on the right wanted to know.

"Weird shit. I mean, fuckin' weird. There was this one with a guy who got his eye cut open with a straight razor, and ants came out of some dude's hand. Like *Friday the Thirteenth*, but this was really old. Nineteen . . . something or other. But he showed us one of this guy Benvideo's movies. *The Adventure of* something or other. It was really strange. And Grange turns on the lights when the movie's over, and it's like, every girl in the class is crying. I mean, the guy's crazy, you know?"

"You mean Bienvido? Or Grange?"

The first student laughed. "Naw, Grange is just a fucking pussy. He was always staring at girl's crotches under their desks, drooling at their tits 'n shit. But naw, this Benvideo was some kinda nut. He, like — I don't know . . . ate his girlfriend, or some shit like that. But, you know, it made me realize how much I want to be a director. I mean, I could do stuff that made more sense than that. And my dad would probably get up the bucks . . ."

Grange shook his head and snorted despite himself. Here before him stood the future of America. Why did he even bother?

"Hey, Professor Grange!"

He turned at the call. Behind him in the line was a young man he didn't recognize, wearing a Bloom County T-shirt and waving and smiling with easy familiarity. He nodded authoritatively. "Good to see you," he said. He felt an impulse to duck his head and slink away, as if he'd been caught doing something dirty. He was acutely aware of the two students ahead of him in line, who had to have heard his name called.

129

"I thought you might show up here." The young man glanced around the lobby. "Class act," he observed.

Grange nodded noncommitally and moved closer to the counter as someone turned away from it trying to manage a Dr. Pepper and two tubs of popcorn lubricated with that petroleum by-product theaters pass off as butter nowadays. The two students bellied up to the counter and ordered. The one who'd taken his class glanced at him in the mirror, then looked away hurriedly.

"Hey, Professor?"

He glanced back grudgingly.

"I read your book about Bienvido."

"Which one is that? I've written three."

"Yeah? Well . . . I could only find one. Um . . . *Bienvido: The Key of the Eye.*"

Grange nodded.

"Well." The young man glanced around him. "You think it's true, about this movie?" he blurted.

"What's that?" Grange asked blithely.

For a moment the student looked uncomfortable. "You know. All that killer-movie crap."

He spread his hands. "It was banned in Europe," he said cryptically.

"Yeah." He slid four fingers into the hair behind his ear, curled them, and pulled hard. Grange frowned. "I have a friend, he's got a print of the movie Bienvido did before this one."

"*Song of the Bone,*" Grange said.

"Yeah." He began twirling his hair, twisting it in his hand. "I saw it a while ago, and it . . . *upset* me."

"It upset a lot of people."

"Yeah. Which is why I wondered if what they say is true. About this movie." The hand lowered. "I mean, I wouldn't believe it. But after that last movie, and how much it —" He thrust both hands into the front pockets of his jeans. "Well, you know."

"Well, it *was* banned in Europe," he said again. The two ahead of him turned away from the counter clutching Cokes and tubs of popcorn. The face of the one who'd been talking about him was red; he avoided looking at Grange. The other one looked as if he were trying not to laugh. Grange ignored them and ordered a Coke and a box of jujubes.

Posters for porn movies flanked the concession stand: *Triple Play* on the left, *Young and Restless* on the right. On the latter poster was a girl in pink panties and black stockings. She was probably in her mid-twenties, but her hair was in pig-tails and her lips were pouty, and somehow she managed to convey a convincing sixteen-year-old's allure.

He wondered what Roberta would think if she knew he was here. Or

Laurie, Roberta's daughter from a previous marriage. Roberta had been a package deal: marrying her had meant instant family. But Grange had never minded playing surrogate father to Laurie. For her he always tried to appear the professorial authority figure, because he knew that young girls responded to it in a way against which no strong-jawed, quick-handed youth could ever compete. He wanted her to like him, not only to gain Roberta's approval, but because he liked Laurie for herself. In fact, the daughter looked so much like a younger version of her mother that Grange could not help but find her tantalizing.

He frowned as the girl behind the counter handed him his drink and candy. Well, *tantalizing* was certainly a loaded word. But he knew what he meant; he didn't have to go justifying himself to his own mind. He returned his attention to the poster, a mental image of Laurie momentarily super-imposed over the porn starlet — which was ridiculous, considering Laurie's boyishness. Grange thanked whatever impulse had prompted Roberta to take Laurie to her grandmother's for dinner tonight.

He paid for his snack and turned away. Behind him the student grinned — it was nearly a leer — and said, "Hey, good luck, Professor Grange."

"I'm sure we'll all pull through," Grange replied, knowing that his sarcasm, as always, would be lost.

"At fifty bucks a shot?" the young man replied. "*Somebody* better not."

Bienvido's first notable film was shot when he was only nineteen. He financed it himself, with money saved from odd jobs and small cons he ran as he worked the towns along the Mediterranean coast. There are also indications that young Luis prostituted himself, accommodating the peculiar tastes of some of the Italian and German officers who sought leisure there. But whether by hook or by crook, he certainly managed to gain entry into that elite stratum of producers, directors, and actors who entangled in various combinations in the resorts, on board the yachts, and on the balconies along the Golfo de Valencia.

Hitler and Mussolini were helping Franco and the Nationalists oppose the Spanish Democratic Party, and the fledgling Nazi war machine needed propaganda. Luis managed to borrow equipment in the way of lights and cameras, and sometimes even entire sets, from film crews shooting features for a (largely German) audience hungry to know that there was indeed a Good Future awaiting them, eager to find vindication in the Reich ways as the right ways, and prideful with the cinematic crystallization of *Deutschland ueber alles*.

SILVER SCREAM

Pages from the Diaries of the Dead was shot in ten days, though those days were spread across a summer month in Franco Spain. It is a stilted and cheap-looking film, and silent to boot (young Luis either could not afford or could not persuade the means for sound), but in it one may see the germination of the style that was to become notorious throughout Europe. As with all Bienvido films, there is no plot, there is only theme. And he does not hesitate to bring in wholly irrelevant images to support this theme.

Bienvido's misogyny, his loathing of father figures, and his "yearning to escape the flesh by way of distortion," are evident from this first effort: in *Pages* a woman is violated by a chair upon which the ghostly image of her tyrannical husband appears; lovers kiss, the kiss is held, the lovers' eyes open and stare unseeing, until we realize that they are dead, and still the kiss is held, beetles crawl from their mouths, and (utilizing the same lighting and make-up techniques employed in the John Barrymore *Jekyll & Hyde*, a tight tracking shot that spirals inward, and brilliantly subtle facial nuances employed by the actors as the camera reveals their hidden sides) the lovers wither and decompose; a man who eats the eyes of a crow during famine becomes able to view the world from soaring heights.

Diaries of the Dead is also notable for the on-camera deaths of actors Carmelita Esprella and Roberto Jose Caspar — establishing the grisly pattern that was to haunt each of Bienvido's future efforts, both in front of the camera and behind it. Near the end of *Diaries* the camera follows Esprella and Caspar onto a rain-swept train station; they turn to wave at the arriving train; Carmelita slips at the edge of the platform; Caspar reaches out to steady her, and they both fall in front of the iron wheels. Mercifully — for the viewer — the sight is obstructed by the platform edge, but the horrified reactions of film crew and extras on the platform inform the tragedy more than the actual sight ever could.

Both actors were rumored to have been Bienvido's lovers at the time. That their deaths affected him personally is undoubtable, but how their deaths affected his future work is best left to examination of the works themselves.

Bienvido retained the train-station footage for the final cut of *Pages from the Diaries of the Dead*. In later years he would remark, "One must be willing to sacrifice anything for the sake of the image. The image is everything. The brain believes the eye. The eye believes the image. I am the image. The eye is the key.

132

THE ANSWER TREE

By shaping what occurs in front of it, I shape what is behind it as well.''

His coat and legal pad had been moved to the end of the row, which was otherwise full. Sitting where his things had been were the two young men who had been ahead of him in the concession-stand line. They conspicuously shoved popcorn into their mouths and avoided looking at him as he sat down and folded the coat across his lap. He sipped his Coke and surveyed the audience.

The majority were white males, middle-class college kids. He seemed to be the oldest person here. There was a nervous hubbub throughout the theater, punctuated by occasional, overloud laughter. In another frame of mind Grange might have been pleased at such a turnout for this rarest of movies by the infamous, yet ironically unheralded, Luis Bienvido. He might have felt smug satisfacation that his own film courses and critical publications had possibly been a factor in turning people on to the director, people who might otherwise have never heard of him, and certainly never would have attended one of his disturbing and idiosyncratic films even if they had.

But he found himself annoyed. Most of his students had been like the ones across the row from him, taking a film course for an easy grade, and leaving it with little else. His books about Bienvido were university-press books that had — like the unappreciated genius of Bienvido himself — gone unheralded. He frowned. It was like playing the violin to water buffalos. There was nothing intrinsic to Bienvido's work that had packed a theater at fifty dollars a ticket. These kids weren't here to watch a movie. They were here to watch someone die.

Manipulation certainly became the hallmark of Bienvido's work. It was only natural, therefore, that he attracted the attention of the Nationalsozialistische Deutsche Arbeiterpartei, which paid his way to Berlin. There he took tea with Joseph Goebbels, Hitler's minister of propaganda, who found him ''enthusiastic and disquieting.''

Financed by the Axis, Bienvido's next film *Wir Warten fur den Roten Zug (Waiting for the Red Train* — a clear reference to the train-platform tragedy) went unreleased. With its fusion of organic and mundane domestic shapes (a marriage bed is slit

133

open to reveal internal organs and later, a fetus; a father's favorite easy chair is found to contain his heart long after his death; a woman gives birth to a button-eyed rag doll that bleeds), Goebbels' Chamber of Culture consider the film "too obscure for the popular appetite."

Red Train contains the famous "interment orgy" montage, where Bienvido incorporated footage he had shot himself, using cameras in hidden rooms, of the sheeplike resignation on the faces of naked Jews waiting in cinder-block rooms as cyanide gas begins to pour from showerheads. The footage was used as "color" — for the effect of the image as mere punctuation for the pensive interment scene.

Hitler requested a screening, and was rumored to have left the theater afterward in an extreme state of excitement.

After the war, black-market release of the *Waiting for the Red Train* gained Bienvido international underground attention, in the form of critical outrage and public shock, if not commercial return. Interestingly, this is the first time the single name "Bienvido" appeared on the credits of one of his films. It would remain such from that point on; Bienvido as institution; Bienvido as "name."

His much-publicized meeting with admirer Salvador Dali — another "name," who showed him off to such contemporaries as Bunuel and Cocteau — resulted in Spanish financing and distribution for his first major film: *The Great Adventure.*

The film went unreleased by the very government that had funded its creation, and again the justification for its supression was the nature of Bienvido's profoundly disturbing eye for the visceral and the sexual. But in much the same way the Marquis de Sade was heralded as the individualist of his age, Bienvido's peers championed the film. Prints were smuggled to the first Cannes Film Festival in 1947, where it earned nothing but a storm of outrage. *Cine* critic Henri L'Enfal wrote (with relative moderation): "Bienvido is gaining a reputation as a propagandist, a master manipulator whose works leave audiences inexplicably moved, influenced, affected, even disturbed. This reviewer has found all these claims to be true: after but a single viewing of *The Great Adventure*, he was left with a pulsing headache which did not abate until the next day."

From such notable derision, Bienvido's place in cinema history became assured.

* * *

THE ANSWER TREE

The house lights dimmed just as Grange brought the box of jujubes to his mouth. The crowd volume rose. Quickly he tamped the end of the box. Several of the soft shapes fell into his mouth and he began to chew. Filling-pullers, Laurie called them. Little tomboy.

The curtains parted and he settled into his seat. The screen lit white, and the movie began.

No trailers, no chain promotion, no cute anti-litter or no-smoking bits. The leader fed in, and automatically he frowned: the print was old and scratchy. Well, what had he expected?

The credits were in French, plain white block letters on black, like negatives of newspaper headlines. They appeared on the screen like stills at a hurried slide show.

L'ARBRE A REPONSES

Applause.

Un Film De Bienvido

More applause. A few strangled cries, as if audience members were dying. Laughter.

Grange checked his penlight, folded his right leg over his left, and clicked the ballpoint. The credits continued, some of the audience members reading them aloud in comical French accents. He wanted to tell them to shut up, but he said nothing. They'd shut up soon enough.

Scénario et Réalisé par Bienvido

The applause swelled, the movie began, and Grange waited.

Paris did not quite receive Bienvido with open arms and an engraved key. Though he had not been a Francophile, he had worked for the Fascists; though he had not been a Nazi, he had worked for Goebbels; though he had not been a propagandist, he had directed a film for the German propaganda ministry. He could not be considered a war criminal, but neither would he ever be treated as *un ami de France*.

In Paris Bienvido lived with Lona de Vreker, a Belgian actress whom the director had met when she was cast in a minor part in *The Great Adventure*. Detractors have often remarked on de Vreker's appearance, a combination of boyishness and youth. She seemed to simultaneously act as Bienvido's son, daughter, wife, and lover, during a time when Bienvido was known to have had both male and female sex partners; he often affectionately referred to her as "my own little sin."

de Vreker's androgynic appeal cannot be denied; for the next two years she was Bienvido's constant companion. Unsurprisingly, she was cast as the lead for his next film.

Song of the Bone is legendary among followers of what is admittedly an esoteric branch of film study; much space has been given over to academic interpretation of its themes and images. It is primal and immediate in its imagery, yet the *effect* the imagery attempts to achieve is uncertain. Bienvido's exact theme is unclear.

Song of the Bone is a difficult film for many reasons, but its primary challenge to the uninitiated viewer is a raw power that seems to bypass the intellect and work directly upon the most primal of human mental functions. It is the film for which Bienvido first employed the term "cinema of instinct," and it is an intensely uncomfortable viewing experience. There is solid evidence that the film has upset the mental balance of more than a few of its viewers. Possibly this is because of an already-extant predisposition on the part of the afflicted, but the movie is affecting even for the most mentally and emotionally stable.

A catalog of its images does not adequately serve to explain the overall impression the movie leaves: the father forcing his daughter to lick the knife he has used to perform an emergency Caesarian; the talking head within the lettuce in the icebox; the dream of the seagull that dives into a road where the fins of sharks sweep the macadam in the wake of trucks that pass above; the haunting recurrent image of the gaunt mother rocking the cradle that contains the decomposed body of her infant.

And Lona de Vreker. Throughout the film Bienvido effectively exploits her androgyny, even celebrates it. In *Song of the Bone* she appears to be both male and female, making love with men as a woman, and with women as a man. This hermaphroditic quality is boldly stated but never explained. Possibly it is meant to suggest a physical expression of Jung's notions of the animus/anima. (Interestingly, Jung was proscribed in Hitler's Germany.) It is when de Vreker meets her *doppelganger* near the end of the film that many of the previous images repeat in significant and ever-shifting juxtapositions, and when the two s/hes make love in a way that renders gender identification and sexual roles impossible to determine, the viewer is left undeniably upset by the confusion.

Here is a scene that could have been played broadly, indeed

with high comedy: yet it upsets. Why? Being a film of pre-conscious images — a cinema of instinct — it is easy to experience the film's effects, yet quite difficult to account for them. Indeed, the act of explication seems to empty these images of meaning; analysis is the opposite of what Bienvido seeks.

It is ironic, then, that analysis is precisely what many of the film's viewers were forced to seek.

Woodwinds swell above nervous cellos.
A field, grainy in overexposed blue light.
A wooden farmhouse materializes.
Smooth glide toward the front door, which opens. Within, filmy curtains diffuse the light, billowing inward in hommage to Cocteau. Up the stairs with amazing smoothness, into the hall, and pause before a bedroom door, which opens.
A man lies dying on a four-poster bed. His daughter sits reading beside him. A pleasant mongrel dog curls on the floor at the foot of the bed.
The daughter reading.
The old man breathing.
The dog sleeping.
Gust of wind billows curtains like mainsails.
The dog looks up, alert, eyes narrowed.
The daughter looks up from her book.
The old man opens his eyes.
The daughter shuts the book.
The dog barks at the window.
"Tu m'ênterreres" says the old man. "Alors tu comprendras. Alors, peut-etre, tu voudras demander."
And dies.
The daughter walks down the stairs. The dog follows.
From the shed beside the house she takes a shovel. The camera swings with the arc of the spade tossing clots of earth.
The dog squirms on its back in the grass.
The old man in a shroud materializes in the grave as it takes shape. As he attains solidity the soil fades in over him by degrees, to the background chuffing of the shovel. The grave is filled. The dog urinates upon the mound. The daughter returns to the house. The house dissolves.
Grange sat stunned.

*   *   *

SILVER SCREAM

It was near the end of principal photography for *Song of the Bone* that the gruesome events at the chalet retreat of Bienvido's friend and sometime producer Gascon D'Arcy took place. The similarities to the Tate/La Bianca murders perpetrated by the Manson "family," still a decade and a half away, have been thoroughly remarked on. Lona de Vreker's frozen remains were found scattered in the snow in front of the chalet; D'Arcy and his mistress were butchered before the fireplace and thrown to mingle in the bathtub; a fourth, never-identified man was completely flensed and decapitated. His blackened skull was found in the ashes of the chalet's long-cold fireplace.

The slaughter apparently took place while Bienvido was in town acquiring supplies to see the group through the blizzard that was coming; shopkeepers later confirmed his presence there. He returned to the chalet and discovered the carnage just as the blizzard descended.

No phones. No contact with the outside world. For the next four days Bienvido was snowbound in the chalet with the dismembered bodies of his lover and his friends, while outside the wind howled and the snow piled at the door.

The killers were never found.

The daughter upon the bed on which her father died. Pregnant, in labor, screaming.

Purple-lit curtains billow, behind them lightning flashing.

Looking toward the house from the back yard. Lone candle-lit window. Screams from within.

A tree grows from the grave.

Inside, the daughter naked, sweating, alone.

The dog pacing nervously.

Looking down at herself, the daughter feels something within. Her screams abate. Motion at her pubic mound.

Around the triangle of her dark pubic hair, evenly spaced blisters.

The dog whimpers.

The tree stretches toward the rain.

The blisters expand, become protuberances. The flesh pulls and tears like taffy.

Long, thin, jointed, furred legs emerge. Spider legs. They lengthen, they bend. They straddle her. In the center of the legs, the spider body: her pubic mound. Labial folds work back and forth, become mandibles.

138

THE ANSWER TREE

The spider begins to lift itself. To wrench itself whole from her.
Outside, the tree, looking toward the house.
The candle-lit window darkens.
The rain stops.
A baby's cry.

In the theater there was an uncertain lull. Then: applause.
Grange let out his breath, unaware that he had been holding it. His
pen began to move. **Establishing, he scribbled. Unusually linear! Story
emphasis. Misogyny/fear of flawed progeny. Father-to-daughter.**

After authorities released him, Bienvido completed *Song of
the Bone* (the title of which, morbidly but intriguingly, was
selected *after* the chalet murders). It was during the editing
process that associates first noticed the changes in Bienvido's
behavior. At first they thought them unremarkable — indeed,
after such a travail, to continue normally would have seemed the
most peculiar thing. Nonetheless, it was Gunther Hewe, Bienvido's favored editor, who noticed that the director had begun to
spend all his time in the tiny editing room in Paris. Bienvido
brought in a cot and had his meals delivered. Ultimately he cut
the film by himself, with minimal assistance from Hewe, and the
result was a movie of such intensity that some viewers have been
permanently scarred by its derangement.
The notoriety of the film was great, but Bienvido received
few offers to direct more films. Quite simply, everyone thought
he was mad.
Madness has never been considered a detriment to the
artistic temperament, however, particularly in Europe, and it was
not long before Bienvido obtained (ironically enough, considering his past associations) French backing for his next, his final, his
least-seen and most notorious, film: *The Answer Tree.*

The child runs out the back door of the house, down the stairs, and across

SILVER SCREAM

the back yard to stop before the tree. Barely discernible looking down through the branches is the child's face looking up. The child picks the green fruit and takes a bite. It is impossible to tell if the child is a boy or a girl. The child smiles at the tree as if it has suddenly said something amusing.

Inside the house the mother lies in the four-poster, hair gray and wild, eyes mad.

The child offers her a bite of the green fruit. She turns her head away. The child touches her hair, clenches it, and tilts up its head to bite from the fruit. A squirt of juice lands upon its mother's cheek.

Grange scribbled. He wrote without looking, hardly conscious of the words flowing from the pen, his eyes fixed upon the images unfolding in front of them.

First Bienvido interview/the green bottle. Temptations of androgyny & incest. Laurie.

He shifted uncomfortably in his seat and pressed his lap with the notepad to relieve the pressure of his erection.

Luis Bienvido approached Salvador Dali about doing production design for *The Answer Tree*, which he claimed would be his *magnum opus*, his "lifework." The flamboyant artist was agreeable, until Bienvido described the film in detail. Dali would never divulge the details of his long conversation with Bienvido, but after hearing his countryman's plans for the new film, even the famous iconoclast refused to have any association with the project.

Bienvido proceeded with his own production designs. The result was a sort of modern *Cabinet of Dr. Caligari*, a world of bleached colors seen through the eyes of a tormented madman.

Using skills perfected during his days on the Spanish Mediterranean, Bienvido used his talents to persuade any number of friends and acquaintances to lend their finances, time, and talents to the production of his film. He went through three cinematographers, six main cameramen, four assistant directors, innumerable technicians. Never was a named producer associated with the project. The entire cast were virtual unknowns. At no point was there a definitive shooting script.

THE ANSWER TREE

Cast members received the pages pertinent to their roles and no more. Unions threatened walkouts, actors threatened breach-of-contract suits, hotels demanded payment for room and board. Somehow Bienvido held the project together through sheer force of will for fifteen hellish weeks of shooting. *The Answer Tree* had become an obsession; he would allow nothing to get in its way.

Eventually shooting completed and cast and crew went their separate ways. Bienvido took his one and one-half million feet of film and ensconsed himself in his old editing room in Paris, less than a mile from where he had once lived with the ill-fated Lona de Vreker. He would not receive visitors; he did not reply to mail or telephone calls; he granted no interviews.

The images flowed before Grange's eyes. The impressions flowed from Grange's pen. Bienvido is the image. The eye is the key. The brain believes.

The cleaning lady found him by the smell. She unlocked the door despite the cautions against her, and there she found Bienvido: slumped over the two-reel editor, hands (one holding a revolver) stretched toward stacked and numbered aluminum cannisters labeled *The Answer Tree*. Bienvido's last film was in the can; the brain that had conceived it was spattered across it.

On the screen the child now grown kills his/her lover by smashing a green bottle across her head.

The daughter/son vindicates parental vestment. Rightness of murder in the face of obstruction of desire. Desire.

Grange's hand scribbled while reflected light played across his face.

Bottle as penis & instrument of paternal authority. Primacy of the penis. Punishment of the flesh. Progeny as embodiment of gender, of sexuality. Progeny as affirmation of the self. Laurie as progeny.

*   *   *

141

SILVER SCREAM

Within a week of its Paris premier the film was pulled. Prints that had been delivered to Parisian and surrounding theaters were recalled. A rumor began to circulate that was simultaneously amazing, ugly, and intriguing: viewing the film could prove fatal. Inevitably at each screening, at least one audience member would be found dead in his theater chair, eyes forever fixed upon the screen. The only cause of death physicians could ever determine was "heart failure," which reveals nothing and everything.

The Answer Tree was immediately supressed. Bootlegged prints made it to Spain (where *The Great Adventure* had been smuggled *from*), and were shown in secret screenings. Whenever they could be located, the prints were seized and burned. The mythos grew.

A curious — yet sadly predictable — phenomenon arose: here was a movie reputed to kill at least one member of every audience who saw it, so naturally people flocked to view it whenever knowledge of a screening was obtained. Theater managers charged the equivalent of up to two hundred dollars to moviegoers, who seemed to consist of two basic types: Bienvido fanatics, and media necrophiles unconvinced of their own mortality, the sort who watched *Wide World of Sports* in eager anticipation of the agony of defeat.

Authorities had difficulty with the legality of supressing showings of *The Answer Tree*. Theater owners and movie audiences howled for their right to screen and view whatever they pleased. Bienvido had died intestate, with no living relatives or heirs — whom would authorities prosecute?

The distributors and the theater owners, it turned out. To screen a movie with full knowledge that it could be fatal to an audience member (however unlikely the notion may seem) was to commit premeditated murder; to distribute such a film was to be an accessory to murder.

With a hue and cry the theater owners claimed that, in that case, all amusement parks containing roller coasters must be shut down immediately. People died on them all the time; they were *designed* to disrupt the heart!

The debate raged. The lawyers and theater owners profited. Meanwhile, screenings were raided and prints were seized and destroyed.

The United States settled the problem with the same ingenuity it had employed to keep Joyce's *Ulysses* out of eager American hands: sight unseen, it declared *The Answer Tree* to be obscene.

142

THE ANSWER TREE

It seems no one has committed the film to videotape, despite substantial standing offers — possibly because prints are nearly impossible to come by, and those who obtain them are reluctant to risk them.

Due to the scarcity of prints, and to the covert nature of their screenings, it is impossible to determine where the hoopla ends and the truth begins. Can the movie really kill people?

It hardly seems likely. One must suppose that, at a screening or two, early on in the film's infamous career, a patron suffered a heart attack, and people blamed what seemed to be the most obvious cause. But customers suffer heart attacks in any number of restaurants, and no one ever assumes there is such a thing as a restaurant that kills at least one patron per evening.

Yet if the restaurant had an unusual or macabre theme — an Edgar Allen Poe restaurant, for example — then it would wear the stamp of doom the very instant a customer coughed out a fishbone.

The film is blamed because it is strange, because it is upsetting, because it is Bienvido. After all, would anyone think to label *The Sound of Music* a killer movie after two or three moviegoer heart attacks?

In darkened theaters across the world, *The Answer Tree* winds on, its only certain victim the mind and eye that created it.

The child of the child of the tree that is the father wanders the winter landscape. Body parts are scattered in the red-stained snow. A graceful, disembodied hand rises, Lady of the Frozen Lake, and points. The child follows.

A couple make love before a burning tree at the edge of the wood. In the crotch of the tree is a skull.

The child holds out the seeds of the father tree. "Où puis-je les plante?"

In their copulation the couple begin to fuse, to merge first at groin, then middle and chest and shoulder, writhing, many-jointed.

Clutching the seeds, the child watches intently until they no longer move, then walks on.

Grange caught his breath. A chill swept down his back and caused his knees to jerk.

All the while, his hand, guided by his brain, which believed his eye, wrote:

Androgyny as innocence. Seeds of consummation. Innocent androgyny of Laurie. The daughter as mother and father. The seeds _are_ father, the father _is_ the seed.

Without actually knowing it, Grange understood what had happened during Bienvido's snow-bound days at the chalet. Escaping the flesh by way of distortion.

The child returns, now an adult, to the field where she has planted her seeds.
Her father sleeps with his head propped against the trunk.
She watches him.
He opens his eyes.
"Bonjour," he says.
"Bonjour." The wind sweeps hair across her face. "Es-tu mon père?"
"Tu es ma fille," he replies, and stands.
They make love in the field beside the four-poster bed on which lies the corpse of the mother of the boyish girl now grown, daughter of the tree now a man.

When the score was not playing, the ratcheting of the projector seemed very loud. Automatically, Grange wrote on.

It is her boyishness I love. Her femininity makes her boyishness desirable. Her mother is the guardian of the moré, the Angel with the Sword.

The brown eye fills the screen.
It shrinks as the camera pulls back.
It is unblinking and lifeless dull.
The eye of a dead dog.
It lies at the foot of the four-poster bed.
The bed in the house from the film's opening.
In bed the old man, the father, young again.

THE ANSWER TREE

In his hand, a pistol painted bottle-green.
He smiles contentedly and raises the gun to his head.
He turns his head at a whine.
Beside the bed, the dog.
It raises a paw to bat at the mattress.
The man's eyes crinkle and he reaches out a hand.
The dog opens its mouth. The pink tongue lolls as the man pats its head.
The dog flinches at the sound of the gunshot.

**cinema of man as animal of instinct to fuck as animal is man to
cinema as instinct to fuck the daughter as extension of the mother as
extension of the self**

Grange mumbled to himself as he wrote. "Cinema of man. Man as animal. Animal of instinct." He scribbled on. "Cinema of man as animal of instinct."

Later, he would look at what he had written, and from the interlocking combinations of phrases would emerge a synthesis, a *gestalt* greater than the sum of its component thoughts.

In the room, the sleeping dog fills the screen.
It wakes, stretches, and yawns.
The pink tongue curls comically.
The dog stands.
In the center of the room is a tree.
Green fruit hangs in profusion.
The dog sniffs at the rough bole.
Behind the tree the curtains billow.
Outside the window the setting sun.
The dog raises a leg and urinates on the tree, then glances toward the
bedroom door. It trots out of the room.
The camera closes toward the window.
Sound of claws as the dog descends the wooden stairs.
Curtains billow with a gust of wind.
Branches tangle overhead.
Stop at the window, framed by curtains. One of the long, green fruits
hangs at the top left corner.
Outside, the back yard, the hills, the setting sun.

SILVER SCREAM

The dog runs into the yard. It stops to sniff at a rectangular patch of ground.
The sun is only a molten drop smearing the edge of a hill.
The dog looks up, toward the window.
The sun disappears, and the screen grows dark.
The curtains settle and the low violins fade.
The dog barks twice.

fulfillment of the self of the desire to be complete to liberate from the flesh of my flesh with my flesh for my flesh to free my flesh from flesh

The screen went white, then dark as the projector shut down. The lights came up and the curtains began to close.

There was silence for a few seconds. Then: scattered applause quickly subsumed by boos and whistles.

These stopped quickly.

In a middle row, near the aisle, a young man in a Bloom County T-shirt sat slack-jawed with glazed, unmoving eyes. His head was at an uncomfortable angle. He did not appear to be breathing. Those around him had stood up and were staring at him, expressions a strange mixture of horror and fascination.

Suddenly the young man grinned and sat up, shaking his head. A disappointed groan circulated, and the young man laughed at the insults flung at him. He looked for Professor Grange to see what his reaction was, but the old fart had already left.

At home Grange typed the final chapter to his last book on Bienvido's final film. He had waited years to see this film so that he could finish the book, and now he was done.

Often he had to stop to blow his nose or wipe his eyes dry on his sleeve.

He had never felt so contented with the perfect understanding of a thing. Imagined images had been crystallized for him; unspoken thoughts articulated. Grange vibrated as responsive chord, thrumming and content.

He finished the article and stacked it neatly atop the Selectric.

THE ANSWER TREE

In the bedroom he opened his underwear drawer, on his side of the dresser, and got out the long-barreled .38.

In the living room he rocked slowly in his favorite easy chair. He loved the sound of his heartbeat, loved being surrounded by the things he had acquired throughout his life and career. He loved the feel of the chair leather against his naked skin, the hard feel of his erection pressing the barrel of the gun.

With his free hand he wiped a tear from the corner of one eye, truly happy for the first time in his life as he thought about seeds and waited for the sound of the car in the driveway.

(*Merci beaucoup*, Dr Marie Zrimc *et* Lisa Margolis — SRB)

NIGHT THEY MISSED THE HORROR SHOW

by

Joe R. Lansdale

(For Lew Shiner. A story that doesn't flinch.)

If they'd gone to the drive-in like they'd planned, none of this would have happened. But Leonard didn't like drive-ins when he didn't have a date, and he'd heard about *Night Of The Living Dead*, and he knew a nigger starred in it. He didn't want to see no movie with a nigger star. Niggers chopped cotton, fixed flats and pimped nigger girls, but he'd never heard of one that killed zombies. And he'd heard too that there was a white girl in the movie that let the nigger touch her, and that peeved him. Any white gal that would let a nigger touch her must be the lowest trash in the world. Probably from Hollywood, New York or Waco, some godforsaken place like that.

Now Steve McQueen would have been all right for zombie killing and girl handling. He would have been the ticket. But a nigger? No sir.

Boy, that Steve McQueen was one cool head. Way he said stuff in them pictures was so good you couldn't help but think someone had written it down for him. He could sure think fast on his feet to come up with the things he said, and he had that real cool, mean look.

Leonard wished he could be Steve McQueen, or Paul Newman even. Someone like that always knew what to say, and he figured they got plenty of bush too. Certainly they didn't get as bored as he did. He was so bored he felt as if he were going to die from it before the night was out. Bored, bored, bored. Just wasn't nothing exciting about being in the Dairy Queen parking lot leaning on the front of his '64 Impala looking out at the highway. He figured maybe old crazy Harry who janitored at the highschool might be right about them flying saucers. Harry was always seeing something. Bigfoot, six-legged weasels, all manner of things. But maybe he was right about the saucers. He'd said he'd seen one a couple nights back hovering over Mud Creek and it was shooting down these rays that looked like wet peppermint

149

sticks. Leonard figured if Harry really had seen the saucers and the rays, then those rays were boredom rays. It would be a way for space critters to get at earth folks, boring them to death. Getting melted down by heat rays would have been better. That was at least quick, but being bored to death was sort of like being nibbled to death by ducks.

Leonard continued looking at the highway, trying to imagine flying saucers and boredom rays, but he couldn't keep his mind on it. He finally focused on something in the highway. A dead dog.

Not just a dead dog. But a DEAD DOG. The mutt had been hit by a semi at least, maybe several. It looked as if it had rained dog. There were pieces of that pooch all over the concrete and one leg was lying on the curb-ing on the opposite side, stuck up in such a way that it seemed to be waving hello. Doctor Frankenstein with a grant from John Hopkins and assistance from NASA couldn't have put that sucker together again.

Leonard leaned over to his faithful, drunk companion, Billy — known among the gang as Farto, because he was fart lighting champion of Mud Creek — and said, "See that dog there?"

Farto looked where Leonard was pointing. He hadn't noticed the dog before, and he wasn't nearly as casual about it as Leonard. The puzzle piece hound brought back memories. It reminded him of a dog he'd had when he was thirteen. A big, fine German Shepherd that loved him better than his Mama.

Sonofabitch dog tangled its chain through and over a barbed wire fence somehow and hung itself. When Farto found the dog its tongue looked like a stuffed, black sock and he could see where its claws had just been able to scrape the ground, but not quite enough to get a toe hold. It looked as if the dog had been scratching out some sort of coded message in the dirt. When Farto told his old man about it later, crying as he did, his old man laughed and said, "Probably a goddamn suicide note."

Now, as he looked out at the highway, and his whisky-laced Coke col-lected warmly in his gut, he felt a tear form in his eyes. Last time he'd felt that sappy was when he'd won the fart lighting championship with a four-inch burner that singed the hairs of his ass and the gang awarded him with a pair of colored boxing shorts. Brown and yellow ones so he could wear them without having to change them too often.

So there they were, Leonard and Farto, parked outside the DQ, leaning on the hood of Leonard's Impala, sipping Coke and whisky, feeling bored and blue and horny, looking at a dead dog and having nothing to do but go to a show with a nigger starring in it. Which to be up front, wouldn't have been so bad if they'd had dates. Dates could make up for a lot of sins, or help make a few good ones, depending on one's outlook.

But the night was criminal. Dates they didn't have. Worse yet, wasn't a girl in the entire highschool would date them. Not even Marylou Flowers, and she had some kind of disease.

All this nagged Leonard something awful. He could see what the problem was with Farto. He was ugly. Had the kind of face that attracted flies.
And though being fart lighting champion of Mud Creek had a certain
prestige among the gang, it lacked a certain something when it came to
charming the gals.

But for the life of him, Leonard couldn't figure his own problem. He
was handsome, had some good clothes, and his car ran good when he didn't
buy that old cheap gas. He even had a few bucks in his jeans from breaking
into washaterias. Yet his right arm had damn near grown to the size of his
thigh from all the whacking off he did. Last time he'd been out with a girl
had been a month ago, and as he'd been out with her along with nine other
guys, he wasn't rightly sure he could call that a date. He wondered about it
so much, he'd asked Farto if he thought it qualified as a date. Farto, who had
been fifth in line, said he didn't think so, but if Leonard wanted to call it one,
wasn't no skin off his dick.

But Leonard didn't want to call it a date. It just didn't have the feel of
one, lacked something special. There was no romance to it.

True, Big Red had called him Honey when he put the mule in the
barn, but she called everyone Honey — except Stoney. Stoney was Possum
sweets, and he was the one who talked her into wearing the grocery bag with
the mouth and eye holes. Stoney was like that. He could sweet talk the
camel out from under a sand nigger. When he got through chatting Big Red
down, she was plumb proud to wear that bag.

When finally it came his turn to do Big Red, Leonard had let her take
the bag off as a gesture of good will. That was a mistake. He just hadn't
known a good thing when he had it. Stoney had had the right idea. The bag
coming off spoiled everything. With it on, it was sort of like balling the Lone
Hippo or some such thing, but with the bag off, you were absolutely certain
what you were getting, and it wasn't pretty.

Even closing his eyes hadn't helped. He found that the ugliness of that
face had branded itself on the back of his eyeballs. He couldn't even imagine
the sack back over her head. All he could think about was that puffy, too-
painted face with the sort of bad complexion that began at the bone.

He'd gotten so disappointed, he'd had to fake an orgasm and get off
before his hooter shriveled up and his Trojan fell off and was lost in the
vacuum.

Thinking back on it, Leonard sighed. It would certainly be nice for a
change to go with a girl that didn't pull the train or had a hole between her
legs that looked like a manhole cover ought to be on it. Sometimes he wished
he could be like Farto who was as happy as if he had good sense. Anything
thrilled him. Give him a can of Wolf Brand Chili, a big moon pie, Coke and
whisky and he could spend the rest of his life fucking Big Red and lighting
the gas out of his asshole.

SILVER SCREAM

God, but this was no way to live. No women and no fun. Bored, bored, bored. Leonard found himself looking overhead for space ships and pepper-mint-colored boredom rays, but he saw only a few moths fluttering drunkenly through the beams of the DQ's lights.

Lowering his eyes back to the highway and the dog, Leonard had a sudden flash. "Why don't we get the chain out of the back and hook it up to Rex there? Take him for a ride."

"You mean drag his dead ass around?" Farto asked.

Leonard nodded.

"Beats stepping on a tack," Farto said.

They drove the Impala into the middle of the highway at a safe moment and got out for a look. Up close the mutt was a lot worse. Its innards had been mashed out of its mouth and asshole and it stunk something awful. The dog was wearing a thick, metal-studded collar and they fastened one end of their fifteen foot chain to that and the other to the rear bumper.

Bob, the Dairy Queen manager, noticed them through the window, came outside and yelled, "What are you fucking morons doing?"

"Taking this doggie to the vet," Leonard said. "We think this sumbitch looks a might peaked. He may have been hit by a car."

"That's so fucking funny I'm about to piss myself," Bob said.

"Old folks have that problem," Leonard said.

Leonard got behind the wheel and Farto climbed in on the passenger side. They manuvered the car and dog around and out of the path of a tractor-trailer truck just in time. As they drove off, Bob screamed after them, "I hope you two no-dicks wrap that Chevy piece of shit around a goddamn pole."

As they roared along, parts of the dog, like crumbs from a flakey loaf of bread, came off. A tooth here. Some hair there. A string of guts. A dew claw. And some unidentifiable pink stuff. The metal-studded collar and chain threw up sparks now and then like firey crickets. Finally they hit seventy-five and the dog was swinging wider and wider on the chain, like it was looking for an opportunity to pass.

Farto poured him and Leonard up Cokes and whisky as they drove along. He handed Leonard his paper cup and Leonard knocked it back, a lot happier now than he had been a moment ago. Maybe this night wasn't going to turn out so bad after all.

They drove by a crowd at the side of the road, a tan station wagon and a wreck of a Ford up on a jack. At a glance they could see that there was a nigger in the middle of the crowd and he wasn't witnessing to the white boys about Jesus. He was hopping around like a pig with a hotshot up his ass, trying to find a break in the white boys so he could make a run for it. But there wasn't any break to be found and there were too many to fight. Nine white boys were knocking him around like he was a pinball and they were a malicious machine.

152

NIGHT THEY MISSED THE HORROR SHOW

"Ain't that one of our niggers?" Farto asked. "And ain't that some of them White Tree football players that's trying to kill him?"

"Scott," Leonard said, and the name was dogshit in his mouth. It had been Scott who had outdone him for the position of quarterback on the team. That damn jig could put together a play more tangled than a can of fishing worms, but it damn near always worked. And he could run like a spotted ass ape.

As they passed, Farto said, "We'll read about him tomorrow in the papers."

But Leonard drove only a short way before slamming on the brakes and whipping the Impala around. Rex swung way out and clipped off some tall, dried sunflowers at the edge of the road like a scythe.

"We gonna go back and watch?" Farto said. "I don't think them White Tree boys would bother us none if that's all we was gonna do, watch."

"He may be a nigger," Leonard said, not liking himself, "but he's our nigger and we can't let them do that. They kill him they'll beat us in football."

Farto saw the truth of this immediately. "Damn right. They can't do that to our nigger."

Leonard crossed the road again and went straight for the White Tree boys, hit down hard on the horn. The White Tree boys abandoned beating their prey and jumped in all directions. Bullfrogs couldn't have done any better.

Scott stood startled and weak where he was, his knees bent in and touching one another, his eyes big as pizza pans. He had never noticed how big grillwork was. It looked like teeth there in the night and the headlights looked like eyes. He felt like a stupid fish about to be eaten by a shark.

Leonard braked hard, but off the highway in the dirt it wasn't quite enough to keep from bumping Scott, sending him flying over the hood and against the glass where his face mashed to it then rolled away, his shirt snagging one of the windshield wipers and pulling it off.

Leonard opened the car door and called to Scott who lay on the ground. "It's now or never."

A White Tree boy made for the car, and Leonard pulled the taped hammer handle out from beneath the seat and stepped out of the car and hit him with it. The White Tree boy went down on his knees and said something that sounded like French but wasn't. Leonard grabbed Scott by the back of the shirt and pulled him up and guided him around and threw him into the open door. Scott scrambled over the front seat and into the back. Leonard threw the hammer handle at one of the White Tree boys and stepped back, whirled into the car behind the wheel. He put the car in gear again and stepped on the gas. The Impala lurched forward, and with one hand on the door Leonard flipped it wider as if he were flexing a wing: The car bumped back on the highway and the chain swung out and Rex clipped

153

the feet out from under two boys as neatly as he had taken down the dried sunflowers popping a White Tree boy.

Leonard looked in his rearview mirror and saw two White Tree boys carrying the one he had clubbed with the hammer handle to the station wagon. The others he and the dog had knocked down were getting up. One had kicked the jack out from under Scott's car and was using it to smash the headlights and windshield.

"Hope you got insurance on that thing," Leonard said.

"I borrowed it," Scott said peeling the windshield wiper out of his tee-shirt. "Here, you might want this." He dropped the wiper over the seat and between Leonard and Farto.

"That's a borrowed car?" Farto said. "That's worse."

"Nah," Scott said. "Owner don't know I borrowed it. I'd have had that flat changed if that sucker had had him a spare tire, but I got back there and wasn't nothing but the rim, man. Say, thanks for not letting me get killed, else we couldn't have run that ole pig together no more. Course, you almost run over me. My chest hurts."

Leonard checked the rearview again. The White Tree boys were coming fast. "You complaining?" Leonard said.

"Nah," Scott said, and turned to look through the back glass. He could see the dog swinging in short arcs and pieces of it going wide and far. "Hope you didn't go off and forget your dog tied to the bumper."

"Goddamn," said Farto, "and him registered too."

"This ain't so funny," Leonard said, "them White Tree boys are gaining."

"Well speed it up," Scott said.

Leonard gnashed his teeth. "I could always get rid of some excess baggage, you know."

"Throwing that windshield wiper out ain't gonna help," Scott said.

Leonard looked in his mirror and saw the grinning nigger in the back-seat. Nothing worse than a comic coon. He didn't even look grateful. Leonard had a sudden horrid vision of being overtaken by the White Tree boys. What if he were killed with the nigger? Getting killed was bad enough, but what if tomorrow they found him in a ditch with Farto and the nigger. Or maybe them White Tree boys would make him do something awful with the nigger before they killed them. Like making him suck the nigger's dick or some such thing. Leonard held his foot all the way to the floor; as they passed the Dairy Queen he took a hard left and the car just made it and Rex swung out and slammed a light pole then popped back in line behind them.

The White Tree boys couldn't make the corner in the station wagon and they didn't even try. They screeched into a car lot down a piece, turned around and came back. By that time the tail lights of the Impala were moving away from them rapidly, looking like two inflamed hemorrhoids in a dark asshole.

"Take the next right coming up," Scott said, "then you'll see a little road off to the left. Kill your lights and take that."

Leonard hated taking orders from Scott on the field, but this was worse. Insulting. Still, Scott called good plays on the field, and the habit of following instructions from the quarterback died hard. Leonard made the right and Rex made it with them after taking a dip in a water-filled bar ditch.

Leonard saw the little road and killed his lights and took it. It carried them down between several rows of large tin storage buildings, and Leonard pulled between two of them and drove down a little alley lined with more. He stopped the car and they waited and listened. After about five minutes, Farto said, "I think we skunked those father rapers."

"Ain't we a team?" Scott said.

In spite of himself, Leonard felt good. It was like when the nigger called a play that worked and they were all patting each other on the ass and not minding what color the other was because they were just creatures in football suits.

"Let's have a drink," Leonard said.

Farto got a paper cup off the floorboard for Scott and poured him up some warm Coke and whisky. Last time they had gone to Longview, he had peed in that paper cup so they wouldn't have to stop, but that had long since been poured out, and besides, it was for a nigger. He poured Leonard and himself drinks in their same cups.

Scott took a sip and said, "Shit, man, that tastes kind of rank."

"Like piss," Farto said.

Leonard held up his cup. "To the Mud Creek Wildcats and fuck them White Tree boys."

"You fuck em," Scott said. They touched their cups, and at that moment the car filled with light.

Cups upraised, the Three Musketeers turned blinking toward it. The light was coming from an open storage building door and there was a fat man standing in the center of the glow like a bloated fly on a lemon wedge. Behind him was a big screen made of a sheet and there was some kind of movie playing on it. And though the light was bright and fading out the movie, Leonard, who was in the best position to see, got a look at it. What he could make out looked like a gal down on her knees sucking this fat guy's dick (the man was visible only from the belly down) and the guy had a short, black revolver pressed to her forehead. She pulled her mouth off of him for an instant and the man came in her face then fired the revolver. The woman's head snapped out of frame and the sheet seemed to drip blood, like dark condensation on a window pane. Then Leonard couldn't see anymore because another man had appeared in the doorway, and like the first he was fat. Both looked like huge bowling balls that had been set on top of shoes. More men appeared behind these two, but one of the fat men turned and

155

held up his hand and the others moved out of sight. The two fat guys stepped outside and one pulled the door almost shut, except for a thin band of light that fell across the front seat of the Impala.

Fat Man Number One went over to the car and opened Farto's door and said, "You fucks and the nigger get out." It was the voice of doom. They had only thought the White Tree boys were dangerous. They realized now they had been kidding themselves. This was the real article. This guy would have eaten the hammer handle and shit a two-by-four.

They got out of the car and the fat man waved them around and lined them up on Farto's side and looked at them. The boys still had their drinks in their hands, and sparing that, they looked like cons in a line up.

Fat Man Number Two came over and looked at the trio and smiled. It was obvious the fatties were twins. They had the same bad features in the same fat faces. They wore Hawaiian shirts that varied only in profiles and color of parrots and had on white socks and too-short, black slacks and black, shiny, Italian shoes with toes sharp enough to thread needles.

Fat Man Number One took the cup away from Scott and sniffed it. "A nigger with liquor," he said. "That's like a cunt with brains. It don't go together. Guess you was getting tanked up so you could put the ole black snake to some chocolate pudding after while. Or maybe you was wantin' some vanilla and these boys were gonna set it up,"

"I'm not wanting anything but to go home," Scott said.

Fat Man Number Two looked at Fat Man Number One and said, "So he can fuck his mother."

The fatties looked at Scott to see what he'd say but he didn't say anything. They could say he screwed dogs and that was all right with him. Hell, bring one on and he'd fuck it now if they'd let him go afterwards.

Fat Man Number One said, "You boys running around with a jungle bunny makes me sick."

"He's just a nigger from school," Farto said. "We don't like him none. We just picked him up because some White Tree boys were beating on him and we didn't want him to get wrecked on account of he's our quaterback."

"Ah," Fat Man Number One said, "I see. Personally, me and Vinnie don't cotton to niggers in sports. They start taking showers with white boys the next thing they want is to take white girls to bed. It's just one step from one to the other."

"We don't have nothing to do with him playing," Leonard said. "We didn't integrate the schools."

"No," Fat Man Number One said, "that was ole Big Ears Johnson, but you're running around with him and drinking with him."

"His cup's been peed in," Farto said. "That was kind of a joke on him, you see. He ain't our friend, I swear it. He's just a nigger that plays football."

"Peed in his cup, huh?" said the one called Vinnie. "I like that, Pork, don't you? Peed in his fucking cup."

156

Pork dropped Scott's cup on the ground and smiled at him. "Come here, nigger. I got something to tell you."

Scott looked at Farto and Leonard. No help there. They had suddenly become interested in the toes of their shoes; they examined them as if they were true marvels of the world.

Scott moved toward Pork, and Pork, still smiling, put his arm around Scott's shoulders and walked him toward the big storage building. Scott said, "What are we doing?"

Pork turned Scott around so they were facing Leonard and Farto who still stood holding their drinks and contemplating their shoes. "I didn't want to get it on the new gravel drive," Pork said and pulled Scott's head in close to his own and with his free hand reached back and under his Hawaiian shirt and brought out a short, black revolver and put it to Scott's temple and pulled the trigger. There was a snap like a bad knee going out and Scott's feet lifted in unison and went to the side and something dark squirted from his head and his feet swung back toward Pork and his shoes shuffled, snapped and twisted on the concrete in front of the building.

"Ain't that somethin'," Pork said as Scott went limp and dangled from the thick crook of his arm, "The rhythm is the last thing to go."

Leonard couldn't make a sound. His guts were in his throat. He wanted to melt and run under the car. Scott was dead and the brains that had made plays twisted as fishing worms and commanded his feet on down the football field were scrambled like breakfast eggs.

Farto said, "Holy shit."

Pork let go of Scott and Scott's legs split and he sat down and his head went forward and clapped on the cement between his knees. A dark pool formed under his face.

"He's better off, boys," Vinnie said. "Nigger was begat by Cain and the ape and he ain't quite monkey and he ain't quite man. He's got no place in this world 'cept as a beast of burden. You start trying to train them to do things like drive cars and run with footballs it ain't nothing but grief to them and the whites too. Get any on your shirt, Pork?"

"Nary a drop."

Vinnie went inside the building and said something to the men there that could be heard but not understood, then he came back with some crumpled newspapers. He went over to Scott and wrapped them around the bloody head and let it drop back on the cement. "You try hosing down that shit when it's dried, Pork, and you wouldn't worry none about that gravel. The gravel ain't nothing."

Then Vinnie said to Farto, "Open the back door of that car." Farto nearly twisted an ankle doing it. Vinnie picked Scott up by the back of the neck and seat of his pants and threw him onto the floorboard of the Impala.

Pork used the short barrel of his revolver to scratch his nuts, then put the gun behind him, under his Hawaiian shirt. "You boys are gonna go to the river bottoms with us and help us get shed of this nigger."

"Yes sir," Farto said. "We'll toss his ass in the Sabine for you."

"How about you?" Pork asked Leonard. "You trying to go weak sister?"

"No," Leonard croaked. "I'm with you."

"That's good," Pork said. "Vinnie, you take the truck and lead the way."

Vinnie took a key from his pocket and unlocked the building door next to the one with the light, went inside, and backed out a sharp-looking, gold Dodge pickup. He backed it in front of the Impala and sat there with the motor running.

"You boys keep your place," Pork said. He went inside the lighted building for a moment. They heard him say to the men inside, "Go on and watch the movies. And save some of them beers for us. We'll be back." Then the light went out and Pork came out, shutting the door. He looked at Leonard and Farto and said, "Drink up, boys."

Leonard and Farto tossed off their warm Coke and whisky and dropped the cups on the ground.

"Now," Pork said, "you get in the back with the nigger, I'll ride with the driver."

Farto got in the back and put his feet on Scott's knees. He tried not to look at the head wrapped in newspaper, but he couldn't help it. When Pork opened the front door and the overhead light came on Farto saw there was a split in the paper and Scott's eye was visible behind it. Across the forehead the wrapping had turned dark. Down by the mouth and chin was an ad for a fish sale.

Leonard got behind the wheel and started the car. Pork reached over and honked the horn. Vinnie rolled the pickup forward and Leonard followed him to the river bottoms. No one spoke. Leonard found himself wishing with all his heart that he had gone to the outdoor picture show to see the movie with the nigger starring in it.

The river bottoms were steamy and hot from the closeness of the trees and the under and overgrowth. As Leonard wound the Impala down the narrow, red clay roads amidst the dense foliage, he felt as if his car were a crab crawling about in a pubic thatch.

He could feel from the way the steering wheel handled, that the dog and the chain were catching brush and limbs here and there. He had forgotten all about the dog and now being reminded of it worried him. What if the dog got tangled and he had to stop? He didn't think Pork would take kindly to stopping, not with the dead burrhead in the floorboard and him wanting to get rid of the body.

Finally they came to where the woods cleared out a spell and they drove along the edge of the Sabine River. Leonard hated water and always had. In the moonlight the river looked like poisoned coffee flowing there.

158

Leonard knew there were alligators and gars big as little alligators and water moccasins by the thousands swimming underneath the water, and just the thought of all those slick, darting bodies made him queasy.

They came to what was known as Broken Bridge. It was an old worn out bridge that had fallen apart in the middle and it was connected to the land on this side only. People sometimes fished off of it. There was no one fishing tonight.

Vinnie stopped the pickup and Leonard pulled up beside him, the nose of the Chevy pointing at the mouth of the bridge. They all got out and Pork made Farto pull Scott out by the feet. Some of the newspaper came loose from Scott's head exposing an ear and part of the face. Farto patted the newspaper back into place.

"Fuck that," Vinnie said. "It don't hurt if he stains the fucking ground. You two idgits find some stuff to weight this coon down so we can sink him."

Farto and Leonard started scurrying about like squirrels, looking for rocks or big, heavy logs. Suddenly they heard Vinnie cry out. "Godamighty, fucking A. Pork. Come look at this."

Leonard looked over and saw that Vinnie had discovered Rex. He was standing looking down with his hands on his hips. Pork went over to stand by him, then Pork turned around and looked at them. "Hey, you fucks, come here."

Leonard and Farto joined them in looking at the dog. There was mostly just a head now, with a little bit of meat and fur hanging off a spine and some broken ribs.

"That's the sickest fucking thing I've ever fucking seen," Pork said.

"Godamighty," Vinnie said.

"Doing a dog like that. Shit, don't you got no heart? A dog. Man's best fucking goddamn friend and you two killed him like this."

"We didn't kill him," Farto said.

"You trying to fucking tell me he done this to himself? Had a bad fucking day and done this."

"Godamighty," Vinnie said.

"No sir," Leonard said. "We chained him on there after he was dead."

"I believe that," Vinnie said. "That's some rich shit. You guys murdered this dog. Godamighty."

"Just thinking about him trying to keep up and you fucks driving faster and faster makes me mad as a wasp," Pork said.

"No," Farto said. "It wasn't like that. He was dead and we were drunk and we didn't have anything to do, so we —"

"Shut the fuck up," Pork said sticking a finger hard against Farto's forehead. "You just shut the fuck up. We can see what the fuck you fucks did. You drug this here dog around until all his goddamn hide came off . . . What kind of mothers you boys got anyhow that they didn't tell you better about animals?"

159

"Godamighty," Vinnie said.

Everyone grew silent, stood looking at the dog. Finally Farto said. "You want us to go back to getting some stuff to hold the nigger down?"

Pork looked at Farto as if he had just grown up whole from the ground. "You fucks are worse than niggers, doing a dog like that. Get on back over to the car."

Leonard and Farto went over to the Impala and stood looking down at Scott's body in much the same way they had stared at the dog. There in the dim moonlight shadowed by trees, the paper wrapped around Scott's head made him look like a giant paper mache doll. Pork came up and kicked Scott in the face with a swift motion that sent newspaper flying and sent a thonking sound across the water that made frogs jump.

"Forget the nigger," Pork said. "Give me your car keys, ball sweat. Leonard took out his keys and gave them to Pork and Pork went around to the trunk and opened it. "Drag the nigger over here."

Leonard took one of Scott's arms and Farto took the other and they pulled him over to the back of the car.

"Put him in the trunk," Pork said.

"What for?" Leonard asked.

"Cause I fucking said so," Pork said.

Leonard and Farto heaved Scott into the trunk. He looked pathetic lying there next to the spare tire, his face partially covered with newspaper. Leonard thought, if only the nigger had stolen a car with a spare he might not be here tonight. He could have gotten the flat changed and driven on before the White Tree boys even came along.

"All right, you get in there with him," Pork said, gesturing to Farto.

"Me?" Farto said.

"Nah, not fucking you, the fucking elephant on your fucking shoulder. Yeah, you, get in the trunk. I ain't got all night."

"Jesus, we didn't do anything to that dog, mister. We told you that. I swear. Me and Leonard hooked him up after he was dead . . . It was Leonard's idea."

Pork didn't say a word. He just stood there with one hand on the trunk lid looking at Farto. Farto looked at Pork, then the trunk, then back to Pork. Lastly he looked at Leonard, then climbed into the trunk, his back to Scott.

"Like spoons," Pork said, and closed the lid. "Now you, whatsit, Leonard? You come over here." But Pork didn't wait for Leonard to move. He scooped the back of Leonard's neck with a chubby hand and pushed him over to where Rex lay at the end of the chain with Vinnie still looking down at him.

"What you think, Vinnie?" Pork asked. "You got what I got in mind?"

Vinnie nodded. He bent down and took the collar off the dog. He fastened it on Leonard. Leonard could smell the odor of the dead dog in his nostrils. He bent his head and puked.

"There goes my shoeshine," Vinnie said, and he hit Leonard a short one in the stomach. Leonard went to his knees and puked some more of the hot Coke and whisky.

"You fucks are the lowest pieces of shit on this earth, doing a dog like that," Vinnie said. "A nigger ain't no lower."

Vinnie got some strong fishing line out of the back of the truck and they tied Leonard's hands behind his back. Leonard began to cry.

"Oh shut up," Pork said. "It ain't that bad. Ain't nothing that bad."

But Leonard couldn't shut up. He was caterwauling now and it was echoing through the trees. He closed his eyes and tried to pretend he had gone to the show with the nigger starring in it and had fallen asleep in his car and was having a bad dream, but he couldn't imagine that. He thought about Harry the janitor's flying saucers with the peppermint rays, and he knew if there were any saucers shooting rays down, they weren't boredom rays after all. He wasn't a bit bored.

Pork pulled off Leonard's shoes and pushed him back flat on the ground and pulled off the socks and stuck them in Leonard's mouth so tight he couldn't spit them out. It wasn't that Pork thought anyone was going to hear Leonard, he just didn't like the noise. It hurt his ears.

Leonard lay on the ground in the vomit next to the dog and cried silently. Pork and Vinnie went over to the Impala and opened the doors and stood so they could get a grip on the car to push. Vinnie reached in and moved the gear from Park to Neutral and he and Pork began to shove the car forward. It moved slowly at first, but as it made the slight incline that led down to the old bridge, it picked up speed. From inside the trunk, Farto hammered lightly at the lid as if he didn't really mean it. The chain took up slack and Leonard felt it jerk and pop his neck. He began to slide along the ground like a snake.

Vinnie and Pork had jumped out of the way and they watched the car make the bridge and go over the edge and disappear into the water with amazing quietness. Leonard, tugged by the weight of the car, rustled past them. When he hit the bridge, wooden splinters tugged at his clothes so hard they ripped his pants and underwear down almost to his knees.

The chain swung out once toward the edge of the bridge and the rotten railing, and Leonard tried to hook a leg around an upright board there, but that proved wasted. The weight of the car just pulled his knee out of joint and tugged the board out of place with a screech of nails and lumber.

Leonard picked up speed and the chain rattled over the edge of the bridge, into the water and out of sight, pulling its connection after it like a pull toy. The last sight of Leonard was the soles of his bare feet, white as the bellies of fish.

"It's deep there," Vinnie said. "I caught an old channel cat there once, remember? Big sucker. I bet it's over fifty feet deep down there."

They got in the truck and Vinnie cranked it.

"I think we did them boys a favor," Pork said. "Them running around with niggers and what they did to that dog and all. They weren't worth a thing."

"I know it," Vinnie said. "We should have filmed this, Pork, it would have been good. Where the car and that nigger lover went off in the water was choice."

"Nah, there wasn't any women."

"Point," Vinnie said, and he backed around and drove onto the trail that wound its way out of the bottoms.

MORE SINNED AGAINST

by

Karl Edward Wagner

Theirs was a story so commonplace that it balanced uneasily between the maudlin and the sordid — a cliché dipped in filth.

Her real name was Katharina Oglethorpe and she changed that to Candace Thornton when she moved to Los Angeles, but she was known as Candi Thorne in the few films she ever made — the ones that troubled to list credits. She came from some little Baptist church and textile mill town in eastern North Carolina, although later she said she came from Charlotte. She always insisted that her occasional and transient friends call her Candace, and she signed her name Candace in a large, legible hand for those occasional and compulsive autographs. She had lofty aspirations and only minimal talent. One of her former agents perhaps stated her *mot juste*: a lady with a lot of guts, but too much heart. The police records gave her name as Candy Thorneton.

There had been money once in her family, and with that the staunch pride that comes of having more money than the other thousand or so inhabitants of the town put together. Foreign textiles eventually closed the mill; unfortunate investments leeched the money. Pride of place remained.

By the time that any of her past really matters, Candace had graduated from an area church-supported junior college, where she was homecoming queen, and she'd won one or two regional beauty contests and was almost a runner-up in the Miss North Carolina pageant. Her figure was good, although more for a truck stop waitress than suited to a model's requirements, and her acting talents were wholehearted, if marginal. Her parents believed she was safely enrolled at U.C.L.A., and they never quite forgave her when they eventually learned otherwise.

Their tuition checks kept Candace afloat as an aspiring young actress/model through a succession of broken promises, phony deals, and predatory agents. Somewhere along the way she sacrificed her cherished virginity a

163

dozen times over, enough so that it no longer pained her, even as the next day dulled the pain of the promised break that never materialized. Her family might have taken back, if not welcomed, their prodigal daughter, had Candace not begged them for money for her first abortion. They refused, Candace got the money anyway, and her family had no more to do with her ever.

He called himself Richards Justin, and there was as much truth to that as to anything else he ever said. He met Candace when she was just on the brink of putting her life together, although he never blamed himself for her subsequent crash. He always said that he was a man who learned from the mistakes of others, and had he said "profited" instead, he might have told the truth for once.

They met because they were sleeping with the same producer, both of them assured of a part in his next film. The producer failed to honor either bargain, and he failed to honor payment for a kilo of coke, after which a South American entrepreneur emptied a Browning Hi-Power into him. Candace and Richards Justin consoled one another over lost opportunity, and afterward he moved in with her.

Candace was sharing a duplex in Venice with two cats and a few thousand roaches. It was a cottage of rotting pink stucco that resembled a gingerbread house left out in the rain. Beside it ran a refuse-choked ditch that had once been a canal. The shack two doors down had been burned out that spring in a shootout between rival gangs of bikers. The neighborhood was scheduled for gentrification, but no one had decided yet whether this should entail restoration or razing. The rent was cheaper than an apartment, and against the house grew a massive clump of jade plant that Candace liked to pause before and admire.

At this time Candace was on an upswing and reasonably confident of landing the part of a major victim in a minor stalk-and-slash film. Her face and teeth had always been good; afternoons in the sun and judicious use of rinses on her mousy hair had transformed her into a passable replica of a Malibu blonde. She had that sort of ample figure that looks better with less clothing and best with none at all, and she managed quite well in a few photo spreads in some of the raunchier skin magazines. She was not to be trusted with a speaking part, but some voice and drama coaching might have improved that difficulty in time.

Richards Justin — Rick to his friends — very studiously was a hunk, to use the expression of the moment. He stood six foot four and packed about 215 pounds of health club-nurtured muscle over wide shoulders and lean hips. His belly was quite hard and flat, his thighs strong from jogging, and an even tan set off the generous dark growth of body hair. His black hair was neatly permed, and the heavy mustache added virility to features that stopped just short of being pretty. He seemed designed for posing in tight jeans, muscular arms folded across hairy chest, and he often posed just so. He claimed to have had extensive acting experience in New York before moving to Los Angeles, but somehow his credentials were never subject to verification.

Candace was a type who took in stray animals, and she took in Richards Justin. She had survived two years on the fringes of Hollywood, and Rick was new to Los Angeles — still vulnerable in his search for the elusive Big Break. She was confident that she knew some friends who could help him get started, and she really did need a roommate to help with the rent — once he found work, of course. Rick loaded his suitcase and possessions into her aging Rabbit, with room to spare, and moved in with Candace. He insisted that he pay his share of expenses, and borrowed four hundred bucks to buy some clothes — first appearances count everything in an interview.

They were great together in bed, and Candace was in love. She recognized the sensitive, lonely soul of the artist hidden beneath his macho exterior. They were both painfully earnest about their acting careers — talking long through the nights of films and actors, great directors and theories of drama. They agreed that one must never compromise art for commercial considerations, but that sometimes it might be necessary to make small compromises in order to achieve the Big Break.

The producer of the stalk-and-slash flick decided that Candace retained too much southern accent for a major role. Having just gone through her savings, Candace spent a vigorous all-night interview with the producer and salvaged a minor role. It wasn't strictly nonspeaking, as she got to scream quite a lot while the deranged killer spiked her to a barn door with a pitchfork. It was quite effective, and a retouched still of her big scene was used for the posters of *Camp Hell!* It was the highwater mark of her career.

Rick found the Big Break even more elusive than a tough, cynical, street-wise hunk like himself had envisioned. It discouraged the artist within him, just as it embarrassed his virile nature to have to live off Candace's earnings continually. Fortunately coke helped restore his confidence, and unfortunately coke was expensive. They both agreed, however, that coke was a necessary expense, career-wise. Coke was both inspiration and encouragement; besides, an actor who didn't have a few grams to flash around was as plausible as an outlaw biker who didn't drink beer.

Candace knew how discouraging this all must be for Rick. In many ways she was so much wiser and tougher than Rick. Her concern over his difficulties distracted her from the disappointment of her own faltering career. Granted, Rick's talents were a bit raw — he was a gem in need of polishing. Courses and workshops were available, but these cost money, too. Candace worked her contacts and changed her agent. If she didn't mind doing a little T&A, her new agent felt sure he could get her a small part or two in some soft-R films. It was money.

165

SILVER SCREAM

Candace played the dumb southern blonde in *Jiggle High* and she played the dumb southern cheerleader in *Cheerleader Superbowl* and she played the dumb southern stewardess in *First Class Only* and she played the dumb southern nurse in *Sex Clinic* and she played the dumb southern hooker in *Hard Streets*, but always this was Candi Thorne who played these roles, and not Candace Thornton, and somehow this made the transition from soft-R to hard-R films a little easier to bear.

They had their first big quarrel when Candace balked over her part in *Malibu Hustlers*. She hadn't realized they were shooting it in both R- and X-rated version. Prancing about in the buff and faking torrid love scenes was one thing, but Candace drew the line at actually screwing for the close-up cameras. Her agent swore she was through if she backed out of the contract. Rick yelled at her and slapped her around a little, then broke into tears. He hadn't meant to lose control — it was just that he was *so* close to getting his break, and without money all they'd worked so hard together for, all they'd hoped and prayed for . . .

Candace forgave him, and blamed herself for being thoughtless and selfish. If she could ball off camera to land a role, she could give the same performance on camera. This once.

Candace never did find out what her agent did with her check from - *Malibu Hustlers*, nor did the police ever manage to find her agent. The producer was sympathetic, but not legally responsible. He did, however, hate to see a sweet kid burned like that, and he offered her a lead role in *Hot 'n' Horny*. This one would be straight X — or XXX, as they liked to call them now — but a lot of talented girls had made the big time doing their stuff for the screen, and Candi Thorne just might be the next super-X superstar. He had the right connection, and if she played it right with him . . .

It wasn't the Big Break Candace had dreamed of, but it was money. And they *did* need money. She worried that this would damage her chances for a legitimate acting career, but Rick told her to stop being a selfish prude and to think of their future together. His break was coming soon, and then they'd never have to worry again about money. Besides, audiences were already watching her perform in *Malibu Hustlers*, so what did she have left to be shy about?

The problem with coke was that Rick needed a lot of it to keep him and his macho image going. The trouble with a lot of coke was that Rick tended to get wired a little too tight, and then he needed downers to mellow out. Smack worked best, but the trouble with smack was that it was even more expensive. Still, tomorrow's male sex symbol couldn't go about dropping ludes and barbs like some junior high punker. Smack was status in this game — everybody did coke. Not to worry: Rick had been doing a little heroin ever since his New York days — no needle work, just some to toot. He could handle it.

166

Candace could not — either the smack or the expense. Rick was gaining a lot of influential contacts. He had to dress well, show up at the right parties. Sometimes they decided it would be better for his career if he went alone. They really needed a better place to live, now that they could afford it.

After making *Wet 'n' Willing* Candace managed to rent a small house off North Beverly Glen Boulevard — not much of an improvement over her duplex in Venice, but the address was a quantum leap in class. Her biggest regret was having to leave her cats: no pets allowed. Her producer had advanced her some money to cover immediate expenses, and she knew he'd be getting it back in pounds of flesh. There were parties for important friends, and Candace felt quite casual about performing on camera after some of the things she'd been asked to do on those nights. And that made it easier when she was asked to do them again on camera.

Candace couldn't have endured it all if it weren't for her selfless love for Rick, and for the coke and smack and pills and booze. Rick expressed concern over her increasing use of drugs, especially when they were down to their last few lines. Candace economized by shooting more — less waste and a purer high than snorting.

She was so stoned on the set for *Voodoo Vixens* that she could barely go through the motions of the minimal plot. The director complained; her producer reminded her that retakes cost money, and privately noted that her looks were distinctly taking a shopworn plunge. When she threw up in her co-star's lap, he decided that Candi Thorne really wasn't star material.

Rick explained that he was more disappointed than angry with her over getting canned, but this was after he'd bloodied her lip. It wasn't so much that this financial setback stood to wreck his career just as the breaks were falling in place for him, as it was that her drug habit had left them owing a couple thou to the man, and how were they going to pay that?

Candace still had a few contacts to fall back on, and she was back before the cameras before the bruises had disappeared. These weren't the films that made the adult theater circuits. These were the fifteen-minute-or-so single-takes shot in motel rooms for the 8-mm. home projector/porno peepshow audiences. Her contacts were pleased to get a semi-name porno queen, however semi and however shopworn, even if the films seldom bothered to list credits or titles. It was easier to work with a pro than some drugged-out runaway or amateur hooker, who might ruin a take if the action got rough or she had a phobia about Dobermans.

It was quick work and quick bucks. But not enough bucks.

Rick was panic-stricken when two large black gentlemen stopped him outside a singles bar one night to discuss his credit and to share ideas as to the need to maintain intact kneecaps in this cruel world. They understood a young actor's difficulties in meeting financial obligations, but felt certain Rick could make a substantial payment within forty-eight hours.

Candace hit the streets. It was that, or see Rick maimed. After the casting couch and exotic partners under floodlights, somehow it seemed so commonplace doing quickies in motel rooms and car seats. She missed the cameras. It all seemed so transient without any playback.

The money was there, and Rick kept his kneecaps. Between her work on the streets and grinding out a few 8-mm. films each month, Candace could about meet expenses. The problem was that she really needed the drugs to keep her going, and the more drugs she needed meant the more work to pay for them. Candace knew her looks were slipping, and she appreciated Rick's concern for her health. But for Rick the Big Break was coming soon. She no longer minded when he had other women over while she was on the streets, or when he stayed away for a day or two without calling her. She was selling her body for his career, and she must understand that sometimes it was necessary for Rick, too, to sleep around. In the beginning, some small compromises are to be expected.

A pimp beat her up one night. He didn't like freelance chippies taking johns from his girls on his turf. He would have just scared her, had she agreed to become one of his string, but she needed all her earnings for Rick, and the truth was the pimp considered her just a bit too far gone to be worth his trouble. So he worked her over but didn't mess up her face too badly, and Candace was able to work again after only about a week.

She tried another neighborhood and got busted the second night out; paid her own bail, got busted again a week later. Rick got her out of jail — she was coming apart without the H, and he couldn't risk being implicated. He had his career to think about, and it was thoughtless of Candace to jeopardize his chances through her own sordid lifestyle.

He would have thrown her out, but Candace paid the rent. Of course, he still loved her. But she really ought to take better care of herself. She was letting herself go. Since her herpes scare they seldom made love, although Candace understood that Rick was often emotionally and physically drained after concentrating his energy on some important interview or audition.

They had lived together almost two years, and Candace was almost 25, but she looked almost 40. After a client broke her nose and a few teeth in a moment of playfulness, she lost what little remained of her actress/model good looks. They got the best cosmetic repair she could afford, but after that neither the johns nor the sleaze producers paid her much attention. When she saw herself on the screen at fifth-rate porno houses, in the glimpses between ducking below the rows of shabby seats, she no longer recognized herself.

But Rick's career was progressing all the while, and that was what made her sacrifice worthwhile. A part of Candace realized now that her dreams of Hollywood stardom had long since washed down the gutter, but at least Rick was almost on the verge of big things. He'd landed a number of modeling jobs and already had made some commercials for local tv. Some recent roles in what Rick termed "experimental theater" promised to draw the attention of talent scouts. Neither of them doubted that the Big Break was an imminent certainty. Candace kept herself going through her faith in Rick's love and her confidence that better times lay ahead. Once Rick's career took off, she'd quit the streets, get off the drugs. She'd look ten years younger if she could just rest and eat right for a few months, get a better repair on her nose. By then Rick would be in a position to help her resume her own acting career.

Candace was not too surprised when Rick came in one morning and shook her awake with the news that he'd lined up a new film for her. It was something about devil worshipers called *Satan's Sluts* — X-rated, of course, but the money would be good, and Candace hadn't appeared even in a peepshow gangbang in a couple months. The producer, Rick explained, remembered her in *Camp Hell!* and was willing to take a chance on giving her a big role.

Candace might have been more concerned about filming a scene with so small a crew and in a cellar made over into a creepy B&D dungeon, but her last films had been shot in cheap motel rooms with a home video camera. She didn't like being strapped to an inverted cross and hung before a black-draped altar, but Rick was there — snorting coke with the half-dozen members of the cast and crew.

When the first few whip lashes cut into her flesh, it took Candace's drugged consciousness several moments to be aware of the pain, and to understand the sort of film for which Rick had sold her. By the time they had heated the branding iron and brought in the black goat, Candace was giving the performance of her life.

She passed out eventually, awoke another day in their bed, vaguely surprised to be alive. It was a measure of Rick's control over Candace that they hadn't killed her. No one was going to pay much attention to anything Candace might say — a burned out porno star and drug addict with an arrest record for prostitution. Rick had toyed with selling her for a snuff film, but his contacts there preferred anonymous runaways and wetbacks, and the backers of *Satan's Sluts* had paid extra to get a name actress, however faded, to add a little class to the production — especially a star who couldn't cause problems afterward.

Rick stayed with her just long enough to feel sure she wouldn't die from her torture, and to pack as many of his possessions as he considered worth keeping. Rick had been moving up in the world on Candace's earnings — meeting the right people, making the right connections. The money from *Satan's Sluts* had paid off his debts with enough left over for a quarter-ounce of some totally awesome rock, which had so impressed his friends at a party that a rising tv director wanted Rick to move in with her while they discussed a part for him in a much talked-about new miniseries.

169

SILVER SCREAM

The pain when he left her was the worst of all. Rick had counted on this, and he left her with a gram of barely cut heroin, deciding to let nature take its course.

Candace had paid for it with her body and her soul, but at last this genuinely was the Big Break. The primetime soaper miniseries, *Destiny's Fortune,* ran for five nights and topped the ratings each night. Rick's role as the tough steelworker who romanced the millowner's daughter in parts four and five, while not a major part, attracted considerable attention and benefited from the huge success of the series itself. Talent scouts saw a new hunk in Richards Justin, most talked-about young star from the all-time hit, *Destiny's Fortune.*

Rick's new agent knew how to hitch his Mercedes to a rising star. Richards Justin made the cover of *TV Guide* and *People,* the centerfold of *Playgirl,* and then the posters. Within a month it was evident from the response to *Destiny's Fortune* that Richards Justin was a hot property. It was only a matter of casting him for the right series. Network geniuses juggled together all the ingredients of recent hits and projected a winner for the new season — *Colt Savage, Soldier of Fortune.*

They ran the pilot as a two-hour special against a major soaper and a tv movie about teenage prostitutes, and *Colt Savage* blew the other two networks away in that night's ratings. *Colt Savage* was The New Hit, blasting to the top of the Nielsen's on its first regular night. The show borrowed from everything that had already been proven to work — "an homage to the great adventure classics of the '30s" was how its producers liked to describe it.

Colt Savage, as portrayed by Richards Justin, was a tough, cynical, broad-shouldered American adventurer who kept busy dashing about the cities and exotic places of the 1930s — finding lost treasures, battling spies and sinister cults, rescuing plucky young ladies from all manner of dire fates. Colt Savage was the protégé of a brilliant scientist who wished to devote his vast fortune and secret inventions to fighting Evil. He flew an autogiro and drove a streamlined speedster — both decked out with fantastic weapons and gimmickry rather in advance of the technology of the period. He had a number of exotic assistants and, inevitably, persistent enemies — villains who somehow managed to escape the explosion of their headquarters in time to pop up again two episodes later.

Colt Savage was pure B-movie corn. In a typical episode, Colt would meet a beautiful girl who would ask him for help, then be kidnapped. Following that there would be fights, car chases, air battles, captures and escapes, derring-do in exotic locales, rescues and romance — enough to fill an hour show. The public loved it. Richards Justin was a new hero for today's audiences — the new Bogart, a John Wayne for the'80s. The network promoted *Colt Savage* with every excess at its command. The merchandising rights alone were bringing in tens of millions.

Rick dumped the director who had given him his start in *Destiny's Fortune* long before he moved into several million bucks worth of Beverly Hills real estate. The tabloids followed his numerous love affairs with compulsive and imaginative interest.

Candace blamed it all on the drugs. She couldn't bring herself to believe that Rick had never loved her, that he had simply used her until she had no more to give. Her mind refused to accept that. It was she who had let Rick down, let drugs poison his life and destroy hers. Drugs had ruined her acting career, had driven her onto the streets to pay for their habit. They could have made it, if she hadn't ruined everything for them.

So she quit, cold turkey. Broken in body and spirit, the miseries of withdrawal made little difference to her pain. She lived ten years of hell over the next few days, lying in an agonized delirium that barely distinguished consciousness from unconsciousness. Sometimes she managed to crawl to the bathroom or to the refrigerator, mostly she just curled herself into a fetal pose of pain and shivered beneath the sweaty sheets and bleeding sores. In her nightmares she drifted from lying in Rick's embrace to writhing in torture on Satan's altar, and the torment of either delirium was the same to her.

As soon as she was strong enough to face it, Candace cut the heroin Rick had left her to make five grams and sold it to one of her friends who liked to snort it and wouldn't mind the cut. It gaver her enough money to cover bills until Candace was well enough to go back on the streets. She located the pimp who had once beat her up; he didn't recognize her, and when Candace asked to work for him, he laughed her out of the bar.

After that she drifted around Los Angeles for a month or two, turning tricks whenever she could. She was no longer competitive, even without the scars, but she managed to scrape by, somehow making rent for the place on North Beverly Glen. It held her memories of Rick, and if she let that go, she would have lost even that shell of their love. She even refused to throw out any of his discarded clothing and possessions; his toothbrush and an old razor still lay by the sink.

The last time the cops busted her, Candace had herpes, a penicillin-resistant clap, and no way of posting bail. Jail meant losing her house and its memories of Rick, and there would be nothing left for her after that. Rick could help her now, but she couldn't manage to reach him. An old mutual

SILVER SCREAM

friend finally did, but when he came to visit Candace he couldn't bear to give her Rick's message, and so he paid her bail himself and told her the money came from Rick, who didn't want to risk getting his name involved.

She had to have a legitimate job. The friend had a friend who owned interest in a plastic novelties plant, and they got Candace a factory job there. By now she had very little left of herself to sell in the streets, but at least she was off the drugs. Somewhat to the surprise of all concerned, Candace settled down on the line and turned out to be a good worker. Her job paid the bills, and at night she went home and read about Richards Justin in the papers and magazines, played back video cassettes of him nights when he wasn't on live.

The cruelest thing was that Candace still nurtured the hope that she could win Rick back, once she got her own act together. Regular meals, decent hours, medication and time healed some wounds. The face that looked back at her from mirrors no longer resembled a starved plague victim. Some of the men at the plant were beginning to stare after her, and a couple of times she'd been asked to go out. She might have got over Richards Justin in time, but probably not.

The friend of a friend pulled some strings and called in some favors, and so the plant where Candace worked secured the merchandising rights to the Colt Savage, Soldier of Fortune Action Pak. This consisted of a plastic Colt Savage doll, complete with weapons and action costumes, along with models of Black Blaze, his supersonic autogiro, and Red Lightning, the supercar. The merchandising package also included dolls of his mentor and regular assistants, as well as several notable villains and their sinister weaponry. The plant geared into maximum production to handle the anticipated rush orders for the Christmas market.

Candace found herself sitting at the assembly line, watching thousands of plastic replicas of Richards Justin roll past her.

She just had to see Rick, but the guards at the gate had instructions not to admit her. He wouldn't even talk to her over the phone or answer her letters. The way he must remember her, Candace couldn't really blame him. It would be different now.

His birthday was coming up, and she knew he would be having a party. She wrote him several times, sent messages via old contacts, begging Rick to let her come. When the printed invitation finally came, she'd already bought him a present. Candace knew that her confidence had not been a mistake, and she took a day off work to get ready for their evening together.

The party had been going strong for some time when Candace arrived, and Rick was flying high on coke and champagne. He hugged her around the shoulders but didn't kiss her, and half carried her over to where many of the guests were crowded around a projection television.

Ladies and gentlemen, here she is — our leading lady, the versatile Miss Candi Thorne.

172

MORE SINNED AGAINST

All eyes flicked from the screen to Candace, long enough for recognition. Then the cheers and applause burst out across the room. Rick had been amusing his guests with some of her films. Just now they were watching the one with the donkey.

Candace didn't really remember how she managed to escape and find her way home.

She decided not to leave a note, and she was prying the blade out of Rick's old razor when the idea began to form. The razor was crudded with dried lather and bits of Rick's whiskers, and she wanted to get it clean before she used it on her wrists. A scene from another of her films, *Voodoo Vixens*, arose through the confusion of her thoughts. She set the razor aside carefully.

Candace made herself a cup of coffee and let the idea build in her head. She was dry-eyed now and quite calm — the hysterical energy that had driven her to suicide now directed her disordered thoughts toward another course of action.

She still had all of her mementos of Rick, and throughout the night she went over them, one by one, coolly and meticulously. She, scraped all the bits of beard and skin from his razor, collected hair and dandruff from his brush and comb, pared away his toothbrush bristles for the minute residues of blood and plaque. She found a discarded handkerchief, stained form a coke-induced nosebleed, and from the mattress liner came residues of their former lovemaking. Old clothes yielded bits of hair, stains of body oils and perspiration. Candace searched the house relentlessly, finding fragments of his nails, his hair, anything at all that retained physical residues of Rick's person.

The next day Candace called in sick. She spent the day browsing through Los Angeles' numerous occult bookshops, made a few purchases, and called up one or two of the contacts she'd made filming *Voodoo Vixens*. It all seemed straightforward enough. Even those who rationalized it all admitted that it was a matter of belief. And children have the purest belief in magic.

Candace ground up all her bits and scrapings of Richards Justin. It came to quite a pile and reminded her of a bag of Mexican heroin.

Candace returned to work and waited for her chance. When no one was watching, she dumped her powdered residue into the plastic muck destined to become Colt Savage dolls. Then she said a prayer of sorts.

Beneath the Christmas tree, Joshua plays with his new Colt Savage doll. *Pow!* An electron cannon knocks Colt out of the sky, crashes him to the rocks below!

173

SILVER SCREAM

Jason pits Colt Savage against his model dinosaurs. *Yahhh!* The dinosaur stomps him!

David is racing Colt Savage in his car, Red Lightning. *Ker-blam!* Colt drives off the cliff at a hundred miles an hour!

Billy is still too young to play with his Colt Savage doll, but he likes to chew on it.

Mark decides to see if Colt Savage and Black Blaze can withstand the attack of his atomic bomb firecrackers.

Jessica is mad at her brother. She sees his Colt Savage doll and stomps on it as hard as she can.

Tyrone is bawling. He pulled the arms off his Colt Savage doll, and he can't make them go back on.

Richards Justin collapsed on set, and only heavy sedation finally stilled his screams. It quickly became apparent that his seizures were permanent, and he remains under sedation in a psychiatric institution. Doctors have attributed his psychotic break to longterm drug abuse.

Nothing excites the public more than a fallen hero. *Richards Justin: The Untold Story*, by Candace Thornton, rose quickly on the best-seller charts. Reportedly she was recently paid well over a million for the film rights to her book.

RETURN OF THE NEON FIREBALL

by

Chet Williamson

"Picture it," Michael Price said over chowder at Mario's, the chi-chi Italian restaurant that had once been Sam's Grill. "Triple features — IT CAME FROM OUTER SPACE, FRANCIS JOINS THE NAVY, HIGH NOON, cartoons, old newsreels, and Jesus Christ the *clock*, remember the clock? 'Only ten minutes until the next feature,' and the dancing hot dogs — *da*-da-*dada*-*dah!* — and cups of soft drinks on little train cars? And don't forget the snack bar — quarter hot dogs, ten cent cups of Coke and popcorn, nickel Raisinets and Goobers —"

"Wait a minute," Lenny Crane said. "Who pays for *that* stuff?"

"*They* do — the patrons — when they come in. Lenny, the rental on these old films is diddley-squat. We'll sell the food at cost so we won't *lose* money, and we charge to get in — four bucks a person or twelve a car, whichever's cheaper. We'll make a good profit on that."

"Mike, the fucking thing is closing in the first place due to lack of business, and you tell me people are going to pay four bucks a head to see stuff they can see on TV?"

"It's not the films — it's the *experience*. It's closing because they've been showing third-run crap you can rent on cassette. The snack bar sells expensive shit, they don't keep the place clean, they tore the old playground down — they tried to make an indoor theatre outside, and that's where they screwed up. Now what *I* say is make it what it used to be, and you'll get people. We can use the line, 'The Fireball Drive-In Theatre — where it's always the fifties,' or something."

Lenny sucked his lower lip. "And what stops people from filling their trunks with five cent Goobers?"

"Tickets they get when they come in that they have to turn in when they buy food. Maybe two or three items per person."

175

"You got this worked out pretty fast."

"I was up all night."

And he had been. From the minute he had read of the closing in the paper, he had thought of nothing else but the Fireball. Though he hadn't been there in twenty years, Mike Price loved the Fireball, just as he loved everything he remembered about being young. Awake all night, he still dreamed. He dreamed about himself in high school — lean, muscular, with that thatch of white-blond hair the girls loved to ruffle. He dreamed about winning football games for the McKinley Marauders, pulling the ball magically out of the air and floating across the goal line on the light feet of youth. He dreamed of his '49 Merc, chopped and channelled, its seats filled with his friends, himself sitting tall behind the wheel, wearing his blue and white varsity sweater. But most of all, he dreamed of the Fireball.

It had blazed its way through his sleeping dreams at night for years, and now, as his life grew sad and empty, it began to light up his days as well, that bright, neon concoction of red and yellow and orange, with a tail of brilliant blue behind it, and the words in letters of fire: "FIREBALL DRIVE-IN THEATRE." It was huge and gaudy and high and beautiful, suspended twenty yards in the air above its cement base. Fall was the best season to see the sign, for it was dark when they started the show, and driving down Route 30 you saw its glow from a mile away, brightening as you drew nearer until you could finally see the comet itself streaking across the horizon.

But for real fun, summer had been the time — arriving at 8:00 when the gates opened, looking for a spot close to the screen, but not close enough for it to shine too brightly on you and your date. If you were with your pals, it was different. Then all you cared about was parking far enough away from the snack bar and from cars with families so that you could drink your bottle of beer and whoop and swear and make cracks at the love scenes without anybody calling the manager. You'd sit back, watch THE BLOB, FIVE GUNS WEST, PSYCHO, HOUSE OF USHER, and feel the warm breeze, the bottle cool against your forehead, and want the screen, the white marquee, the neon fireball to shine forever.

But it wouldn't, not if it was sold to anyone but him. It would be stripped away, and a housing development would rise where the old speaker posts and snack bar used to be, or a factory would rear itself up upon the rows that rippled like the waves of the sea when you drove directly toward the screen after the movie. And that night he sat and thought about how another treasured chunk of his youth would be wiped out, just like the old high school, or the soda fountain down on Bainbridge Street where they had made the best goddam vanilla cokes on the planet. The next morning he had called Lenny Crane.

"How much they want for the thing?" Lenny asked.

Mike pulled out a slip of paper and slid it across the table. "I checked this morning."

176

"Jesus, that's a lot."

"It's worth it."

"Can you affort half of this?" Mike nodded. "I don't believe you."

"If I sell the store I can."

"Sell the store?"

"It's a shitty store. I don't want it anymore."

"Whatta you mean you don't *want* it anymore? What's wanting got to do with it? For crissake, that was your old man's store, Mike. You don't piss away a family business like that." Lenny shook his head. "Sylvia was still alive, you wouldn't be acting like this. You're acting like a *kid*, Mike."

"Don't lecture me, Lenny."

"But why a drive-in theater?"

Mike puffed a sigh wreathed in age. "I'm not having any fun, Lenny. I want to have fun again. The Fireball was always fun."

"Yeah," Lenny agreed. "We had some good times there. But I don't know, I mean, can you really afford to take a chance like this? What if it flops?"

"So who am I saving my money for? Goddam it, Lenny, I got no kids, Sylvia's gone . . ."

"You might get married again."

"Shit. Look at me."

"What? You're forty-five, same as me."

"Bullshit. You're good looking and rich. I'm bald and fat and . . . *not* rich."

"Come on, knock it off." Lenny waved his hands in the air. "What about all the time it would take, Mike? After all, I got a finance business to run."

"We'd only be open weekends. Friday through Sunday. I'd do all of the work needed doing during the week — advertising, maintenance, all that."

"What, you wanta be a fucking janitor too?"

"Why not?"

Lenny sighed. "Some guys with money buy model trains, or gliders, or expensive stamps. Me, I play racquetball and tennis and put it in the bank and get laid by pretty girls now and then, and that's about all. Maybe I need a hobby." He gave a lopsided grin and shook his head. "But, holy shit, a drive-in theater? You let me think about it, huh?"

"Remember, Lenny. Convertibles and summer nights. VERTIGO and THE DEADLY MANTIS and . . ."

"Okay, *okay*, go sell some clothes, all right?"

All the way back to his shop Mike Price thought *please God, let him do it, let him do it*, praying for the lost good times to come back again.

* * *

SILVER SCREAM

And somebody heard him. The next day Lenny called and told him that although it was a helluva time to start a new business in this deader'n shit town, he couldn't resist giving it a try. Besides, if it turned out to be a bust, it wouldn't have to be a complete loss — they could always sell the land.

They bought the theatre and all the equipment the following week. Mike sold his store to come up with his half, but not for as much as he had hoped. He had to cash in his bonds and take out a big chunk from the IRA's he'd set up for his retirement. He didn't tell Lenny about it.

But goddam it if it wasn't worth it several weeks later, on that warm, breezy Friday evening in mid-May when the neon fireball lit up again, and cars lined up for a quarter mile to get in. Leny sold the tickets, and Mike ran the snack bar with the help of three giggly teenage girls. There was a double feature — THE FIREBALL, a 1950 Mickey Rooney movie about roller derbies, and IT CONQUERED THE WORLD — neither of them classics, but the names looked glorious on the marquee, and Mike had gotten photographers from the three local newspapers to come out and record it for posterity.

It was a great night. The weather cooperated, the three security men Lenny had hired arrested no one, children played in the well-lit playground, people mobbed the snack bar at intermission, and at the end of the show a winning ticket stub holder received a Dustbuster Plus vacuum cleaner, the first prize in a series of drawings to be held every Friday night.

After everyone else went home, and the Del-Vikings' last notes faded away on the P.A. system, Lenny and Mike remained to count the cash. "Looks like you were right," Lenny said, smiling. "*If* it keeps up."

"It'll keep up," Mike said quietly.

"Hey, what's wrong?"

"Wrong?"

"For a successful impresario, you don't seem too happy."

Mike shook his head. "I'm happy enough. It went fine."

"It sure as hell did," Lenny laughed, gesturing to the piles of bills.

"It's just that . . ."

"Just that what?"

"It wasn't as much *fun* as I thought it would be," Mike said with a sigh.

Lenny nodded. "I know. I think I know what you mean. But it's *never* gonna be what it was. We were young then. But what it is now is pretty damn good. Hell, partner, we made the fifties live again."

"Almost."

"Yeah, almost." Lenny looked down again at the money on the table, and with the tip of his finger shot a coin across to Mike. "There. That's your souvenir. '51 Franklin half."

Mike picked it up. "You get this tonight?"

Lenny nodded. "Car full of kids, really up for it. Came in an old car, all dressed up like the fifties. One of the girls had a *poodle* skirt on, for crissake."

178

RETURN OF THE NEON FIREBALL

"And they gave you this?"

"Uh-huh. Bought tickets with it. I said hey, you know this is a valuable coin, but the kid just looked at me like I was crazy and said, yeah, it's worth a whole fifty cents. So I thought what the hell, if he didn't want it. Keep it if you want." Lenny stretched, yawned, and stood up. "Well, I'm going home. If you can take the stuff in to the bank tomorrow, I'd appreciate it. I got clients in the morning."

After Lenny left, Mike sat for some time turning the half dollar over in his hands. It was bright and shiny, and showed little wear, and he began to go through the stacks of coins looking for other old ones. He found two, both quarters — the first a 1945 Standing Liberty, the other a 1953 Washington. With the fifty cent piece, they totalled a dollar.

Then he started on the bills. It was nearly two in the morning before he found them all — a five and six ones, all dated 1956 and before. Other than those, the oldest bills in the pile went back only to the mid-seventies.

One five, six ones, a dollar in change. Twelve dollars altogether, the admission price for one carful. A carful of kids, according to Lenny, who were really up for it.

That night Mike dreamed about double dating with Becky Geyer. They were watching the movie out of the corners of their eyes, most of their attention devoted to necking. Mike had his hand under Becky's sweater and on top of her bra, and from the panting in the back seat Phil Strickler, his class president, was doing pretty well with Crissy Medwick, the prettiest of the cheerleaders except for Becky. If Mike looked real hard out of his right eye, he could just make out Phil's hand losing its definition, becoming a lump that crept snakelike under the material of Crissy's skirt, higher and higher until the poodle embroidered on it seemed to shift in discomfort while Crissy moaned an insincere protest . . .

The poodle . . .

Mike awoke sweating, felt his way to the refrigerator, and drank half a can of beer to cool himself off.

The next evening, Saturday, Mike sat in the ticket kiosk with Lenny, leaving the snack bar to the girls. Only one car of fifties vintage came through, a '55 T-bird with classic plates, occupied by a local real estate broker and his wife. The crowd was even larger that night, and afterwards, when the cars had gone and the two of them were counting the receipts, Mike asked casually if Lenny remembered what kind of car the kids with the old coin had been driving.

"Didn't look too close," Lenny said. "Ford, Merc, something like that."

"Pretty old?"

"Shit, yeah. Had that clumsy, round styling, y'know? Didn't look like a reconditioned one, though. Dull paint job, and the interior looked worn."

"You think it might've been a Merc?"

179

SILVER SCREAM

"Maybe." Lenny looked up from the piles of singles. "Why?"

"Just wondered," Mike said.

That night he dreamed about LaVern Baker wailing from the Merc's tinny speaker while he screamed down the back road playing chicken, swerving at the final moment, skidding off the blacktop into the field, corn shocks scattering like frightened birds, and laughing and laughing while his heart beat so fast that it filled the car, buoyed it up, made it fly, with a fiery comet's tail dragging behind it that froze in the cold upper sky, hardening to thick bright tubes of neon.

There were fewer cars on Sunday, but the attendance was still respectable and highly profitable, and Mike thought with deep satisfaction that he was not the only one who needed to escape, to retreat into a bright and peaceful past.

Monday through Thursday, while Lenny worked in his office in town, Mike played janitor, accountant, and purchasing agent, faithfully recording income and expenses, buying the snack bar food for the next weekend, repairing the speakers that had been snapped from their wires, and walking down the softly curving rows, picking up the beer bottles, soda cans, popcorn boxes, candy wrappers (and yes, one used condom, by God), and dropping them into his wheeled cart under the warm May sun.

He didn't mind it. He had never worked beneath the sky before, and he liked the scent of approaching summer, the crunch of the loose stones under his feet, the sounds of birds roosting in the grove behind the last row of the theatre. When he closed his eyes, the breeze brushed his face so lightly that he could almost believe it was once more smooth and beardless, young. He dreamed at night, imagined by day, and waited for Friday, when the Fireball would shine again.

Lenny frowned when he saw Mike approaching the kiosk. "Hey," he said. "What's up?"

"I thought you might be lonely," Mike answered.

"Don't you think you oughta be at the snack bar?"

"The girls can handle it."

"They screwed up last Saturday. Not enough doggies out of the freezer, remember?" He looked pointedly at Mike. "You wanta take tickets tonight or what?"

"Would you mind? Just trading for tonight? I'm a little tired."

Lenny sighed. "Yeah okay." He climbed off the stool, then looked at Mike again. "You feel sick or anything?"

"No."

RETURN OF THE NEON FIREBALL

"Mike. Tell me. This place getting to you?"

"No," he said defensively.

"Okay." Lenny nodded, but there was doubt in his eyes. "Just . . . don't take things too seriously, y'know? I mean, this is just fun, a fun way to make a buck, right? When we were kids it was fun too. But it wasn't all *that* great. It wasn't everything." Lenny nodded again, agreeing with himself, and walked to the snack bar, leaving Mike alone in the ticket kiosk.

The cars started to arrive within a few minutes, and Mike took the money, counting heads and giving out change and food tickets automatically, waiting, watching for one special car.

It was nearly dark by the time it arrived, a '49 Merc, chopped and chan-nelled. The color was a faded baby blue, accented by bright orange flames painted on the rear fenders. The front bumper bore a blue and white McKinley High sticker. Mike recognized the car, and thought he recognized the people inside, four of them.

"Twelve dollars," he said in a harsh whisper. The driver took out a light tan wallet with a western design on the leather and counted out some bills, then reached behind him to take the money the boy in the back seat was offering.

"There ya go, pardner," the driver said, giving Mike the money and keeping his hand extended for the change.

"Do you . . ." Mike cleared his throat roughly. "Do you kids go to McKinley?"

"Yeah." The driver nodded. "McKinley. Why?"

Mike shook his head. McKinley. It had been John F. Kennedy High for almost twenty years, one martyred president's name replacing another's in white metal letters above the tired entrance.

"Hey." Mike looked at the driver. "How 'bout the change?"

Mike handed the boy three singles and the snack bar tickets, which the boy looked at strangely. Then he shrugged. "Thanks, daddio."

The car pulled away from the kiosk fast, making loose gravel fly up in narrow twin geysers. Mike watched it go. It was not until he saw the car park in the center of the lot, five rows back from the screen, that he responded to the driver of the next car. "Hey, buddy," he finally heard the man say, "are you okay?"

"Yes. Yes, fine." He took money and made change, glancing every few seconds, his heart pounding and stomach churning, toward the middle of the fifth row where the Merc sat. Time and again he wiped the sweat from his forehead and prayed that the car wouldn't disappear, not before he got to it, not before he could talk to them again.

Night came, the screen glowed, the stream of cars became short and staggered groups, then a single car every minute or so. Mike thought he could still see the tubular, whale-like shape of the Merc, imagined he could see the four heads within. At last there were no more cars coming in, and he turned off the kiosk light, locked the door, and walked down and across the rows until he was behind the Mercury. The two heads in back were together, kissing. Those in front were together too, but watching the film, Kirk Douglas in INDIAN FIGHTER.

He didn't want to startle them, so he rapped on the left rear fender before coming to the window. The pairs of heads parted like a shadowy mitosis, and as Mike moved up the length of the car he saw, by the light of the screen, the white poodle on the skirt of the girl in the back seat. The driver looked at Mike and frowned. "So what is it? Necking illegal?"

"No . . . no. I just . . ." Mike gave a short, brittle laugh. "I just thought I recognized you."

"You recognized us." They were all looking at him now, questions on their dark faces, discomfort in the smoky air of the car. The boy in back took a drag on his cigarette and blew in Mike's direction.

"Yes. I know you." He looked at the girl in the passenger seat. "Becky," he said. "Becky Geyer." He turned his head toward the back seat. "Phil Strickler. Crissy. Crissy Medwick." Then he looked at the driver and could not speak.

"So far so good," the boy said. "What about me?" He smiled like a shark, showing white, even teeth that complemented his white-blond hair, as his hands tightened on the steering wheel, and the muscles of his arms and chest stood out tautly.

"I . . ." Mike could not say it. "Tell me. You tell me . . ."

"He's Mike Price," grunted the boy in the back seat. "You know who he is, you know who we all are, now what's your beef, dad? You wanta check us for beer or what?"

Mike shook his head, suddenly feeling very old, very tired, but very excited as well. "No, no trouble. I just want to . . . to talk to you."

"Why?" the driver asked.

"Because I'm *one* of you!"

The girl in the back seat laughed.

"One of us," the driver said flatly.

"Yes!"

"You're not one of us."

"But I *am*! Let me explain . . . let me talk to you." He grasped the door handle. "Let me in . . ."

The boy pushed the cylinder down, locking the door. "After the movies. When everyone's gone. We'll wait." He put his arm around the girl and turned back toward the screen, away from the older man.

Michael Price walked back to the ticket kiosk and sat inside in the dark. When the first feature ended he did not go into the snack bar to help Lenny and the girls. He only waited.

RETURN OF THE NEON FIREBALL

Ten minutes into the second feature he heard footsteps on the loose stones. "Mike!" Lenny said beside him. "What are you doing out here? You sick?"

"Just thinking."

"We coulda used some help in there. Busy as hell."

"I'm sorry."

"You coming in?"

"Not right away." Neither spoke for a moment. "Lenny . . . do you think if you want things bad enough . . . they come to you?"

Lenny sucked his lower lip. "Nothing comes to you. You get it for yourself. I'm going in. Why don't you come with me?"

"No. I'd rather stay here."

"Come on in, Mike. Things look too different out here." Lenny turned and walked back to the snack bar. Mike stayed in the kiosk.

The movie finally ended and the cars formed into a long procession, red and white lights gleaming as they left the presence of the darkened screen. When all the cars but one had vanished, Mike walked across the empty lot to where the Mercury sat, its engine running, its lights on. The driver looked at him with a strangely blank expression.

"One of us," he said again, as though no time had passed.

"Yes. I am."

"If you want to be one of us," the boy said," there's only one way."

He raced the engine and patched out of the space, yanking the wheel around and roaring down the gentle curve of the fourth row. Mike threw up an arm against the barrage of stones that shot from beneath the tires. The Mercury slowed as it reached the row's end, then turned completely around so that it faced down the fifth row, its headlights shining directly into Mike's startled eyes.

He stood for a moment, pinned in the high-beams, before he understood. The Merc's engine roared out its challenge, and he turned and started toward his Buick, parked next to the snack bar.

Lenny met him halfway there. "Mike, what the hell are those kids doing?"

"They're . . . it's okay. They're waiting for me."

"For you?" He got into step beside Mike, moving toward the Buick. The Merc roared again, lurched like a caged beast. Stones flew. "Jesus Christ," Lenny swore. "What's *with* them? They're acting like . . ." A dim memory moved within him. ". . . play chicken."

Mike put the Buick in reverse and started to back out, but Lenny shot an arm through the window and grabbed the wheel, making him brake.

"Let go!"

"What are you *doing*?"

"They're *waiting* for me, Lenny!"

183

"Who? Who are *they?*"

"Phil, Crissy, Becky . . . Becky Geyer . . ."

"In that car? You're nuts! Those're *kids!*"

"You remember, Lenny, you remember what they looked like, you saw them the other night!"

"I only saw the driver, for crissake . . ."

"That was *me!* Me and my friends!"

"You? Your *friends?*" Lenny shook his head, confused. "Hell, Mike, they were never your friends, they didn't even *talk* to you . . ."

"*Me,* Lenny! Me and my car! My Merc!"

"God *damn* it, what is *wrong* with you? You never had a car, Mike you always came in *my* car, you and me . . ."

"But it was *me,*" Mike sobbed. "You remember *me!*"

"The blond kid? That was never you," Lenny said, near tears himself now, remembering the pudgy, unpopular junior he'd pitied and befriended, remembering Michael Price. "That wasn't *you* . . ."

"Let *go!*" shrieked Mike, slamming a fist down on Lenny's knuckles so that Lenny cried out and released the wheel. Mike hit the accelerator, and the Buick surged backwards with a rattle of stones, then swung left, raced down the row, swerved, fishtailed, straightened out, moved toward the screen, turned again, and stopped.

The two cars faced down the hundred yards of gravel that defined the fifth row, the curve of it making the beams of their headlights cross several rows further back. Speaker posts marked the boundaries of their arena, the worn, metal surfaces gleaming dully in the beams of the headlights. The Merc roared, and the sound seemed louder than before. The Buick tried to respond, but its tone was ratchety, unskilled, its fuel-saving engine unable to issue screaming challenges in the night. At last Lenny realized what was going to happen.

"No!" he cried, running toward Mike's Buick. "You can't! Mike, goddammit, stop it! *Stop!*"

"I've done it before!" Mike yelled through the open window. "I know how!"

"Never!" answered Lenny. "You never! . . ."

The Merc streaked forward like a sprinter from the blocks, and Mike slammed his foot to the floor. The cars rushed toward the center, the beams of their headlights straightening, meeting, driving the light before them until it met in the center of the row, a rising flare of whiteness.

Neither turned.

The impact shook the world.

"Oh Christ," whispered Lenny. "Oh Christ Jesus . . ." He started to walk toward the spot, then ran, then slowed, and walked again, stopped.

There was no Merc. There was only the Buick, its lights extinguished, crumpled as though it had run into an invisible wall, a dead beast lying in a pool of darkness.

They had to cut Mike out of the car with torches.

In the office behind the snack bar Lenny told the troopers that he had heard the crash, run outside, and found the car.

"There must have been another vehicle," a trooper said.

"I didn't see it."

"He had to have hit *something*."

Lenny shook his head and the troopers frowned. There hadn't been a sign of another car, no impressions in the stones, no shattered pieces from whatever it was the dead man hit at forty miles per hour. "We'll check the body shops around here," the trooper said. "We'll find out who he hit, or who hit him."

Lenny shook his head again. Again the troopers frowned.

The Fireball was closed the next week, but the following Friday it opened with an Abbott and Costello double bill. Lenny hired a ticket seller, and stayed with the high school girls in the snack bar. He didn't want to be alone. Twenty minutes after the first film began, the new girl came in from the kiosk with the money. "Look at this," she said, dumping change into Lenny's hand.

He looked down at the forties and fifties coinage and felt ice on his spine. "Who gave you these?" he asked so harshly that the girl's smile vanished.

"Some kids in an old car."

"A Mercury?"

"I don't know. I don't know old cars."

"Two guys, two girls?"

"I . . . I think so, yeah."

Lenny walked out into the night and made his way through the maze of cars to the fifth row near the center. The Mercury sat there, undamaged. He made himself walk on until he stood by the left rear fender, until he could see the face of the driver reflected in the outside mirror.

Then he turned and walked back toward the safer light, wondering how much he could get for the land after he'd torn down the screen and dismantled and destroyed the brilliant neon fireball, trying desperately to forget the driver's face, that fleshy, forty-five year old face smiling at the movie, at the girl beside him, trying without success to forget Michael Price, happy, among his friends at last, and for the first time.

*   *   *

NIGHT CALLS
THE GREEN FALCON

by

Robert R. McCammon

Chapter One
NEVER SAY DIE

He was in the airplane again, falling toward the lights of Hollywood.

Seconds ago the craft had been a sleek silver beauty with two green-painted propellers, and now it was coming apart at the seams like wet cardboard. The controls went crazy, he couldn't hold the stick level, and as the airplane fell he cinched his parachute pack tighter around his chest and reached up to pop the canopy out. But the canopy was jammed shut, its hinges red with clots of rust. The propellers had seized up, and black smoke whirled from the engines. The plane nosed toward the squat, ugly buildings that lined Hollywood Boulevard, a scream of wind passing over the fuselage.

He didn't give up. That wasn't his way. He kept pressing against the canopy, trying to force the hinges, but they were locked tight. The buildings were coming up fast, and there was no way to turn the airplane because the rudder and ailerons were gone too. He was sweating under his green suit, his heart beating so hard he couldn't hear himself think. There had to be a way out of this; he was a never-say-die type of guy. His eyes in the slits of the green cowl ticked to the control panel, the jammed hinges, the dead stick, the smoking engines, back to the control panel in a frantic geometry.

The plane trembled; the port side engine was ripping away from the wing. His green boots kicked at the dead rudder pedals. Another mighty heave at the canopy, another jerk of the limp control stick — and then he knew his luck had, at long last, run out. It was all over.

Going down fast now, the wings starting to tear away. Klieg lights swung back and forth over the boulevard, advertising somebody else's premiere. He marked where the plane was going to hit: a mustard-yellow, five-floored brick building about eight blocks east of the Chinese Theater. He was going to hit the top floor, go right into somebody's apartment. His hands in their green gloves clenched the armrests. No way out . . . no way out . . .

He didn't mourn for himself so much, but someone innocent was about to die and that he couldn't bear. Maybe there was a child in that apartment, and he could do nothing but sit in his trap of straps and glass and watch the scene unfold. No, he decided, as the sweat ran down his face. No, I can't kill a child. Not another one. I *won't*. This script has to be rewritten. It wasn't fair, that no one had told him how this scene would end. Surely the director was still in control. Wasn't he? "Cut!" he called out, as the mustard-yellow building filled up his horizon. "Cut!" he said again, louder — then screamed it: "CUT!"

The airplane crashed into the building's fifth floor, and he was engulfed by a wall of fire and agony.

Chapter Two
AN OLD RELIC

He awoke, his flesh wet with nightmare sweat and his stomach burning with the last flames of an enchilada tv-dinner.

He lay in the darkness, the springs of his mattress biting into his back, and watched the lights from the boulevard — reflections of light — moved across the cracked ceiling. A fan stuttered atop his chest-of-drawers, and from down the hall he could hear the LaPrestas hollering at each other again. He lifted his head from the sodden pillow and looked at his alarm clock on the table beside his bed: twenty-six minutes past twelve, and the night had already gone on forever.

His bladder throbbed. Right now it was working, but sometimes it went haywire and he peed in his sheets. The laundromat on the corner of Cosmo Street was not a good place to spend a Saturday night. He roused himself out of bed, his joints clicking back into their sockets and the memory of the nightmare scorched in his mind. It was from Chapter One of "Night Calls The Green Falcon", RKO Studios, 1949. He remembered how he'd panicked when he couldn't get the plane's canopy up, because he didn't like close places. The director had said, "Cut!" and the canopy's hinges had been oiled and the sequence had gone like clockwork the second time around.

The nightmare would be back, and so would the rest of them — a reel of car crashes, falls from buildings, gunshots, explosions, even a lion's attack. He had survived all of them, but they kept trying to kill him again and again. Mr. Thatcher at the Burger King said he ought to have his head looked at, and maybe that was true. But Mr. Thatcher was only a kid, and the Green Falcon had died before Mr. Thatcher was born.

188

NIGHT CALLS THE GREEN FALCON

He stood up. Slid his feet into slippers. Picked his robe off a chair and shrugged into it, covering his pajamas. His eyes found the faded poster taped to the wall: NIGHT CALLS THE GREEN FALCON, it said, and showed an assemblage of fist fights, car crashes and various other action scenes. IN TEN EXCITING CHAPTERS! the poster promised. STARRING CREIGHTON FLINT, "THE GREEN FALCON".

"The Green Falcon has to piss now," he said, and he unlocked the door and went out into the hallway.

The bathroom was on the other side of the building. He trudged past the elevator and the door where the LaPrestas were yelling. Somebody else shouted for them to shut up, but when they got going there was no stopping them. Seymour the super's cat slinked past, hunting rats, and the old man knocked politely at the bathroom's door before he entered. He clicked on the light, relieved himself at the urinal and looked away from the hypodermic needles that were lying around the toilet. When he was finished, he picked up the needles and put them in the trash can, then washed his hands in the rust-stained sink and walked back along the corridor to his apartment.

Old gears moaned. The elevator was coming up. It opened when he was almost even with it. Out walked his nextdoor neighbor, Julie Saufley, and a young man with close-cropped blond hair.

She almost bumped into him, but she stopped short. "Hi, Cray. You're prowlin' around kinda late, aren't you?"

"Guess so." Cray glanced at the young man. Julie's latest friend had pallid skin that was odd in sun-loving California, and his eyes were small and very dark. Looks like an extra in a Nazi flick, Cray thought, and then returned his gaze to Julie, whose dark brown hair was cut in a Mohawk and decorated with purple spray. Her spangled blouse and short leather skirt were so tight he couldn't fathom how she could draw a breath. "Had to use the bathroom," he said. Didn't that just sound like an old fool? he asked himself. When he was forty years younger such a statement to a pretty girl would have been unthinkable.

"Cray was a movie star," Julie explained to her friend. "Used to be ... what did they call them, Cray?"

"Serials," he answered. Smiled wanly. "Cliff-hangers. I was the —"

"I'm not paying you for a tour of the wax museum, baby." The young man's voice was taut and mean, and the sound of it made Cray think of rusted barbed-wire. A match flared along the side of a red matchbook; the young man lit a cigarette, and the quick yellow light made his eyes look like small ebony stones. "Let's get done what we came here for," he said, with a puff of smoke in Cray Flint's direction.

"Sure." Julie shrugged. "I just thought you might like to know he used to be famous, that's all."

"He can sign my autograph book later. Let's go." Spidery white fingers slid around her arm, and drew her away.

189

SILVER SCREAM

Cray started to tell him to release her, but what was the use? There were no gentlemen anymore, and he was too old and used-up to be anyone's champion. "Be careful, Julie," he said as she guided the man to her apartment.

"My name's Crystal this week," she reminded him. Got her keys out of her clutch purse. "Coffee in the morning?"

"Right." Julie's door opened and closed. Cray went into his room and eased himself into a chair next to the window. The boulevard's neon pulse painted red streaks across the walls. The street denizens were out, would be out until dawn, and every so often a police car would run them into the shadows but they always returned. The night called them, and they had to obey. Like Julie did. She'd been in the building four months, was just twenty years old, and Cray couldn't help but feel some grandfatherly concern for her. Maybe it was more than that, but so what? Lately he'd been trying to help her get off those pills she popped like candy, and encouraging her to write to her parents back in Minnesota. Last week she'd called herself Amber; such was the power of Hollywood, a city of masks.

Cray reached down beside his chair and picked up the well-worn leather book that lay there. He could hear the murmur of Julie's voice through the paper-thin wall; then her customer's saying something. Silence. A police car's siren on the boulevard, heading west. The squeak of mattress springs from Julie's apartment. Over in the corner, the scuttling of a rat in the wall. Where was Seymour when you needed him? Cray opened his memory book, and looked at the yellowed newspaper clipping from the Belvedere, Indiana *Banner* on March 21st, 1946, that said HOMETOWN FOOTBALL HERO HOLLYWOOD BOUND. There was a picture of himself, when he was still handsome and had a headful of hair. Other clippings — his mother had saved them — were from his highschool and college days, and they had headlines like BOOMER WINS GYMNASTIC MEDAL and BOOMER BREAKS TRACK MEET RECORD. That was his real name: Creighton Boomershine. The photographs were of a muscular, long-legged kid with a lop-sided grin and the clear eyes of a dreamer.

Long gone, Cray thought. Long gone.

He had had his moment in the sun. It had almost burned him blind, but it had been a lovely light. He had turned sixty-three in May, an old relic. Hollywood worshipped at the altar of youth. Anyway, nobody made his kind of pictures anymore. Four serials in four years, and then —

Cut, he thought. No use stirring up all that murky water. He had to get back to bed, because morning would find him mopping the floor in the Burger King three blocks west and Mr. Thatcher liked clean floors.

He closed the memory book and put it aside. On the floor was a section of yesterday's L.A. *Times*; he'd already read the paper, but a headline caught his attention: FLIPTOP KILLER CHALLENGES POLICE. Beneath that was a story about the Fliptop, and eight photographs of the street people

190

whose throats had been savagely slashed in the last two months. Cray had known one of them: a middle-aged woman called Auntie Sunglow, who rocketed along the boulevard on roller skates singing Beatles songs at the top of her lungs. She was crazy, yes, but she always had a kind tune for him. Last week she'd been found in a trash dumpster off Sierra Bonita, her head almost severed from her neck.

Bad times, Cray mused. Couldn't think of any worse. Hopefully the police would nail the Fliptop before he — or she — killed again, but he didn't count on it. All the street people he knew were watching their backs.

Something struck the wall, in Julie's apartment. It sounded like it might have been a fist.

Cray heard the springs squalling, like a cat being skinned alive. He didn't know why she sold her body for such things, but he'd learned long ago that people did what they had to do to survive.

There was another blow against the wall. Something crashed over. A chair, maybe.

Cray stood up. Whatever was going on over there, it sounded rough. Way too rough. He heard no voices, just the awful noise of the springs. He went to the wall and pounded on it. "Julie?" he called. "You all right?"

No answer. He put his ear to the wall, and heard what he thought might have been a shuddering gasp.

The squall of the springs had ceased. Now he could hear only his own heartbeat. "Julie?" He pounded the wall again. "Julie, answer me!" When she didn't respond, he knew something was terribly wrong. He went out to the corridor, sweat crawling down his neck, and as he reached out to grip the doorknob of Julie's apartment he heard a scraping noise that he knew must be the window being pushed upward.

Julie's window faced the alley. The fire escape, Cray realized. Julie's customer was going down the fire escape.

"Julie!" he shouted. He kicked at the door, and his slipper flew off. Then he threw his shoulder against it, and the door cracked on its hinges but didn't give way. Again he rammed into the door, and a third time. On the fourth blow the door's hinges tore away from the wood and it crashed down, sending Cray sprawling into the apartment.

He got up on his hand and knees, his shoulder hurting like hell. The young man was across the untidy room, still struggling with the reluctant windowsill, and he paid Cray no attention. Cray stood up, and looked at the bed where Julie lay, naked, on her back.

He caught his breath as if he'd been punched in the stomach. The blood was still streaming from the scarlet mass of Julie Saufley's throat, and it had splattered across the yellow wall like weird calligraphy. Her eyes were wet and aimed up at the ceiling, her hands gripped around the bars of the iron bedframe. Without clothes, her body was white and childlike, and she

191

hardly had any breasts at all. The blood was everywhere. So red. Cray's heart was laboring, and as he stared at the slashed throat he heard the window slide up. He blinked, everything hazy and dreamlike, and watched the young blond man climb through the window onto the fire escape.

Oh God, Cray thought. He wavered on his feet, feared he was about to faint. Oh my God . . .

Julie had brought the Fliptop Killer home to play.

His first impulse was to shout for help, but he squelched it. He knew the shout would rob his breath and strength, and right now he needed both of them. The LaPrestas were still fighting. What would one more shout be? He stepped forward. Another step, and a third one followed. With the rusty agility of a champion gymnast, he ran to the open window and slid out to the fire escape.

The Fliptop Killer was about to go down the ladder. Cray reached out, grasped the young man's t-shirt in his freckled fist, and said hoarsely, "No."

The man twisted toward him. The small black eyes regarded him incuriously: the emotionless gaze of a clinician. There were a few spatters of blood on his face, but not many. Practice had honed his reflexes, and he knew how to avoid the jetting crimson. Cray gripped his shirt; they stared at each other for a few ticks of time, and then the killer's right hand flashed up with an extra finger of metal.

The knife swung at Cray's face, but Cray had already seen the blow coming in the tension of the man's shoulder and as he let go of the shirt and scrambled backward the blade hissed past.

And now the Fliptop Killer stepped toward him — a long stride, knife upraised, the face cold and without expression, as if he were about to cut a hanging piece of beef. But a woman screamed from an open window, and as the man's head darted to the side Cray grasped the wrist of his knife-hand and shouted, "Call the po—"

A fist hit him in the face, crumpling his nose and mashing his lips. He pitched back, stunned — and he fell over the fire escape's railing into empty space.

Chapter Three
A RED MATCHBOOK

His robe snagged on a jagged edge of metal. The cloth ripped, almost tore off him, and for three awful seconds he was dangling five floors over the alley but then he reached upward and his fingers closed around the railing.

The Fliptop Killer was already scrambling down the fire escape. The woman — Mrs. Sargenza, bless her soul — was still screaming, and now

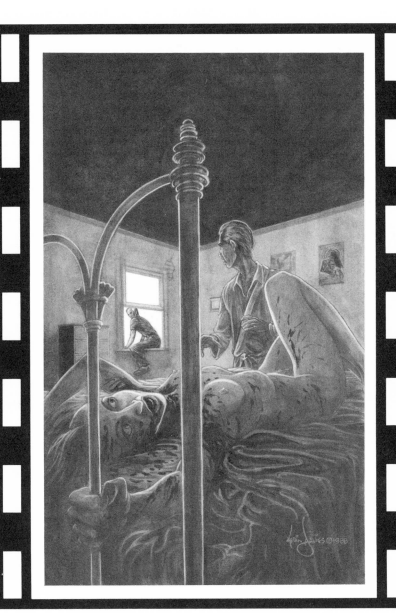

somebody else was hollering from another window and the Fliptop Killer clambered down the alley with the speed and power of a born survivor.

Cray pulled himself up, his legs kicking and his shoulder muscles standing out in rigid relief. He collapsed onto his knees when he'd made it to the landing's safety. He thought he might have to throw up enchiladas, and his stomach heaved but mercifully there was no explosion. Blood was in his mouth, and his front teeth felt loose. He stood up, black motes buzzing before his eyes. Looked over the edge, gripping hard to the railing.

The Fliptop Killer was gone, back to the shadows.

"Call the police," he said, but he didn't know if Mrs. Sargenza had heard him though she disappeared from her window and slammed it shut. He was trembling down to his gnarly toes, and after another moment he climbed back into the room where the corpse was.

Cray felt her wrist for a pulse. It seemed the sensible thing to do. But there was no pulse, and Julie's eyes didn't move. In the depths of the wound he could see the white bone of her spine. How many times had the killer slashed, and what was it inside him that gave him such a maniacal strength? "Wake up," Cray said. He pulled at her arm. "Come on, Julie. Wake up."

"Oh, Jesus!" Mr. Myers from across the hall stood in the doorway. His hand went to his mouth, and he made a retching sound and staggered back to his apartment. Other people were peering in. Cray said, "Julie needs a doctor," though he knew she was dead and all a doctor could do was pull the bloodied sheet over her face. He still had her hand, and he was stroking it. Her fingers were closed around something; it worked loose, and fell into Cray's palm.

Cray looked at it. A red matchbook. The words GRINDERSWITCH BAR printed on its side, and an address just off Hollywood and Vine, three blocks over.

He opened the red matchbook. Two matches were missing. One of them had been used to light the Fliptop Killer's cigarette, out in the hallway. The Fliptop Killer had been to the Grinderswitch, a place Cray had walked past but never entered.

"Cops are on their way!" Mr. Gomez said, coming into the room. His wife stood at the door, her faced smeared with blue anti-aging cream. "What happened here, Flint?"

Cray started to speak, but found no words. Others were entering the room, and suddenly the place with its reek of blood and spent passions was too tight for him; he had a feeling of suffocation, and a scream flailed behind his teeth. He walked past Mr. Gomez, out the door and into his own apartment. And there he stood at the window, the brutal neon pulse flashing in his face and a red matchbook clenched in his hand.

The police would come and ask their questions. An ambulance without a siren would take Julie's corpse away, to a cold vault. Her picture would be

194

in the *Times* tomorrow, and the headline would identify her as the Fliptop Killer's ninth victim. Her claim to fame, he thought, and he almost wept. *I saw him,* he realized. *I saw the Fliptop. I had hold of the bastard.*

And there in his hand was the matchbook Julie had given him. The bartender at the Grinderswitch might know the Fliptop. The bartender might *be* the Fliptop. It was a vital clue, Cray thought, and if he gave it up to the police it might be lost in shufflings of paper, envelopes and plastic bags that went into what they called their evidence storage. The police didn't care about Julie Saufley, and they hardly cared about the other street victims either. No, Julie was another statistic — a "crazy", the cops would say. The Fliptop Killer loved to kill "crazies".

Julie had given him a clue. Had, perhaps, fought to keep it with her dying breath. And now what was he going to do with it?

He knew, without fully knowing. It was a thing of instincts, just as his long-ago gymnastic training, track-and-field and boxing championships were things of instincts. Inner things, that once learned and believed in could never be fully lost.

He opened the closet's door.

A musty, mothball smell rolled out. And there it was, on its wooden hanger amid the cheap shirts and trousers of an old dreamer.

It had once been emerald-green, but time had faded it to more of a dusky olive. Bleach stains had mottled the flowing green cape, and Cray had forgotten how that had happened. Still, he'd been a good caretaker: various rips had been patched over, the only really noticeable mark was a poorly-stitched tear across the left leg. The cowl, with its swept-back, crisply wing-like folds on either side of the head and its slits for the eyes, was in almost perfect condition. The green boots were there on the floor, both badly scuffed, and the green gloves were up on the shelf.

His Green Falcon costume had aged, just like its owner. The studio had let him keep it, after he came out of the sanitarium in 1954. By then serials were dying anyway, and of what use was a green suit with a long cape and wings on the sides of its cowl? In the real world, there was no room for Green Falcons.

He touched the material. It was lighter than it appeared, and it made a secret — and dangerous — whispering noise. The Green Falcon had made mincemeat out of a gallery of villains, roughnecks and killers, every Saturday afternoon in the cathedrals of light and shadow all across America. Why, then, could the Green Falcon not track down the Fliptop Killer?

Because the Green Falcon is dead, Cray told himself. Forget it. Close the door. Step back. Leave it to the police.

But he didn't close the door, nor did he step back. Because he knew, deep at his center, that the Green Falcon was not dead. Only sleeping, and yearning to awaken.

195

He was losing his mind. He knew that clearly enough, as if somebody had thrown ice water in his face and slapped him too. But he reached into the closet, and he brought the costume out.

The siren of a police car was approaching. Cray Flint began to pull the costume on, over his pajamas. His body had thinned, not thickened, with age; the green tights were loose, and though his legs were knotty with muscles they looked skinny and ill-nourished. His shoulders and chest still filled out the tunic portion of the costume, though, but his thin, wiry arms had lost the blocky muscularity of their youth. He got the costume zipped up, worked his feet into the scuffed boots, then put on the cape and laced it in place. The dust of a thousand moth wings shimmered gold against the green. He lifted the gloves off the shelf, but discovered the moths had enjoyed an orgy in them and they were riddled with holes. The gloves would have to stay behind. His heart was beating very hard now. He took the cowl off its hanger. The police car's siren was nearing the building. Cray ran his fingers over the cowl, which still gleamed with a little iridescense, as it had in the old days.

I shouldn't do this, he told himself. *I'm going crazy again, and I'm nothing but an Indiana boy who used to be an actor . . .*

I shouldn't . . .

He slipped the cowl over his head, and drew its drawstring tight. And now he saw the world through cautious slits, the air coming to his nostrils through small holes and smelling of mothballs and . . . yes, and something else. Something indefinable: the brassy odor of a young man's sweat, the sultry heat of daredeviltry, maybe the blood of a split lip incurred during a fight scene with an over-eager stuntman. Those aromas and more. His stomach tightened under the green skin. *Walk tall and think tall,* he remembered a director telling him. His shoulders pulled back. How many times had he donned this costume and gone into the battle against hoodlums, thugs and murderers? How many times had he stared Death in the face through these slits, and walked tall into the maelstrom?

I'm Creighton Flint, he thought. And then he looked at the faded poster that promised a world of thrills and saw STARRING CREIGHTON FLINT, "THE GREEN FALCON".

The one and only.

The police car's siren stopped.

It was time to go, if he was going.

The Green Falcon held the matchbook up before his eyeslits. The Grinderswitch was a short walk away. If the Fliptop Killer had been there tonight, someone might remember.

He knew he was one stride away from the loony bin, and if he went through that door dressed like this there was no turning back. But if the Green Falcon couldn't track down the Fliptop, nobody could.

NIGHT CALLS THE GREEN FALCON

It was worth a try. Wasn't it?

He took a deep breath, and then the one stride followed. He walked out into the hallway, and the residents gathered around Julie Saufley's door saw him and everyone of them recoiled as if they'd just seen a man from Mars. He didn't hesitate; he went past them to the elevator. The little numerals above the door were on the upward march. The policemen were coming up, he realized. It would not be wise to let them see the Green Falcon.

"Hey!" Mr. Gomez shouted. "Hey, who the hell are *you?*"

"He must be nuts!" Mrs. LaPresta said, and her husband — in a rare moment — agreed.

But Cray was already heading toward the door marked STAIRS. The cape pinched his neck and the mask was stuffy; he didn't remember the costume being so uncomfortable. But he pulled open the door and started quickly down the stairway, the matchbook clenched in his hand and the smell of Julie's blood up his nostrils.

He was puffing by the time he reached the ground floor. But he crossed the cramped little lobby, went out the revolving door and onto Hollywood Boulevard where the lights and the noise reminded him of a three-ring circus. But he knew full well that shadows lay at the fringes of those lights, and in those shadows it was dangerous to tread. He started walking west, toward Vine Street. A couple of kids zipped past him on skateboards, and one of them gave a fierce tug at his cape that almost strangled him. Horns were honking as cars passed, and ladies of the night waved and jiggled their wares from the street corner. A punk with his hair in long red spikes peered into Cray's eyeholes and sneered, "Are you for *real*, man?" The Green Falcon kept going, a man with a mission. A black prostitute jabbed her colleague in the ribs, and both of them hooted and made obscene noises as he passed. Here came a group of Hare Krishnas, banging tambourines and chanting, and even their blank eyes widened as they saw him coming. But the Green Falcon, dodging drunks and leather-clad hustlers, left them all in the flap of his cape.

And then there was the Grinderswitch Bar, jammed between a porno theater and a wig shop. Its blinking neon sign was bright scarlet, and out in front of the place were six big Harley-Davidson motorcycles. Cray paused, fear fluttering around in the pit of his stomach. The Grinderswitch was a place of shadows; he could tell that right off. There was a meanness even in the neon's buzz. Go home, he told himself. Forget this. Just go home and —

Do what? Vegetate? Sit in a lousy chair, look at clippings and reflect on how lucky you are to have a job sweeping the floor at a Burger King?

No. He was wearing the armor of the Green Falcon now, and why should he fear? But still he paused. To go into that place would be like walking into a lion's den after rolling around in fresh meat. Who was Julie Saufley, anyway? His friend, yes, but she was dead now, and what did it matter? Go home. Put the costume back on its hanger, and forget. He looked at the door, and knew that beyond it the monsters waited. Go home. Just go home.

Chapter Four
ONE-EYED SKULLS

He swallowed thickly. *Walk tall and think tall,* he told himself. If he did not go in, the very name of the Green Falcon would be forever tainted. Pain he could take; shame he could not.

He grasped the door's handle, and he entered the Grinderswitch.

The six motorcycle owners, husky bearded men wearing black jackets that identified them as members of the ONE-EYED SKULLS gang, looked up from their beers. One of them laughed, and the man sitting in the center seat gave a low whistle.

The Green Falcon paid them no attention. Bass-heavy music pounded from ceiling-mounted speakers, and on a small upraised stage a thin blond girl wearing a g-string gyrated to the beat with all the fervor of a zombie. A few other patrons watched the girl, and other topless girls in g-strings wandered around with trays of beers and cheerless smiles. The Green Falcon went to the bar, where a flabby man with many chins had halted in his pouring of a new set of brews. The bartender stared at him, round-eyed, as the Green Falcon slid onto a stool.

"I'm looking for a man," Cray said.

"Wrong joint, Greenie," the bartender answered. "Try the Brass Screw, over on Selma."

"No, I don't mean that." He flushed red under his mask. Trying to talk over this hellacious noise was like screaming into a hurricane. "I'm looking for a man who might have been in here tonight."

"I serve beer and liquor, not lonely hearts club news. Take a hike."

Cray glanced to his left. There was a mug on the bar full of GRINDER-SWITCH matchbooks. "The man I'm looking for is blond, maybe in his early or mid-twenties. He's got pale skin and his eyes are very dark — either brown or black. Have you seen anybody who —"

"What the hell are you doin' walking around in a friggin' green suit?" the bartender asked. "It's not St. Patrick's Day. Did you jump out of a nut-house wagon?"

"No. Please, try to think. Have you seen the man I just described?"

"Yeah. A hundred of 'em. Now I said move it, and I'm not gonna say it again."

198

NIGHT CALLS THE GREEN FALCON

"He took one of those matchbooks," Cray persisted. "He might have been sitting on one of these stools not long ago. Are you sure you —"

A hand grasped his shoulder and swung him around. Three of the bikers had crowded in close, and the other three watched from a distance. A couple of go-go dancers rubbernecked at him, giggling. The bass throbbing was a physical presence, making the glasses shake on the shelves behind the bar. A broad, brown-bearded face with cruel blue eyes peered into Cray's mask; the biker wore a bandana wrapped around his skull and a necklace from which rusty razor blades dangled. "God Almighty, Dogmeat. There's somebody *inside* it!"

The biker called Dogmeat, the one who'd whistled as Cray had entered, stepped forward. He was a burly, gray-bearded hulk with eyes like shotgun barrels and a face like a pissed-off pit bull. He thunked Cray on the skull with a thick forefinger. "Hey, man! You got some screws loose or what?"

Cray smelled stale beer and dirty armpits. "I'm all right," he said, with just a little quaver in his voice.

"I say you *ain't*," Dogmeat told him. "What's wrong with you, comin' into a respectable joint dressed up like a Halloween fruitcake?"

"Guy was just on his way out," the bartender said. "Let him go." The bikers glared at him, and he smiled weakly and added, "Okay?"

"No. Not okay," Dogmeat answered. He thunked Cray's skull again, harder. "I asked you a question. Let's hear you speak, man."

"I'm . . . looking for someone," Cray said. "A young man. Blond, about twenty or twenty-five. Wearing a t-shirt and blue jeans. He's got fair skin and dark eyes. I think he might have been in here not too long ago."

"What're you after this guy for? He steal your spaceship?" The others laughed, but Dogmeat's face remained serious. Another thunk of Cray's skull. "Come on, that was a joke. You're supposed to laugh."

"Please," Cray said. "Don't do that anymore."

"Do what? This?" Dogmeat thunked him on the point of his chin.

"Yes. Please don't do that anymore."

"Oh. Okay." Dogmeat smiled. "How about if I do this?" And he flung his half-full mug of beer into Cray's face. The liquid blinded Cray for a few seconds, then washed out of his mask and ran down his neck. The other One-Eyed Skulls howled with laughter and clapped Dogmeat on the back.

"I think I'd better be going." Cray started to get up, but Dogmeat's hand clamped to his shoulder and forced him down with ridiculous ease.

"Who are you supposed to be, man?" Dogmeat asked, feigning real interest. "Like . . . a big bad superhero or somethin'?"

"I'm nobo—" He stopped himself. They were watching and listening, smiling with gap-toothed smiles. And then Cray straightened up his shoulders, and it came out of him by instinct. "I'm the Green Falcon," he said.

199

There was a moment of stunned silence, except for that thunderous music. Then they laughed again, and the laughter swelled. But Dogmeat didn't laugh; his eyes narrowed, and when the laughter had faded he said, "Okay, Mr. Green Falcon sir. How about takin' that mask off and . . . like . . . let's see your secret identity." Cray didn't respond. Dogmeat leaned closer. "I *said*, Mr. Green Falcon sir, that I want you to take your mask off. Do it. *Now.*"

Cray was trembling. He clenched his fists in his lap. "I'm sorry. I can't do that."

Dogmeat smiled a savage smile. "If you won't, I will. Hand it over."

Cray shook his head. No matter what happened now, the die was cast. "No. I won't."

"Well," Dogmeat said softly, "I'm really sorry to hear that." And he grasped the front of Cray's tunic, lifted him bodily off the stool, twisted and threw him across a table eight feet away. Cray went over the table, crashed into a couple of chairs and sprawled to the floor. Stars and rockets fired in his brain. He got up on his knees, aware that Dogmeat was advancing toward him. Dogmeat's booted foot drew back, the kick aimed at the Green Falcon's face.

Chapter Five
THE STAR AND QUESTION MARK

A shriek like the demons of Hell singing Beastie Boys tunes came from the speakers. "Christ!" Dogmeat shouted, clapping his hands to his ears. He turned, and so did the other One-Eyed Skulls.

A figure stood over at the record's turntable near the stage, calmly scratching the tonearm back and forth across the platter. The Green Falcon pulled himself up to his feet, and stood shaking the explosions out of his head. The figure let the tonearm skid across the record with a last fingernails-on-chalkboard skreel, and then the speakers were silent.

"Let him be," she said, in a voice like velvet smoke.

The Green Falcon's eyes were clear now, and he could see her as well as the others did. She was tall — maybe six-two or possibly an inch above that — and her amazonian body was pressed into a tigerskin one-piece bathing suit. She wore black high heels, and her hair was dyed orange and cropped close to her head. She smiled a red-lipped smile, her teeth startlingly white against her ebony flesh.

"What'd you say, bitch?" Dogmeat challenged.

"Gracie!" the bartender said. "Keep out of it!"

She ignored him, her amber eyes fixed on Dogmeat. "Let him be," she repeated. "He hasn't done anything to you."

"Lord, Lord." Dogmeat shook his head with sarcastic wonder. "A talkin' female monkey! Hey, I ain't seen you dance yet! Hop up on that stage and shake that black ass!"

"Go play in somebody else's sandbox," Gracie told him. "Kiddie time's over."

"Damned right it is." Dogmeat's cheeks burned red, and he took a menacing step toward her. "Get up on that stage! Move your butt!"

She didn't budge.

Dogmeat was almost upon her. The Green Falcon looked around, said, "Excuse me," and lifted an empty beer mug off a table in front of a pie-eyed drunk. Then he cocked his arm back, took aim, and called out, "Hey, Mr. Dogmeat!"

The biker's head swivelled toward him, eyes flashing with anger.

The Green Falcon threw the beer mug, as cleanly as if it were a shotput on an Indiana summer day. It sailed through the air, and Dogmeat lifted his hand to ward it off but he was way too late. The mug hit him between the eyes, didn't shatter but made a satisfying clunking sound against his skull. He took two steps forward and one back, his eyes rolled to show the blood-shot whites, and he fell like a chopped-down sequoia.

"Sonofabitch!" the brown-bearded one said, more in surprise than anything else. Then his face darkened like a stormcloud and he started toward the Green Falcon with two other bikers right behind him.

The Green Falcon stood his ground. There was no point in running; his old legs would not get him halfway to the door before the bikers pulled him down. No, he had to stand there and take whatever was coming. He let them get within ten feet, and then he said, in a calm and steady voice, "Does you mother know where you are, son?"

Brown Beard stopped as if he'd run into an invisible wall. One of the others ran into him and bounced off. "*Huh?*"

"Your mother," the Green Falcon repeated. "Does she know where you are?"

"My . . . my mother? What's she got to do with this, man?"

"She gave birth to you and raised you, didn't she? Does she know where you are right now?" The Green Falcon waited, his heart hammering, but Brown Beard didn't answer. "How do you think your mother would feel if she could see you?"

"His mother wouldn't feel nothin'," another of them offered. "She's in a home for old sots up in Oxnard."

"You shut up!" Brown Beard said, turning on his companion. "She's not an old sot, man! She's just . . . like . . . a little sick. I'm gonna get her out of that place! You'll see!"

"Quit the jawin'!" a third biker said. "We gonna tear this green fruit apart or not?"

201

SILVER SCREAM

The Green Falcon stepped forward, and he didn't know what he was about to say but lines from old scripts were whirling through his recollection like moths through klieg lights. "Any son who loves his mother," he said, "is a true American, and I'm proud to call him friend." He held his hand out toward Brown Beard.

The other man stared at it, and blinked uncertainly. "Who . . . who the hell *are* you?"

"I'm the Green Falcon. Defender of the underdog. Righter of wrongs, and champion of justice." *That's not me talking,* he realized. *It's from* Night Calls the Green Falcon, *Chapter Five.* But he realized also that his voice sounded different, in a strange way. It was not the voice of an old man anymore; it was a sturdy, rugged voice, with a bass undertone as strong as a fist. It was a hero's voice, and it demanded respect.

No one laughed.

And the biker with the brown beard slid his hand into the Green Falcon's, and the Green Falcon gripped it hard, and said, "Walk tall and think tall, son."

At least for a few seconds, he had them. They were in a thrall of wonder, just like the little children who'd come to see him during the public relations tour in the summer of 1951, when he'd shaken their hands and told them to respect their elders, put up their toys, and do right: the simple secret of success. Those children had wanted to believe in him, so badly; and now in this biker's eyes there was that same glimmer — faint and faraway, yes — but as clear as a candle in the darkness. This was a little boy standing here, trapped in a grown-up skin. The Green Falcon nodded recognition, and when he relaxed his grip the biker didn't want to let go.

"I'm looking for a man whom I think is the Fliptop Killer," the Green Falcon told them. He described the blond man who'd escaped from the window of Julie Saufley's apartment. "Have any of you seen a man who fits that description?"

Brown Beard shook his head. None of the others offered information, either. Dogmeat moaned, starting to come around. "Where is he?" Dogmeat mumbled. "I'll rip his head off."

"Hey, this joint's about as much fun as a mortician's convention," one of the bikers said. "Women are ugly as hell, too. Let's hit the road."

"Yeah," another agreed. "Ain't nothin' happening' around here." He bent down to help haul Dogmeat up. Their leader was still dazed, his eyes roaming in circles. The bikers guided Dogmeat toward the door, but the brown-bearded one hesitated.

"I've heard of you before," he said. "Somewhere. Haven't I?"

"Yes," the Green Falcon answered. "I think you probably have."

The man nodded. Pitched his voice lower, so the others couldn't hear: "I used to have a big stack of Batman comics. Read 'em all the time. I used to think he was *real*, and I wanted to grow up just like him. Crazy, huh?"

"Not so crazy," the Green Falcon said.

The other man smiled slightly, a wistful smile. "I hope you find who you're lookin' for. Good luck." He started after his friends, and the Green Falcon said, "Do right."

And then they were gone, the sounds of their motorcycles roaring away. The Green Falcon glanced again at the bartender, still hoping for some information, but the man's face remained a blank.

"You want a beer, Greenie?" someone asked, and the Green Falcon turned to face the tall black go-go dancer.

"No, thank you. I've got to go." To where he didn't know, but the Grinderswitch was a dead end.

He had taken two steps toward the door when Gracie said, "I've seen him. The guy you're after." The Green Falcon abruptly stopped. "I know that face," Gracie went on. "He was in here maybe two, three hours ago."

"Do you know his name?"

"No. But I know where he lives."

His heart kicked. "Where?"

"Well . . . he might live there or he might not," she amended. She came closer to him, and he figured she was in her late twenties but it was hard to tell with all the makeup. "A motel on the Strip. The Palmetto. See, I used to . . . uh . . . work there. I was an escort." She flashed a quick warning glance at the bartender, as if she just dared him to crack wise. Then back to the Green Falcon again. "I used to see this guy hanging out around there. He comes in here maybe two or three times a week. Asked me out one time, but I wouldn't go."

"Why not?"

She shrugged. "Too white. Amazin' Grace doesn't have to go out with just anybody. I choose my own friends."

"But you remember seeing him at the Palmetto?"

"Yeah. Or at least somebody who fits that description. I'm not saying it's the same guy. Lots of creeps on the Strip, and those hot springs motels lure most of them one time or another." She licked her lower lip; the shine of excitement was in her eyes. "You really think he's the Fliptop?"

"I do. Thank you for telling me, Miss." He started toward the door, but again her husky voice stopped him.

"Hey, hold on! The Palmetto's about ten or twelve blocks east. You got a car?"

"No."

"Neither do I, but there's a cab stand down the street. I'm just clocking out. Right, Tony?"

"You're the star," the bartender said, with a wave of his hand.

"You want some company, Greenie? I mean . . ." She narrowed her eyes. "You're not a crazy yourself, are you?" Gracie laughed at her own question. "Hell, sure you are! You've *got* to be! But I'm heading that way, and I'll show you the place if you want. For free."

"Why would you want to help me?" he asked.

Gracie looked wounded. "I've got civic pride, that's why! Hell, just because I strut my butt in this joint five nights a week doesn't mean I'm not a humanitarian!"

The Green Falcon considered that, and nodded. Amazin' Grace was obviously intelligent, and she probably enjoyed the idea of a hunt. He figured he could use all the help he could get. "All right. I'll wait while you get dressed."

She frowned. "I *am* dressed, fool! Let's go!"

They left the Grinderswitch and started walking east along the boulevard. Gracie had a stride that threatened to leave him behind, and his green suit drew just as many doubletakes as her lean ebony body in its tigerskin wrapping. The cab stand was just ahead, and a cab was there, engine running. A kid in jeans and a black leather jacket leaned against the hood; he was rail-thin, his head shaved bald except for a tuft of hair in the shape of a question mark on his scalp.

"You got a fare, kid," Gracie said as she slid her mile-long legs in. "Move it!"

The kid said, "I'm waitin' for —"

"Your wait's over," Gracie interrupted. "Come on, we don't have all night!"

The kid shrugged, his eyes vacant and disinterested, and got behind the wheel. As soon as the Green Falcon was in, the kid shot away from the curb with a shriek of burning rubber and entered the flow of westbound traffic.

"We want to go to the Palmetto Motel," Gracie said. "You know where that is?"

"Sure."

"Well, you're going the wrong way. And start your meter, unless we're going to ride for free."

"Oh. Yeah." The meter's arm came down, and the mechanism started ticking. "You want to go east, huh?" And without warning he spun the wheel violently, throwing the Green Falcon and Gracie up against the cab's side, and the vehicle careened in a tight U-turn that narrowly missed a collision with a BMW. Horns blared and tires screeched, but the kid swerved into the eastbound lane as if he owned Hollywood Boulevard. And the Green Falcon saw a motorcycle cop turn on his blue light and start after them, at the same time as a stout Hispanic man ran out of a Chock Full 'O Nuts coffee shop, yelling and gesturing frantically.

"Must be a caffeine fit," Gracie commented. She heard the siren's shrill note and glanced back. "Smart move, kid. You just got a blue-tailed fly on your ass."

The kid laughed, sort of. The Green Falcon's gut tightened; he'd already seen the little photograph on the dashboard that identified the cab driver. It was a stout Hispanic face.

"Guy asked me to watch his cab while he ran in to pick up some coffee," the kid said, with a shrug. "Gave me a buck, too." He looked in the rearview mirror. The motorcycle cop was waving him over. "What do you want me to, folks?"

The Green Falcon had decided, just that fast. The police might be looking for him since he'd left the apartment building, and if they saw him like this they wouldn't understand. They'd think he was just a crazy old man out for a joyride through fantasy, and they'd take the Green Falcon away from him.

And if anyone could find the Fliptop Killer and bring him to justice, the Green Falcon could.

He said, "Lose him."

The kid looked back, and now his eyes were wide and thrilled. He grinned. "Roger willco," he said, and pressed his foot to the accelerator.

The cab's engine roared, the vehicle surged forward with a power that pressed the Green Falcon and Gracie into their seats, and the kid whipped around a Mercedes and then up onto the curb where people screamed and leaped aside. The cab, its exhaust pipe spitting fire, rocketed toward the plate glass window of a lingerie store.

Gracie gave a stunned little cry, gripped the Green Falcon's hand with knuckle-cracking force, and the Green Falcon braced for impact.

Chapter Six
HANDFUL OF STRAWS

The kid spun the wheel to the left, and the cab's fender knocked sparks off a brick wall as it grazed past the window. Then he veered quickly to the right, clipped away two parking meters, and turned the cab off Hollywood onto El Centro Avenue. He floorboarded the gas pedal.

"Let me outta here!" Gracie shouted, and she grasped the door's handle but the cab's speedometer needle was already nosing past forty. She decided she didn't care for a close acquaintance with asphalt, and anyway the Green Falcon had her other hand and wasn't going to let her jump.

The motorcycle cop was following, the blue light spinning and the siren getting louder. The kid tapped the brakes and swerved in front of a gasoline truck, through an alley and behind a row of buildings, then back onto El Centro and speeding southward. The motorcycle cop came out of the alley and got back on their tail, again closing the gap between them.

"What's your name?" the Green Falcon asked.

"Me? Ques," he answered. "Because of —"

"I can guess why. Ques, this is very important." The Green Falcon leaned forward, his fingers clamped over the seat in front of him. "I don't want the policeman to stop us. I'm —" Again, lines from the scripts danced through his mind. "I'm on a mission," he said. "I don't have time for the police. Do you understand?"

Ques nodded. "No," he said. "But if you want to give the cop a run, I'm your man." The speedometer's needle was almost to sixty, and Ques was weaving in and out of traffic like an Indy racer. "Hold on," he said.

Gracie screamed.

Ques suddenly veered to the left, almost grazing the fenders of cars just released from a red light at the intersection of El Centro and Fountain Avenue. Outraged horns hooted, but then the cab had cleared the intersection and was speeding away. Ques took a hard right onto Gordon Street, another left on Lexington and then pulled into an alley behind a Taco Bell. He drew up close to a dumpster and cut the headlights.

Gracie found her voice: "Where the hell did you learn to drive? The demolition derby?"

Ques got himself turned around in the seat so he could look at his passengers. He smiled, and the smile made him almost handsome. "Close. I was third unit stunt driver in *Beverly Hills Cop II*. This was a piece of cake."

"I'm getting out right here." Gracie reached for the door's handle. "You two never saw me before, okay?"

"Wait." The Green Falcon grasped her elbow. The motorcycle cop was just passing, going east on Lexington. The siren had been turned off, and the blue light faded as he went on.

"Not in the clear yet," Ques said. "There'll be a lot of shellheads looking for us. We'd better sit here a while." He grinned at them. "Fun, huh?"

"Like screwing in a thornpatch." Gracie opened the door. "I'm gone."

"Please don't go," the Green Falcon said. "I need you."

"You need a good shrink is what you need. Man, I must've been crazy myself to get into this! You thinking you could track down the Fliptop!" She snorted. "Green Falcon, my ass!"

"I need you," he repeated firmly. "If you've got connections at the Palmetto, maybe you can find someone who's seen him."

"The Fliptop?" Ques asked, his interest perked again. "What about that sonofabitch?"

"I saw him tonight," the Green Falcon said. "He killed a friend of mine, and Grace knows where he might be."

206

"I didn't say that, man. I said I knew where I'd seen a guy who looked like the guy who's been coming into the Grinderswitch. That's a big difference."

"Please stay. Help me. It's the only lead I've got."

Gracie looked away from him. The door was halfway open and she had one leg out. "Nobody cares about anybody else in this city," she said. "Why should I stick around and get my ass in jail . . . or *worse?*"

"I'll protect you," he answered.

She laughed. "Oh, yeah! A guy in a green freaksuit's going to protect me! Wow, my mind feels so much better! Let me go." He hesitated, then did as she said. She sat on the seat's edge, about to get out. About to. But a second ticked past, and another, and still she sat there. "I live on Olympic Boulevard," she said. "Man, I am a *long* way from home."

"Green Falcon, huh?" Ques asked. "That what you call yourself?"

"Yes. That's . . ." A second or two of indecision. "That's who I am."

"You got information about the Fliptop, why don't you give it to the cops?"

"Because . . ." *Why not, indeed?* he asked himself. "Because the Fliptop's killed nine times, and he's going to kill again. Maybe tonight, even. The police aren't even close to finding him. *We* are."

"No, we're not!" Gracie objected. "Just because I saw a guy at a motel a few times doesn't mean he's the Fliptop! You've got a handful of straws, man!"

"Maybe I do. But it's worth going to the Palmetto to find out, isn't it?"

"You just don't want to go to the cops because you're afraid they'll pitch you into the nuthouse," Gracie said, and the way the Green Falcon settled back against the seat told her she'd hit the target. She was silent for a moment, watching him. "That's right, isn't it?"

"Yes," he said, because he knew it was. "I . . ." He hesitated, but they were listening and he decided to tell it as it had been, a long time ago. "I've spent some time in a sanitarium. Not recently. Back in the early 'fifties. I had a nervous breakdown. It . . . wasn't a nice place."

"You used to be somebody, for real?" Ques inquired.

"The Green Falcon. I starred in serials." The kid's face showed no recognition. "They used to show them on Saturday afternoons," Cray went on. "Chapter by chapter. Well, I guess both of you are too young to remember." He clasped his hands together in his lap, his back bowed. "Yes, I used to be somebody. For real."

"So how come you went off your rocker?" Gracie asked. "If you were a star and all, I mean?"

He sighed softly. "When I was a young man I thought the whole world was one big Indiana. That's where I'm from. Some talent scouts came through my town one day, and somebody told them about me. Big athlete,

207

they said. Won all the medals you can think of. Outstanding young American and all that." His mouth twitched into a bitter smile. "Corny, but I guess it was true. Heck, the world was pretty corny back then. But it wasn't such a bad place. Anyway, I came to Hollywood and I started doing the serials. I had a little talent. But I saw things . . ." He shook his head. "Things they didn't even know about in Indiana. It seemed as if I was on another world, and I was never going to find my way back home. And everything happened so fast . . . it just got away from me, I guess. I was a star — whatever that means — and I was working hard and making money, but . . . Cray Boomershine was dying. I could feel him dying, a little bit more every day. And I wanted to bring him back, but he was just an Indiana kid and I was a Hollywood star. The Green Falcon, I mean. Me. Cray Flint. Does that make any sense to you?"

"Not a bit," Gracie said. "Hell, *everybody* wants to be a star! What was wrong with you?"

His fingers twined together, and the old knuckles worked. "They wanted me to do a public relations tour. I said I would. So they sent me all across the country . . . dressed up like this. And the children came out to see me, and they touched my cape and they asked for my autograph and they said they wanted to grow up just like me. Those faces . . . they gave off such an innocent light." He was silent, thinking, and he drew a deep breath and continued because he could not turn back. "It was in Watertown, South Dakota. April 26th, 1951. I went on stage at the Watertown Palace theater, right after they showed the tenth and final chapter of 'Night Calls the Green Falcon'. That place was packed with kids, and all of them were laughing and happy." He closed his eyes, his hands gripped tightly together. "There was a fire. It started in a storeroom, in the basement." He smelled acrid smoke, felt the heat of flames on his face. "It spread so *fast*. And some of the kids . . . some of them even thought it was part of the show. Oh God . . . oh my God . . . the walls were on fire, and children were being crushed as they tried to get out . . . and I heard them screaming. Green Falcon! Green Falcon!" His eyes opened, stared without seeing. "But the Green Falcon couldn't save them, and thirty-one children died in that fire. He couldn't save them. Couldn't." He looked at Ques, then to Gracie and back again, and his eyes were wet and sunken in the mask's slits. "When I came out of the sanitarium, the studio let me keep the costume. For a job well done, they said. But there weren't going to be any more Green Falcon serials. Anyway, everybody was watching television, and that was that."

Neither Ques nor Gracie spoke for a moment. Then Gracie said, "We're going to take you home. Where do you live?"

"Please." He put his hand over hers. "I can find the Fliptop Killer. I know I can."

"You *can't*. Give it up."

208

NIGHT CALLS THE GREEN FALCON

"What would it hurt?" Ques asked her. "Just to drive to that motel, I mean. Maybe he's right." He held up his hand before she could object. "*Maybe.* We could drive there and you could ask around, and then we'll take him home. How about it?"

"It's crazy," she said. "And *I'm* crazy." But then she pulled her leg back in and shut the door. "Let's try it."

The Palmetto Motel was a broken-down stucco dump between Normandie and Mariposa, on the cheap end of Hollywood Boulevard. Ques pulled the cab into the trash-strewn parking lot, and he spoke his first impression: "Place is a crack gallery, folks." He saw shadowy faces peering through the blinds of second-floor windows, and blue firelight played across a wall. "Bullet holes in a door over there." He motioned toward it. "From here on we watch our asses." He stopped the cab next to a door marked OFFICE and cut the engine.

"It's sure enough gone to Hell since I worked here," Gracie said. "Nothing like addicts to junk a place up." Not far away stood the hulk of a car that looked as if it had been recently set afire. "Well, let's see what we can see." She got out, and so did the Green Falcon. Ques stayed behind the wheel, and when Gracie motioned him to come on he said nervously, "I'll give you moral support."

"Thanks, jerkoff. Hey, hold on!" she said, because the Green Falcon was already striding toward the Office door. He grasped the knob, turned it, and the door opened with a jingle of little bells. He stepped into a room where lights from the boulevard cut through slanted blinds, and the air was thick with the mingled odors of marijuana, a dirty carpet, and . . . what else was it?

Spoiled meat, he realized.

And that was when something stood up from a corner and bared its teeth.

The Green Falcon stopped. He was looking at a stocky, black-and-white pit bull, its eyes bright with the prospect of violence.

"Oh shit," Gracie whispered.

Soundlessly, the pit bull leaped at the Green Falcon, its jaws opened for a bone-crushing bite.

Chapter Seven
THE WATCHMAN

The Green Falcon stepped back, colliding with Gracie. The pit bull's body came flying toward him, reached the end of its chain and its teeth

209

clacked together where a vital member of the Green Falcon's anatomy had been a second before. Then the dog was yanked back to the wall, but it immediately regained its balance and lunged again. The Green Falcon stood in front of Gracie, picked up a chair to ward the beast off, but again the chain stopped the pit bull short of contact. As the animal thrashed against its collar, a figure rose up from behind the counter and pulled back the trigger on a double-barrelled shotgun.

"Put it down," the man told the Green Falcon. He motioned with the shotgun. "Do it or I swear to God I'll blow your head off." The man's voice was high and nervous, and the Green Falcon slowly put the chair down. The pit bull was battling with its chain, trying to slide its head out of the collar. "Ain't nobody gonna rob me again," the man behind the counter vowed. Sweat glistened on his gaunt face. "You punks gonna learn some respect, you hear me?"

"Lester?" Gracie said. The man's frightened eyes ticked toward her. "Lester Dent? It's me." She took a careful step forward, where the light could show him who she was. "Sabra Jones." The Green Falcon stared at her. She said, "You remember me, don't you Lester?"

"Sabra? That really you?" The man blinked, reached into a drawer and brought out a pair of round-lensed spectacles. He put them on, and the tension on his face immediately eased. "Sabra! Well, why didn't you say so?" He uncocked the shotgun and said, "Down, Bucky!" to the pit bull. The animal stopped its thrashing, but it still regarded the Green Falcon with hungry eyes.

"This is a friend of mine, Lester. The Green Falcon." She said it with all seriousness.

"Hi." Lester lowered the shotgun and leaned it behind the counter. "Sorry I'm a little jumpy. Things have changed around here since you left. Lot of freaks in the neighborhood, and you can't be too careful."

"I guess not." Gracie glanced at a couple of bullet holes in the wall. Flies were buzzing around the scraps of hamburger in Bucky's feedbowl. "Used to be a decent joint. How come you're still hanging around here?"

Lester shrugged. He was a small man, weighed maybe a hundred and thirty pounds, and he wore a Captain America t-shirt. "I crave excitement. What can I say?" He looked her up and down with true appreciation. "Life's being pretty good to you, huh?"

"I can't complain. Much. Lester, my friend and I are looking for somebody who used to hang around here." She described the man. "I remember he used to like Dolly Winslow. Do you know the guy I mean?"

"I think I do, but I'm not sure. I've seen a lot of 'em."

"Yeah, I know, but this is important. Do you have any idea what the guy's name might have been, or have you seen him around here lately?"

"No, I haven't seen him for awhile, but I know what his name was." He grinned, gap-toothed. "John Smith. That's what all their names were." He glanced at the Green Falcon. "Can you breathe inside that thing?"

"The man we're looking for is the Fliptop Killer," the Green Falcon said, and Lester's grin cracked. "Do you know where we can find Dolly Winslow?"

"She went to Vegas," Gracie told him. "Changed her name, the last I heard. No telling where she is now."

"You're lookin' for the Fliptop Killer?" Lester asked. "You a cop or somethin'?"

"No. I've got . . . a personal interest."

Lester drummed his fingers on the scarred countertop and thought for a moment. "The Fliptop, huh? Guy's a mean one. I wouldn't want to cross his path, no sir."

"Anybody still around who used to hang out here?" Gracie asked. "Like Jellyroll? Or that weird guy who played the flute?"

"That weird guy who played the flute just signed a million-dollar contract at Capitol Records," Lester said. "We should all be so weird. Jellyroll's living uptown somewhere. Pearly's got a boutique on the Strip, makin' money hand over fist. Bobby just drifted away." He shook his head. "We had us a regular club here, didn't we?"

"So everybody's cleared out?"

"Well . . . not everybody. There's me, and the Watchman."

"The Watchman?" The Green Falcon came forward, and the pit bull glowered at him but didn't attack. "Who's that?"

"Crazy old guy, lives down in the basement," Lester said. "Been here since the place was new. You won't get anything out of him, though."

"Why not?"

"The Watchman doesn't speak. Never has, as far as I know. He goes out and walks, day and night, but he won't tell you where he's been. You remember him, don't you, Sabra?"

"Yeah. Dolly told me she saw him walking over on the beach at Santa Monica one day, and Bobby saw him in downtown L.A. All he does is walk."

"*Can* he speak?" the Green Falcon asked.

"No telling," Lester said. "Whenever I've tried talking' to him, he just sits like a wall."

"So why do you call him the Watchman?"

"You know the way, Sabra." Lester motioned toward the door. "Why don't you show him?"

"You don't want to see the Watchman," she said. "Forget it. He's out of his mind. Like me for getting into this. See you around, Lester." She started out, and Lester said, "Don't be such a stranger."

Outside, Gracie continued walking to the cab. The Green Falcon caught up with her. "I'd like to see the Watchman. What would it hurt?"

"It would waste my time and yours. Besides, he's probably not even here. Like I said, he walks all the time." She reached the cab, where Ques was waiting nervously behind the wheel.

"Let's go," Ques said. "Cars have been going in and out. Looks like a major deal's about to go down."

"Hold it." The Green Falcon placed his hand against the door before she could open it. "If the Watchman's been here so long, he might know something abut the man we're looking for. It's worth asking, isn't it?"

"No. He doesn't speak to *anybody*. Nobody knows where he came from, or who is he, and he likes it that way." She glanced around, saw several figures standing in a second-floor doorway. Others were walking across the lot toward a black Mercedes. "I don't like the smell around here. The faster we get out, the better."

The Green Falcon stepped back, and let her get into the cab. But he didn't go around to the other door. "I'm going to talk to the Watchman," he said. "How do I get to the basement?"

She paused, her eyelids at half-mast. "You're a stubborn fool, aren't you? There's the way down." She pointed at a door near the office. "You go through there, you're on your own."

"We shouldn't leave him here," Ques said. "We ought to stay —"

"Shut up, cueball. Lot of bad dudes around here, and I'm not getting shot for anybody." She smiled grimly. "Not even the Green Falcon. Good luck."

"Thanks for your help. I hope you —"

"Can it," she interrupted. "Move out, Ques."

He said, "Sorry," to the Green Falcon, put the cab into reverse and backed out of the lot. Turned left across the boulevard, and headed west.

And the Green Falcon stood alone.

He waited, hoping they'd come back. They didn't. Finally, he turned and walked to the door that led to the Palmetto Motel's basement, and he reached for the knob.

But somebody came out of another room before he could open the door, and the Green Falcon saw the flash of metal.

"Hey, *amigo*," the man said, and flame shot from the barrel of the small pistol he'd just drawn.

Chapter Eight
YOURS TRULY

The Hispanic man lit his cigarette with the flame, then put the pistol-shaped lighter back into his pocket. "What kinda party you dressed up for?"

NIGHT CALLS THE GREEN FALCON

The Green Falcon didn't answer. His nerves were still jangling, and he wasn't sure he could speak even if he tried.

"You lookin' for a score or not?" the man persisted.

"I'm . . . looking for the Watchman," he managed to say.

"Oh. Yeah, I should've figured you were. Didn't know the old creep had any friends." Somebody called out, "Chico! Get your ass over here, *now!*" The man sneered, "When I'm ready!" and then he sauntered toward the group of others who stood around the Mercedes. The Green Falcon went through the door and into darkness.

He stood on a narrow staircase, tried to find a lightswitch but could not. Two steps down and his right hand found a lightbulb overhead, with a dangling cord. He pulled it, and the lightbulb illuminated with a dim yellow glow. The concrete stairs descended beyond the light's range, the walls made of cracked gray cinderblock. The Green Falcon went down, into a place that smelled as damp and musty as a long-closed crypt. Halfway down the steps, he halted.

There had been a sound of movement, over on the right. "Anyone there?" he asked. No answer, and now the sound had ceased. Rats, he decided. Big ones. He came to the bottom of the stairs, darkness surrounding him. Again he felt for a lightswitch, again with no reward. The smell was putrid: wet and decaying paper, he thought. He took a few steps forward, reaching out to both sides; his right arm brushed what felt like a stack of magazines or newspapers. And then the fingers of his left hand found a wall and a lightswitch, and when he flicked it a couple of naked bulbs came on.

He looked around at the Watchman's domain.

The basement — a huge, cavernous chamber — might have put the periodicals department of the L.A. Public Library to shame. Neat stacks of books, newspapers, and magazines were piled against the walls and made corridors across the basement, their turns and windings as intricate as a carefully-constructed maze. The Green Falcon had never seen anything like it before; there had to be thousands — no, hundreds of thousands — of items down here. Maps of Los Angeles, Hollywood, Santa Monica, Beverly Hills and other municipalities were mounted on the walls, tinged with green mold but otherwise unmarred. Here stood a stack of telephone books six feet tall, there were multiple stacks of old *Hollywood Reporters*. The place was an immense repository of information, and the Green Falcon was stunned because he'd never expected anything like this. A bank of battered filing cabinets stood against one wall, more newspapers stacked on top of them. There had to be thirty years of accumulated magazines and papers just in this part of the basement alone, and the chamber stretched the length of the motel. He couldn't restrain his curiosity; he went to one of the filing cabinets, which had precise little alphabet letters identifying their contents, and opened a drawer. Inside were hundreds of notebook pages covered with what appeared to be license-plate numbers and the make and color of the cars that carried them, all written in an elegant, almost calligraphic hand-writing. Another drawer held lists of items found in various trashcans at scores of locations and dates. A third drawer bulged with pages that seemed to record the routes of pedestrians through the city streets, how long to the second they stayed in this or that store or restaurant, and so forth.

And it dawned on the Green Falcon that this was exactly what the Watchman did: he watched, recorded, filed away, all to the service of some bizarre inner logic, and he'd been doing it for years.

Something moved, back beyond the room in which the Green Falcon stood. There was a quick rustling sound of papers being disturbed . . . then silence. The Green Falcon wound his way through the maze, found another lightswitch that illuminated two more bulbs at the rear of the basement. Still more periodicals, maps and filing cabinets stood in that area of the basement as well, but there was a cot, too, and a desk with a blue blotter.

And a man in a long, dirty olive coat, huddled up with his back wedged into a corner and his Peter Lorre eyes looked as if they were about to pop from their sockets.

"Hello," the Green Falcon said quietly. The man, gray-bearded and almost emaciated, trembled and hugged his knees. The Green Falcon walked closer and stopped, because the Watchman was shaking so hard he might have a heart attack. "I've come to talk to you."

The Watchman's mouth opened in his sallow face, gave a soft gasp and closed again.

"I'm looking for someone you might help me find." The Green Falcon described the man. "I think he might be the Fliptop Killer, and I understand a man fitting that description used to come around here. He might have been friends with a girl named Dolly Winslow. Do you know the man I'm talking about?"

Still no response. The Watchman looked as if he were about to jump out of his skin.

"Don't be afraid. I'm the Green Falcon, and I wish you no harm."

The Watchman was so terrified there were tears in his eyes. The Green Falcon started to speak again, but he realized the futility of it. The Watch-man was a human packrat, and Amazin' Grace had been right: there was nothing to be gained here.

He almost took off his mask and threw it aside in disgust. What had made him think he could track down the Fliptop? he asked himself. A red matchbook from a dead girl's hand? A glimpse of the killer's face, and an ill-founded yearning for a counterfeit past? It was ridiculous! He was standing in a motel's dank basement with a drug deal going on over his head, and he'd better get out of here as fast as he could before he got his throat cut. "I'm sorry to have bothered you," he told the Watchman, and he started walking toward the stairs. He heard the Watchman gasp and crawl across the floor, and he looked back to see the man rummaging with frantic speed inside an old mildewed cardboard box.

214

NIGHT CALLS THE GREEN FALCON

This is no place for me, the Green Falcon realized. In fact, there was no place at all left for the Green Falcon, but Cray Flint's mop was waiting at the Burger King.

He kept going to the stairs, burdened with age.

"Dear Davy," the voice rang out. "I am sorry I can't come to Center City this summer, but I'm working on a new mystery . . ."

The Green Falcon stopped.

". . . and I'm very busy. I just wanted you to know that I appreciate your letter, and I like to hear from my fans very much. Enclosed is something I want you to have, and I hope you'll wear it with pride. Remember to respect your elders, put up your toys, and do right . . ."

He turned, his heart pounding.

"Yours truly, The Green Falcon." And the Watchman looked up, smiling, from the yellowed, many-times-folded letter in his hands. "You signed it," he said. "Right here. Remember?" He held it up. Then scrambled to the box again, rummaged and came up with an old wallet covered in multi-colored Indian beads. He flipped it open and showed what was pinned inside. "I kept it, all this time. See?"

The plastic button said THE GREEN FALCONEERS. "I see." Cray's voice cracked.

"I did right," Davy said. "I always did right."

"Yes." The Green Falcon nodded. "I know you did."

"We moved from Center City." Davy stood up; he was at least six inches taller than the Green Falcon. "My dad got a new job, when I was twelve. That was —" He hesitated, trying to think. "A long time ago," he decided. A frown slowly settled on his deeply-lined face. "What happened to you?"

"I got old," the Green Falcon said.

"Yes sir. Me, too." His frown started to slip away, then took hold again. "Am I still a Falconeer?"

"Oh, yes. That's a forever thing."

"I thought it was," Davy said, and his smile came back.

"You've got a nice collection down here." The Green Falcon walked amid the stacks. "I guess gathering all this takes a lot of time."

"I don't mind. It's my job."

"Your job?"

"Sure. Everybody's got a job. Mine is watching things, and writing them down. Keeping them, too."

"Have you actually read all these papers and magazines?"

"Yes sir. Well . . . most of them," he amended. "And I remember what I read, too. I've got . . . like . . . a Kodak in my brain."

Did he mean a photographic memory? the Green Falcon wondered. If so, might he recall the man Gracie remembered? "Davy," he said, in his heroic voice, "I've come to you because I need your help. I'm trying to find the Fliptop Killer. Have you heard of him?"

215

SILVER SCREAM

Davy nodded without hesitation.

"Can you think of a man like the one I described? A man who was a friend of —"

"Dolly Winslow," Davy finished for him. "Yes sir. I remember him. I never liked him, either. He laughed at people when he didn't think they were looking."

So far so good. The Green Falcon felt sweat on the back of his neck. "I want you to concentrate very hard, like a good Falconeer. Did you ever hear the man's name?"

Davy rubbed his mouth with the back of his hand, and his eyes took on a steely glint. He walked to a filing cabinet, bent down and opened the bottom drawer. Looked through dozens of envelopes. And then he pulled one of them out, and he brought it to the Green Falcon. On it Davy had written: 23. "Dolly's room," he said. "He cleaned his wallet out in her trash can one night."

The Green Falcon went to the desk and spilled the envelope's contents out on the blotter. There was a torn-open Trojans wrapper, two dried-up sticks of Doublemint gum, a few cash register receipts, a ticket stub to a Lakers game, and . . .

"His name's Rod Bowers. It's on the library card," Davy said. "His address, too."

The library card had been torn into quarters, but Davy had taped it back together again. And there was the name and address: RODNEY E. BOWERS, 1416 D Jericho Street, Santa Monica.

"That was over a year ago, though. He might not be there now," Davy said.

The Green Falcon's hands were shaking. Davy had taped together another piece of paper: a receipt that had been torn into many fragments. On that receipt was the name of a business: The House of Blades. On December 20th, 1986, Rodney Bowers had bought himself a Christmas present of a John Wayne Commemorative Hunting knife.

"Did I do right?" Davy asked, peering over the Green Falcon's shoulder.

"You sure did, son." He grasped the younger man's arm. "You're . . ." He said the first thing that came to mind: "The number one Falconeer. I have to go, now. I've got a job to do." He started striding, his pace quick, toward the stairs.

"Green Falcon, sir?" Davy called, and he paused. "I'll be here, if you ever need my help again."

"I'll remember," the Green Falcon answered, and he climbed the stairs with the taped-together library card and the House of Blades receipt gripped in his hand.

He went through the door into the parking-lot — and instantly heard someone shouting in Spanish. Somebody else was hollering from the second-floor, and there were other angry voices. The man named Chico was standing next to the Mercedes, and suddenly he drew a pistol — not a cigarette-

216

lighter this time, but a .45 automatic. He shouted out a curse and began firing into the Mercedes, glass from the windshield exploding into the air. At the same time, two men got out of another car, flung themselves flat on the pavement, and started spraying Chico with gunfire. Chico's body danced and writhed, the .45 going off into the air.

"Kill 'em!" somebody yelled from the second-floor. Machine-gun fire erupted, and bullets ricocheted off the concrete in a zigzagging line past the Green Falcon.

Oh my God! Cray thought. And he realized he'd come out of the basement into the middle of a drug deal gone bad.

The two men on the pavement kept firing. Now figures were sprinting across the parking-lot, shooting at the men on the second-floor. Machine-gun bullets cut one of them down, and he fell in a twitching heap. The Green Falcon backed up, hit the wall and stayed there — and then a man in a dark suit turned toward him, a smoking Uzi machine-gun in his hand, his face sparkling with the sweat of terror. He lifted the weapon to spray a burst at the Green Falcon.

Chapter Nine
HELL OR HIGH WATER

A black-and-white streak shot across the parking-lot, and the pit bull hit the gunman like a miniature locomotive. The man screamed and went down, the Uzi firing an arc of tracers into the sky. And Lester ran past, stopped almost in front of the Green Falcon, fired a shotgun blast at another man and then skidded on his belly behind the protection of a car.

The Green Falcon ran toward the street — and was almost struck by a cab that whipped into the lot with a shriek of burning rubber.

Ques hit the brake, and Gracie shouted, "Come on, fool!" as she threw the door open. The Green Falcon heard a bullet hiss past his head, and then he grasped the door and hung on as Ques reversed out of the lot and sped away on Hollywood.

Gracie pulled the Green Falcon in, and they got the door closed but Ques still kept a leaden foot on the accelerator. "Slow down!" she told him. "We don't want the cops stopping us!" He didn't respond, and she slapped him on the question mark. "SLOW DOWN!"

Ques did, but only by a little. "They had guns," he said shakily. "*Real* guns!"

"What'd you expect drug dealers to carry? Slingshots?" She looked at the Green Falcon. "You in one piece?" He nodded, his eyes huge behind his

217

mask. "We were circling the block, waiting for you to come out. We figured you'd never get out of this neighborhood alive. We were almost right, huh?"

"Yes," he croaked.

"Welcome to the big city. You find the Watchman?"

"I did." He drew a couple of deep breaths, could still smell the gunsmoke. "And something else, too." He gave the library card to Ques. "That's where we're going. I think it's the Fliptop Killer's name and address."

"Not *that* again!" Gracie protested. "Man, we're taking you home!"

"No. We're going to Santa Monica. You don't have to get out of the cab if you don't want to — in fact, I'd rather you didn't. But I'm going to find the Fliptop, with you or without you."

"It'll be without me, all right," she answered, but the way he'd said that let her know he was through talking about it. The man had a mission, and he was going to do it come hell or high water. She settled back into her seat, muttering, and Ques turned toward the Santa Monica Freeway.

The address was near the beach, so close they could smell the sea. The building was dark-bricked, one of those old Art Deco places that probably used to be a hotel when Santa Monica was young. Ques pulled the cab to a halt in front of it and cut the engine.

"I want both of you to stay here," the Green Falcon said. "I'm going in alone." He started to get out, but Gracie caught his arm.

"Hey, listen. If the Fliptop's really in there, this is the time to call the cops. No joke."

"I don't know that he's in there. It's an old library card; he might have moved. But if he's there, I've got to see his face for myself. Then we can call the police."

"She's right," Ques told him. "Listen, it's crazy to go in there. You don't have a gun or anything."

"The Green Falcon," he said adamantly, "never carries a gun."

"Yeah, and the Green Falcon's only got one life, fool!" Gracie didn't release her grip. "Playtime's over. I mean it. This isn't some old serial, this is real life. You know what reality is?"

"Yes, I do." He turned the full wattage of his gaze on her. "The reality is that . . . I think I'd rather die as the Green Falcon than live as an old man with a screwed-up bladder and a book of memories. I want to walk tall, just once more. Is that so terrible?"

"It's nuts," she answered. "And *you're* nuts."

"So I am. I'm going." He pulled loose from her and got out of the cab. He was scared, but not as much as he thought he'd be. It wasn't as bad as indigestion, really. And then he went up the front steps into the building, and he checked the row of mailboxes in the alcove.

The one for apartment D had BOWERS on it.

Apartments A, B, and C were on the first floor. He climbed the stairs, aided by a red-shaded light fixture on the wall, and stood before Apartment D's door.

NIGHT CALLS THE GREEN FALCON

He started to knock. Stopped his hand, the fist clenched. A thrill of fear coursed through him. He stood there, facing the door, and he didn't know if he could do it or not. He wasn't the Green Falcon; there was no such entity, not really. It was all a fiction. But Julie's death was not a fiction, and neither was what he'd been through tonight to reach this door. The sane thing was to back off, go down those stairs, get to a phone and call the police. Of course it was.

He heard a car's horn blare a quick tattoo. The cab, he thought. Ques, urging him to come back?

He knocked at the door, and waited. His heart had lodged in his throat. He tensed for a voice, or the sudden opening of the door.

The stairs creaked.

He heard the cab's horn again. This time Ques was leaning on it, and suddenly the Green Falcon knew why.

He turned, in awful slow-motion, and saw the shadow looming on the wall.

And there he was: the young blond, dark-eyed man who'd slashed Julie's throat. Coming up the staircase, step by step, not yet having seen the Green Falcon. But he would, at any second, and each step brought them closer.

The Green Falcon didn't move. The killer's weight made the risers moan, and he was smiling slightly — perhaps, the Green Falcon thought, musing over the feel of the blade piercing Julie's flesh.

And then the Fliptop Killer looked up, saw the Green Falcon at the top of the stairs, and stopped.

They stared at each other, standing not quite an arm's length apart. The killer's dark eyes were startled, and in them the Green Falcon saw a glint of fear.

"I've found you," the Green Falcon said.

The Fliptop Killer reached to his back, his hand a blur. It returned with the bright steel of the hunting knife, taken from a sheath that must fit down at his waistband. He moved fast, like an animal, and the Green Falcon saw the blade rising to strike him in the throat or chest.

"*It's him!*" Gracie shouted, as she burst into the alcove and to the foot of the steps.

The killer looked around at her — and it was the Green Falcon's turn to move fast. He grasped the man's wrist and struck him hard in the jaw with his right fist, and he felt one of his knuckles break but the killer toppled backward down the stairs.

The man caught the railing before he'd tumbled to the bottom, and he still had hold of the knife. A thread of blood spilled from his split lower lip, his eyes dazed from a bang of his skull against a riser. The Green Falcon was coming down the steps after him, and the Fliptop Killer struggled up and backed away.

SILVER SCREAM

"Watch out!" the Green Falcon yelled as Gracie tried to grab the man's knife. The killer swung at her, but she jumped back and the blade narrowly missed her face. But she had courage, and she wasn't about to give up; she darted in again, clutching his arm to keep the knife from another slash. The Green Falcon tensed to leap at the man, but suddenly the killer struck Gracie in the face with his left fist and she staggered back against the wall. Just that fast, the man fled toward the front door.

The Green Falcon stopped at Gracie's side. Her nose was bleeding and she looked about to pass out. She said, "Get the bastard," and the Green Falcon took off in pursuit.

Out front, the Fliptop Killer ran to the parked cab. Ques tried to fight him off, but a slash of the blade across Ques' shoulder sprayed blood across the inside of the windshield; the Fliptop Killer looked up, saw the man in the green suit and cape coming after him. He hauled Ques out of the cab and leaped behind the wheel.

As the cab's tires laid down streaks of rubber, the Green Falcon grasped the edge of the open window on the passenger side and just had an instant to lock his fingers, broken knuckle and all, before the cab shot forward. Then he was off his feet, his body streamlined to the cab's side, and the vehicle was roaring north along serpentine Jericho Street at fifty miles an hour.

The Green Falcon hung on. The killer jerked the wheel back and forth, slammed into a row of garbage cans and kept going. He made a screeching left turn at a red light that swung the Green Falcon's body out from the cab's side and all but tore his shoulders from their sockets, but still the Green Falcon hung on. And now the Fliptop Killer leaned over, one hand gripping the wheel, and jabbed at the Green Falcon's fingers with the knife. Slashed two of them, but the Green Falcon's right hand darted in and clamped around the wrist. The cab veered out of its lane, in front of a panel truck whose fender almost clipped the Green Falcon's legs. The killer thrashed wildly, trying to get his knife-hand free, but the Green Falcon smashed his wrist against the window's frame and the fingers spasmed open; the knife fell down between the seat and the door.

Beachfront buildings and houses flashed by on either side. The cab tore through a barricade that said WARNING NO VEHICLES BEYOND THIS POINT.

The Green Falcon tried to push himself through the window. A fist hit his chin and made alarm bells go off in his brain. And then the Fliptop Killer gripped the wheel with both hands, because the cab was speeding up a narrow wooden ramp. The Green Falcon had the taste of blood in his mouth, and now he could hear a strange thing: the excited shouts of children, the voices of ghosts on the wind. His fingers were weakening, his grip about to fail; the voices, overlapped and intermingled, said *Hold on Green Falcon hold on . . .*

220

And then, before his strength collapsed, he lunged through the window and grappled with the Fliptop Killer as the cab rocketed up onto a pier and early-morning fishermen leapt for their lives.

Fingers gouged for the Green Falcon's eyes, could not get through the mask's slits. The Green Falcon hit him in the face with a quick boxer's left and right, and the killer let go of the wheel to clench both sinewy hands around the Green Falcon's throat.

The cab reached the end of the pier, crashed through the wooden railing, and plummeted into the Pacific Ocean twenty feet below.

Chapter Ten
NIGHTMARE NETHERWORLD

The sea surged into the cab, and the vehicle angled down into the depths.

The Fliptop Killer screamed. The Green Falcon smashed him in the face with a blow that burst his nose, and then the sea came between them, rising rapidly toward the roof as the cab continued to sink.

The last bubbles of air exploded from the cab. One headlight still burned, pointing toward the bottom, and for a few seconds the instrument panel glowed with weird phosphorescence. And then the lights shorted out, and darkness claimed all.

The Green Falcon released his prey. Already his lungs strained for a breath, but still the cab was sinking. One of the killer's thrashing legs hit his skull, a hand tearing at his tunic. The Green Falcon didn't know which was up and which was down; the cab was rotating as it descended, like an out-of-control aircraft falling through a nightmare netherworld. The Green Falcon searched for an open window but found only the windshield's glass. He slammed his fist against it, but it would take more strength than he had to break it.

Cut, he thought. Panic flared inside him, almost tore loose the last of the air in his lungs. *Cut!* But there was no director here, and he had to play this scene out to its end. He twisted and turned, seeking a way out. His cape was snagged around something — the gear shift, he thought it was. He ripped the cape off and let it fall, and then he pulled his cowl and mask off and it drifted past him like another face. His lungs heaved, bubbles coming out of his nostrils. And then his flailing hands found a window's edge; as he pushed himself through, the Fliptop Killer's fingers closed on his arm.

The Green Falcon grasped the man's shirt, and pulled him through the window too.

221

Somewhere below the surface, he lost his grip on the Fliptop Killer. His torn tunic split along the seams, and left him. He kicked toward the top with the legs that had won a gold medal in his junior year swim meet, and as his lungs began to convulse his head broke the surface. He shuddered, drawing in night air.

People were shouting at him from the pier's splintered rail. A wave caught him, washed him forward. The rough surface of a barnacled piling all but ripped the green tights off his legs. Another wave tossed him, and a third. The fourth crashed foam over him, and then a young arm got him around the neck and he was being guided to the beach.

A moment later, his knees touched sand. A wave cast him onto shore, and took the last tatters of his Green Falcon costume back with it to the sea.

He was turned over. Somebody trying to squeeze water out of him. He said, "I'm all right," in a husky voice, and he heard someone else shout, "The other one washed up over here!"

Cray sat up. "Is he alive?" he asked the tanned face. "Is he alive?"

"Yeah," the boy answered. "He's alive."

"Good. Don't let him go." Cray snorted seaweed out of his nostrils. "He's the Fliptop Killer."

The boy stared at him. Then shouted to his friend, "Sit on that dude 'til the cops get here, man!"

It wasn't long before the first police car came. The two officers hurried down to where Cray sat at the edge of the land, and one of them bent down and asked his name.

"Cray Fl. . ." He stopped. A piece of green cloth washed up beside him, was pulled back again just as quickly. "Cray Boomershine," he answered. And then he told them the rest of it.

"This guy got the Fliptop!" one of the kids standing nearby called to his friend, and somebody else repeated it and it went up and down the beach. People crowded around, gawking at the old man who sat in his pajamas on the sand.

The second police car came, and the third one brought a black go-go dancer and a kid with a question mark on his scalp and a bandage around his shoulder. They pushed through the crowd, and Gracie called out, "Where is he? Where's the Green Fal—"

She stopped, because the old man standing between two policemen was smiling at her. He said, "Hello, Gracie. It's all over."

She came toward him. Didn't speak for a moment. Her hand rose up, and her fingers picked seaweed out of his hair. "Lord have mercy," she said. "You look like a wet dog."

"You got that sucker, didn't you?" Ques watched the cops taking the Fliptop, in handcuffs, to one of the cars.

"We got him," Cray said.

NIGHT CALLS THE GREEN FALCON

A tv news truck was pulling onto the beach. A red-haired woman with a microphone and a guy carrying a video-camera and powerpack got out, hurrying toward the center of the crowd. "No questions!" a policeman told her, but she was right there in Cray's face before she could be restrained. The camera's lights shone on him, Gracie and Ques. "What happened here? Is it true that the Fliptop Killer was caught tonight?"

"No questions!" the policeman repeated, but Gracie's teeth flashed as she grinned for the camera.

"What's your name?" the woman persisted. She thrust the microphone up to Cray's lips.

"Hey, lady!" Ques said. The microphone went to him. "Don't you recognize the Green Falcon?"

The newswoman was too stunned to reply, and before she could find another question a policeman herded her and the cameraman away.

"We're going to the station and clear all this mess away," the officer who had hold of Cray's elbow said. "All three of you. Move it!"

They started up the beach, the crowd following and the newswoman trying to get at them again. Gracie and Ques got into one of the police cars, but Cray paused. The night air smelled sweet, like victory. The night had called, and the Green Falcon had answered. What would happen to him, Gracie and Ques from this moment on, he didn't know. But of one thing he was certain: they had done right.

He got into the police car, and realized he still wore his green boots. He thought that maybe — just maybe — they still had places to go.

The police car carried them away, and the tv news truck followed.

On the beach, the crowd milled around for awhile. Who was he? Somebody asked. The Green Falcon? Did he used to be somebody? Yeah, a long time ago. I think I saw him on a rerun. He lives in Beverly Hills now, went into real estate and made about ten million bucks but he still plays the Green Falcon on the side.

Oh yeah, somebody else said. I heard that too.

And at the edge of the ocean a green mask and cowl washed up from the foam, started to slip back into the waves again.

A little boy picked it up. He and his dad had come to fish on the pier this morning, before the sun came up and the big ones went back to the depths. He had seen the cab go over the edge, and the sight of this mask made his heart beat harder.

It was a thing worth keeping.

He put it on. It was wet and heavy, but it made the world look different, kind of.

He ran back to his dad, his brown legs pumping in the sand, and for a moment he felt as if he could fly.

BARGAIN CINEMA

by

Jay Sheckley

"Chuck, look."

The serrated molybdenum knife moved back and forth across a cardboard photo of a chuckroast.

"No, sweetheart," Chuck said. "You're no steak." With a stubby forefinger he followed the knife's motorized path, pointing out the serving spears.

Patty admired the gleaming electroplate blade. Admiring it, she twisted a stringy lock of blonded hair around her finger.

"Come on," Chuck said. "Get a look at these."

Hungrily Patty examined the case of hunting knives. What kinds there were — folding knives, imitations of Swiss Army issue, small oval blades incised with woodland animals. "Look, a bobcat!" she said. "Oh, a cute beaver!"

"We don't need it for the picture on it," Chuck said.

"Yeah," Patty said. "That's for sure." They looked at each other shyly, knowing that no one knew their Plan. No one who hadn't seen the movie.

"For a buck more than those animals," Chuck said, "we could get *that* one."

"Ooh." Patty imagined Chuck's hand wrapped around the dagger's real brass hilt, coming at her.

The brass-hilted dagger was the most expensive knife in Gristleton. $49.95. But nothing was too good that Tuesday. "Die with love and a flourish." That's what the movie had been about.

Bargain Cinema was two blocks from Patty's apartment. So every Saturday — regardless of the program — Chuck and Patty would go there, arm-in-arm.

225

Often the rumpled ticket-taker remembered them, and would refuse their dollar-fifty admissions. "Go on in," he'd croak affectionately. "You're nice kids."

They *were* nice kids, too. They knew each other from Marrowville High, and hadn't gone out with anyone else in three years. Well, once Chuck had kissed some girl named Diane Tartare at a big party in Gristleton. But that was all over with. It wasn't worth risking their happiness. Even though their happiness bored them.

They needed glamor. Chuck cooked at a ChewyBurger stand. Patty was the receptionist at Red's Lockers. Neither earned much or knew how to manage money. For fun Chuck had an old Chevy; Patty dyed her hair. Sometimes she dyed it Gravy Brown, sometimes Charcola Black, and now Buttersauce Yellow. "Sure I like it," Chuck said. Patty's hair looked like threshed straw. Chuck said, "You could be a movie star."

Patty smiled. She nestled into her liver-colored parka as if it was a good fur. Glamor. It was all they needed. A dashing trim for their secure couplehood.

The Italian movie *Amplitude* gave them direction. It gave them hope that they could triumph over the commonness and the pettiness of love. "They risked all," the Bargain Cinema poster said, "to be lovers like the world had never seen. Violent and tender, shocking and beautiful: Was it murder or eternal romance? AMPLITUDE — Rated R."

Chuck and Patty did not even glance at the marquee. This had been a Saturday, Movie Night. That was enough for them.

"Go on in," the ticket-taker said. "You're nice kids."

The nice kids went on in. They didn't smoke marijuana in the theater. They didn't spill popcorn. They didn't shout. They abstained from public necking.

Arms around one another's shoulders, they watched the screen couple make their vows. After the movie, they went out for a couple of Cokes and some pie.

"I hate foreign movies," Patty said. "But this one was okay."

"Yeah," Chuck said. He was finishing his pie.

"Should've been in English." Patty said. "Nobody reads that fast."

"Uh-huh." Chuck sucked the last of his Coke up the straw. Patty hadn't finished her mincemeat.

"Can you tell me it?"

"What?"

"The story," Patty said. "How the guy comes to slit her throat for love."

"Eat your pie," Chuck said. He was paying for it.

"If you tell me."

"Eat," Chuck said. "Okay — it was like this. The guy — he had a funny name — he loved that girl, right? And she loved him. But they didn't get

226

married 'cause when their friends got married they saw it wasn't no good. So they wanted to love each other like they already were."

"That's us," Patty said. "Isn't it, Chuck?"

"Yeah," he said. "But eat. So then she got knocked up, or something makes her father yell at the guy, and then the guy and his girl have a fight."

"They have a fight," Patty said with enthusiasm, "and then they get together again and kiss and there's all that music."

"Right," Chuck said. "But they saw there was going to be trouble. They loved each other. They knew they would fight or get bored or break up or just forgive each other, year after year. So he says, 'Don't forgive me, I'm not going to live like that,' or something."

"Then," Patty said, "they came up with the Plan."

"I thought you didn't understand it."

"It was in *Italian!* How can I be sure?"

"Okay, okay, I'll tell you," Chuck said. "Eat. So she says she doesn't want to lose him, or ever be with another man. She wants him to change her so the bad things can't happen. She asks him to kill her."

"*Yeah,*" Patty said.

"And he says no, no way man, that's too dangerous. But he loves her. Finally he agrees to it."

"That's beautiful," Patty said.

"It's scary, if you ask me."

"But he did it," Patty said, "because he loved her."

"And because they had problems," Chuck said, "and so she wouldn't screw around."

"That's not why!" Patty said. She was pouting. "It's so their love would be *pure*. What's-his-name was the bravest man I've ever seen!"

"Oh yeah?" Chuck said. They were both starting to take it personally. "Yeah? Even the *girl* was a lot braver than *you*."

"Sure," Patty said. "You're just embarrassed green that you could *never* do a thing like that. Even for me."

"What do *you* know?" Chuck said.

Two weeks later they bought the knife.

After the Plan, how happy they were! Nobody understood but them. They took long drives among farmlands, and made every detail part of their vow. No one understood but them.

Once Patty asked, "What will you say when somebody tells you I've been found dead?"

"I'll try to act natural," Chuck said. "Maybe I'll cry. I'll say, 'Shit, you're kidding!'" Patty kissed him. How happy they were!

This, they knew, was Love. This was Glamor: intimacy and risk. Their fates were bound together by their pact. More than making love — this was something they would do only once, only with one another.

On the final day the knife was selected. "Meet you at the car," Patty whispered. Alone, she paid cash for the dagger; then upstairs in the ladies' room she combed her stiff hair, and tucked her new top neatly into her new jeans. She felt high . . .

Patty jumped into the car.

"Got it?" Chuck said. It was like a bank robbery.

"Here." Patty handed him the paper bag and the sales receipt. "You have everything?"

"Checklist," Chuck said, "blanket, bottle of wine —"

"What kind?"

"It's here somewhere." Chuck fished around on the Chevy's floor and found a bottle. "Here: Uncle Jack's Grape Wine."

"Yuck."

"Oh come on, sweetheart," Chuck said. "Not now. We're never going to argue again, right?"

"I'm sorry."

"Let's see — I also have three Quaaludes."

"Really?" Patty said. "Downs?"

"Only the best," Chuck bragged, "for my best girl. You want to do this thing now?"

"No," Patty said.

"No?" Chuck was amazed. "Why didn't you say so before? Jeez."

"No, no," Patty said. "I didn't mean it like that. I want to do it. Really. But now I'm hungry."

They dined at Burger Bonanza. They had two Bigburgers each. Under the table their ankles touched. They spent five dollars and forty cents but it was worth it. They were stuffed.

It was six thirty when they left Burger Bonanza. By the time they got out to the old barn the light was fading fast. There, in view of the full moon, they spread the blanket and undid the twist-off cap on the wine.

"Better take these now," Chuck said. He handed her the Quaaludes.

"Three?" she said. "Don't you want one?"

"I don't want to get sloppy," Chuck said. He tried to sound like he knew what he was doing. "But I *will* help you kill the wine."

Patty laughed and took her medicine. They drank and huddled and waited for Patty to relax.

BARGAIN CINEMA

The last thing she said was, "You'll fix us, won't you, Chuck."
There was no counting time. The moon was high. Finally the pills
acted like tiny weights in her lips and cheeks. Chuck zipped Patty's parka.
She must be getting cold. Then he unzipped it a little so the neckline was
accessible.

He recalled one of his last conversations with her. "Well, why don't *you*
kill *me?*" he had asked. Patty had said, "No! It should be like it was in the
movies." Now she murmured drunkenly. *I'll never hear her speak again.* He
felt the burden of his duty like a hideous bird that had him by the neck. He
could hardly breathe; yet the cool, fresh air burned his throat. He wanted to
leave and never see Patty again. *I love her,* he told himself.

The knife was in her small hands. She slept with it, as she once slept
with a Barbie Doll. *Better hurry.*

He took the knife. *This is so difficult. I am a man; a man can do this.*

Chuck slung the faintly conscious girl across his lap. Her head lolled
back; the expanse of her throat gleamed.

Like it was in the movies. Or how could I keep her? He had to have the
nerve. A *man.*

He raised the knife; slashed at her.

"No!" she cried, waking. She tensed, trembling in the unsureness of his
cut. She felt suddenly defiant and alone; uncoupled, intending to live.

"Lie back," Chuck hissed. He stroked her cheek. "I'll get it right." *She's
suffering,* he thought, *I'm failing.*

Patty's left hand came up, clasped her throat. She picked at the new
flap of flesh. She felt damaged; he should finish. "Chuck," she said dreamily.

She leaned back limply into his lap, returned her hand to her side,
sighed. Her fingers were sticky and slimy . . . blood? Yes, of course. "Dear
Chuck," she whispered. She thought she was composing a gentle letter to
him from far away. Then the blade became decisive and changed them
forever.

The night air was cold. A new silence pointed at Chuck. He was
shaking.

For a moment he didn't know why any of this was here; a blanket, a
bottle of Uncle Jack's Grape Wine, a girl all messy under the big moon, her
head separate from her body.

Chuck was very cold. There was a thick jelly between his fingers.
Somewhere a dog barked twice.

Chuck was supposed to leave. Now. *Now.* He wiped his hands on the
coarse wet weeds. He wrapped the blanket across the corpse. Before, he

thought he would say, "Goodbye, sweetheart" and kiss her. But his gut hurt him and Patty wasn't there playing movies any more. Chuck recited "Shit-you're-kidding, shit you're kidding" all the way to the car.

And the car started like a dream; the headlights were twin projectors. From his seat he watched his own life, moving slowly.

LIFECAST

by

Craig Spector

By the time the temperature hit ninety-nine degrees, Philip Thomas was completely insane.

He sat by the table in the cramped, airless confines of his kitchen, sweat pasting his *Dawn of the Dead* t-shirt to his back and sides. A white plastic egg timer sat on the table before him, ticking off the seconds. He still had some time to go, but he was getting impatient. The phone would be ringing any minute, sure as shit. It ought to be ready by now.

Phil cracked the door of the oven and peered in at the contents. Waves of heat leached out, adding a horrible stench to the already unbearable air in the kitchen. The contents of the oven peered back, unseeing.

Ready enough.

Inside, nestled in a baking pan, was an exact alginate replica of a human face. In the past hour it had dehydrated considerably, shrivelling from its normal adult size to that of a child — two, three years, tops.

And getting younger by the minute.

Phil stared into the oven. It was an act of madness for several reasons, perhaps the least of which being that it was August in New York, which was a very good time to be someplace else. Another high pressure system had stalled over the entire eastern seaboard, and it had turned the concrete canyons of Manhattan into the world's largest convection oven, baking the unfortunate inhabitants into a miserable, short-tempered stupor. Nights were no better, as the accumulated heat of the day radiated out from the walls, the streets, everywhere. On his block alone — a dreary strip of brownstones slicing across Avenue D in an area of the East Village that passed clear through trendy, into simple squalor — there had been two shootings, three stabbings, and more fistfights than he cared keep track of. All related, directly or otherwise, to the heat. It was felony weather, every brutal second ticking off like a time bomb waiting to blow.

Phil could relate. He was feeling a bit murderous himself lately.

And inside the oven, the alginate was still shrinking.

He smiled; showtime. When he closed his eyes, he could almost hear the screams.

Philip Thomas was a tad young to go over the edge: on the dawn side of twenty-two, with a lingering air of adolescent awkwardness that belied what experience he had. But he made up for his youth, with talent and intensity and an obsessiveness that bordered on mania. He was tall, thin, pale and stoop-shouldered from too many bright summer days spent hunkered over clay models and molds in the basement. Gaunt, haunted features shrouded coal-black eyes that picked up every detail and stored them forever, and but the barest hint of facial growth struggled to offset a prematurely receding hairline. He looked like a tuberculous Edwardian poet, if you were feeling neo-romantic, or a twerp-faced geek if you weren't. In truth, he was neither.

In truth, Philip Thomas was an artist.

He stood there, flaking dried bits of rubbery goo off his fingers and checking the alginate's progress with a perverse and resounding glee. Amazing stuff, alginate. It was a makeup artist's best friend: a chalky white powder, actually made from sea algae. Dry, it was inert and generally useless. But add liquid, mix it up, and presto! It became a gelatinous blob, which set to a rubber-like consistency in minutes and picked up the tiniest detail of anything it touched.

As with every other aspect of his craft, Phil took alginate very, very seriously. In his brief, struggling career he'd slathered veritable mountains of the stuff across the heads or tits or bellies or behinds of one low-rent starlet or has-been actor after another, in anticipation of their upcoming hatchet-in-the-face scene, or wet t-shirt/chain-saw sequence, or chest-burster *Alien*-ripoff, or whatever other bit of cinematic Cheez-whiz to which Herschel Floyd would periodically enslave him.

Of course, for most applications you generally mixed it with water, but today called for an extra special effect.

And, except for the smell, blood worked surprisingly well.

Phil winced as a stinging trickle of sweat found his eyes. He slipped on an oven mitt, gingerly lifting the pan up and out of the heat. This was a delicate phase of the process; no sense in rushing things.

He carried the pan out of the kitchen and into the living room, where

LIFECAST

the heat went from unbearable to merely suffocating. Demons, mutants and mangled limbs greeted him from every surface of the room, throwing monstrous shadows across the walls and ceiling. They were his creations, and his friends: the great horned troll adorning the mantlepiece of the bricked-up fireplace, and the dwarfish minions flanking it, all cutting-room floor fatalities from *Voodoo Vacation*; the pair of hacked-off, shredded arms which looked so real in person and so ridiculous in *Class of Splatter High*. The human-faced spider-thing, with eyes of glistening marbles, that sadly spun its web across the mirror over the mantle, a pre-production reject from *Invasion of the Maggot Eaters*. Screaming skulls and mutant body parts adorned the bookshelves; even the cupboard at the end of the room held the headless female torso from *Slaughterhouse Slumber Party*, replete with pitchfork tines protruding below the breasts in neatly-spaced holes.

"Evening, dear," he said, laying the pan on another cluttered table. He flicked on his work light and began inspecting the cooling features. This was serious. Every crease, every wrinkle had to be absolutely perfect, even if the ritual didn't strictly require it.

The face in the pan was Herschel Floyd's taken from the plaster positive Phil had made for *Chainsaw Cheerleaders*. (In sleazoid Hitchcockian imitation, Herschel's ego asserted itself via cameo appearance as the exploding head during the obligatory bone-squat/make-out scene, thus achieving him immortality while compelling some feckless bimbo to quaff the big-veined man-thing in take after take.) The positive from which the mold was taken was propped on the table, facing him: eyes closed, mouth frozen open like Mr. Bill in Hell, bearded jowls drooping, looking altogether more like a deathmask than a lifecast.

"Both, actually," he said to the face. He held up the negative, a bowl-shaped shell of the original with the features on the inside. The alginate's shrinkage had left the features looking more like a pissed-off raisin than a man: all pinched in and wrinkled, its little mouth a puckered sphincter in the center.

"Your true character revealed, Hersch, ol' buddy." He looked at the shrunken form. "I do good work, yes?"

There was no reply: its lips were sealed.

"Aw, poor little fellah." Phil took an exacto knife and rectified the problem. "That's better, isn't it?" he twisted the alginate slightly, forcing the tiny mouth into a hideous tiny grin. "I've got big plans for you, you know." He addressed it in his best Mr. Rogers voice. "Can you say, 'san-tah-*reeh*-ah'?" The tiny face nodded in his grasp.

"I knew you could."

Phil Thomas had paid his dues — films that were low-budget, more often *no*-budget, forcing him to make miracles out of next to nothing in the worst of all possible circumstances. He'd been abused and jerked off, conscripted into constructing the requisite monsters and mayhem out of foam latex and chicken wire, squibs and stage blood and pure heart-sweat, all in the hope of that one big break.

Three years into the business, and that one big break was still as elusive as ever. But Phil had gotten better. Much better. It was inevitable: no matter how vile or trashy the production as a whole, it was still *his* heart up there, *his* soul on the screen with his creations.

It was more than just a job, after all.

It was his life.

Phil smiled, laid the alginate face down and began sifting a few c.c.'s of Ultrocal-30 plaster mix into a bowl. "You've no one to blame but yourself, you know." He talked to the mask as he worked, a by-product of habitual solitude. "You shouldn't expect to go fucking with a man's lifelong ambition and go unpunished, should you?" He glared at the mask.

"Of course not."

And makeup had been Phil Thomas' dream ever since he first saw Lon Chaney as the Phantom of the Opera, skulking out of the sewers of Paris and into his living room courtesy of WTAR's Creature Feature matinee. He went apeshit over the Creature From The Black Lagoon. He devoured the drawings in Creepy and Eerie comics before he was even old enough to read the words; in school he was extremely popular around Halloween and when they needed someone to run the magic show at the Spring Fair, and virtually ignored throughout the rest of the year.

All of which was fine by Phil. He was a loner by nature, given to pursuing his hobbies under his parents' indulgent inattention. Young Philip Thomas liked magic tricks, music, models, monsters.

And movies.

Especially horror movies.

They were the best, the ones that hit everyone right in the yahooties. Philip was culturally weaned in the seventies, at the dawning of the Age of Excessiveness; a time of ruptured ideals and empathy overload, with all icons fair game and no taboo beyond reproach. A lot of people were shocked at the new explicitness, the brazen disregard for propriety and restraint.

To Phil it seemed the most natural thing in the world.

By the time puberty kicked his glands into gear he'd witnessed thirteen thousand, nine hundred and forty-two murders and/or random killings, in varying degrees of detail, and easily twice that number of maimings, tortures and sexual assaults. He'd seen Linda Blair's head twist clean around as she turbo-fucked a crucifix in *The Exorcist,* observed tongues being ripped out with red-hot pincers as he collected his very own set of 'stomach distress bags' from *Mark of The Devil,* yucked it up with *Count Yorga, Vampire* and a veritable host of Hammer horror films by junior high.

By the time he saw the zombies overrunning the shopping malls in *Dawn Of The Dead,* destiny had called.

LIFECAST

Philip Thomas had found his niche.

But he wanted more than to just sit on the one side of the silver screen as the dark, awesome magic came to life. He wanted to make the line disappear altogether. He wanted to create the illusions, himself.

And he wanted to make them flawlessly, perfectly real.

Sloppiness always spoiled the effect: nylon wires hanging out of a creature's back, seams where the latex didn't lay properly, the flat, waxy pallor of an obviously fake head that took an all-too-real axe — such gaffes Philip Thomas could not abide. He was fanatical about details, even unto the tiniest minutiae of continuity. If the killer got sprayed with blood running out of the farmhouse, then the spatter pattern had god-damned well better stay the same when he is next seen running through the woods with a chainsaw.

He would have offered heart and soul to any of a handful of truly great filmmakers, and any of them surely would have seen the extent of his talent. He came to New York because it was the next best place to L.A., and not too far from that oh-so vital familial support network. So he came to the big city, to hustle and schmooze and weasel his way into the promised land.

And he succeeded, after a fashion. Philip Thomas' hard work did not go unnoticed, and within six months of his arrival, he was hired to assist on his first feature length film.

"So who do I end up working with?" he asked the stifling air. His creations regarded the query in silent assent. "Do I get Cronenberg? Friedkin? Romero?"

"No. Floyd," he answered, the name flat as copper plating on his tongue. "I got fucking Floyd."

Herschel Floyd, the producer/director-*scheissmeister*, grand high potentate of Trauma Production, Inc. — formerly Goldenrod Productions, masters of the technicolor blowjob. That was before, of course — before video supplanted film as the preferred medium for adult entertainment, and the bulk of the porn film industry sank like a mastodon in a tarpit.

In a luckier world, he'd have gone down with the herd.

"But this is not a very lucky world, is it?" Phil asked the face in his hands. It frowned. "Nosirree."

Because Herschel Floyd fancied himself as more than a sleaze merchant. Herschel Floyd was an *auteur*. Herschel Floyd had mutated with survival instincts that would shame a cockroach, shifting into the one genre where people with a little bit of money, even less imagination and absolutely no talent could still make a killing.

And straight into a crash course with Philip Thomas.

Of course, he'd brought along the same delicate sensibilities that had allowed him to spawn such rip-off megahits as *Bondage Bitches in Heat*, *Beach Blanket Bimbo*, or a host of others. Which meant that Herschel Floyd made tons-o'-bucks, none of which ever seemed to find its way into the next production budget. He drove a black Mercedes coupe with a cellular phone in it, did prodigious quantities of cocaine and otherwise brandished his zeal in a way that attracted the young, the unconnected and the eternally hopeful.

And when he had gotten the hungry ones assembled, their vision burning to express itself, he did the only thing an *auteur* of his calibre could ever possibly do.

Hack. Chop. Slash.

Phil glared at the lifecast, blinking back saline beads from the corners of his eyes. "So what else is new? Herschel Floyd: killer of hopes, mangler of dreams. You attach yourself to real talent like a leech and don't drop off until you've sucked them dry." Herschel Floyd's ash-white image remained fixed, immutable. "You humiliate and bully creative people until they're only hope of survival is to become a twisted reflection of yourself."

"And worse yet," he added, under his breath and over the growing knot in his throat, "worst of all . . .

"We let you get away with it."

It was understandable, at first. He didn't know squat about the lurid guts of the dreaded Industry, and had simply tried to do his best. But the work on Slaughterhouse Slumber Party *was ultimately buried by lame editing, a bone-dumb plot and Herschel's insistence on casting ex-Penthouse Pets and softcore burnouts for the female leads on the basis of their under-the-desk auditions. Of cours, the kudos afforded his work in the otherwise scathing reviews in* Cinefex, Fangoria, Cineteratologist *and the other FX rags took a little of the sting out of seeing his work brutalized. And, slime though he was, Herschel was smooth, a consummate master of the buttered back-entry. Thus, when Herschel called him to work on* Trauma's *next project, Phil still had that brittle crust of hope, that this time, this time would be different.*

He should have known.

Toxic Shock Avenger, the terrifying tale of a deformed boy menacing a wealthy all-girl summer camp with lethal tampons, was a nightmare quickly becoming a disaster. Phil had driven himself, under Herschel Floyd's aesthetic sword of Damocles, to the point of near-collapse on the project; designing and redesigning the prosthetics for the dreaded applicator scenes, making the Avenger's super-absorbent head seem really believable.

The on-location conditions were, of course, appalling: weeks at an abandoned dioxin dump in New Jersey, where one of the locals bragged that the EPA had declared its inspection results safe because "they only test six inches down, and we buried it two whole feet". One of the actresses — a former Miss November — quit after an unsightly rash broke out on her thighs. Meals — if you considered such delicacies as cold, blue-green spaghetti (so congealed that it retained the shape of the spatula a full half-hour after it was scooped) food — were served on tables made from plywood

236

LIFECAST

sheets laid on recently-emptied waste barrels. The relentless heatwave made the prosthetics finicky and the chemicals he worked with unstable; Phil spent half his time inhaling noxious fumes and the other half trying to avoid blowing up.

But it was worth it. The Avenger was scary, dammit, a goddamned masterpiece. The best work he'd ever done.

Until Herschel. Gak. Spew. *Plork.*

The bastard ruined it, somehow: when they screened the dailies, the head came off looking rubbery and stupid, the horror reduced to cheesy laughability. Herschel blamed Phil. Of course, Phil knew whose fault it really was, whose negligent vision was ultimately responsible for the insipid awfulness unfolding before him. But that didn't stop the creep from screaming "Who's the incompetent twit that did this shit?" as Phil sank into his seat in the screening room. "Thomas, you asshole! This shit doesn't look real! It's doesn't work! It's garbage! Jeezus, we're gonna have to reshoot all of this shit! You call yourself a makeup artist?! Jeezus!! You're fired! Get the fuck outahere!"

Phil had fled then, unable to cope with the abusive tantrums any longer. This was not the first time, but that was hardly the point. Something in him just snapped. The harangue continued on, echoing off the walls, burning in his mind long after he'd gone.

"You call this magic?! I want to see some fucking magic, goddammit! Get me somebody who can do it right! Now!!"

That was two days ago.

"I got some magic for you now, alrightee," he muttered. "This one's so good that even your participation couldn't fuck it up." He surveyed the array of objects surrounding Floyd's lifecast on the cluttered tabletop: the telephone answering machine, a TDK hi-bias cassette, a wooden box drilled with airholes, a pair of heavy duty rubber-and-canvas workgloves, the large votive candle that he'd scored at *Los Campeneros* bodega on Avenue D, and the bowl of Ultrocal.

And, stippling the plaster surface of the lifecast, perhaps the most important ingredients of all. They were very small, unnoticeable to all by the most observant gaze. They'd been plucked accidently from the bristling expanse of Herschel's face, back when the original cast had been taken. A few stray whiskers, lifted by the pull of the alginate, then transferred again to the plaster positive, where they even now protruded like saplings on a snow-covered mountainside.

Phil looked at the candle. Its inscription read *Siete Potencias Africana.* It had a little picture on it, a crucified Jesus surrounded by a rooster, a ladder, snakes, swords, spear and skulls, with a wall of fire behind Him and ringed by what Phil presumed were pictures of the seven 'saints': African gods brought by slaves to Cuba, and annexed into legitimacy by the Church. *Chango, Orula, Ogum, Elegua, Obatalia, Yemalia,* and *Ochum.* The Seven African Powers.

237

SILVER SCREAM

He'd seen the candles every day for years now, crowding the bottom shelf near the door at *Los Campeneros*, wedged between the Nine Lives Super Supper cans and Goya bean section. They were big and gawdy and ugly as sin, with a cryptic inscription in Spanish on the back, and were every one manufactured by the Blessed Miracle Candle Company of East Laredo, Texas. Just light the candle, recite the prayer, and *bang! zoom!* your wish would be granted.

Maybe it was the crazy-making heat, which nudged adolescent revenge fantasies clear into the kill-zone. Maybe it was the fact that last night his video store had finally gotten him a copy of *The Believers*, which he'd missed in the theatres because he was too busy slaving for Herschel Floyd, and he loved the scene where the spiders crawled out of Helen Shaver's face. Maybe it was because he recognized the candle even before Martin Sheen did, and it inspired him.

And maybe it was because he knew that his phone would be ringing any minute now, because he just knew that Herschel Floyd knew that Phil was the best; certainly, the best Trauma Productions could ever hope for. He'd call, all right, with weasledick apologies and backhanded complements and just enough empty promises to suck him back into the fold.

The last time Floyd fired him Phil had held out, until Floyd actually agreed to *double* his salary. A big hundred bucks a week — *if* the checks cleared. Last time, Phil had been a sucker enough to take it.

This time, he wanted a little something extra.

He lit the candle and fed the cassette into his stereo, which was his pride and joy and his sole valuable possession. He'd taken the liberty of pre-recording the chant, so that he could better concentrate on the moment. Mood was everything. He'd even mixed in a recording of African rhythms he'd found buried in his record collection, as a kind of a soundtrack. The sound swelled in the room, and his own voice came back as if from another planet . . .

"OH SIETE POTENCIAS AFRICANAS QUE SE ENCUENTRAN ALREDEDOR DE NUESTRO SENOR, HUMILDEMENTE ME ARRO DILLO ANTE TU MILAGROSO CUADRO A PEDIR SOCCORO . . ."

Phil giggled; it sounded great. Real spookshow. He donned the work-gloves and reached for the box. The weight shifted as he picked it up; from inside came the frantic skittering of tiny claws. Phil checked the dexterity of the gloves: so-so, the fingertips a bit too thick and squared and clubby for any real precision. He managed to pick up the exacto knife, thinking *I'll have to be quick about it.* He pried up the lid, reached in and ensnared one of the screeching prisoners. Good reflexes. He pulled it out.

It was a rat: the youngest one, eight, ten ounces maybe, its eyes shiny-bright and black as night. A heckuva lot easier to come by than a live chicken in Manhattan, and a lot more appropriate. He'd caught a few last night, just

238

by setting the box-trap in the back alley. He hadn't bothered to feed them yet; they were panicked and pissed. The one in his hand tried to bite through the offending digits, got a mouthful of neoprene and duckcloth instead. Phil squeezed it so tightly that it screeched in helpless rage and flipped it over onto its back.

"Nighty-night," he offered by way of eulogy.

And he buried the blade in the soft fur of its breast.

"... *PIDANLE QUE ALEJE DE MI CAMINO Y DE MI CASA ESAS ESCOLLAS QUE CAUSAN TODOS MIS MALES* ..." the tape droned, "... *PARA QUE NUNCA VUELVAN A ATORMENTARME* ..."

Blood pooled instantly around the hilt, matting the rat's fur as its body went all stiff and trembly. Death was a foregone conclusion: the blade was sharp and long enough to crack its sternum like a dirt-gray walnut, skewering the heart-muscle beneath in an invasion of cold razored steel. It expended a few feeble kicks, and then it was lights out in ratville.

Before this afternoon, he'd never cold-bloodedly *killed* anything before. The first one he did to make the alginate. It gave him a giddy, queasy rush in the pit of his stomach. This one felt kinda neat.

It felt like he could get used to it.

The gloves were hotter than hell in the already stifling room, causing the palms of his hands to sweat like crazy. He peeled one off, the better to work with, leaving on the other to hold the ratty carcass. He held it over the bowl of Ultrocal and opened its throat, letting the blood squirt down to spatter the mound of powder. There was a surprising amount of it in such a tiny creature; it filled the bottom of the bowl, turning the Ultrocal into a frothy mush.

When it was drained he laid the corpse on the table, close enough to the box that the others could smell it. They reacted very, very strongly, gnawing and clawing and shoving whiskered snouts through the airholes, "Mmmmm, yummy nums," he cooed. "Soon, soon." The rats were not amused.

Inside the bowl, the plaster and blood was combining.

Outside, the temperature read ninety-nine degrees.

He peeled off the other glove and tossed it aside. His palm was moist with perspiration, as much from anticipation now as from the heat. He mixed the plaster, dipping his fingers deep into the bowl and stirring it into a creamy red paste. When it was done he picked up a pair of tweezers.

"Now, this won't hurt a bit," he murmured, then he thought about it a moment. "Wait a minute; who am I kidding?" He smiled grimly at the cast, and plucked a few whiskers off its surface.

"You're not going to believe this, but I read somewhere — I think it was *Psychology Today*, but don't quote me on that — that voodoo requires only the tiniest bit of the victim in order to work. A fingernail paring, a drop of vital fluid, a single hair" — he held the tweezers up to the light — "each contains all the genetic indentification necessary. Neat, huh?"

239

SILVER SCREAM

The lifecast said nothing as he placed the hairs in a crucifix pattern — forehead, chin, cheek, cheek — in the alginate shell. The fresh blood gave off a ripe, heady odor that permeated the still air of the room. The music on the tape throbbed. In Phil's imagination, which was working overtime, he saw it coming: like a black cloud, boiling up on the horizon. Alginate was versatile: you could shrink it, expand it, liquify it and remold it into yet another shape, again and again and again. It was infinitely finer than the banal repetitiveness of another dumb psycho-slasher pseudo-plot: he could literally let his imagination run wild. He wondered how Herschel Floyd's shrunken face would look grafted onto his armpit, say, or onto the end of his fat wanger.

The phone rang. *Showtime.*

"Lights . . .", he whispered, clicking off the worklamp. The candle's glow remained, wavering like a beacon. ". . . camera . . ."

The phone rang again.

". . . action."

He picked up. "Hello?"

"Phil, baby! Whoa, what's that shit in the background?! Turn it down, guy!"

Phil turned the tape down. A whine of static told him that Herschel was on the car-phone; probably cruising Eleventh Avenue, for a new female lead. "Herschel. What a surprise."

"Heh-hey, guy! We missed you today!"

"I bet you did." Phil began brushing the paste into the alginate shell. "What exactly do you want?"

"I want *you*, babe. On the set tomorrow, bright an' early."

"Forget it." Phil kept brushing; thick, hasty strokes.

"Aw, don't be that way, guy." Herschel's tone was silk-smooth and oh-so-hip. Mellow, even. "You know how I get when I'm under the gun. I get crazy, okay. I say things. But you know I love ya. You're the best . . ."

He was really laying it on. Phil kept right on brushing, coat after coat. The blood-smell was thick in the air. The rats were getting agitated; he could hear them ripping splinters out of the interior of the box. The room seemed to close in around the candle, hot and stifling. The chanting continued, building in intensity.

". . . and hey, I'll even double your salary again. Two-hundred big ones, kiddo, every week. Accounting will kill me, but hey, you get what you pay for, right? And besides, we really need you here. The Avenger needs you. *I* need you. Trauma needs your magic touch, guy. Whaddaya *ssssaaaay* . . .?"

One of the problems with Ultrocal-30 is that it gets hard suddenly. It has a lot to do with temperature, and timing. Sometimes it could be a real pain.

Then again, sometimes the timing was just right.

"D'ja say something, Hersch?" Phil paused the tape. The voice on the

other end of the line was one long, unhealthy vowel movement, spiralling up and up what sounded like intense pain.

"Herschel? Are you alright? Speak up!"

"Aaaaaaaaeeeeeiiiiihhhh . . ."

He was reminded of the old Warner Brothers cartoon, the one where Bugs Bunny tortures the fat opera singer by filling his throat spritzer with liquid alum, and the opera singer goes "figaro . . . figaro . . . figaro" as his head gets smaller and smaller and smaller.

It was kind of funny.

For about two seconds.

Then the rush hit: his heart pounding suddenly in his throat, cold sweat breaking out from every pore on his body as he realized that this was real, this wasn't just an adolescent revenge-fantasy anymore, this was it — he was really fucking *doing* it! He wished he could have a camera rolling, lens focused in tight close-up to drink in every awful detail. He closed his eyes, head reeling, as the mind-movie came to life . . .

. . . skin, muscle and ligament pulling taut, stretching his eyelids until the socketed orbs burst, follicles shrinking around the bristle of his beard until each shaft poked up thick as a pencil stub and then shrinking further still, until it was stretched tighter than the sheets on a boot camp bed; cartilage compacting, skull pressing in to trash-mash the brain, arteries blowing like high-pressure hoses, spraying blue-black blood to put out the fire that was the heat of the power, the heat of the plaster setting in his hands . . .

From the receiver came the sound of many things breaking, and a rush of car horns. A breeze stirred through the windows, hot as dragon's breath. Phil's vision glitched back to real-time, sweat pouring off him. Terror and adrenaline comingled, fueling the buzz in his brain. There was power in the room, uncoiling as days upon weeks upon months upon years of frustration came to a head.

"Hey, Hersch baby!" he howled. "How do you like my new effect, you bush-league douchebag amateur! Is it *real* enough for you?? Do you think it *works*?!"

He was screaming now, his face flushed with excitement and rage. "You want my 'magic touch', huh?! Is that what you want?! Huh?!

"Well, touch *this*, motherfucker!"

He stood up, the shrunken mask still in his hands, and shoved it into the trap.

"Touch *this*!"

The rodents fell upon the bloody fetish in a feeding frenzy: tearing it to shreds, taking little pieces out of the box, each other, everything. From over the phone came a high-pitched screech and the sound of tires skidding out of control. More horns, blaring hysterically. Phil cranked the volume of the stereo back up, louder than before; it was the point in the recording where

LIFECAST

he'd gone a little overboard, snatching at foreign bits of phrases as the rhythms built in intensity, until he was practically speaking in tongues, wailing little more than garbled incoherencies. It made for a great soundtrack, true.

But very sloppy ritual.

Phil fell back from the table, as the box wrenched sideways to crash on the floor. The shadows closed in, a hot blanket enfolding him. The phone slipped thuddingly from his grasp, but Floyd's screams carried well.

They were matched, in perfect stereo, by his own.

He realized, in that dreadful instant of ultimate collaboration, that he'd underestimated something fundamental regarding the nature of the dark arts, and the even darker powers he'd called upon: how very much in common they had. They, too, hated to be abused.

And They required very little of the victim to work. A bit of hair, a fingernail, a drop of blood.

Or sweat.

Phil shrieked and lunged toward the big mirror over the mantle, his voice spiraling up and up. It was small consolation for him to consider that a lesser artist probably could not have pulled it off at all. Blunders notwithstanding, he had given birth to the perfect effect; the line finally disappeared altogether.

His dream and his reality fused.

From the telephone, a symphony of screaming metal. Before his bulging eyes, a twisted reflection. Flawlessly real.

And perfectly ravenous.

By the time he got both hands to his face, it could fit neatly into the palm of one; by the time the first whiskered snout poked its way through the soft flesh of his cheek, he was too far gone to care.

The rats remained long after the tape had played itself through. They dined by candlelight, and invited many friends.

SIRENS

by

Richard Christian Matheson

A mansion.
Black.
Curtains breathing slowly.
A bed. Sheets twining in her young hands. Bad dreams. Chaotic.
Helpless.
She turns, wakes. Terrified.
There is no time to react. Something takes her. No shape; dimension.
She is flung, a roped calf, onto the floor. Her throat fattens. She
screams; dread.
Her eyes.
The whites grow, absorbing terror. She's held. Squeezed. Restrained.
Perfect body stripped. Legs pulled apart; an ugly runway.
Something undetailed, fleshy climbs between them. Begins to enter.
Pulse; a stapling dampness. Her slender wrists are held. No blood.
White fingers grasp uselessly. She sees nothing. There is nothing to
see. She shakes, struggles. Feels a slap; cruel.
The cheek goes hot like a pipe bowl burning. Sweat shivers.
Dirty fingernails scar her breasts. Red braille rises. Nipples are twisted,
sucked. Licked by more than one tongue.
Scores of them. Wet, sour. Rough. Every kind of tongue.
She screams.
A hundred hands without arms cover her mouth. She searches for
faces. Finds blackness.
More flesh enters. Everywhere. Like knives using her for a sheath.
Pain.
Her features are beautiful. Even in agony.
She hears laughter, low and hateful. A poison chorus. It wants her.

245

SILVER SCREAM

They want her. Blunt, shapeless fingers brand her face, pull at her, touch everything.

She stares helplessly at photographs of herself on the wall; the smile, the hair. The image.

Perfection.

Her tan legs are spread wider. Angry fingers reach into her. Her mouth bleeds, lips kissed hard; bitten. Dark laughter rises. Her make-up bottles are grabbed. Explode against walls; thrown. Liquid skin runs like blood. Lipstick is scrawled over her mouth and breasts.

She is spread more, arms and legs held; a bruised X.

They begin to moan. Faceless numbers of them. Vague. Bodiless.

She is slapped, scratched.

Her skin is numb.

The groans fill the humid room. She is pressed deeply into the mattress like a child's open hand into clay.

One by one, they do it to her. Lick her neck. Fill her mouth.

Ten. Twenty.

Fifty.

A hundred. A thousand. Always more.

She loses count and as the sheets drench red, her mind is towed into blackness.

The ambulance.

She is belted-down in back, teeth beating.

Eyes wide. Wet.

The attendant wipes her forehead. Tells her she'll be alright.

Tells her they'll get them.

Tells her she's beautiful.

The driver agrees. Keeps driving; sirens scraping night.

He remembers movies he saw her in. All his friends do. The men remember it all. Nude scenes. Love scenes. Seducing the camera; the world.

He remembers getting hard. Wanting her.

He glances into the rearview, fixes on the rise of her chest; the illicit view of her breasts.

The perfection blood can't ruin.

Another cut opens on her breast as the driver stares; imagining how she'd be under him; how he'd do it to her.

Then another as he thinks harder.

*   *   *

246

HELL

by

Richard Christian Matheson

August. Two-thirteen, a.m.

L.A. was turning on a spit and teenagers were in cars everywhere, cooking alive, tortured. The insanity of summer's sauna made the city grow wet and irritable, and blood bubbled at a sluggish boil in the flesh. Animals slept deeply, too hot to move, fur smelling of moist lethargy. Chewing gum came to life on sidewalks and the glow of fires created arsonist sunsets on the foothills which rimmed the city.

Lauren pulled her VW Rabbit into the view area off Mulholland, damp hair sticking to her forehead in fang shapes. The Rabbit rolled against the headstone at the parking slot's end that prevented berserkos from driving over the edge and she killed the engine. Hollywood was spread before her, eating electricity, *hibachi*-bright. To her side, in the other parked cars, she saw silhouette couples, in back seats, groping, fucking; glistening under the swelter.

Her skull slowly steamed open and she punched on the AM-FM as insects broiled on her radiator; tiny steaks. She tuned in a station and a moody deejay came-to over the airwaves, laughing softly like a rapist. Lauren was numb from the burning night and rolled-down her window more, letting in the oven.

"Here's a track the needle *loves* to lick." He made a faint licking noise. Laughed more, soft and cruel. "Mick and the boys givin' us some sympathy for a bad man. In case you're wonderin' about L.A.'s needle . . . it's in the red, babies. Hundred and two in the dark. I feel hot . . . How 'bout you?"

He chuckled as if tying a woman up and lowering onto her terrified body. Then "Sympathy For the Devil"'s rhythmic trance began and Lauren

247

leaned back, staring out the windshield, sweat glazing her forehead. Hot wind blew air that felt sour and old and smog stuck to everything. They called it riot weather after the Watt's riots back in the Sixties.

Bad wind. Poison days.

She rubbed her eyes and remembered that kerosene summer a million years ago. It had put a blister on top of L.A. and all those welfare cases cooking-up in their crackerbox hells went insane. Killed. Looted. Shoved broken glass into cop's throats and watched them bleed to death for fun. People said it was the thermometer that finally triggered it. Just a hot, wet summer day that made people itch and drink and lose their tempers and carve each other up for relief.

She tapped tiredly on the wheel, following Jagger's voice as it stabbed, pulled the knife out and stabbed again. Ran fingers through sweat-salted hair, feeling as if she'd taken her clothes out of a dryer half-wet and put them on.

The song thinned to nothing and the deejay was groaning, sounding like it was all over and he needed a cigarette. She wiped her forehead, starting to feel sick from the heat which crept in her windows. She unbuttoned her blouse lower, inviting what breeze hadn't been baked solid. Felt her mouth parting, her breathing slow. The two cars beside hers started and pulled away, leaving her surrounded by shapes the exhaust formed under moonlight.

The deejay came out of a commercial for a de-tox clinic and hissed lewd amusement.

"Hope you're with the one who makes you get *hideous* out there." He paused and Lauren could see him grinning cynically like a psycho killer in a courtroom, enjoying the grotesque evidence. "Temperature . . . a hundred and two and a half. How 'bout some Doors? 'Back Door Man,' summer of '69. Where were you?" Sensual, torturer's breathing. "And . . . who were you tormenting?"

The night felt suddenly swampier as requiem notes hit the air and Lauren closed her eyes, spinning, sweating, feeling creeks of perspiration run down her ribs. She drifted farther, remembering a beach party in August of '69 when she'd taken her first acid trip and glided for twelve hours in a Disney borealis, able to listen to handfuls of sand that spoke to her in frantic whispers. What was it it had said? She tried to remember . . . something about mankind suffering. Hating itself. It had terrified her.

She opened her eyes trying to forget, as another car pulled into the slot beside hers — a teenage, muscle cruiser; primered, deafening. Heavy metal howled and though the windows were tinted, she could see cigarette tips roving inside, as whoever drove watched the city.

She wiped sweat which slid between her breasts and watched two other cars racing closer, up Mulholland, headlights jabbing; hunting. The cars finally prowled into the view area, one beside her, one behind. She felt massive engines shaking the pavement and the cars on either side were so close she couldn't open the doors. The one on the right had tinted windows like the one on the left. Inside both she saw cigarettes, maybe joints, making slow moving graffitti patterns. Heard muted laughter; unsettling voices. Male and female.

Restless.

She tried her doors and neither would open; blocked.

The deejay sighed depressively. "Another knifing downtown. Simply Blues Bar." A yawn. The sound of something icy and long being swallowed. "Some people just shouldn't drink. Let's get back to the Doors."

Lauren pushed harder on her driver's door that felt fused shut. There was no play in it and she yelled to the driver to move his car. But there was no answer and when she did the same on the other side, still nothing. She knocked sweating hands on the windows of both cars and Morrison started screaming.

". . . well the music is your only friend.
Dance on fire as it intends.
Music is your only friend. Until the end."

Lauren started the Rabbit, jammed it into reverse, hit the gas and let out the clutch. Her tires gushed black but the car behind her didn't move. She started to panic, unable to escape, and screamed at the drivers pressing against her, on three sides, to move their cars. She caught her expression in the Rabbit's rearview; a fleeting look of terror.

"The face in the mirror won't stop,
the girl in the window won't drop.
A feast of friends — 'Alive!' she cried.
Waiting for me outside. Outside!"

She pounded harder on the windows of both cars but no one responded. Just more murmured amusement behind tinted glass. Cigarette tips burning, shifting like creature eyes. She slid across the front seat again, grunting trapped, primitive sounds and banged on the tinted windows of the opposite car. She could see her helpless features reflected in the black glass and gripped the door more tightly as she screamed.

"Before I sink
into the big sleep.
I want to hear the scream
of the butterfly."

SILVER SCREAM

The Doors kicked her harder and her hands began to bruise; yellow-purple flesh replacing pink. Her throat was etched by screams and though she couldn't make out voices, the laughter in the surrounding cars grew louder. She began to cry and the deejay chuckled.

"Just stepped outside and the flames are rising. Don't forget to use your lotion guys and gals." He made an obscene squirting sound. "Quick thought for the night: maybe we're all cooking alive and don't know it. Let's party."

He killed the Doors.

Napalm headbleed came next, making Lauren's heart beat too fast.

She looked up when the car behind hers began to rumble like a piece of earth moving equipment and started forward, shoving the Rabbit's front tires over the cement block. Then, the rear tires. It pushed harder, engine screaming, tires spinning. Ahead, the sequin sea of L.A. glittered.

Lauren tried frantically to get out. The other cars rolled over their own cement blocks and stopped her, jamming either side like grisly escorts.

She looked ahead, saw the cliff's edge and grabbed the wheel tightly, trying to lock the tires. But the Rabbit kept sliding closer to the edge, tires gouging fat scars in the dirt. She held down the horn, trying to let someone know, then covered her face with both hands, plunging into blackness; a burning spray twisting end over end.

As the three cars drove away into the gloom the deejay made a sound of exquisite pain. "Another ghastly evening in the City of Angels. In case you're keeping score, the temperature just went up another degree . . . and you're *losing*."

The six headlights stared around a curve and disappeared, looking for places to go; things to do. Sirens wailed and moved toward Mulholland as the deejay blew smoke into the mike, spun a ballad and cooed Auschwitz delight.

"Stay bad, babies . . . the night is young. And there's no way out."

A LIFE IN THE CINEMA

by

Mick Garris

The Mexican woman's freak baby might have been the worst thing ever to happen to her, but it could have been the best thing in the world to ever happen to me.

I'd much rather show it than tell it, but that's just not the way things work out in this town. You hear all that shit about only being as good as your last picture, and all those other hoary old saws about the Industry-with-a-capital-I, but that's ancient Hollywood masturbatory storytelling. If you're smart, you get your next picture set up before the last one comes out. You're as good as your last *two*.

I guess.

It started with film school. We didn't have the kind of money you need to go to S.C. and use all that stuff Steven and George bought for them, but I did get a scholarship to UCLA. So you make do, right?

It was *great*! I mean, just imagine having all that equipment to use for nothing! Sure, most of the study work had to be done on video, but the thesis was always shot on film, with sync sound, even optical titles. I shot mine in 35mm 'scope and dolby stereo.

One good thing about UCLA is the agent connection. You make a good film or write a good script, and every door in Century City suddenly opens up to you. It's like dogs smelling a bitch in heat. Make a short film on your own, and even it it's *Raiders of the Lost Ark*, nobody's ever going to see it unless it comes from film school.

So that's what happened. It took me a year and a half to finish *Words Without Voices*, but it was worth it. I badgered my way into incredible locations, built weird, wonderful sets that represented every dreamscape you could imagine (and many you couldn't, I'm sure), got a full orchestral original score, and made my 24-minute epic.

251

SILVER SCREAM

If you know lighting, manipulation, composition, and you throw away the zoom lens, directing's easy.

After copyrighting the film in *my* name, and not the school's (they weren't going to make money off of my talent), I submitted it to film festivals around the world, and started collecting ribbons. First place at AFI Fest, first place at USA Film Festival, honorable mention in Seattle (fuck 'em. Who cares about Seattle?).

And then, you learn about taking meetings. I got calls from ICM, William Morris, CAA, Triad, the whole catalogue. The hungry young guys have the most hustle, but the old Jewish farts have the connections and the clients. Maybe you wouldn't want to eat with them, but they know how to get a deal green-lighted. I learned quick that it's the agent, not the agency, that makes the difference. The old guys are never too eager to take on the new clients, but some of them can be convinced. Eventually.

All of them wanted me to leave a cassette of my film — can you imagine that? I shot it in Panavision, spent weeks on the stereo mix, and they're going to glance at it through phone calls on a nineteen inch screen. *I* know these lazy bastards all have screening rooms, so I insisted that they run the film in 35. I was nice about it and everything, but very persistent, so they'd know they were dealing with an artist.

Well, I got the pick of the litter. I made a couple of mistakes, first, like everybody does. One of these ten-percenters got real excited about getting me a *Miami Vice* meeting; as if I would even consider television drek. Another one thought getting me a sequel would speed things up. Right. Do *Police Academy 7* and Hollywood spreads its legs. Then, who knows? Maybe *Hardbodies 4!*

So finally, old Rosen at CAA and I reach an understanding. I mean, you don't want to watch this toothless clown take meals, but he knows how to throw his ninety-eight pounds around. We don't want to make development deals, he says, we want to make *movies*. No TV, no cable. Theatrical features only. *My* scripts, no options. Pay *and* play.

It's good cop/bad cop time. I'm taking meetings in high-altitude offices on every lot, with Sean and Mike and Len and Jeffrey and the big boys, discovering how easy all of this can be. Thank God for film school. These guys love to talk about how there's such a void left by Preston Sturges and Alfred Hitchcock and how there's never been an American equivalent to *The Bicycle Thief*, and all that other dinosaur shit I flunked in Film History 101. And then I talk Carpenter, Dante, Hooper, my gods. They like that, but only if you talk *Poltergeist* and not *Lifeforce*, *Halloween* and not *The Thing*. The supreme measure of art is boxoffice.

So I pitch them my movies, and listen to their reactions. They give me their "thoughts", and I get all excited about some of their ideas, as though they just made my story better than I ever could have alone. Then I hang back and consider their "notes" a few moments, before telling them why those ideas don't work. They get a feeling of give and take, that I'm willing to listen to their suggestions, and yet that I'm strong enough to defend my own ideas. They like me.

My job is to charm them, then Rosen gets to be the asshole. But that's okay, he's used to that. He *likes* that. He wheels and deals, gets the studios fighting over me, the price goes into the stratosphere, and I get to make my movie in Burbank.

Now there's an experience. At UCLA, you've got everybody and his grandmother thrilled to death to be a part of a movie (tell them it'll be on cable, and you can hose any of the women who took their clothes off for free on camera). Everybody works twenty hours a day, just for the sake of making your movie. Commitment, creativity, drive: everybody wants to help out.

But the studio experience is something else again. First, there's the unions; you've never seen so many people to do so few things. You kick out a plug, a union electrician has to plug it in. You're just about to shoot the crucial shot you and the cameraman (excuse me — *cinematographer*) have been setting up for the last three hours, and the assistant director calls lunch. Of course, everybody dicks around when they get there, so you can't start on time, but there is no going over, or you're into triple golden time.

And then there's the twenty-seven teamster drivers who are assigned to the show, sitting on their asses in their air-conditioned station wagons, waiting around at $2,500 a week, in case somebody needs a Diet Dr. Pepper at the Company Store.

But that's the least of it. That shit I can understand. These guys make a living, they do their work, and they get paid. The Suits are worse. I mean, I wear a tie on the set; when you can still get into Disneyland on a Junior ticket, and shaving is an exercise in wishful thinking, you do anything you can to direct from a position of power. But these fuckers in their Armanis, with their cigars and soft voices are the reason why all the movies you see are shit. Okay, here's how they think. What's "good" mean to you. Quality? Great. You and I think alike. But "good" to these guys is "familiar". Good is somebody else's hit. God forbid you make something unique, with an original vision. No, they want the "heart" of *E.T.*, the "visual kineticism" of *Star Wars*, the "pacing" of *Beverly Hills Cop*, the "gloss" of *Top Gun*, shit like that. All they know how to sell is what they know how to sell. And that, not very well.

So once we're in preproduction, there are the fights. They want story-boards, and I don't work with storyboards. We hire a storyboard artist to keep them happy, knowing full well I'm never going to look at the fucking little cartoons once I'm on the set.

Then there's casting. Oh, God, you wouldn't believe the names they want in my movie. If it were up to me — believe me, it wasn't — I'd cast all

SILVER SCREAM

unknowns. I want you to see the characters I've created, not famous actors in the roles. But no. I write the scientist role patterned on an old high school biology teacher of mine, and they want Tom Cruise. Tom fucking Cruise to play a biogeneticist! For the social worker they can get Kelly LeBrock . . . but they'd have to give her husband executive producer credit. Ultimately, it doesn't matter who I want, because with money and schedule and billing and studio problems, nobody is available anyway. At least not until you get down to the bottom of the list. Dreg city.

And then, of course, there is the wonderfully creative hand of Mr. Flotsam, our esteemed producer. He "developed" this "package", and his involvement is primarily to bring in Tangerine Dream for the music, and he gets a presentation credit for that. For that he should get a black eye! This film demands a full orchestra, and I get three fucking synthesizer programmers who can't even speak English.

Somehow, we get into production. Once the train starts, there is no stopping it. ILM is already shooting plates for the effects shots, the dailies are coming in, the Suits are bitching about diffusion and coverage and boom shadows. They haven't the slightest idea how a movie is made. All I can say is Trust Me. I know what I'm doing. You're going to love it when it's cut. Of course, that's not enough for them. They're insisting on more coverage, at the same time they're bitching about going over schedule and budget. And this isn't *Howard the Duck* or *Ishtar* — this is just a lousy ten million bucks they're talking about!

Okay, I admit I can be a bit tyrannical on the set. But do you blame me? My name is on the line. Written and directed by. Me. Nobody notices the accountant's name. Nobody cares about the editor, or *cinematographer*, or the atmosphere, or matte artist. Nobody gives fuck one about costume design. So, yeah. If it's going to get done, it's going to get done right . . . even if it means a little more time and money. What are they going to do, fire me and replace me, twenty days into a thirty-five day shoot?

So maybe a couple of *thespians* cried . . . it's the performance that counts, not how you get it. The only thing anybody can judge is what's on the screen. And actors! They'll do *anything*! Unless they're "names", of course. Then the fucking prima donnas won't even give you so much as a little nipple.

You've never seen a less cooperative group of people. I never set out to win a popularity contest; I just wanted to make my film.

So we made it. It wasn't that much over budget; I mean, it wasn't *Heaven's Gate*, or anything like that. So they sneaked my cut, like the Director's Guild requires. The preview cards were okay — not as good as we hoped, but okay. And it wasn't made for the carbohydrate crowd anyway. This is a sophisticated film, and they preview it for the horny-handed machinists and their toothless girlfriends in Long Beach. Brilliant. So the

254

A LIFE IN THE CINEMA

studio, of course, recut it and completely fucked the whole thing up, and tested their abortion in San Diego — my home town! Thanks, guys. Somehow the trades found out about the San Diego sneak, and they crucified us. I mean slit us up the middle and yanked out the entrails. Those guys like nothing more than shitting on an artist. If they know so much about making movies, let them try it! Fuck critics. If you ever met a critic, you wouldn't want to eat with him, either.

So much for flavor of the month. It plays the art house graveyard in four major markets, no TV support, no radio, just some print ads in the hip weekly papers that nobody pays for anyway. It plays in the 50-seat house at the Herpes Cineplex, and even Rosen doesn't answer my calls anymore. My one solace is that it killed Annamarie Longines' career in features. She got a sitcom last season, but it was gone after three weeks. They put it up against Cosby. I gloated.

Okay, so the Brothers Warner (or, at least, their corporate equivalent) give me the boot. So what? There's six or seven other majors. Yeah, right, except that with the executive circle jerk that goes on, the VP assigned to your picture will be at Universal next week; his girlfriend is being hosed by an exec at Columbia, who's now at Tri-Star until his father-in-law makes him exec VP at Disney to keep him from telling about the episode in the private jet with the male lead in their new picture.

So the old grey fag gets protection, and I get a chainsaw right in the career.

CAA dumped me, the development deals undeveloped, and before I know it, I'm sniffing around New World, Atlantic, New Line, and the other independents. I'm hosing this 43-year-old Jewish American Princess agent who wants me to call her Mama. You should see the claw marks on my back. She's got an office with no secretary in Pacoima or some god-awful place in the Valley, but the phone never rings. Never. She's hardly worth spilling my precious bodily fluids over. Or your time. Sorry.

She calls in a few favors, getting me meetings with Rehme and Corman and the other guys. I go in, tie and all, and it's inevitably the same song: "I'm sorry, Mr. Corman was called out of town at the last minute. But he personally asked Mr. Third-string Pimpleface Nobody to hear your pitch."

Needless to say, my pitches were never home runs. The galling thing is that these guys are constantly hiring first-time directors — guys who've only made videos of their kids' birthday parties before wind up getting ten grand to do these veg-o-matic killer thrillers that gross 67 million. I've done a studio picture, for Christ's sake, and get the bottom rung shoved up my ass.

By now my beach condo had flown to repossessionland. Ditto my 941. I met Rebecca in a corridor at DEG; I think we were both thinking of fucking the same producer. Her dream was jumping from soaps to features; personally, I thought she only made widescreen by doing hardcore, but who am I to

255

say so? Shacking up in Rebecca's West Hollywood apartment meant that I could dump Mama as a fuckmate, but keep her on the string as an agent. Rebecca also had a car.

By now, I'm starting to think TV sitcom work ain't so bad. The door has slammed in my face so hard that "Charles in Charge" starts to seem pretty Goddamn funny.

I had to get out, go somewhere, anywhere. Get away from the TV.

Rebecca was out on an interview, so I jumped the bus downtown. It's not what you think. Downtown LA has no orange trees, no limos or movie stars, nothing you'd ever want to send pictures of to Mom. Just corporate highrises, and a crumbling, decaying but lively city center, virtually 100% Latino: street vendors hustling in Spanish, salsa blasting from cheap, torn speakers, outlet stores, huge, fantastic old movie palaces now dowdy and rotting, showing three Spanish-language hits for two bucks, 24 hours a day. It's much more like Mexico City than the center of an American metropolis.

All I can do is wander and watch, chewing churros as the cops make the winos perambulate along. Gulping fresh Mexican juice from the vendors while a pimp opens his whore's face in a piss-scented doorway. I like it here; the street's like a 360-degree Sensurround movie.

One of the things I like best is the collapsible green magazine rack on every corner. They're filled with weird Mexican adult comic books, bosomy romance pulps, and unbelievably bloody wrestling magazines — really great stuff. They cost next to nothing . . . and are worth every centavo. Even if you don't speak Spanish, like me.

But this time, I found more than masked wrestlers in bondage.

The old woman minding the stand had a basket in the shade, which she kept rocking with her foot. I saw the blanket in the basket squirm; she noticed me looking, and moved in front of it.

"*Muchacho*?" I asked, because I had nothing else to say.

"*Muchacha.*"

Like it really mattered if it was a boy or a girl. A baby's a baby, right? They all look like Alfred Hitchcock, anyway.

Then the kid started to cry, this weird, soft mewling sort of sound. I sneaked a peek over the Santo magazine. The crying got louder, but the old lady wouldn't move. She just kept watching me like she was mad at me or something. I can't help it; I watch stuff. All the time. I guess I'm nosy . . . but show me a filmmaker who isn't a voyeur, and I'll show you a TV hack.

The kid's catlike bellow was a primal screech by now, and even the old lady could no longer pretend to ignore it. She picks up the baby and lifts her blouse to release a stretched, hanging blob of a tit. She carefully lifts the edge of the baby blanket, and springs a leaking, incredibly long and erect nipple into the begging mouth.

She turns to see me watching her, and our eyes lock. I can't look away, and her grim face defies my stare.

A LIFE IN THE CINEMA

Finally, the infant has taken its fill, and releases its hold on her breast. The leaking prong of her nipple springs up, and is quickly tucked away, after splashing drops of lactose on the baby's face.

As she wiped its face, I caught my first glance of it.

This was no child. I didn't know what it was, but it was nothing I'd seen before. It was slippery-looking, completely hairless with dark, rubbery skin. It looked more like a human than any other kind of animal, but just barely. It seemed like it had been burned or something, except that its skin was wet, oily. It had lips like a fish, large and gasping, breathing like a rich fat man puffs on a Havana, wet and floppy.

I tried to get a better look, but she kept shielding it from me, covering it with the blanket and blocking it from view with her girth. I tried to wear as much sympathy as I could get on my face, a mask of soft, gentle caring. I had to see this kid more closely.

Talk was useless; she couldn't speak English, and Spanish is Greek to me. But I reached out with Allstate-sized helping hands to touch the baby. She was hesitant and defensive, but when she saw I had no intention of hurting or making fun of the thing, she let me lift the blanket, still watching my face the whole time.

Close up, with time to really see it, this freak baby was incredible. I knew immediately that I was back in business. And if you judge this thing the way you do a real baby, it *was* a girl. I had Rebecca's rent money in an envelope in my back pocket, and gave it to the old woman. I'm not sure why. I guess I just had to touch it. This thing would make the most incredible story ever; it all rushed through my mind in the time it took for the lights to flash around the marquee of the Million Dollar Theatre: all the words that had been shoved down my throat from the critics and the development meetings.

Heart. Story. Character. All that shit.

I just wanted to hold the thing, feel its reality, touch it. But I didn't just want to do some latex life story. *Words Without Voices* had soured me on special effects. This thing was *real*, and *that's* what I had to show the world. No state-of-the-art Rob Bottin special effect could ever hope to compete with the beating-heart, coursing-blood reality of this slippery, shifting-irised creature squirming in the blanket in my hands.

This baby was my movie.

I couldn't tell how old it was; how do you judge the age of something you've never seen before? It couldn't have been more than a couple months. When it realized that somebody new was holding it, its eyes locked onto mine, and we were both transfixed. The muddy irises seemed to swirl like whirlpools, clearing and changing to blue, then becoming so clear that I swear I could see the brain behind them. I could feel its heartbeat rippling through my hands as I stared into its cortex, distantly hearing it mewl, and

257

seeing music deep within. Not like musical notes, but actually seeing the music itself. I don't know how else to explain it, except to compare it to the acid trips my stepfather always talks about.

This kind of eye contact seemed to tire the kid out, and the huge eyes filled with dead brown mud again, then slowly drifted closed. When I looked up, Mamacita was vamoosed.

Not that I minded. She had a chance to dump the freak, and jumped at it. If I had to sell year-old wrestling magazines to farmworkers on a street-corner, I'd probably have done the same thing.

But I lucked out. I had this incredible treasure in my hands; I would get another chance to thrill the world. And a month's rent for Rebecca's West Hollywood digs would pay for the old bitch's flop for five years. Later I would realize that she got the better end of the deal.

Rebecca was freaked but fascinated by the little slug in the bassinette in the kitchen. I decided to leave the details out of the story until later — especially the part about the rent money. I'd deal with that when the Arab came around asking for it.

"You said you always wanted a baby," I told her. She was not amused. But I knew how to handle her. She wouldn't have any trouble dealing with the freak if she knew she'd get at least a featured role in the picture at scale-plus-ten. We quickly discovered how simple the care and feeding of the little monster was; it sucked on anything and everything that found its way into its disgusting little smacking lips. Once Rebecca was leaning over it to get a good look, and the little sucker went for her breast right through the shirt. I tried to joke her into suckling it, but her sense of humor has its limits.

I named it Asta.

I gave Mama in Pacoima the heave-ho, and set about scaling every bridge I ever burned. I bullied, badgered and blackmailed my way into meetings everywhere in town, from the sleaziest Troma to the most muscle-bound Paramount. At first it was always the third-stringers, like before; the studios are cautious. You can get the meetings; they don't want to close the door on anybody who might make a hit movie for somebody else, and not be able to get them back. The guy who flops with *THX 1138* at Warners might go on to do *Star Wars* at Fox. The door is shut, but not locked.

Anyway, I've got meetings with sons of mucky-mucks at *other* studios, and we talk "Heart" and "Story" and "Character", and we shoot boxoffice shit, and then I bring up The Idea. It's always the same reaction: "Yeah, but it's been done. The unfortunate baby is really more a Movie-of-the-Week, don't you think? But I'd be glad to put you in touch with our TV people." And that's supposed to signal the end of the meeting.

I won't let go. We talk *Elephant Man* and *Mask* and *E.T.* and all that other heartfelt mutant crap, and my eyes go misty and caring and gentle. They start to get uncomfortable. I tell them how The Idea could be done so cheaply, and how much I learned by the last experience. Then I shrug like it's obviously brick wall time, and I say thank you, and walk out like a broken man. But they can't see my smile.

Before the door closes all the way, I pretend to spot the box I have sitting in the reception area, like I forgot about it. And before Mr. Pimple can finish punching up his next phone call, I scoop it up and swing around to face him, with Asta in my arms under a Smurf baby blanket. "Oh, by the way . . . you want to see it?"

Of course he's too busy, and he has no idea that what I'm talking about is real, and he wants me the hell out of his office. Fruitless meetings never end. So I don't give him a chance to answer. I rush up, put the thing under his nose, and pull back the Smurf.

The guy shits his pants. He wants to know if the guys who did "Nightmare on Elm Street Part 3" made it, and I have to say over and over, no, it's real.

They don't believe me. I hold it closer, so close they can smell the acrid urine-stink that seeps from its skin, and invite them to touch her. Every single one I ever asked has declined.

It's amazing how quickly I get access to the ladder. I meet Sonny's boss, then her boss, then his boss, then his boss, and finally it's the rarefied penthouse office of Daddy himself.

At this point, Rosen's calling me back; he's caught wind of the tarbaby story, and he wants to break some backs at the majors. I don't blame the guy for dropping me, after all, I was poison. And Rosen doesn't give a shit about relationships or being my pal. He's a businessman. Right. He yanks mine and I squeeze his, and we both come dollars. He knows I know he can negotiate the hell out of my deals, so I give him the nod. It's old home week, and he's got the studios beating each other up for the baby story.

Praise Jesus.

We set the deal up in Culver City. I'm writer, producer and director; no presentation credit, but I'm not crying. We want to keep the budget low, shoot in some right-to-work state in the South, and I finally get to cast my talented unknowns, and throw Rebecca a three-line bone. Now that I'm producing, I can see the wisdom of keeping costs low, so that it's tougher for the studio to hide the profits if the film does business. We're talking a below-the-line of maybe three-point-five. And most of the above-the-line is me.

I decided early not to allow the cast and crew to see the kid until we actually shot the birth scene. I knew the reality of their reactions would make the scene really sing. I couldn't wait.

Everybody loved the scripts: even the Heart and Story and Characters. But wait until they saw Pee Wee. I was worried that during three or four months of preproduction, Asta might grow out of her weirdness. The freakishness might just be a stage. I held my breath every morning before checking under that Smurf blanket. But the thing wasn't changing at all.

SILVER SCREAM

In truth, I *did* learn a lot from the Warners experience. I'm prepared this time, I become the cast and crew's best pal, actually let them make suggestions, and pretend to consider them for a moment before I turn them down to do it my way. They like that.

Everything is going fine. We've run a day or two over schedule, but stay under budget, so the Suits are happy. They like the dailies, love the coverage and what we call the Look of Show.

I couldn't be happier. During breaks, I'm rocking my Winnebago with Cindy, my superstar discovery, chewing her implants and filling her with my goo. But the headier foreplay is thinking about the birth scene, scheduled for the Monday of week four.

Everybody's asking to see the puppet, who made the baby, when are we going to see the poor little thing. I just smile, playing the wise man with the secret.

B day.

Crew call is 7:00 a.m., and I get there an hour early. Asta's been a little fussy, but seems okay. She's comfortable and well fed; I've got her in a basket that once held Snookie's Cookies.

Everybody's excited about the big scene. We'll be shooting Asta for the next three weeks, but this is her debut. I want to shoot the freak in continuity, just in case it changes at all during production. The locations that feature it are limited, so it's easy to shoot those scenes in order.

So we've got Cindy Starlet's belly as padded as Dr. Ellenbogen stuffed her breasts, and she's on her back, hyping up. For authenticity's sake she has been taking Lamaze classes at the clinic. Whatever works.

Rebecca's in the corner studying her line, looking sexy in her nurse outfit. She has no idea about me and Cindy, not that it matters if she did. I can afford my own place now.

Vilmos has just about finished lighting. I rush off and bring in the basket from my Winnie, and keep it hidden from view as I move onto my mark. I'm doing my cameo as the doctor who delivers the thing, so I'm in total control. I even gave myself a crucial close-up.

I'm mildly surprised to see that Cindy isn't wearing anything under the hospital gown. She winks, knowing I'm the only one in a position to know, and I give her little curls a tickle. She tries not to react in front of the others.

Then I bring Asta up onto the table, covered in her little blanket. Still, nobody but me has seen the thing, and my heart is pounding through the stethoscope hanging from my ears.

I place the baby thing between Cindy's legs (I like putting things between Cindy's legs). I'm the only one who can see Asta, and I enjoy watching it move wetly up against Cindy's private parts. Cindy tries not to react to the rippling wet pressure. Then, the inquisitive little beggar's lips seek out something that resembles a nipple down there, and starts to suckle.

A LIFE IN THE CINEMA

"Quiet! Rolling!" Cindy can scarcely breathe . . . but she isn't about to blow the shot.

"Speed!" I can't believe what only I can see, but manage to stifle my laughter, and gently try to move it away from Cindy's happy button. I guess I'm sensitive that way.

"Slate it!"

"Settle! Okay, Cindy . . . Action!"

And the camera makes its slow, relentless push in to the table. Cindy and I have spray sweat on our brows; I notice Rebecca watching me sneak a private grope under Cindy's sheet. But she won't bitch while the camera is rolling. It's perfect. Drama, tension, Cindy really making me believe she's delivering a difficult baby. Maybe this method shit isn't so bad; she was probably really dilating under there.

The camera is almost on top of her now, she's spasming with pain, and I'm struggling heroically to save the baby. Special effects releases the wash of fluid from hoses run through the table, and I lift Asta from between Cindy's thighs, holding the thing up in the blue light directly in front of the camera.

Asta played it beautifully, letting loose with that long, weak tremolo, spooking everyone on the stage into bug-eyed silence. I kept it rolling for a full two extra minutes, and when I finally yelled "Cut!", cast and crew alike burst into spontaneous applause. I bowed, holding the thing up in front of them, and Hollywood welcomed me home.

When I was sure that there was no camera bobble or sound problem, there was no way I was going to tempt fate. The take was perfect, and we wouldn't do another for Prudential.

I cleared the gawkers away, and set up for the close-up. Asta was no trouble at all under the lights. It just lay there, as if waiting for direction. Vilmos asked me if I wanted to use a doll for a stand-in to set the lights, and like a supreme dick, I said no. No doll is going to have the same reflective qualities of this kid's weird flesh. And it didn't seem to mind, anyway.

Well, I don't know how the word got out so quick, but Welfare showed up on the set before we even ran through the close-up. They were furious, screaming child abuse. There's some law about not being able to have an infant under stage lights for more than thirty seconds, and there must be a state welfare worker and a nurse and a teacher present at all times, or some shit like that.

I tell them there's no child here, that it's special effects. Or an animal. They want to know where the wrangler is. Right. Freak wrangler. By then, we're all yelling, so the AD calls a break, and everybody else is glad to sneak away.

While the welfare bitch and I are getting close to fisticuffs, the second AD gently taps my shoulder. What he whispers makes the whole argument moot. After biting his head off for butting in, I push him aside and rush over to the now-dark delivery table, where Asta is lying. I try to stand in the way, but the bitch in the grey suit is right behind me, wanting to see.

I let her.

Because the little freak wasn't moving, or breathing, or eating, or smelling, or fucking *living*.

Inside my head, there were fireworks, suicide, guns and cacophony. But I stood stock still, my face a bland, vapid wall of I-told-you-so. While the woman was trying to puzzle out the rapidly rubberizing little torso on the table, I slowly turned to look her in the eye, and using all my power, said softly, "Is this really something that concerns you?"

We both turned to see what it was not: a glass-eyed, latex-skinned dummy prop. I remember being astonished at how phony it looked with its lights out, that devoid of life it looked like a castoff from *Ghoulies* or something.

"There's your baby," I gloated, and she split, pissed off, even disappointed.

I called a wrap, and while everybody started to get ready for the next day's shoot, I took the little body and retired to the Winnebago. Cindy was waiting for me, looking all smiley and coquettish about the secret gumming she got under the sheet. I threw her out. She looked all upset and hurt, but fuck her. This was the end of my career.

I locked the door, and sat the little creep on the table and stared at it. The thing now looked ridiculously fake, its skin drying and looking like inner tube rubber — even down to the white dust of powder. The eyes were sightless, soulless, clear glass windows to a dark room.

Before I knew it, Rebecca was knocking on the door, but I just ignored her. She gave up quickly; she must not have been as pissed as I thought she would be.

I started yelling at the little pile of shit on the table, backhanding it to the floor. I'm sorry now, but you've got to comprehend the stress I was under. This little fucker was the key to everything I'd worked so long and hard for, and now all that was smoke. Fuck!

Suicide was an alternative, but I'm too much of a coward to pull the trigger, and not enough of a coward to go quickly. But as I stared into its ugly rubber mug, a simpler choice came to mind. We had the most important shot in the can already. The establishing shot of the monster was there. I could use the whole take. We'd already moved in to a good tight shot anyway, and there was no way the audience wouldn't buy it. Shot properly, maybe one of these effects tyros could help me pull off the rest of the show. Looking at the thing now, with its wick extinguished, the difference between life and latex was obvious . . . but there was no other way out.

We shut down the production for a few weeks while we sent out emergency bids to Stan Winston and Chris Walas and some non-union guys.

SILVER SCREAM

When I showed them the kid the next day, they all thought it was nice, but a little simplistic in design. They all wanted to know who made it, and why didn't I just use them? I told them I'd made it myself, based on a dream I'd had, but I needed someone who could articulate and manipulate it better than I could. It had to be exactly the same look, I told them, only with more life.

After the bids came in, we went with a local Texas kid who cost us a third of the big boys, and was willing to work thirty-hour days for the honor.

As I was waiting in the screening room to see the birth scene, I held my breath. All the big cheeses were there for the dailies; they knew it was the most important moment in the picture. I had only seen it on the Moviola so far. But it was perfect. Everything in perfect focus, no bobbles, and the kid looked great. Unbelievable. When the Suits all gasped at the reveal, I started to breath easy. By now, they all assumed that this thing had always been a special effect, anyway, and were almost glad to shut down for a couple weeks to keep the quality up.

All we had to do was hook them with the real baby footage, and they'd buy the rubber surrogate.

I went home that night feeling almost relaxed. New place, no furniture in it yet: just a bed, a hi-fi VCR, and a projection TV. And a wicker basket with Asta in it. Once the latex clone was finished, I promised to give the thing a decent burial out back . . . but only if the rubber one was perfect.

I didn't have to shoot the next day, so I had my own mini-movie-marathon: *It's Alive, Rosemary's Baby,* and *Taboo IV,* which put me to sleep, but with a raging erection.

It was an engorgement that would not subside in slumber, but rather kept time with my heartbeat until the door opened late that night. I opened my eyes. Unexpectedly, delightfully, Rebecca and Cindy entered in a shaft of light that penetrated the sparse, diaphanous nightclothes they wore. However unlikely, they seemed the best of friends, and got even friendlier when they joined me in the kip.

Our acrobatics were like a letter to Penthouse, and featured every erotic combination you could imagine . . . and six or seven more. It was a release I hadn't felt since preproduction began. I had a mouth at either end of me, and the two of them brought me to the most devastating, sphincter-clenching orgasm of my life!

But on the second jolt, I woke up, my little friend pumping, my eyes rolled back in abandoned ecstasy.

As the waves of orgasm died down, I gradually resumed consciousness. I opened my eyes for real . . . and almost threw up. That slippery fucking maggot kid from the cookie basket was between my legs, impaled on my divining rod taken so deeply down its throat that I must have fertilized its stomach. The thing was ravenously sucking my milk until I was dry. Its skin was slippery again, oily and alive, as it slid hungrily over my flesh.

A LIFE IN THE CINEMA

Barely conscious at four in the morning, and dazed from the force of the orgasm, I could only stare through slitted, puffy eyes at the monstrosity devouring me. The incredible suction slackened as it sensed there was no more juice to be had, and I weakly backhanded the thing. It didn't even react; gathering my strength in disgust, I hit out with full force, knocking the piece of shit against the wall, where it hit with a splat before sliding stickily and lifelessly down the wall.

I stood up, my head throbbing with every heartbeat, and walked dizzily across the room, following my still-extended wand until I was right over Asta. There was a trail of blood on the wall, as if pointing at the gooey little heap that lay on the floor. Guilt, disgust, and horror welled up in the pit of my stomach, and lurched out of my mouth and onto the dead heap.

First with the stage lights and now, literally at my own hand, I had killed the thing again.

I jumped into my sweats, and scooped the horrid pile into a plastic bag, then carried it out into the yard. There was no moon, which was fine with me, so I took the mess and buried it deep behind the barbecue pit. Blood-blisters on my hands, I rushed back into the barren house.

I stayed in bed the whole next day, just thinking about the little monster. There was no innocence there. This was no child, no infant. In the months I had been in possession of it, there had been no sign of growth or maturity or change. The thing is what it is, not what it's going to be. What that is, I don't know, but I soon would make an educated guess.

All I know is that day I was as fucked up as I've ever been — my ecstasy had been linked end-to-end with extreme revulsion. I'd been blown by the ghost of a monster baby. Not recommended. And then the fucking toilets backed up. I know that may seem mundane in this perspective, but it has everything to do with it. When I tried to flush, there was merely a gurgle, and I knew at once the damned machine was playing with its food. The lid was lowered and the plumber called.

I forgot about it until I had to go again that afternoon. Ready for relief, I lifted the lid, only to see that fucking squirmer Asta settled in the bowl, basking in dinner. I tried to flush it down to greet the legendary sewer 'gators, but the plumbing just backed up, spewing fouled water onto the bathroom floor.

Again, in anger, humiliation, and disgust, I beat the shit out of it, mangled the tortured little body, and killed it a third time. Big fucking deal. It would be back . . . no matter how often, or distant, or deeply I buried the thing.

The old Mexican woman knew I was her salvation the first time she saw me. I know that now. I must have destroyed the baby two dozen times by now, but it'll keep coming back. To feed.

I can only imagine how long its last host continued to lactate and suckle the parasite that had claimed and controlled her. It's like giving a stray cat a dish of milk — you'll never shake the fucking thing. My lust to own it was the closest thing to love it ever felt, and now we're paired. Mated. For life.

It comes, each day after I kill it, to partake of my body's castoffs — my cells, my essence. It sweats my saliva, lives on my excreta, rejuvenated by my spermatozoa.

God help me if it tastes my blood.

In the months since we shot the birth scene, sleep has been only a distant dream that comes fleetingly. The phone used to ring before I pulled it out, and many people have come to the door and given up trying to find me. Whenever my defenses drop, it comes home to ravage me. I fade into exhausted sleep, knowing I'll wake to find it devouring me, my sex slid deep into its female region, another slippery appendage behind and inside me, taking, not wasting anything, not even tears.

This thing will live as long as I do. Maybe longer.

I had to have the little fucker to exploit. It was the strongest emotion I could feel, and now I'm paying up. I know of one sure way to end the torment. I can't believe I've put it off so long. Asta may be indestructible, but I am not. I have only a single regret.

I know I'll never make another movie.

SPLATTER: A CAUTIONARY TALE

by

Douglas E. Winter

Apocalypse Domani

In the hour before dawn, as night retreated into shadow, the dream chased Rehnquist awake. The gates of hell had opened, the cannibals had taken to the streets, and Rehnquist waited alone, betrayed by the light of the coming day. Soon, he knew, the zombies would find him, the windows would shatter, the doors burst inward, and the hands, stained with their endless feast, would beckon to him. They would eat of his flesh and drink of his blood, but spare his immortal soul; and at dawn, he would rise again, possessed of their hunger, their quenchless thirst, to view a grave new world through the vacant eyes of the dead next door.

The Beyond

"And you will face the sea of darkness, and all therein that may be explored." Tallis tipped his wine glass in empty salute. "So much for the poet." He glanced back along the east wing of the Corcoran Gallery, its chronology of Swiss impressionists dominated by Zweig's "L'Aldila," an oceanscape of burned sand littered with mummified remains. His attorney, Gavin Widmark, steered him from the bar and forced a smile: "Perhaps a bit more restraint." Tallis slipped a fresh glass of Chardonnay from the tray of a passing waiter. "Art," he said, his voice slurred and overloud, "is nothing but the absence of restraint." Across the room, a blonde woman faced them with a frown. "Ah, Thom," Widmark said, gesturing toward her. "Have you met Cameron Blake?"

SILVER SCREAM

Cannibal Ferox

Memory: the angry rain washing over Times Square, scattering the Women's March Against Pornography into the ironic embrace of ill-lit theater entrances. She stood beneath a lurid film poster: "Make Them Die Slowly!" it screamed, adding, as if an afterthought, "The Most Violent Film Ever!" And as she waited in the sudden shadows, clutching a placard whose red ink had smeared into a wound, she surveyed the faces emerging from the grindhouse lobby: the wisecracking black youths, shouting and shoving their way back onto the streets; the middleaged couple, moving warily through the unexpected phalanx of sternfaced women; and finally, the young man, alone, a hardcover novel by Thomas Tallis gripped to his chest. His fugitive eyes, trapped behind thick wire-rimmed glasses, seemed to caution Cameron Blake as she stood with her sisters, hoping to take back the night.

Dawn of the Dead

At the shopping mall, the film posters taunted Rehnquist with the California dream of casual, sunbaked sex: for yet another summer, teen tedium reigned at the fourplex. He visited instead the video library, prowling the everthinning shelves of horror films — each battered box a brick in the wall of his defense — and wondering what he would do when they were gone. At the cashier's desk, he had seen the mimeographed petition: PROTECT YOUR RIGHTS — WHAT YOU NEED TO KNOW ABOUT H.R. 1762. But he didn't need to know what he could see even now, watching the shoppers outside, locked in the timestep of the suburban sleepwalk. "This was an important place in their lives," he said, although he knew that no one was listening.

Eaten Alive

"After all," said Cameron Blake as another slide jerked onto the screen, a pale captive writhing in bondage on a dusty motel-room bed, "what is important about a woman in these films is not how she feels, not what she does for a living, not what she thinks about the world around her . . . but simply how she bleeds." The slide projector clicked, and the audience fell silent. The next victim arched above a makeshift worktable, suspended by a meat hook

268

that had been thrust into her vagina. Moist entrails spilled, coiling, onto the gore-stained floor below. From the back of the lecture hall, as the shocked whispers rose in protest, came the unmistakable sound of someone laughing.

Friday the 13th

He had decided to rent an eternal holiday favorite, and now, on his television screen, the bottle-blonde game-show maven staggered across the moonlit beach, her painted lips puckered in a knowing smile. "Kill her, Mommy, kill her," she mouthed, a sing-song soliloquy that he soon joined. The obligatory virgin fell before her, legs sprawled in an inviting wedge, and the axe poised, its shiny tip moistened expectantly with a shimmer of blood. Rehnquist closed his eyes; all too soon, he knew, we would visit the hospital room where the virgin lay safe abed, wondering what might still lurk at Camp Crystal Lake. But he imagined instead a different ending, one without sequel, one without blood, and he knew that he could not let it be.

The Gates of Hell

On the first morning of the hearings on H.R. 1762, Tallis mounted the steps to the Rayburn Building to observe the passionate parade: the war-film actor, pointing the finger of self-righteous accusation; the bearded psychiatrists, soft-spoken oracles of aggression models and impact studies; the school-teachers and ministers, each with a story of shattered morality; and then the mothers, the fathers, the battered women, the rape victims, the abused children, lost in their tears and in search of a cause, pleading to the politicians who sat in solemn judgment above them. He saw, without surprise, that Cameron Blake stood with them in the hearing room, spokesman for the silent, the forgotten, the bruised, the violated, the sudden dead.

Halloween

That night, alone in his apartment, Rehnquist huddled with his videotapes, considering the minutes that would be lost to the censor's blade. Sometimes,

SILVER SCREAM

when he closed his eyes, he envisioned stories and films that never were, and that now, perhaps, never would be. As his television flickered with the ultimate holiday of horror, he watched the starlet's daughter, pressed against the wall, another virgin prey to an unwelcome visitor; but as her mouth opened in a soundless scream, his eyes closed, and he saw her in her mother's place, heiress to that fateful room in the Bates Motel, a full-color nude trapped behind the shower curtain as the arm, wielding the long-handled knife, stiffened and thrust, stiffened and thrust again. And as her perfect body, spent, slipped to the blood-sprinkled tile, he opened his eyes and grinned: "It *was* the Boogeyman, wasn't it?"

Inferno

"No, my friends," pronounced the Reverend Wilson Macomber, scowling for the news cameras as he descended the steps of the Liberty Gospel Church in Clinton, Maryland. "I am speaking for our children. It is *their* future that is at stake. I hold in my hand a list . . ." The flashguns popped, and the mini-cams swept across the anxious gathering, then focused upon the waiting jumble of wooden blocks, doused with kerosene. Macomber suddenly smiled, and his flock, their arms laden with books and magazines, videotapes and record albums, smiled with him. He thrust a paperback into the eye of the nearest camera. "This one," he laughed, "shall truly be a firestarter." He tossed the book onto the waiting pyre, and proclaimed, with the clarity of unbending conviction, "Let there be light." And the flames burned long into the night.

Just Before Dawn

As she rubbed at her eyes, the headache seemed to flare, then pass; she motioned to the graduate student waiting at the door. Cameron Blake saw herself fifteen years before, comfortable in t-shirt and jeans, hair tossed wildly, full of herself and the knowledge that change lay just around the corner. She saw herself, and knew why she had left both a husband and a Wall Street law firm for the chance to teach the lessons of those fifteen years. Change did not lie in wait. Change was wrought, often painfully, and never without a fight. In the student's hands were the crumpled sheets of an awkward polemic: "Only Women Bleed: DePalma and the Politics of Voyeurism." In her eyes were the wet traces of self-doubt, but not tears; no,

270

never tears. Cameron Blake smoothed the pages and unsheathed her red pen. "Why don't we start with *Body Double?*"

The Keep

Tallis silenced the stereo and stared into the blank screen of his computer. He had tried to write for hours, but his typing produced only indecipherable codes: words, sentences, paragraphs without life or logic. Inside, he could feel only a mounting silence. He looked again to the newspaper clippings stacked neatly on his desk, a bloody testament to the power of words and images: Charles Manson's answer to the call of the Beatles' "Helter Skelter"; the obsession with *Taxi Driver* that had almost killed a president; the parents who had murdered countless infants in bedroom exorcisms. He drew his last novel, *Jeremiad*, from the bookshelf, and wondered what deaths had been rehearsed in its pages.

The Last House on the Left

Congressman James Stodder overturned the cardboard box, scattering its contents before the young attorney from the American Civil Liberties Union. He carefully catalogued each item for the subcommittee: black market photographs of the nude corpse of television actress Lauren Hayes, taken by her abductors moments after they had disembowelled her with a garden trowel; a videotape of Lucio Fulci's twice-banned *Apoteosi del Mistero*; an eight-millimeter film loop entitled *Little Boy Snuffed*, confiscated by the FBI in the back room of an adult bookstore in Pensacola, Florida; and a copy of the Clive Barker novel *Requiem*, its pages clipped at its most infamous scenes. "Now tell me," Stodder said, his voice shaking and rising to a shout, "which is fact and which is fiction?"

Maniac

Rehnquist keyed the volume control, drawn to the montage of violent film clips that preceded the C-SPAN highlights of the Stodder subcommittee. A film critic waved a tattered poster, savoring his moment before the cameras: "This is," he exclaimed, "the single most reprehensible film ever made. The question that should be asked is: are people so upset because the murderer is so heinous or because the murderer is being portrayed in such a positive and supportive light?" Rehnquist twisted the television dial, first to the top-rated police show, where fashionable vice cops pumped endless shotgun rounds into a drug dealer; then to the news reports of bodies stacked like cords of wood at a railhead in El Salvador; and finally to the solace of MTV, where Mick Jagger cavorted in the streets of a ruined city, singing of too much blood.

Night of the Living Dead

In the beginning, he remembered, there were no videotapes. There were no X ratings, no labels warning of sex or violence, no seizures of books on library shelves, no committees or investigations. In the beginning, there were dreams without color. There was peace, it was said, and prosperity; and he slept in that innocent belief until the night he had awakened in the back seat of his car, transfixed by the black-and-white nightmare, the apocalypse alive on the drive-in movie screen: "They're coming to get you, Barbara," the actor had warned. But Rehnquist knew that the zombies were coming for him, the windows shattering, the doors bursting inward. The dead, he had learned, were alive and hungry — hungry for him — and the dreams, ever after, were always the color red.

Orgy of the Blood Parasites

The gavel thundered again, and as the shouts subsided, Tallis returned to his prepared statement. "Under the proposed legislation," he read, without waiting for silence, "whether or not the depiction of violence constitutes pornography depends upon the perspective that the writer or the film director adopts. A story that is violent and that simply depicts women" — he winced at the renewed chorus of indignation — "that simply depicts women in positions of submission, or even display, is forbidden, regardless of the literary or political value of the work taken as a whole. On the other hand, a story that depicts women in positions of equality is lawful, no matter how graphic its violence. This . . ." He paused, looking first at James Stodder, then at each other member of the subcommittee. "This is thought control."

SPLATTER: A CAUTIONARY TALE

Profondo Rosso

Widmark led him through the gauntlet of reporters outside the Rayburn Building. Tallis looked to the west, but saw only row after row of white marble facades. "This is suicide," Widmark said. "You realize that, don't you? Take a look at this." He flourished an envelope stuffed with photocopies of news clippings and book reviews, then handed Tallis a letter detailing the lengthy cuts that Berkley had requested for the new novel. Tallis tore the letter in half, unread. "I need a drink," he said, and waved to the blonde woman who waited for him on the steps below. No one noticed the young man in wire-rimmed glasses who stood across the street, washed in the deep red of the setting sun.

Quella Villa Accanto il Cimitero

Rehnquist had found the answer on the front page of the *Washington Post*, while reading its reports of the latest testimony before Stodder's raging subcommittee. There, between boldfaced quotations from a midwestern police chief and a psychoanalyst with the unlikely name of Freudstein, was a clouded news photograph labelled GEORGETOWN PROFESSOR CAMERON BLAKE; its caption read, "Violence in fiction, film, may as well be real." His fingers had traced the outline of her face with nervous familiarity — the blonde hair, the thin lips, parted in anxious warning, the wide dark eyes of Barbara Steele. When he raised his hand, he saw only the dark blur of newsprint along his fingertips. He knew then what he had to do.

Reanimator

They shared a booth at the Capitol Hilton coffee shop, trading Bloody Marys while searching for a common ground. The conversation veered from Lovecraft to the latest seafood restaurant in Old Town Alexandria; then Tallis, working his third cocktail, told of his year in Italy with Dario Argento, drawing honest laughter with an anecdote about the mistranslated script for *Lachrymae*. She countered with the story of the graduate student who had

273

called him the most dangerous writer since Norman Mailer. "That's quite a compliment," he said. "But what do you think?" Cameron Blake shook her head: "I told her to try reading you first." As they left the hotel, he paused at the newsstand to buy a paperback copy of *Jeremiad.* "A gift for your student," he said, but when he reached to take her hand, she hesitated. In a moment, he was alone.

Suspiria

"Hello." It was his voice, hardly more than a sigh, that surprised Cameron Blake. The door slammed shut behind her, and he passed from the shadows into light, barring her way. She stepped back, taking the measure of the drab young man who had invaded her home; she thought, for a moment, that they had once met, strangers in a sudden rain. "I want to show you something," Rehnquist said; but as she pushed past him, intent on reaching the telephone, the videocassette that he had offered to her slipped away, shattering on the hardwood floor. In that moment, as the tape spooled lifelessly onto the floor, their destiny was sealed.

The Texas Chainsaw Massacre

Tallis hooked the telephone on the first ring. He had been waiting for her to call, but the voice at the other end, echoing in the hiss of long distance, was that of Gavin Widmark; it was his business voice, friendly but measured, and could herald only bad news. Berkley, despite three million copies of *Jeremiad* in print, had declined to publish the new novel. If only he would consider the proposed cuts . . . If only he would mediate the level of violence . . . If only . . . Without a word, Tallis placed the receiver gently back onto its cradle. He tipped another finger of gin into his glass and stared into the widening depths of the empty computer screen.

The Undertaker and His Pals

She knew, as Rehnquist unfolded the straight razor, that there would be no

274

escape. A dark certainty inhabited his eyes as he advanced, the light shimmering on the blade, and she pressed against the wall, watching, waiting. "For you, Cameron," he said. The razor flashed, kissing his left wrist before licking evenly along the vein. She squeezed her eyes closed, but he called to her — "For you, Cameron" — and she looked again as the fingers of his left hand toppled to the carpet in a rain of blood. "For you, Cameron." The razor poised at his throat, slashing a sudden grin that vomited crimson across his chest, and as he staggered out into the street, blood trailing in his wake, she found that she could not stop watching.

Videodrome

Every picture tells a story, thought Detective Sergeant Richard Howe, stepping aside to clear the police photographer's field of vision. He knew that the prints on his desk tomorrow would seem to depict reality, their flattened images belying what he had sensed from the moment he arrived: the bloodstains splattering the floor of the Capitol Hill townhouse had been deeper and darker than any he had ever seen. He would not easily forget the woman's expression when he told her that the shorn fingertips were slabs of latex, the blood merely a concoction of corn syrup and food coloring. He looked again to the shattered videocassette, sealed in the plastic evidence bag: DIRECTED BY DAVID CRONENBERG read the label. He couldn't wait for the search warrant to issue; turning over this guy's apartment was going to be a scream.

The Wizard of Gore

When the first knock sounded at the door, Rehnquist set aside his worn copy of *Jeremiad*, marked at its most frightening passage: "and at dawn, he would rise again, possessed of their hunger, their quenchless thirst, to view a grave new world through the vacant eyes of the dead next door." At his feet curled the thin plastic tubing, stripped from his armpit and drained of stage blood. "It's not real," he said, and the knocking stopped. "It's *never* been real." The window to his left shattered, glass spraying in all directions; then the door burst inward, yawning on a single hinge, and the hands, the beckoning hands, thrust toward him. The long night had ended. The zombies had come for him at last.

SILVER SCREAM

Xtro

The Reverend Wilson Macomber rose to face the Stodder subcommittee, his deep voice echoing unamplified across the hearing room. "I don't know if anybody else has done this for you all, but I want to pray for you right now, and I want to ask everyone in this room who fears God to bow their head." He pressed a tiny New Testament to his heart. "Dear Father . . . I pray that you would destroy wickedness in this city and in every wicked city. I pray that you draw the line, as it is written here, and those that are righteous, let them be righteous still, and they that are filthy, let them be filthy still . . ." At the back of the hearing room, his face etched in the shadows, Tallis shifted uneasily. In Macomber's insectile stare, mirrored by the stony smile of James Stodder, the haunted eyes of Cameron Blake, he knew that it was over. As the vote began on H.R. 1762, he turned and walked away, into the sudden light of a silent day.

Les Yeux sans Visage

Months later, in another kind of theater, green-shirted medical students witnessed the drama of stereotactic procedures, justice meted out in the final reel. "The target," announced the white-masked lecturer, gesturing with his scalpel, "is the cingulate gyrus." Here he paused for effect, glancing overhead to the video enlargement of the patient's exposed cerebral cortex. "Although some prefer to make lesions interrupting the fibers radiating to the frontal lobe." The blade moved with deceptive swiftness, neither in extreme closeup nor in slow motion; but the blood, which jetted for an instant across the neurosurgeon's steady right hand, was assuredly real.

Zombie

In an hour like many other hours, Rehnquist smiled as the warder rolled his wheelchair along the endless white corridors of St. Elizabeth's Hospital. He smiled at his newfound friends, with their funny number-names; he smiled at the darkened windows, criss-crossed with wire mesh to keep him safe; he

276

smiled at the warmth of the urine puddling slowly beneath him. And as the wheelchair reached the end of another hallway, he smiled again and touched the angry scar along his forehead. He asked the warder — whose name, he thought, was Romero — if it was time to sleep again. He liked to sleep. In fact, he couldn't think of anything he would rather do than sleep. But sometimes, when he woke, smiling into the morning sun, he wondered why it was that he no longer dreamed.

FILM AT ELEVEN

by

John Skipp

It started out like just another Thursday in Hell.

She awoke in her bed at eight a.m. The air was thick with heat and sweat. Dale was naked and snoring beside her, his fists unfurled in sleep. She heard the screen door at the front of the house scream open, then slam shut. Tiny footsteps hit the sidewalk and receded into the world.

Nikki was safe: for now, at least.

And Dottie Neff was alone.

With him.

She let the day's pain seep back into her body gradually, let her memory piece together what it could. Sleep had put a buffer between Wednesday's Hell and the new one a-bornin', but that mercy fried quickly in the sweet light of day. Then the damage began to itemize itself, meticulous but in no particular order.

This morning brought the skull-ache first. It centered on the jaws, the temples, and the space immediately behind her eyes. By the time her brain began to throb, the rest of her body was catching up: the wrenched left arm, the throbbing nipples, the pummeled pussy, all on fire. Before she even began to move, the entire inventory had been laid out.

Then she remembered poor ol' Buzz Royer, which reminded her of the plan, and the ghostly sweet sweet taste of freedom came flooding back to warm and haunt her.

It didn't make Hell go away, of course; when she moved the pain got instantly worse. "Oh, God," she moaned, but she did so quietly. There was much to do, in the next hour or so; the last thing she wanted was to wake up Dale. Not with that flavor so close to her tongue.

Not when she was so close.

Her feet edged off the side of the bed and wobbled to the floor. The rest of her followed, wobbling naked toward the open bedroom door. He had not bothered to close it before launching into last night's hate-making ritual. So Nikki, as usual, had heard it all.

But for the last time, Dottie silently swore. *Baby, I promise.*

Today we say goodbye . . .

She shuffled into the hallway and headed for the back of the house. There was a full-length mirror on the bathroom door at the end of the hall. She saw herself in it, could not look away.

The woman who stared back was thirty-two, five foot six, one hundred and sixty-nine. She had big brown eyes with tiny pupils and dark puffy bruises around them. A styleless mop of mud-brown hair, limp as roadkill, crowned her head. There was no tone to the pale white flesh, just bulge and stoop and sag. In fact, there was nothing to commend this woman at all. Except.

Except that she was ready.

And that, with every step she took, she seemed to grow . . .

june 17

dear oprah winfrey

i don't know how to start this. i've never written to a big star like yourself before! i never thought i had anything that important to say, you know? but i watch your show all the time, and it moved me so much. your so brave and strong and funny. i just wish that i was like you. i think you are the greatest woman in the whole world. i really mean that.

but the problem is i'm not like you at all. i don't have any guts. i think the bravest thing i ever did was writing you this letter, and i bet i don't even have the nerve to mail it.

you see, i have problems. most of them are my fault. i know, but i just don't know how to get around them. when i think about how messed up my life has gotten, sometimes it doesn't seem like theres any hope at all. it's just too complicated. do you know what I mean?

but then i watch your show, and i get hope. i see all these women overcoming all these incredible things. just being so honest and open about thier feelings, and i wish that i could do that, but i can't.

sometimes it gets me really scared, like when you had on

the rapists for two days, or those people who wrote books about murderers like son of sam. and sometimes you make me laugh, like when you had on burt reynolds or mel gibson and that black man. and then sometimes you really just make me think, like when you had shirley maclaine. i mean, that stuff was just so far out, i didn't know *what* to think!

but most of the time, it makes me cry. (not that i need any help, thank you!) its just that i see so much of my own life, things that help me explain whats going on in my own life, and i don't know why but most of the time it just makes me more confused.

i geuss the reason i'm writing today is because you just had on that woman doctor susan forward again. you know, the one who wrote *men who hate women and the women who love them?* i had never heard the word misojony before, but i'll never forget it now, because my boyfriend is just like that. he puts me down all the time. he doesnt let me have any friends. when i try to make myself look pretty, like i buy a new dress or put on makeup or get a haircut or something, he says things like what the blank is *that* suppose to be, anyway? i swear it drives me crazy sometimes.

the problem is that i think i could fight him except for my mind doesn't work too well. my doctor, doctor himmler, says that i get seizures in my brain, in the frontal lobe. thats why my thoughts race around so crazy. the drugs he gives me help alot, 1600 mgs. of lithium and 500 mgs. of a new drug called tegretol, which he says suppresses the convulsions. but i still can't get a handle on what i'm doing, and besides my boyfriend is even more messed up than me. he's got a different doctor than me, and he gets lots of percodans and this cough syrup that i think is called hycutus, and all i know is that it has a lot of codeine in it, and it makes him so crazy and mean once he gets going that a lot of times i'm afraid for my life.

the worst part is that i've got a little daughter. her name is nichole, but i call her nikki. she's only six years old. and she doesnt understand whats happening, but i know that she hates dale and i think she hates me for letting him live here, and i would throw him out except i'm afraid he wouldnt leave, he'd just beat me worse and maybe hurt nikki too. i dont think that i could live if he ever did anything to nikki.

so you see what my problem is. i dont know what to do. i dont even know what i'm writing you for except that if you were on my side i know i could do anything. i guess that its too much to ask, sense i'm just somebody off of the streets, but if i was on your show one day, i swear to god i'd spill my guts, and maybe somebody would know how bad i hurt and help me, and maybe other women who are in the same situation could get help. thats the most beatiful thing about your show. you find out that your not alone. thats the most beatiful thing that anyone could ever give a person.

i love you, oprah, and i hope you read this letter. if you cant ever write back, i understand. i wish you all the happiness in the world, and thank you for what you've given me.

all my love,
dorothy abigail neff.

MARK AS EXHIBIT A

After she had thrown up and taken her pills, control began to set in. She could feel it as a cool power running taut down her spine. She could feel it in her movements, the assuredness of them, the sense that she was moving herself and not just being dragged along behind. She was drawing on parts of herself that hadn't seen light in a long time. But they were still there. And they still worked.

She checked herself out in the bathroom mirror. The swelling on her face was expansive and colorful. It would look great on the Channel 8 News Break, she felt quite sure. A picture's worth a thousand words . . .

. . . and of course that took her back to poor Buzz Royer, the beetle-black flatness of his eyes in those, his final moments onscreen. There was something in the way that he parted his lips to swallow Death: not like an invasion, but like a lover's tongue . . .

. . . and then she was back in the bathroom, and the clock was ticking. 8:11.

Time to move.

She had started out okay enough. Dad was a $50,000 a year sales manager for York Caterpillar. Mom was up to her bouffant hairdo in garden clubs and church activities. They loved her just fine, albeit always from a distance. They taught her to be well-mannered, obedient and clean, and above all to put on a happy face.

FILM AT ELEVEN

Dottie had mediocred her way through school, never seeing the point and not entirely wrong in that. She was bright enough, but it was hard to whip up much enthusiasm. The important thing was to make nicey-nice, to not make waves, and to keep on smilin'. There were always friends, and there were always parties, and someday there'd be a man who would take care of her in style.

But then the recreational drugs had begun to get serious roughly one year after graduation; time began to slide by on a moist trail of cheap wine, overpriced columbian, angel dust and ludes. It was the early seventies, and the mighty counter-culture of the previous decade had shot its mighty wad. Left behind in archeological splendor were the sex, the drugs, the rock 'n roll, the threadbare middle-class rebellion; but its lofty values were nowhere to be found, either driven underground or sputtered off into the ozone.

It was an empty time to be young and white in America: and while some covered for it with a brave new cynicism, the Dotties of the world muddled en masse toward the center, where they had no fucking idea as to what was going on. Fake it. Hang out. Don't worry about tomorrow, it'll take care of itself. Don't bother building for it, either. Just gimme another hit.

Her parents responded by throwing her out, after all the hand-wringing and shouting was through. She spent the next few years doing a retro tapdance of her father's footsteps, selling hot pretzels, silly shoes and the last of the great black lite posters as the different jobs shuffled her from one York Mall emporium to the other. The party was dimming, but so was her soul; despite a gnawing dissatisfaction, life appeared to go on.

By the time she met her one true love, she was almost twenty-seven years old. His name was Barry Strasbaugh, and he was tall and skinny, with a nose like a large kosher dill; but he treated her sweetly, and he had a steady job, and she knew for a fact that he wasn't fucking around behind her back.

Most of all, he did not try to change her. He accepted her for what she was. There was no greater gift than that.

She accepted it, and gave him all her love in return.

A year of considerable happiness followed, the dream not decaying until after the marriage, roughly five months into her first to-term pregnancy. That was when her inability to cut back on the drink and smoke and pills began to erode his patience. The fact that his habits remained unchanged was quite beside the point, he felt. After all, he wasn't the one who was pregnant.

By the time Nicole arrived, Barry was yelling most of the time, and Dottie had made the big leap to tequila, vodka, and gin. Little Nikki was tiny indeed — a month premature, at five pounds seven ounces — and

SILVER SCREAM

there was some doubt as to whether she would live. But after three insurance-free and financially devastating weeks in the hospital, their daughter was released into the world of hurt.

It was good of Barry to wait for the baby before he started to slap Dottie around. At that point, he didn't know what else to do. It didn't help matters, but it gave him something to do with his hands when he wasn't busy drinking, playing cards with the boys, or test-driving tanks out at Bowen-McLaughlin.

The marriage lasted for nearly three years. During that time, she made seven trips to the hospital: two mild concussions, one slightly more serious one, a fractured rib, a badly sprained ankle, a stomach ulcer, and one rather lengthy stay in Three Northeast, the psychiatric wing of York Hospital. It was during that sojourn that Barry took his leave for good, bestowing Nikki's sickly presence on Dottie's long-suffering parents.

Under the expert care of the astoundingly-named Dr. Himmler, Dottie went through six weeks that verified her residence in Hell. She remembered very little of her stay, except in snatches that could just as easily have been dreams. She remembered long stretches of questions and answers, where next to none of the words made sense. She remembered A.A. meetings and sessions with priests. She remembered someone giving her injections in her feet. She remembered a number of strange locations: a slum where crumbling doorways were being rebuilt, a room where lots of teenagers were milling around, a place distinguished by white walls and a steady rocking motion. She remembered waking up to sharp pain in her rectum, then fading out again.

At the end, she was diagnosed as suffering from irregular brain seizures. This was not good news. Dr. Himmler, however, had just the thing for her: more drugs. He also set her up on the public dole through the Pennsylvania Department of Mental Health, which paid for everything from her house to her food stamps to her drugs and doctor's appointments. She left the hospital in a cerebrally passive state, free of every nasty habit but smoking and the inability to hold a concrete thought for more than three minutes at a time.

Time heals, and Dottie's seemed to stretch forever; so when six months down the road found her both drinking and thinking again, nobody was too surprised. Though she couldn't find a steady job, or hold it if she did: there was a series of off-the-books housecleaning assignments that kept her in margaritas and occasional clothes for Nikki. For a while, life was almost bearable again.

And then, one night at the Gaslight Tavern, she met Dale. And Hell resumed in earnest . . .

*　*　*

FILM AT ELEVEN

july 20

dear oprah,

its been a while since my last letter. since then, things have gotten much worse. sometimes dale takes as many as twelve percodans at a time, and if he isnt hitting me then he's passed out in bed. he got fired from his job at borg warner. and the money i get from the state isnt enough to keep us all alive. sometimes he goes out and tries to bum some, but his family and friends gave up on him a long time ago, just like mine did with me. i geuss i can't blame them, but its still so hard.

i keep trying to think of something that will make this important, something that makes it different from every other sob story you ever heard. i can't. if there was anything special about me, i probably woundnt be in this mess.

no, maybe i'm wrong. i'm sitting here writing this, and suddenly its all making sense somehow. i'm not just an ordinary person, because ordinary people dont sink this low. i'm a *very* special person, in a very strange way. i'm god's own special fuckup, youll pardon my french. i'm as fucked up as a person can be.

its like, eveybody is born with thier own special guardian angel, you know what i mean? and you live and you live, but every time it comes down to the point of disaster, he's there for you. he sees you thru it, and he kinda gives you a little pat on the head and says its okay, dottie. you made a couple wrong turns there, but i still love you.

now you still have yours. thats real clear. i watch you up there on the tv screen, and its perfectly obvious that you know why you were born. you laugh and you cry and you ask all the right questions, and you bring millions of us together five days a week to help us remember why god bothered to make us in the first place. its the little voice of the angel in your ear going remember me? come on! we got places to go and people to see!

but i lost mine, i swear to god, and now i dont know what to do. its like i went this way and he went that, and the next thing we knew we were out in the wilderness with thousands of miles between us and no way back, because there is no way back. everybody always told me you cant go back and i cant help but beleive them now because i'm totally totally lost.

so what can i think? i'll tell you what. i think that i was supposed to lose it. i think that i'm suppose to be an example of what *not* to do, you know what i'm saying? i feel like a soldier thats marching off to war, and he knows hes going to die, and he

285

knows that theres no way out of it, and the only thing he can figure is that theres a bigger picture somewhere, and he'll be one of the details. one of the bodies in a pile on a page in a textbook on history that somebody will make thier little kids read so that maybe they wont make the same mistake, theyll hold on to that angel and theyll never let go until its time to die and they fly away forever. could that be what its like?

i dont know. tell the truth, i probably never will. i cant stop thinking that if i got on your show, and fifty million people were watching, that maybe my guardian angel would see and get back to me in time.

but i didnt have the guts to send my last letter, so i bet i wont send this one either. sometimes i dont think i'll see my angel again until i die, and all that makes me want to do is die faster. you know what i mean?

i dont know what i mean. i have convulsions in my brain. how are you suppose to think with convulsions in your brain? so maybe i'm not so wrong after all. what do you think?

i love you, oprah. i'm sorry.

love,
dorothy abigail neff

MARK AS EXHIBIT B

Most of the hardest work had already been done last night, before Dale staggered home and raped and beat her. She had had her shit that much together. And so much of it was simple opportunism: the piles of clothing strewn about, the loose newspaper, the cheap furniture and carpet and paneling that constituted her home.

Plus one other little thing . . .

From there, it was largely a matter of strategic placement and timing. Yes, timing was clearly of the essence; that, and the purchase of three cans of lighter fluid. From there, all that remained was getting dressed.

And making a phone call.

And doing it up.

Dottie slid into the green halter top and frayed cutoffs that she had left in the living room the night before. There was no shortage of footwear by the side of the front door. She opted for the tawny brown leather thongs.

As she put them on, she thought *these are the clothes that you're going to die in.* The thought didn't bother her nearly as much as she felt it should have. Funny thing about that. When she thought about Buzz Royer, with his jet-black suit and ridiculous striped tie and balding pate, she felt a burst of ugly pity that was quickly subsumed by the knowledge that he'd died just as he lived. And if that meant he was a fool, then at least he died consistent, he didn't try to be somebody else as he went out.

She hoped to achieve at least that much honesty.

All the way down Lehman St., she was astounded by how *bright* everything was. Not just the sun, which had been scorching the poor long-suffering earth with record heat for the last ten days. It was everything: the crisp green and brown of tree and lawn, the white and brick and tan of the houses that lined the street, the multi-colored cars and flowers, the blue and white of the sky. She felt as if a thick swath of tinted film had been lifted from before her eyes. It was almost like tripping, euphoria and all.

There was a pay phone in the back of Jim & Nina's Pizzeria. The massive air conditioner on the wall above kicked the hundred and ten degrees around the little room with gargantuan futility, but its pointless roar more than shielded her words from the ears of the counter girl. Dottie unravelled the moist strip of paper from her back pocket, slipped a quarter in the slot, and dialed.

Seven rings later, a man's voice informed her that she had reached the Channel 8 news department.

"I'd like to report a fire," she said.

august 7

dear oprah,

if your reading this, i must be dead. dont feel bad. i certainly dont. death cant be any worse than living has been, and i have a feeling that its gonna be a whole lot better.

but i want you to know what happened, because i want you to understand. then maybe you can do a show without me, but people will still get the story, and maybe others wont have to do what i did just to let the world know that they cant take it anymore.

it all started yesterday, when i was watching tv, during the morning, my station is channel 2 from baltimore. it shows you at nine, then phil donohue at ten (i like him, but hes not like you. i geuss its because hes not a woman. sometimes i feel like hes talking down to me, and i get enough of that from dale.) anyway, and then the wheel comes on at 11, and i love pat sajak, i think

287

hes so funny. so i watch straight through to 11:30, and by then dale usually wakes up long enough to choke down some food before passing out again.

but yesterday, just as they were going into the bonus round, they cut in with a special news report. you probably heard about it. this man named buzz royer shot himself in the head in front of national tv at a press conference. i dont know if you saw it, but it was pretty amazing.

i mean, here was this poor man, and you could just see how bad he was hurting inside. i think they had caught him stealing money from the government, he was state treasurer or something. anyway, he was in some deep shit, you could tell right away.

so there he was, standing behind his little podium, and all of a sudden he pulls this gun out of this manila envelope, and everybody starts yelling, and he sticks it in his mouth, and the next thing you know theres this horrible noise and he disappears behind the podium, and before i had a chance to think it was over.

but you know what i thought when i got the chance?

i thought *i can do that.*

i mean, it was over so quickly. the worst part must have been the press conference. thinking about it. talking to all these people as if he was going to be around to have a drink with them later, pretending that he didnt know that it was all over but the shooting. (bad pun. i'm sorry.)

but pulling the trigger, that only took a second. a second and it was over. i mean, you couldn't even see him, thats how over it was. and i thought god, if thats all it takes, then what the hell am i waiting for anyway?

the worst part, of course, is thinking about nikki. but i cant help but feel that shell be happier with her real father, or maybe with my parents, or even if somebody has to adopt her. at least she wont be stuck with me and dale any more. and at least i know that i got her away before dale did anything.

god, if ony you coulda seen how dale treated me back when we met. people warned me about him, but i couldnt believe it because he seemed like such a sweet guy. we used to go out drinking and to parties, and then we would come home and make love and just talk for hours and hours. back then he used to listen to what i had to say. i think he was like me, just so blown away by the idea that someone could actually love him that he would have given anything just to be with me. i know thats how i felt.

but then, once he had me, everything changed. it was like he was scared to be without me, scared that anyone else would find me attractive (ha ha!), scared that i would leave him. and then it got to the point where we would go to a party and he couldnt even drink beer or hed upchuck, but he always had that bottle of cough syrup with him. did you ever see someone just sit there and swig cough syrup? at first its almost funny, and then you realize how sick it is.

its like that woman doctor said. self-esteem, pure and simple. just like the overeaters, the shoplifters, the adulterers, and even the rapists and murderers ive seen on your show. it always seems to come back to that. if he had any self-esteem, he wouldnt have to put me down. but he doesnt. i think that the only person he hates more than me is himself, and if he could just admit that, maybe he wouldnt have to hate either one of us.

of course, if i had any, i wouldnt put up with him either.

i geuss i should tell you that dale was a singer. i hear that he was really great, tho hed stopped pretty much by the time i met him. he said he always knew he was gonna be a star, but then he never left town, and after a while he started losing his hair, and his back started to give him trouble, and i geuss he just got tired. but something must have died when he decided to give up, because everyone says that hes been fucked up ever since.

oh well. at any rate, i'll be gone some time tomorrow morning, by way of the old buzz royer alternitive. dale and the rest of the world can straighten out their own god damn act. not that i blame him or anybody else. you get born, things happen, and eventually you die. thats just the way it goes.

i love you, oprah. i wish you all the best. hope to see you on the other side, even tho i wonder if we will wind up in the same place. you know what they say about suicide, after all.

but i believe that if i can hear my angels voice at all, hes telling me that its time to go now.

goodbye.

love,

dorothy abigail neff.

MARK AS EXHIBIT C

Dale Snyder awoke to smoke and heat and the fog inside his brain. His first reaction was one of muddled alarm: his washed-out red white and blue eyes flew open; he began to cough; he fell backwards off the bed. There were a hundred and eighty pounds of him, spanning an even six feet. They hit the floorboards hard. Even through the drugs, it hurt like a bastard.

"DOTTIE!" he yelled, dragging himself to hands and knees. His voice felt like stars of burning glass in his throat. "WHAT THE FUCK IS GOING ON HERE? DOTTIE!"

There was no answer, just a dull rumble of voices from somewhere in the house. Dale struggled to his feet, murkily assessed the state of the room and his own chances of survival. So far, it didn't look too bad. There were no flames in the room; just a fair amount of smoke rolling in under the door. He eyed the open windows for a second; in a pinch, they'd be all he needed for escape.

But first, he wanted to check the rest of the place out. There was a good chance, he reasoned now, that Dottie had simply fucked something up. She never cooked, so that couldn't be the problem; most likely, she had dumped a hot ashtray into the trash, or maybe passed out with a lit cigarette. Whatever it was, the dumb cunt was about to become very sorry, there was no fucking doubt about that.

His toes caught on last night's discarded underwear, and he slipped them on awkwardly; he didn't want to be caught with his balls hanging out if the fire trucks showed up. Then, his confidence bolstered, he made his wobbly way toward the door.

The knob was room temperature. That was good news, at least. He fitted his sweaty palm around it and twisted. It opened, no problem; the fleeting paranoia that she might have been trying to burn him alive vanished as quickly as it had flitted across his mind . . .

. . . *and his mind was a madhouse. he hated to admit it but it was the fucking truth and had been for quite some time. this early in the morning it was a wonder that he could think at all, much less motorvate himself across the floor, and though he knew it was absurd he couldn't shake the idea that she had planned this. she had something up her sleeve. it would have been better if he really had killed her last night, or the night before that, or maybe even a year ago, instead of just beating her around all the time; it would have been better if he'd listened to the voice that never never wanted to stop . . .*

. . . and then he was in the hallway, and it was both better and worse than he had expected. The stretch between front door and back was relatively clear of everything but smoke; but there were licks of orange light in the kitchen, casting inverse shadows.

And the living room wall was lined with flame.

He stood there, indecisive, in the broiling hallway heat. The noise of voices was clearer now, clearly coming from the front. Maybe it was firemen. Maybe it was pigs. He was surprised to hear women's voices, but these days you never knew.

Then the laughter began, and the theme music kicked in, and Dale's vision went as red as the reflections on the wall before him.

It was the fucking tv.

It was the fucking tv, and Dottie was probably passed out in front of it, curled up in the old brown ottoman with her big tits scraping the air, her wide mouth open, and her already useless brain turned to punk wood by smoke inhalation. It made him crazy just thinking about it.

And that was the weird thing. He knew he should be gearing up to save her, to grab her ass up and cart her off to salvation. The good guy side of his brain knew just what to do, rationale complete down to the little tin Good Citizenship medal affixed to his righteously thudding chest.

But there was another voice in his head; one that slid more easily through the codeine and percodan murk. It was the one that could describe, in tiny detail, what her face would look like as it was held down to the flames. Her eyelids would be shut, of course, but he was willing to bet that the balls beneath would start to sizzle something fierce once those little flaps of skin baked away. Her hair would be a bicentennial celebration of colorful sparks by then; and with all the goddam fat in her cheeks, the odds in favor of an unquenchable grease fire were good, very good indeed . . .

. . . and the good guy voice told him to shut up, reminded him of why he hadn't killed her yet or taken out a little frustration on her bitch of a daughter; and that reason was the law and the way it had of taking things into its own long arms. The law could fuck up your life forever. The law could bust right in through the door. All dipshit morality aside, the law was a very good reason to play nicey-nice and just keep smiling.

But the pictures were too clear.

He started thinking about his hands, what would happen to them if he held her down in the flames that long. *Damage*: that was what. Serious damage. Maybe it would be better if he kicked her into the flames: on the other hand, where was the fun in that? You wanted to see. You wanted to feel . . .

There was a half-sane voice in his head, more biology than logic. It moved him forward, along the wall that was not burning. It moved him to the lip of the living room, bid his head poke around the corner and survey the scene.

It could not believe what it bade his eyes see.

Because she was not frying in the ottoman, though the ottoman was burning up a storn. She wasn't even fucking asleep. She was just *standing* there, by the open front door, with nothing but screen door separating her from the great outdoors. In her left hand, she clenched her pocketbook tightly.

In her right hand, she held his gun . . .

*   *   *

. . . and they hadn't come, they still hadn't come, nearly fifteen minutes later and still the Channel 8 news team had yet to appear. She had run the three blocks back from Jim & Nina's, hastily checked to see that Dale was still out of it, and then doused strategic portions of the house with lighter fluid. The first match had been the hardest to light, but once things got going, it was hard to stop.

Which was why the place was now getting hotter than hell.

Which was why she wished they would please God hurry.

She didn't hear the footsteps behind her until it was far too late. Between the crackle of flame and the laugh of Oprah Winfrey, she didn't have a chance. The grip on the gun barrel had twirled her around before she could start to turn on her own.

All illusion of control vanished in an instant.

As her boyfriend began to scream . . .

. . . and then he was hitting her, backhanded slaps to the face, the way he usually started. She fell back against the door, and it started to open, and before he could catch her she had hit the concrete step outside, her purse flying off into the yard. She made a bad sound in landing, and her eyes unfocused, but it did not occur to him that she might not be able to hear what he had to say next.

"WHAT THE FUCK IS THE MATTER WITH YOU!" he bellowed. He bent over her, and the hand holding the gun came back across her lips, moving fast. He felt something give, and marvelled at the sensation: he had never taken out teeth before, or made flesh tear to quite that extent. She coughed, and the blood sprayed back at him; he caught it on his tongue, and the taste wasn't bad.

"YOU HEARD ME, YOU COW!" he screamed again, and her eyes seemed to struggle toward focus. He was smiling now, he couldn't help it, he had gone too far and there was no question of turning back, so he abandoned himself to the will of the voice, the voice that did not want to stop, the voice that said *now, baby, now* . . .

. . . as the van pulled up to the curb and made its screeching halt Dottie saw it upside-down, a vision that fought its way through the blankness. She saw the words CHANNEL 8 stenciled across its side, saw the two figures scurrying out the doors, saw the video camera that one of them hoisted to its shoulder . . .

292

FILM AT ELEVEN

. . . and she realized that this was it, except that maybe it wasn't, the gun was no longer in her hand and she was choking on something hard and sharp, and the part of her brain that was not going into unprecedented spasms suffered a sudden and keen sense of loss as she was hoisted upright, and her eyes went back to seeing nothing again . . .

. . . and Dale put two and two together. It did not spell four. It spelled something better. For the first time in too long to count, he thought that maybe Dottie *had* something there, she wasn't just the utterly stupid twat that she'd led him to believe she was. Maybe she'd gotten a glimpse of what it takes to hit the big time after all.

You start a fire. The news team comes.

You die in public.

A star is born.

"This is *great!*" he gushed. "This is fucking perfect! You stupid fucking bitch, you UNDERSTAND!"

It was the chance of a lifetime.

Now it was simply a matter of making it all pay off.

He had dragged her inside, where the flames were mounting. Those pretty old pictures of her still remained. He saw a can of lighter fluid, and the scenario was complete. He let her drop.

Picked up the can.

Spritzed her good.

And kicked her into the flames.

She came up quickly, animate and ablaze. She did a quick spin and collapsed at his feet. He flipped her over with his foot, and her face was on fire; the black hole of her open and screaming mouth was the only thing unlit. "*Wee HAH!*" he enthused. "*Thank* you, baby!"

Then he kicked her sparkling ass out into the yard.

The camera missed nothing within its range. It locked on the crawling, burning body. The door opened again, and the skinny balding crazy man in the white BVDs came staggering out of the house, waving a gun, yelling something that the mike couldn't quite pick up. The gun was aimed and fired: a red explosion cascaded down from the flaming belly.

Still the body continued to crawl, close enough now to distinguish as a woman. It reached out its hand to the camera lens, stretching fingers of fire from ten yards away. Then the man fired again, and its head came apart in black smoking chunks.

The camera's perspective began to back away, its operator's voice droning omigod, omigod. *Too late. The man was running now, eyes huge and smiling triumphantly as he screamed,* "OH NO YA DON'T! MY NAME IS DALE SNYDER, AND I'M A FUCKING STAR . . .!"

Then the man began to sing, aiming his gun at the camera.

When the camera moved, he fired again.

MARK AS EXHIBIT D

Two things:

When the pain was gone, the angel was waiting on the other side. It patted her on her little head and said *it's okay. Dottie. You made a couple of wrong turns, but I still love you.*

Then it sent her back to do it again.

Until she got it right.

And meanwhile, back in Hell, there was a film at eleven: substantially edited down, of course.

For the sake of the children.

And the meek in spirit.

THE SHOW GOES ON

by

Ramsey Campbell

The nails were worse than rusty; they had snapped. Under cover of several coats of paint, both the door and its frame had rotted. As Lee tugged at the door it collapsed toward him with a sound like that of an old cork leaving a bottle.

He hadn't used the storeroom since his father had nailed the door shut to keep the rats out of the shop. Both the shelves and the few items which had been left in the room — an open tin of paint, a broken-necked brush — looked merged into a single mass composed of grime and dust.

He was turning away, having vaguely noticed a dark patch that covered much of the dim wall at the back of the room, when he saw that it wasn't dampness. Beyond it he could just make out rows of regular outlines like teeth in a gaping mouth: seats in the old cinema.

He hadn't thought of the cinema for years. Old resurrected films on television, shrunken and packaged and robbed of flavor, never reminded him. It wasn't only that Cagney and Bogart and the rest had been larger than life, huge hovering faces like ancient idols; the cinema itself had had a personality — the screen framed by twin theater boxes from the days of the music hall, the faint smell and muttering of gaslights on the walls, the manager's wife and daughter serving in the auditorium and singing along with the musicals. In the years after the war you could get in for an armful of lemonade bottles, or a bag of vegetables if you owned one of the nearby allotments; there had been a greengrocer's old weighing machine inside the

SILVER SCREAM

paybox. These days you had to watch films in concrete warrens, if you could afford to go at all.

Still, there was no point in reminiscing, for the old cinema was now a back entry for thieves. He was sure that was how they had robbed other shops on the block. At times he'd thought he heard them in the cinema; they sounded too large for rats. And now, by the look of the wall, they'd made themselves a secret entrance to his shop.

Mrs. Entwistle was waiting at the counter. These days she shopped here less from need than from loyalty, remembering when his mother used to bake bread at home to sell in the shop. "Just a sliced loaf," she said apologetically.

"Will you be going past Frank's yard?" Within its slippery wrapping the loaf felt ready to deflate, not like his mother's bread at all. "Could you tell him that my wall needs repairing urgently? I can't leave the shop."

Buses were carrying stragglers to work or to school. Ninety minutes later — he could tell the time by the passengers, which meant he needn't have his watch repaired — the buses were ferrying shoppers down to Liverpool city center, and Frank still hadn't come. Grumbling to himself, Lee closed the shop for ten minutes.

The February wind came slashing up the hill from the Mersey, trailing smoke like ghosts of the factory chimneys. Down the slope a yellow machine clawed at the remains of houses. The Liver Buildings looked like a monument in a graveyard of concrete and stone.

Beyond Kiddiegear and The Wholefood Shop, Frank's yard was a maze of new timber. Frank was feeding the edge of a door to a shrieking circular blade. He gazed at Lee as though nobody had told him anything. When Lee kept his temper and explained, Frank said "No problem. Just give a moan when you're ready."

"I'm ready now,"

"Ah, well. As soon as I've finished this job I'll whiz round." Lee had reached the exit when Frank said, "I'll tell you something that'll amuse you . . ."

Fifteen minutes later Lee arrived back, panting, at his shop. It was intact. He hurried around the outside of the cinema, but all the doors seemed immovable, and he couldn't find a secret entrance. Nevertheless he was sure that the thieves — children, probably — were sneaking in somehow.

The buses were full of old people now, sitting stiffly as china. The lunchtime trade trickled into the shop: men who couldn't buy their brand of cigarettes in the pub across the road, children sent on errands while their lunches went cold on tables or dried in ovens. An empty bus raced along the deserted street, and a scrawny youth in a leather jacket came into the shop, while his companion loitered in the doorway. Would Lee have a chance to defend himself, or at least to shout for help? But they weren't planning theft, only making sure they didn't miss a bus. Lee's heart felt both violent and fragile. Since the robberies had begun he'd felt that way too often.

The shop was still worth it. "Don't keep it up if you don't want to," his father had said, but it would have been admitting defeat to do anything else. Besides, he and his parents had been even closer here than at home. Since their death, he'd had to base his stock on items people wanted in a hurry or after the other shops had closed: flashlights, canned food, light bulbs, cigarettes. Lee's Home-Baked Bread was a thing of the past, but it was still Lee's shop.

Packs of buses climbed the hill, carrying home the rush-hour crowds. When the newspaper van dumped a stack of the evening's *Liverpool Echo* on the doorstep, he knew Frank wasn't coming. He stormed round to the yard, but it was locked and deserted.

Well then, he would stay in the shop overnight; he'd nobody to go home for. Why, he had even made the thieves' job easier by helping the door to collapse. The sight of him in the lighted shop ought to deter thieves — it better had, for their sakes.

He bought two pork pies and some bottles of beer from the pub. Empty buses moved off from the stop like a series of cars on a fairground ride. He drank from his mother's Coronation mug, which always stood by the electric kettle.

He might as well have closed the shop at eight o'clock; apart from an old lady who didn't like his stock of cat food, nobody came. Eventually he locked the door and sat reading the paper, which seemed almost to be written in a new language: *Head Raps Shock Axe*, said a headline about the sudden closing of a school.

Should he prop the storeroom door in place, lest he fall asleep? No, he ought to stay visible from the cinema, in the hope of scaring off the thieves. In his childhood they would hardly have dared sneak into the cinema, let alone steal — not in the last days of the cinema, when the old man had been roaming the aisles.

Everyone, perhaps even the manager, had been scared of him. Nobody Lee knew had ever seen his face. You would see him fumbling at the dim gaslights to turn them lower, then he'd begin to make sounds in the dark as though he was both muttering to himself and chewing something soft. He would creep up on talkative children and shine his flashlight into their eyes. As he hissed at them, a pale substance would spill from his mouth.

But they were scared of nothing these days, short of Lee's sitting in the shop all night, like a dummy. Already he felt irritable, frustrated. How much worse would he feel after a night of doing nothing except wasting electricity on the lights and the fire?

He wasn't thinking straight. He might be able to do a great deal. He emptied the mug of beer, then he switched off the light and arranged himself on the chair as comfortably as possible. He might have to sit still for hours.

He only hoped they would venture close enough for him to see their faces. A flashlight lay ready beside him. Surely they were cowards who would run when they saw he wasn't scared of them. Perhaps he could chase them and find their secret entrance.

For a long time he heard nothing. Buses passed downhill, growing emptier and fewer. Through their growling he heard faint voices, but they were fading away from the pub, which was closing. Now the streets were deserted, except for the run-down grumble of the city. Wind shivered the window. The edge of the glow of the last few buses trailed vaguely over the storeroom entrance, making the outlines of cinema seats appear to stir. Between their sounds he strained his ears. Soon the last bus had gone.

He could just make out the outlines of the seats. If he gazed at them for long they seemed to waver, as did the storeroom doorway. Whenever he closed his eyes to rest them he heard faint tentative sounds: creaking, rattling. Perhaps the shop always sounded like that when there was nothing else to hear.

His head jerked up. No, he was sure he hadn't dozed: there had been a sound like a whisper, quickly suppressed. He hunched himself forward, ears ringing with strain. The backs of the cinema seats, vague forms like charcoal sketches on a charcoal background, appeared to nod toward him.

Was he visible by the glow of the electric fire? He switched it off stealthily, and sat listening, eyes squeezed shut. The sudden chill held him back from dozing.

Yes, there were stealthy movements in a large enclosed place. Were they creeping closer? His eyes sprang open to take them unawares, and he thought he glimpsed movement, dodging out of sight beyond the gap in the wall.

He sat absolutely still, though the cold was beginning to insinuate a cramp into his right leg. He had no way of measuring the time that passed before he glimpsed movement again. Though it was so vague that he couldn't judge its speed, he had a nagging impression that someone had peered at him from the dark auditorium. He thought he heard floorboards creaking.

Were the thieves mocking him? They must think it was fun to play games with him, to watch him gazing stupidly through the wall they'd wrecked. Rage sprang him to his feet. Grabbing the flashlight, he strode through the doorway. He had to slow down in the storeroom, for he didn't want to touch the shelves fattened by grime. As soon as he reached the wall he flashed the light into the cinema.

The light just managed to reach the walls, however dimly. There was nobody in sight. On either side of the screen, which looked like a rectangle of fog, the theater boxes were cups of darkness. It was hard to distinguish shadows from dim objects, which perhaps was why the rows of seats looked swollen.

The thieves must have retreated into one of the corridors, toward their secret entrance; he could hear distant muffled sounds. No doubt they were waiting for him to give up — but he would surprise them.

He stepped over a pile of rubble just beyond the wall. They mustn't have had time to clear it away when they had made the gap. The flashlight was heavy, reassuring; they'd better not come too near. As soon as he reached the near end of a row of seats and saw that they were folded back out of his way, he switched off the light.

Halfway down the row he touched a folding seat, which felt moist and puffy — fatter than it had looked. He didn't switch on the light, for he oughtn't to betray his presence more than was absolutely necessary. Besides, there was a faint sketchy glow from the road, through the shop. At least he would be able to find his way back easily — and he'd be damned if anyone else got there first.

When he reached the central aisle he risked another blink of light, to make sure the way was clear. Shadows sat up in all the nearest seats. A few springs had broken; seats lolled, spilling their innards. He paced forward in the dark, stopping frequently to listen. Underfoot, the carpet felt like perished rubber; occasionally it squelched.

At the end of the aisle he halted, breathing inaudibly. After a while he heard movement resounding down a corridor to his left. All at once — good Lord, he'd forgotten that — he was glad the sounds weren't coming from his right, where the Gents' had been and still was, presumably. Surely even thieves would prefer to avoid the yard beyond that window, especially at night.

Blinking the light at the floor, he moved to his left. The darkness hovering overhead seemed enormous, dwarfing his furtive sounds. He had an odd impression that the screen was almost visible, as an imperceptible lightening of the dark above him. He was reminded of the last days of the cinema, in particular one night when the projectionist must have been drunk or asleep: the film had slowed and dimmed very gradually, flickering; the huge almost invisible figures had twitched and mouthed silently, unable to stop — it had seemed that the cinema was senile but refusing to die, or incapable of dying.

Another blink of light showed him the exit, a dark arch a head taller than he. A few scraps of linoleum clung to the stone floor of a low corridor. He remembered the way: a few yards ahead the corridor branched; one short branch led to a pair of exit doors, while the other turned behind the screen, toward a warren of old dressing rooms.

When he reached the pair of doors he tested them, this time from within the building. Dim light drew a blurred sketch of their edges. The bars which ought to snap apart and release the doors felt like a single pole encrusted with harsh flakes. His rusty fingers scraped as he rubbed them together. Wind flung itself at the doors, as unable to move them as he was.

He paced back to the junction of the corridors, feeling his way with the toes of his shoes. There was a faint sound far down the other branch. Perhaps the thieves were skulking near their secret entrance, ready to flee. One blink of the light showed him that the floor was clear.

The corridor smelled dank and musty. He could tell when he strayed near the walls, for the chill intensified. The dark seemed to soak up those of his sounds that couldn't help being audible — the scrape of fallen plaster underfoot, the flap of a loose patch of linoleum which almost tripped him and which set his heart palpitating. It seemed a very long time before he reached the bend, which he coped with by feeling his way along the damp crumbling plaster of the wall. Then there was nothing but musty darkness for an even longer stretch, until something taller than he was loomed up in front of him.

It was another pair of double doors. Though they were ajar, and their bars looked rusted in the open position, he was reluctant to step through. The nervous flare of his light had shown him a shovel leaning against the wall; perhaps it had once been used to clear away fallen plaster. Thrusting the shovel between the doors, he squeezed through the gap, trying to make no noise.

He couldn't quite make himself switch off the flashlight. There seemed to be no need. In the right-hand wall were several doorways; he was sure one led to the secret entrance. If the thieves fled, he'd be able to hear which doorway they were using.

He crept along the passage. Shadows of dangling plaster moved with him. The first room was bare, and the color of dust. It would have been built as a dressing room, and perhaps the shapeless object, huddled in a corner and further blurred by wads of dust, had once been a costume. In the second deserted room another slumped, arms folded bonelessly. He had a hallucinatory impression that they were sleeping vagrants, stirring wakefully as his light touched them.

There was only one movement worth his attention: the stealthy restless movement he could hear somewhere ahead. Yes, it was beyond the last of the doorways, from which — he switched off the flashlight to be sure — a faint glow was emerging. That must come from the secret entrance.

He paused just ahead of the doorway. Might they be lying in wait for him? When the sound came again — a leathery sound, like the shifting of nervous feet in shoes — he could tell that it was at least as distant as the far side of the room. Creeping forward, he risked a glance within.

Though the room was dimmer than fog, he could see that it was empty:

not even a dusty remnant of clothing or anything else on the floor. The meager glow came from a window barred by a grille, beyond which he heard movement, fainter now. Were they waiting outside to open the grille as soon as he went away? Flashlight at the ready, he approached.

When he peered through the window, he thought at first there was nothing to see except a cramped empty yard: gray walls which looked furred by the dimness, gray flagstones, and — a little less dim — the sky. Another grille covered a window in an adjoining wall.

Then a memory clenched on his guts. He had recognized the yard.

Once, as a child, he had been meant to sneak into the Gents' and open the window so that his friends could get in without paying. He'd had to stand on the toilet seat in order to reach the window. Beyond a grille whose gaps were thin as matchsticks, he had just been able to make out a small dismal space enclosed by walls which looked coated with darkness or dirt. Even if he had been able to shift the grille he wouldn't have dared to do so, for something had been staring at him from a corner of the yard.

Of course it couldn't really have been staring. Perhaps it had been a half-deflated football; it looked leathery. It must have been there for a long time, for the two socketlike dents near its top were full of cobwebs. He'd fled, not caring what his friends might do to him — but in fact they hadn't been able to find their way to the yard. For years he hadn't wanted to look out of that window, especially when he'd dreamed — or had seemed to remember — that something had moved, gleaming, behind the cobwebs. When he'd been old enough to look out of the window without climbing up, the object was still there, growing dustier. Now there had been a gap low down in it, widening as years passed. It had resembled a grin stuffed with dirt.

Again he heard movement beyond the grille. He couldn't quite make out that corner of the yard, and retreated, trying to make no noise, before he could. Nearly at the corridor, he saw that a door lay open against the wall. He dragged the door shut as he emerged — to trap the thieves, that was all; if they were in the yard that might teach them a lesson. He would certainly have been uneasy if he had still been a child.

Then he halted, wondering what else he'd heard.

The scrape of the door on bare stone had almost covered up another sound from the direction of the cinema. Had the thieves outwitted him? Had they closed the double doors? When he switched on the flashlight, having fumbled and almost dropped it lens first, he couldn't tell: perhaps the doors were ajar, but perhaps his nervousness was making the shadow between them appear wider than it was.

As he ran, careless now of whether he was heard, shadows of dead gaslights splashed along the walls, swelling. Their pipes reminded him obscurely of breathing tubes, clogged with dust. In the bare rooms, slumped dusty forms shifted with his passing.

301

The doors were still ajar, and looked untouched. When he stepped between them, the ceiling rocked with shadows; until he glanced up he felt that it was closing down. He'd done what he could in here, he ought to get back to the shop — but if he went forward, he would have to think. If the doors hadn't moved, then the sound he had almost heard must have come from somewhere else: perhaps the unlit cinema.

Before he could help it, he was remembering. The last weeks of the cinema had been best forgotten: half the audience had seemed to be there because there was nowhere else to go, old men trying to warm themselves against the grudging radiators; sometimes there would be the thud of an empty bottle or a fallen walking stick. The tattered films had jerked from scene to scene like dreams. On the last night Lee had been there, the gaslights had gone out halfway through the film, and hadn't been lit at the end. He'd heard an old man falling and crying out as though he thought the darkness had come for him, a little girl screaming as if unable to wake from a nightmare, convinced perhaps that only the light had held the cinema in shape, prevented it from growing deformed. Then Lee had heard something else: a muttering mixed with soft chewing. It had sounded entirely at home in the dark.

But if someone was in the cinema now, it must be the thieves. He ought to hurry, before they reached his shop. He was hurrying, toward the other branch of the corridor, which led to the exit doors. Might he head off the thieves that way? He would be out of the building more quickly, that was the main thing — it didn't matter why.

The doors wouldn't budge. Though he wrenched at them until his palms smarted with rust, the bars didn't even quiver. Wind whined outside like a dog, and emphasized the stuffy mustiness of the corridor.

Suddenly he realized how much noise he was making. He desisted at once, for it would only make it more difficult for him to venture back into the cinema. Nor could he any longer avoid realizing why.

Once before he'd sneaked out to this exit, to let in his friends who hadn't been able to find their way into the yard. Someone had told the usherette, who had come prowling down the central aisle, poking at people with her flashlight beam. As the light crept closer, he had been unable to move; the seat had seemed to box him in, his mouth and throat had felt choked with dust. Yet the panic he'd experienced then had been feeble compared to what he felt now — for if the cinema was still guarded against intruders, it was not by the manager's daughter.

He found he was trembling, and clawed at the wall. A large piece of plaster came away, crunching in his hand. The act of violence, mild though it was, went some way toward calming him. He wasn't a child, he was a shopkeeper who had managed to survive against the odds; he had no right to panic as the little girl had, in the dark. Was the knot that was twisting harder,

harder in his guts renewed panic, or disgust with himself? Hoping that it was the latter, he made himself hurry toward the auditorium.

When he saw what he had already noticed but managed to ignore, he faltered. A faint glow had crept into the corridor from the auditorium. Couldn't that mean that his eyes were adjusting? No, the glow was more than that. Gripping the edge of the archway so hard that his fingers twitched painfully, he peered into the cinema.

The gaslights were burning.

At least blurred ovals hovered on the walls above their jets. Their light had always fallen short of the central aisle; now the glow left a swatch of dimness, half as wide as the auditorium which it divided. If the screen was faintly lit — if huge vague flattened forms were jerking there, rather than merely stains on the canvas — it failed to illuminate the cinema. He had no time to glance at the screen, for he could see that not all the seats were empty.

Perhaps they were only a few heaps of rubbish which were propped there — heaps which he hadn't been able to distinguish on first entering. He had begun to convince himself that this was true, and that in any case it didn't matter, when he noticed that the dimness was not altogether still. Part of it was moving.

No, it was not dimness. It was a glow, which was crawling jerkily over the rows of seats, toward the first of the objects propped up in them. Was the glow being carried along the central aisle? Thank God, he couldn't quite distinguish its source. Perhaps that source was making a faint sound, a moist somewhat rhythmic muttering that sounded worse then senile, or perhaps that was only the wind.

Lee began to creep along the front of the cinema, just beneath the screen. Surely his legs wouldn't let him down, though they felt flimsy, almost boneless. Once he reached the side aisle he would be safe and able to hurry, the gaslights would show him the way to the gap in his wall. Wouldn't they also make him more visible? That ought not to matter, for — his mind tried to flinch away from thinking — if anything was prowling in the central aisle, surely it couldn't outrun him.

He had just reached the wall when he thought he heard movement in the theater box above him. It sounded dry as an insect, but much larger. Was it peering over the edge at him? He couldn't look up, only clatter along the bare floorboards beneath the gaslights, on which he could see no flames at all.

He still had yards to go before he reached the gap when the roving glow touched one of the heaps in the seats.

If he could have turned and run blindly, nothing would have stopped him; but a sickness that was panic weighed down his guts, and he couldn't move until he saw. Perhaps there wasn't much to see except an old coat, full of lumps of dust or rubble, that was lolling in the seat; nothing to make the flashlight shudder in his hand and rap against the wall. But sunken in the gap between the lapels of the coat was what might have been an old Hallo-ween mask overgrown with dust. Surely it was dust that moved in the empty eyes — yet as the flashlight rapped more loudly against the wall, the mask turned slowly and unsteadily toward him.

Panic blinded him. He didn't know who he was nor where he was going. He knew only that he was very small and at bay in the vast dimness, through which a shape was directing a glow toward him. Behind the glow he could almost see a face from which something pale dangled. It wasn't a beard, for it was rooted in the gaping mouth.

He was thumping the wall with the flashlight as though to remind himself that one or the other was there. Yes, there was a wall, and he was backing along it: backing where? Toward the shop, his shop now, where he wouldn't need to use the flashlight, mustn't use the flashlight to illuminate whatever was pursuing him, mustn't see, for then he would never be able to move. Not far to go now, he wouldn't have to bear the dark much longer, must be nearly at the gap in the wall, for a glow was streaming from behind him. He was there now, all he had to do was turn his back on the cinema, turn quickly, just turn —

He had managed to turn halfway, trying to be blind without closing his eyes, when his free hand touched the object which was lolling in the nearest seat. Both the overcoat and its contents flet lumpy, patched with damp and dust. Nevertheless the arm stirred; the object at the end of it, which felt like a bundle of sticks wrapped in torn leather, tried to close on his hand.

Choking, he pulled himself free. Some of the sticks came loose and plumped on the rotten carpet. The flashlight fell beside them, and he heard glass breaking. It didn't matter, he was at the gap, he could hear movement in the shop, cars and buses beyond. He had no time to wonder who was in there before he turned.

The first thing he saw was that the light wasn't that of streetlamps; it was daylight. At once he saw why he had made the mistake: the gap was no longer there. Except for a single brick, the wall had been repaired.

He was yelling desperately at the man beyond the wall, and thumping the new bricks with his fists — he had begun to wonder why his voice was so faint and his blows so feeble — when the man's face appeared beyond the brick-sized gap. Lee staggered back as though he was fainting. Except that he had to stare up at the man's face, he might have been looking in a mirror.

He hadn't time to think. Crying out, he stumbled forward and tried to wrench the new bricks loose. Perhaps his adult self beyond the wall was aware of him in some way, for his face peered through the gap, looking triumphantly contemptuous of whoever was in the dark. Then the brick fitted snugly into place, cutting off the light.

Almost worse was the fact that it wasn't quite dark. As he began to claw at the bricks and mortar, he could see them far too clearly. Soon he might see what was holding the light, and that would be worst of all.

THE CUTTER

by

Edward Bryant

My memory is still intact. I remember the scene as well as I can recall any other episode from my childhood. The year was 1951 and I was six years old.

I was right there with the men — the scientists and the soldiers — as they cautiously crept through the dark, close tunnels of the Arctic base. The steady metronome of the geiger counter clicked ever faster, eventually crackling into a ripping-canvas sound as the probe neared the metal storage locker.

Capt. Hendry paused a moment. The scientists, Carrington and Stern, exchanged glances. The tall, storklike newspaperman, Scotty, didn't look happy at all. The other men leveled their guns at the cabinet. There was something in there. Something from another world. It was ravenous for human blood, and it had already killed.

Capt. Hendry nodded. The man called Bob gingerly reached forward and flipped the door-catch. The locker opened as the music crashed to a climax and I jumped.

The frozen carcass of a sled dog rolled out and thudded to the floor. I stared. So did the men.

Dr. Stern looked disappointed. Dr. Carrington, I couldn't tell. Capt. Hendry smiled grimly and shrugged. Crossing to the other side of the room, he motioned for the rest of us to follow.

We were right behind him when he twisted the knob on the door to the next passageway. The door swung open without warning to reveal the creature standing on the other side. It raised its clawed hands and swiped at Capt. Hendry.

I wet my pants.

SILVER SCREAM

As I said before, it was 1951 and I was six. I hadn't read the publicity and hadn't heard Phil Harris sing about "The Thing" on the radio. I had never heard of John W. Campbell's story. I didn't care whether Christian Nyby or Howard Hawks had really directed.

All I knew was I had lived through a scene up on the flickering screen that had branded itself in my brain far deeper than anything that was to come until a few years later when I sat in the same theater and watched Janet Leigh's dark blood swirl down the drain in *Psycho*.

Twenty years after I first saw it, I watched *The Thing* at a science fiction film festival in Los Angeles. I sat there as entranced as the first time, but now I didn't wet my pants. There was not even the temptation. The absolutely shocking scene I'd remembered wasn't there. Sure, there were the components — the dog falling out of the locker and the part where Kenneth Tobey's character opened the door to the greenhouse and there was the Thing waiting for him. But the juxtaposition that had left me with nightmares for months just wasn't there. I told a friend about it, but he laughed and reminded me that the human mind does that frequently with books and movies, not to mention the whole rest of human experience. We edit in our heads. We change things from reality. After a while, we accept the altered memories as gospel. It's a human thing.

Yeah. Right. What I didn't tell my friend was that I knew for a fact that I had once watched the scene I'd remembered. Frame for frame. I didn't tell him, but I'd known the man who'd re-edited the movie. Little had Hawks — or Nyby, for that matter — known. I used to work for that man. The cutter.

I had been there the final days. And worse, that last night.

"Well, Robby Valdez," said Mr. Carrigan. "You're early again." He paused and smiled. "You are always early."

I never knew what I was supposed to say, so I said nothing and simply stared down at my sneakers.

"So how's your family?" said Mr. Carrigan. My dad was still down in Cheyenne drooling over the new Ford Thunderbird he'd never be able to afford in a million years. He was supposed to be looking for work. I knew my mother was cleaning up after supper and thinking how much money she could win if she could just get on *The $64,000 Question*. My sister would be in her room listening to her Elvis Presley records and skipping her homework, humming through her cleft palate and dreaming of someone who would never want her. I had homework I needed to do, but I knew I'd rather be down here at the Ramona Theater helping out Mr. Carrigan. How was my sad family? Don't exaggerate, my mom would have cautioned me.

"Fine," I said.

Mr. Carrigan wasn't listening, not really. He was staring over my head and I guessed he was looking at the black crepe he'd draped over the posters for *East of Eden* and *Rebel Without a Cause* bracketing the signed studio still of James Dean. "So senseless," he said softly. "Such a terrible waste."

"Did you ever do any work on those two movies?" I said, meaning the Dean pictures.

Mr. Carrigan looked mildly alarmed and darted quick looks around the lobby, of course, there was no one here this early. The box office wasn't even open. The high school girl who ran the concession counter was probably still putting on her uniform and fixing her hair.

"Say nothing of that, Robby. It's our secret."

"Right," I said. I knew very well I was supposed to tell no one of Mr. Carrigan's genius for changing things. I never confided in anyone. Not even later, after the thing with Barbara Curtwood. After all, what good would it have done then?

"All right," said Mr. Carrigan. "Let's get to work. You get the fresh candy out of the storeroom and restock the counter. I've got things to do in the projection room." He smiled. "Oh, and I like the coonskin cap very much," he said.

"Davy Crockett," I said. "My aunt and uncle gave it to me. It's early Christmas."

"In September." Mr. Carrigan stopped smiling. "Thanks for reminding me. Barbara's birthday is soon. I should get her something nice."

I said nothing. I knew he was talking about Barbara Curtwood. He was in love with her. My mom talked about that. But then so did most of the people in town. Not about Mr. Carrigan and Barbara Curtwood, but about just her and how she ran around. She worked at the dress shop and spent — so my mom said to my dad — her nights either at the bars or somewhere else. I didn't know what the somewhere else was, because my mother's voice always dropped lower then and my father would laugh.

It hurt me to think about Mr. Carrigan and Miss Curtwood. Even at ten, I knew how much he loved her and how little she thought of him. About the only thing they had in common was the movies. She came to just about every show at the Ramona. Usually she came with a date. Every week or two, the man she came with would be someone brand new.

Even as young as I was, I had some idea that Mr. Carrigan was about the only man Miss Curtwood would have nothing to do with, and it pained him a lot. But he kept on. Sometimes he'd talk to me about it.

"Think she'd want a Davy Crockett cap?" I said. "I don't think she came to see *King of the Wild Frontier.*"

Mr. Carrigan looked at me in a funny way. "I don't think so. Something a bit . . . more grown-up, perhaps." His mouth got a little pinched. "*King of the Wild Frontier.* Now *there* is a film I could have done something with."

"You didn't change it?"

He shook his head. "I was working on another project. A new thriller called *Tarantula*. I had to move the Disney film right along the circuit. But the monster movie, I was able to get my friend at the distributor's to send me a print early. I've been working on it."

"Oh boy," I said. "That's super. I've seen the ads for *Tarantula* in the *Rocky Mountain News.* I know it'll be good."

"It was good," said Mr. Carrigan. He looked down modestly. "Now it will be great."

"I'm sorry I can't think of anything right for Miss Curtwood," I said seriously.

"I'll come up with something." He went through the door to the projection room. I hauled a carton of stale Guess Whats over to the candy case.

It wasn't until I was an adult and moved away from my tiny hometown that I realized what a genius Mr. Carrigan must have been. Who else could have taken movies, including some really bad ones, and re-cut them into stranger, more ambitious forms? The score was sometimes a little choppy, but we were a small town and we didn't really notice or care. We were just there to be entertained. Little did we understand the novelty, the singularity of what we were seeing.

Nobody but me knew what Mr. Carrigan did. And nobody but me knew how he reversed all that work, re-editing the movies into their original form, painfully chopping and splicing the film back into the way it had been, more-or-less, and sending it on the bus to its next stop on the Wyoming small-town circuit.

I guess if he'd stayed in Hollywood, he could have become a star. I mean as a film editor. A cutter, he called it. But something had happened — I never knew what — and he'd come out here and started a whole new life. I always wanted to live in a small town, he'd told me. I'd grown up in one. I thought he was crazy for saying that. But he convinced me he was searching for the best of all possible worlds.

One thing about Mr. Carrigan, he was an optimist. That's what he called himself.

"Robby," he said to me many, many times. "You can alter reality. If you don't like the way things are, you can change them."

I remember I wanted to believe him. I wanted to change things, right enough. I wanted my dad not just to get a good job, but to keep it. I wanted my mom to get on a quiz show and win more than anybody. I thought, sometimes when I wasn't hating her, that I'd like my sister to be able to see Elvis on the *Ed Sullivan Show.* I mean *all* of Elvis, not just from the waist up like the camera showed. But I knew from a year of working after school and on weekends for Mr. Carrigan that it isn't often a person can really change things. And when you can edit something, sometimes the price is way too high.

We were showing a double-feature of *Creature With the Atom Brain* and *It Came from Beneath the Sea* that Friday night. After Polly, the high school junior who was selling popcorn and candy showed up and Mr. Carrigan turned on the marquee lights and people started lining up to get tickets, I stood off to the side in the lobby and just watched. I was supposed to be an usher if some of the older patrons needed to be helped find their seats. I didn't think this double feature would bring in a lot of old people.

There were some parents and a number of grown-ups who weren't here with kids at all. They were mostly talking about "Ike." I knew vaguely that President Eisenhower had suffered a heart attack and was in a hospital down in Denver. It made me feel sort of strange to know that the President of the whole United States was just a hundred and seventy miles south of me.

Tonight people were wearing jackets. This September was more like autumn than Indian summer.

I noticed that the man with Barbara Curtwood had on a leather jacket that must have come off two or three calves. He was big man and it was a large jacket. I didn't recognize him, which was a surprise since just about everybody in this town knew everybody else. Anyhow, he bought the tickets, escorted Miss Curtwood to the line at the concession counter, and then went into the men's room.

I realized Mr. Carrigan was standing right beside me. "Tell Polly to give Miss Curtwood her candy for free. Her soda too. Whatever she wants."

I stared up at him.

"Now. Do it."

I did it.

Miss Curtwood got a large Coke, a giant popcorn, and a roll of Necco wafers. She didn't even blink when Polly told her it was a present from Mr. Carrigan. She turned from the counter, walking right by him, saying absolutely nothing.

"Barbara," Mr. Carrigan said.

She stopped dead still.

"Your birthday is coming up."

311

SILVER SCREAM

"So?" she said, staring down at him. She shook her hair back. Miss Curtwood was a funny kind of blonde. My mom said it came out of a bottle. She was tall and had what my friends later in junior high called "big tits." Tonight she was dressed in a checkered skirt with a white blouse and pink sweater. Some people though she was pretty. Me, I wasn't so sure. There was something about her that made me want to run. She reminded me of the cruel witch in *Snow White*. The hair color was wrong, but maybe if the witch had bleached it —

Mr. Carrigan smiled at her. "I thought maybe — if you weren't doing anything — well, perhaps on your birthday we might have supper at the Dew Drop Inn."

Miss Curtwood actually giggled. Some of the people waiting to get popcorn stared. "You're kidding," she said, a little too loud.

"Actually," said Mr. Carrigan, "I'm not."

"You're at least ten years older than I am."

Mr. Carrigan smiled. "Perhaps twelve."

"You're an old pervert." More people stared.

Mr. Carrigan was starting to turn red. "I think I'd better go see about preparing the projectors."

Miss Curtwood sneered at him. "Nothing will change, you old creep." People in the lobby started to mumble to one another. Parents hurried their children past the popcorn and into the theater.

"*Anything* can be changed," said Mr. Carrigan.

"Not how I feel about you."

"Even you could change."

"Not a chance," she said venomously.

"Something wrong, sweetheart?" It was the big man, her date, back from the bathroom. "Is this old square bothering you?"

"He owns the theater," I squeaked. Both of them glanced down at me.

"Go inside and see if anyone needs help finding seats," Mr. Carrigan said to me.

I looked from Miss Curtwood and the big man to Mr. Carrigan and back again.

"*Now.* I'll talk with you after the show." His voice was firm. I did as I was told. I noticed that Miss Curtwood and the man came into the auditorium about three minutes later. They took the stairs up to the balcony. The man was red-faced. Miss Curtwood had tight hold of his arm. The people downstairs pointed and whispered to each other.

I was glad when the lights went down, the curtains parted, and the previews of coming attractions began. But somehow I knew that when the double feature was over, I'd have a special mess to clean up by the big man's seat. There was. The floor was sticky with Coke, and bits of popcorn were scattered all over. Along with all the rest of it, there was something strange,

THE CUTTER

half-covered by the Necco wrapper. It was like a deflated balloon, five or six inches long, with something gooey inside. I didn't want to touch it, so I used the candy wrapper to pick it up and put it in the trash. I also suspected I shouldn't ask Mr. Carrigan about it, although I thought I saw him watching me as I looked at the thing. But he didn't say anything.

After I'd finished cleaning up, Mr. Carrigan asked me to come to his office. He looked older. I'd never stopped to wonder before just how old he was. At that point in my life, I thought all adults were ancient. But now I realized Mr. Carrigan was at least as old as my father. He walked with a stoop I hadn't noticed before. He moved slowly, as though he were in pain. He asked me if I wanted a Coca Cola. I shook my head. He asked me to sit down. I took the metal folding chair. He sat down then too, on the other side of the desk, and looked at me for a long minute across the heaps of paper, splicing equipment, film cannisters, and the cold, half-filled coffee cups.

"I really love her, you know."

I looked back at him dumbly. Why was he telling me this?

"Miss Curtwood. Barbara. You know who I'm talking about."

I nodded, but still said nothing.

"Do you think I'm not entirely rational about this all?"

I kept perfectly still.

Mr. Carrigan grimaced. "I know I'm not. It's an obsession. I have no explanation for it. All I know is what I feel for Barbara is love that transcends easy explanation — or perhaps *any* explanation at all." He put his elbows on the cluttered desk, laced his fingers, and set his chin in the cradle. "She's not even what I want. Not really. I would prefer her to be shorter and more delicate. She's not. I love red-headed women. Barbara is a blonde. She is far too —" Mr. Carrigan hesitated "— far too buxom. And there is more which is less apparent. Barbara wished to have no children. She told me this. I would like a family, but —" He closed his eyes. I wondered if he was going to cry. He didn't, but he kept his eyes closed for a long time. "She is everything I should loathe, yet I find myself fatally attracted."

Another minute went by. Two. I stirred restlessly on the hard metal seat.

Mr. Carrigan looked up. "Ah, Robby. I'm sorry I'm keeping you. I simply needed to talk, and you are my only friend." He smiled. "Thank you very much."

"You're welcome," I said automatically, not really understanding what I had done for him.

"I'm going to see Barbara on her birthday," he said, still smiling. "She said so tonight."

313

SILVER SCREAM

"I'm glad," I managed to say, wondering if I should be crossing my fingers for him.

"Life is strange, isn't it, Robby?" Mr. Carrigan stayed seated and motioned me toward the door. "If you wait long enough, you can change things the way you want. If you want things badly enough. If you're willing to do what needs to be done."

Later, I tried to remember back, listening in my memory to tell if his voice had sounded odd. It hadn't, not as best I could recall. Mr. Carrigan had sounded cheerful, as happy as I'd ever heard him.

"She's going to stay after the last show on her birthday. And then we will go to the Dew Drop Inn for a late supper. She told me so. When her — friend — tried to argue, she told him to shut up, that she knew her mind and this was what she wanted to do. I must admit it, I was amazed." The smile spread across his face, the muscles visibly relaxing. He looked straight at me. "Thank you, Robby."

"For what?" I said, a little bewildered.

"For seeing me like this. For being someone who saw my happiness and will remember it."

I was *very* bewildered now.

"Good night, Robby. Please convey my best to your family."

I knew I was dismissed and so I left, mumbling a still confused good night.

All these years later, I've come to live in Los Angeles and it's where I'll probably die. Southern Californa drew me away from my small town. It must have been the movies. I walk Hollywood Boulevard, ignore the sleaze, the tawdriness, and pretend I move among myths. I tread Sunset and sometimes stop to look inside the windows of the restaurants and the shops. I soak up the sun, even while realizing that the smog-refracted rays must surely be mutating my tissues into something other than the flesh I grew up in.

No one ever sees me, but I realize that must be because they are akin to the figures moving on the flickering screen and I am the audience. But I am not only the audience, I control the projector. And, like Mr. Carrigan, I am the cutter.

Miss Curtwood's birthday was Friday, the first night of *Tarantula*. The crowd was large, but I didn't notice. I was just impatient to see everyone seated so that I could take my place in the far back row of the theater and watch the magic wand of the projector beam inscribe pictures on the screen.

I did see Miss Curtwood come down the sidewalk to the Ramona. I knew a ticket was waiting in her name at the box office. She was by herself.

Her friend, the big man in the leather jacket, arrived ten minutes later, just before the previews started. He sat on the other side of the theater from Miss Curtwood. I noticed. I saw Mr. Carrigan paying attention to that too.

Then *Tarantula* started. I forgot about everything else until the movie was done. When the jet pilots — Clint Eastwood, John Wayne, and the others — were strafing the giant spider, the Russians could have dropped their H-bombs and I wouldn't have noticed.

The lights came up and the crowd seemed happy enough. I know I was. The people drifted out and I lost track of the big man and his leather jacket. Miss Curtwood was one of the last to get up and leave.

She saw me and came across the row. "Where is Mr. Carrigan's office?"

"Back down the hall past the women's restroom, just before the door for the supply room." I pointed.

"This is very important," said Miss Curtwood. "Tell Mr. Carrigan to come to the office in twenty minutes. No more, no less. Do you understand?"

"I guess so."

"Do you or don't you?" Her voice was hard. Her blue eyes looked like chips of ice.

"Yes," I said.

"Then go and tell him."

I found Mr. Carrigan out in the lobby holding the door for the last of the patrons. I said to him what Miss Curtwood had told me to say.

"I see," said Mr. Carrigan. Then he told me to go home.

"But what about the cleaning?" I said.

"Tomorrow will be soon enough."

"But the pop," I said, "will be all hardened on the floor."

"The floor," said Mr. Carrigan, "needs a good mopping anyway."

"But —"

"Go," said Mr. Carrigan firmly.

I left, but something made me wait just down the block. I watched from the shadows between dim streetlights as Mr. Carrigan locked the lobby doors. The marquee light blinked off. Then the lights in the lobby. Another minute passed. A second.

I heard something that sounded like gunshots, five of them. Somehow I knew they were shots, even though they were muffled, sounding nothing like what I'd heard in westerns and cops-and-robbers movies.

For a moment, I didn't know what to do. Then I went down to the alley and felt my way through the trash cans and stacked empty boxes to the

Ramona's rear emergency exit. As usual, the latch hadn't completely caught and so I slipped in. Past the heavy drapes, the inside of the auditorium was completely dark. I walked up the aisle, somehow sure I should make no noise. At the top of the inclined floor, I looked down the corridor and saw light spilling from Mr. Carrigan's office.

I called his name. No one answered.

"Mr. Carrigan?" I said again.

This time a figure stepped from the office into the light. It was him. "What are you doing here, Robby?"

"I heard something weird. It sounded like shots."

Mr. Carrigan looked very pale. The skin of his face was drawn tight across the bones. "They were shots, Robby."

"What happened?" I said. "Do you need some help?"

"No," he answered. "I need no help at all, but thank you anyway." He smiled in a funny sort of way.

"What do you want me to do?"

"Go home," he said. He looked suddenly tired. "Go home and call the sheriff and tell him to come down here to the theater right away. Can you do that?"

"Yes," I said without hesitation.

"*Will* you do that?"

"Yes."

"That's good. That's very good." He started to turn back through the pooled light and into the office again, but hesitated. "Robby, remember what I've said so many times about how you can change things for the better?"

"Yes," I said again.

"Well, you can. Remember that." And then he was gone.

I stared at the wedge of light for a few seconds, and then walked back toward the rear of the theater. I didn't go outside. Instead, I just sat behind the screen, there on the dirty wooden floor, thinking about the larger-than-life figures I'd seen dance above me so many times.

After ten or fifteen minutes, I heard another shot. This time it was louder, but I guess that's because I was inside the theater.

I slowly walked back up the aisle. Once I'd reached the corridor, I turned toward the light. I looked inside. Then I went out to the lobby and put a nickel in the pay phone and called the sheriff. I didn't want to phone him from Mr. Carrigan's office.

My parents didn't want me to hear what was decided in the coroner's report, but that didn't matter because it was all over town. And besides, I'd seen it, and even at ten, I could figure some of it out.

Miss Curtwood had gone to Mr. Carrigan's office as she'd said she would, but she had been joined by the big man with the leather jacket. They had taken everything off, the jacket, her dress, everything. They had lain down on the desk together, after shoving all the things lying on it to the floor.

THE CUTTER

When Mr. Carrigan came into his office, they were both there to moan and laugh at him.

If Mr. Carrigan had laughed too, there was no way of telling. But the sheriff did know Mr. Carrigan had taken a .45 revolver out of a desk drawer and fired five times. Some minutes later, he had pulled the trigger a sixth time, this time with the muzzle tight against his right eye.

That was just before I'd phoned.

What I knew, and what none of the other kids at school knew, not even the sheriff's bratty daughter, was that most people in town didn't know everything that must have been in the coroner's report originally.

I remembered everything in detail, like a picture on the screen. I didn't know what it all meant, most of it, until long after. But the images were sharp and clear, waiting for my eventual knowledge.

The first thing I saw when I poked my head through the light outside the office doorway was the big man and Mr. Carrigan, each of them lying in blood with parts of their heads gone. But what I really remember was Miss Curtwood.

Now I know truly how much she had become as Mr. Carrigan really wanted her. Her hair was no longer blonde. It was wet and red. She was not a buxom woman any longer. Nor was she tall. Mr. Carrigan had carefully arranged her legs, but you couldn't ignore the sections that had been removed.

There were other changes I hadn't realized he had wanted.

September evenings are never as crisp and chilly in Los Angeles as they are back home. I miss that.

I just got back from visiting my sister and her family. After Mom and Dad died, she moved out here and married a guy who works at some plant out in Garden Grove. They have a son and a daughter. The son is what the doctors call disturbed. He goes to special classes, but mainly he sits alone in his room. God only knows what he thinks. The daughter has run away from home three times. The first time, they found her at Disneyland; the last two times, with one guy or another in the Valley. The family pictures look like my sister and me as kids.

Everything reminds me of something or someone else.

I bought a .45 revolver just like the one Mr. Carrigan kept in his desk.

There are times I carry it with me to the movies. I sit in the back row and wonder whether the things I see on the screen are edited just as the director planned. Then I go back to my Hollywood apartment and try to sleep. I am the cutter of my own dreams. The fantasies here have never worked out as I'd hoped.

SILVER SCREAM

Sometimes I think about changing my sister's life. And perhaps my own as well. After all, our parents' lives became better, thanks to a late-model T-bird and a drunken real estate developer. With no dreams left to search for, I have only nightmares to anticipate.

The Thing waits for me on the other side of the door.

That which I've never told anyone. The knowledge that behind every adult smile is an ivory rictus. Skeletal hardness underlies the warm flesh. My mother told all her friends I was such a *happy* child. Anyone can be wrong.

I feel like I've built a cage of my own bones.

Mr. Carrigan was right, of course, in the final and most profound analysis. You *can* make anything better. Life can be changed. It can become death.

(for Warren Zevon)

PILGRIMS TO THE CATHEDRAL

by

Mark Arnold

God doesn't love a deconsecrated drive-in: this might be the moral of the story; it's certainly the conclusion. On the other hand, some outdoor theaters *have* converted to other uses without provoking any odd response, or have mellowed from XXX to G rated fare while sprouting gangrenous little amusement parks, carny appendages for a clientele being shepherded about in their Pampers and peejays. So perhaps the message is an obverse comment on the life and soul of James Hern Slavin.

Or else there maybe just is no moral, only a chronicle about the unpleasant intersection of two belief systems. There's no getting around this point, and no particular suspense served in holding it back: this is a story of a collision course, and at the end of it a lot of people are dead.

It's also a story of an American curiosity; an architecture of kitsch and shabby dreams.

As a conscious pursuit, it might have been doomed. But as serendipitous enterprise, an indifferently managed house of cards, the Zone was merely cursed by being in the wrong place.

319

SILVER SCREAM

Granted the Zone was ahead of its time and too intense to be truly commercial, evolving from a half-assed business into a work of obsessive art. In some locales, though, it might have flourished. In Oklahoma or Texas, maybe. As a blue-collar homeboy hurrah in parts of Georgia or North Carolina; paradoxically, as a glam-palace in Marin or Malibu. Solvent or not, it should have become notorious: Calvin Trillin and Charles Kuralt should have done pieces on it, it was the kind of Gothic oddity that Linda Ellerbee and Lloyd Dobbins would have loved.

But the Trilite Zone Drive-In could not have shown a high profile anywhere in Mad River County — not even in Charity, a hippie college town that had closed in upon itself like a blossom, awaiting a decade more to its liking — and the worst possible part of the county for this kind of whimsy was Leviticus.

Leviticus, Ohio was not ever and will never be a village friendly to a three screen tri-triple bill drive-in movie and bootleg white lightning bar that decadent visionaries called the Cathedral of Sleaze.

Not that Earl Bittner had any vision in mind when he bought the place — he was too fried. Shaggy, unwashed, and nearly incoherent beyond bemused whistles, perplexed shrugs and non-plussed eye rolls, Earl wasn't the sort normally tolerated around Leviticus. But this was about the time of the climax to Watergate: God, patriotism and the presidency were dying while hordes of drug-eyed freaks, trauma shocked vets, fanatics, psychics, psychotics and loonies seemed to be ever-growing and spreading. It had been a rough few years, and even the folks of Leviticus were disposed to make allowances, so long as the crazies stayed quiet on the edge of town. Which was the first serendipity, since Earl bought the site of the old Buckeye Drive-In because it was secluded, cheap and barren, and he needed a place to park his butt without getting hassled.

Indeed, the Buckeye seemed a good place to be left alone. Nearly twenty years defunct after a single half-season's operation, its inception hadn't even qualified as a folly — just a damned stupid idea. It was located in a hollow beneath a trash forest, an abandoned farm, and cornfields, three miles from the nearest two-lane state route and nearly a mile from any recognizable road. Nevertheless, some optimist had, once upon a time, poured enough money in high quality cement to accommodate some 2000 cars, built a two-tiered flattop pagoda snack bar-projection booth, erected an electric marquee forty feet long but only eight feet high, and then gone broke so fast there hadn't been time to hock the projectors or sell off the speaker poles. A tax loss so forgotten that it was never even scavenged, the derelict stoicly weathered a generation of Southwest Ohio winters, as if awaiting another quixotic moron.

It did not, in fact, occur to Earl to refurbish the Buckeye, when he moved into the projection booth. He just wanted to veg out and grow seedier;

his apparent life goal was to become a coot. But not a hermit — although whether Earl invited visitors or acquiesced to them wasn't certain. Still, they found him, as many as a dozen on any given evening: barflies needing a place to crash for a night; hitchhikers passing through the county on their way to wherever; backpacking college students; and teens who discovered Earl didn't much care if they used his parking lot to hang out in. Through social osmosis and alchemy, a lowlife underground began re-animating the Buckeye.

County and state patrols slithered by an occasion, causing a scurrying into cars filled with sullen young glares; twice, village police got calls to investigate rumors of a cult. But Earl's place was private property just outside village limits on the Tecumseh Township border and thus nobody's headache; and Earl Bittner could hardly be considered even a minimalist swami — he was at least as bewildered as anyone there.

The parade of transients was healthy for Earl — while he never became, in his life, articulate, at least he retained the concept "speech", and he expanded his repertoire of grimaces. He was home every night, galumphing aimlessly from party to party, the perfect nocturnal host. Earl's only commandments were: no gunfire; no pitbull matches; no battering; no rape. The first two infractions occured once apiece; the latter two would start to take place at times and progress as far as the first cry for help. In all instances the perpetrators abruptly found themselves grabbed by dim, gentle Earl: eyes knit together and squinting, he'd mutter, "Well shit on *this*, man, shit on *this*." Then lights would go out.

Dim, gentle Earl was 6'7", and weighed about 410.

Most guests, then, found four rules a reasonable number. Earl acquired a coterie and his place acquired a nickname — the DMZ, or, more commonly, the Zone.

And that was the second serendipity.

Meanwhile, in other parts of the nation, the vision of a Peoples' Revolutionary Amerika had precipitously fizzled. Which left a lot of the radical vanguard without a hell of a lot to do. Typically distressed was James Hern Slavin, who'd parlayed wrested leadership of a campus political alliance into control of both a large food co-op and small listener sponsored radio station, only to see all three go belly-up for lack of ideologically rigorous donors and volunteers. Most of his militant peers were drifting into law school, real estate, or cocaine; some sat around waiting to discover EST. But Jim Slavin wanted a Cause. He wanted to lead. He enjoyed people taking orders.

SILVER SCREAM

He considered commandeering an alternative school, but it, too, was bankrupt. Then he essayed an abortive foray into grassroots electoral politics — democracy proved too compromised and too risky. At length Jim realised that he yearned to break his materialistic shackles and become enlightened; he decided the fast track was the New Age.

Then Guru Maharaj Ji was proclaimed, by his own mother, to be the final avatar of God. When Jim Slavin first heard of Maharaj Ji, the Godhead was fourteen years old, and often confused with the Maharishi. The differences were that one was a fat old man who giggled a lot, the other was fat, giggly and young; one attracted rock stars, the other, for some reason, radpoliticos.

Now, a few years later, the young messiah still claimed to be God . . . *and* fourteen. What intrigued Slavin was the reaction he got whenever he argued the hard reality of calendars to Maharaj Ji disciples. He emphatically pointed out that if a person is fourteen, 365 days later he is fifteen. If God, then a fifteen year old God, and next year, a *sixteen* year old God.

Wrong, he was told — there was no good reason why God couldn't stay fourteen for a few years if He damn well felt like it.

The potency of such conviction swayed Jim Slavin. Changing his name to Chimoy Haneesh, he found faith — if not in Maharaj Ji, at least in the possibilities of organized religion.

Time, in Mad River County, tends to be measured by the passing of seasons, which tends to obscure the passage of years. And three years, for Earl Bittner and the Zone, drifted until the advent of a wild-eyed cross between James Dean and Joey Ramone, a proto-postpunk from Montclair, New Jersey.

Brandon Pugnale didn't remember where he'd been the day J.F.K. was shot, and didn't care. He was nineteen, and he twitched; he'd survived two teen suicide attempts and a stress-induced nervous collapse; he'd decided the world was in an irreversible decline that would end in nuclear annihilation, and was convincing himself he didn't care about that, either. Brandon felt that, being bright and young, he probably ought to embrace either revolting idealism or disgusting pragmatism, but lacked faith in both.

The only thing Brandon believed in was trash, Lou Reed street people and championship wrestling, White Castles and Tico-Tacos, plastic crucifix musical nightlights and 3D postcards, art deco cafeterias and black painted walls. Trash was all Brandon Pugnale was willing to live for, the sublime essense that never betrayed him. But he had no hope of turning his belief into either a commitment or a career.

PILGRIMS TO THE CATHEDRAL

Brandon discovered the Zone on a cold and drooling wet early-April night. He'd just flunked his sophomore year as a business major at Kent State, and had about a month to figure his next move before the damage became evident. He didn't really wish to stay in Ohio, which was a pisshole. But New Jersey was a pisshole with parents. Montclair was near New York, which had CBGB and Max's; but the bands they booked were from Ohio. Brandon felt no desire for a quotidian world of leisure suits and singles clubs, and couldn't delude himself that the West Coast would be any better than the East. On impulse, he decided to cruise down through Charity and check out its college, which was reputed to be very weird, very expensive, and very desperate for students.

But Charity didn't exist, or had moved, or the roadmap lied. Or something — the village wasn't where it was supposed to be. The run down from Kent was longer than Brandon had thought, the rain got worse all day, and by the time he realized he'd lost his destination, he'd also lost the interstate. He found only hibernating farms, some incongruously fortresslike tract developments, and the spooky, whitewashed, distressingly Christian villages of Lamentations, Leviticus and Judges. In all three, his outsized Harley-Davidson jacket and unmuffled Yahama 450 guaranteed glares and no directions to either a main road or motel.

It was dark when Brandon saw the single light of a combination fire station and tavern a mile beyond Judges, Ohio. The bartender (and chief?) would neither serve nor speak to Brandon; but there was a teenager feeding quarters to a decrepit Gottlieb table. The pinball machine hadn't been serviced in years; half the rollovers were locked in place, the left flipper was lame, and most of the lights were burned out. So was the kid, for that matter — aboriginally ignorant about the existence of highways and Holiday Inns, at least he successfully told Brandon how to find Earl Bittner's place. The rain let up to a drizzle.

The turn-off lacked a street sign, but someone had considerately spray-painted the word ZONE across the blacktop. Brandon liked the name. The drizzle ended, and the cloud cover lifted to the treetops as Brandon found the hollow and the darkened marquee. He wheeled toward a cluster of cars, then saw they were all junkers, neatly arranged to face the skeletal struts that had once borne the screen.

Most drive-ins, like circuses and stage theaters, look small and tawdry when closed. Not the Zone. Immense even in daylight, by night it seemed infinite; acres of black tarmac spreading to merge with the hollow's false horizons. The dozen abandoned cars facing the phantom screen seemed huddled and vulnerable. Then Brandon heard a clomping, squelching tread in the silence. A megalithic shadow detached itself from the refreshment stand and Brandon was seized by panicky *deja vu* of being alone in *terra incognita* after following a retard's directions . . . *Deliverance* . . . *Texas Chainsaw Massacre* . . . *The Hills Have Eyes* . . .

"Ah . . . Hi," he tried. No response. "It's like, uh, 'are you open?'" Grateful that he'd not dismounted, Brandon edged his foot toward the bike's kickstand.

The figure, not stopping, grunted.

Brandon gripped the handlebar clutch. "Look, it's like . . . I'm lost, see, and this kid a few miles from here said it's like 'people can crash at Earl Bittner's and told me to come here but if it's not okay . . .'"

"S'okay," the monolith mumbled, his voice high, nasal and cracking. He rolled his eyes as if exasperated by an idiot question. The gesture and voice were oddly reassuring; the hulk seemed less ominous than asea.

"Well, ah, okay then thanks. Look, it's like 'is there anyplace I can get something to eat?' I been on the road all day — there a Pizza Hut or deli or anything around . . ."

Earl Bittner grunted, turned, and plodded back to the pagoda; suddenly, banks of pink and yellow strip lighting lit the snack bar. Brandon stared, feeling vaguely surreal, then revved up and wheeled across the parking lot.

Earl's hospitality was bachelor simplicity on a grand scale: a six-gallon laundry tub of fearsome chili, perpetually simmering and replenished for nearly three years; cases of lunch-box bagged Fritos; popcorn in the tank of the Buckeye's popper, a machine so antique it dispensed butter; crusted jars of instant coffee and creamer; and soda coolers filled with 140° bootleg corn liquor. Earl waved Brandon toward indifferently cleaned collections of bowls, mugs and spoons. Dinner chat was limited to introductions and Earl's refusal to accept money for his chili and moonshine. Accommodations would be any abandoned car on the lot, or the floor behind the refreshment stand.

A pick-up truck, horn honking, squealed past the snack bar and, splashing puddles, weaved around metal poles to a far corner of the lot. Earl clomped off to play host. The cloudfront passed; greenish-gray moonlight on the Zone piqued Brandon's curiosity. Mad River County began to seem less hostile; warmed and fed, Brandon decided to stick around for a day or two, and continue his search for a college. He wandered across the lot, trying to envision the Zone in what he imagined must have been its salad days: jalopies, Elvis, pony-tails, Beach Party Bingo, I Was a Teenage Scuzzball. He'd been born and raised in mall dominated metro-suburbia, long past the heyday of drive-ins and all their nasty glory . . . the evening chill offset by cayenne, white lightning kindled an alcoholic inkling of awe and revelation. Earl joined him, bearing mugs of hootch.

"This is a great place, man," Brandon said.

Earl grunted, but Brandon was feeling enlightened and expansive.

"So, what're you? Fixing this thing up, or what? I mean you own this place, right? So it's like, 'are you gonna do business,' gonna reopen it or what?" Brandon had another drink.

PILGRIMS TO THE CATHEDRAL

"Re-*open* it?" Earl looked around. "Think it's al-*ready* pretty open."

"What're you, kidding? You fucking kidding me? This is a fucking *great* place! So how come you're not turning it back into a drive-in?"

"*Back* into. A *drive*-in?" The idea had simply never been suggested to Earl.

Brandon, drunk and arms swinging manically, barely noticed. "Are you kidding me? I mean, show cheesy movies and horror and skinflicks, sell popcorn, beer — I mean this is a fucking *theater*, man! It's all here, just use it, it's like 'you got your ticket booth, you got your projection booth, your snack bar'. You got your marquee! It's like, 'how much more do you need?'"

A bit more, as it turned out. But Earl squinted at the lot, quite possibly seeing it objectively for the first time since he'd bought it. His eyes began to gleam with wonder and his right cheek began to spasm. At length the tic firmed into a half-smile. Earl Bittner was finding something to believe in. He could believe in the Zone.

Still, he shook his head and sighed. "Naw, I don't — I don't know shit. Shit about that stuff . . ."

"What — *what're* you? I mean, *what* — picking movies? I got a cousin does that. Business? That shit's easy, man, it's like, 'trust me!' I'm an M.B.A. Really. And all this stuff's *nothing*."

"I." Earl stopped and rolled his eyes. "I don'*know* any'a that stuff . . ."

"Yeah, but I do; I mean it's like, 'I could set you up, and . . .'" and Brandon Pugnale realised he'd just found an alternative to Kent and Montclair, a future embodying his vision of trash ". . . y'know? I really could." He looked up to the nonexistent screen, filling in lurid scenes and splashes of color washing over a hot summer parking lot filled with Trans Ams and Camaros, teeming with teenage girls in misapplied make-up, halter tops, sweaty, beerstained jeans stretched across their oversized Ohio asses. "It could be real . . ." he admiringly whispered, "real . . . real sick." Brandon laughed, clapped his hand and shouted, "Oh, *shit*, man — we gotta *do* it, y'know? It's like — we have just *got* to do this!"

Then he threw up.

Thus was the Zone reborn and baptised.

Drive-in movies were, at the time, adjudged to be endangered, or already extinct. America was rocked by gas shortages, inflation, and threats of rationing; entrepreneurs sought fuel substitutes in everything from rocks to grass clippings; and unnecessary motoring was considered almost sinful. Moreover, all movie receipts had been falling for nearly a decade, as bijous fissioned into puny screening rooms, managers hoping to half-fill hundred seat houses. Media pundits differed only in their choice of apocalypse: either the economy would collapse, in which case everyone would stay home and watch tv; or the economy would improve, in which case everyone would stay home and watch *pay* tv.

SILVER SCREAM

But Earl Bittner and Brandon Pugnale were unaware of fiscal forecasts. They were oblivious to Ohio's eroding industrial base and declining farm land prices. They didn't notice that, above their heads, "For Sale" signs went up on the forsaken farm and forest while the cornfields were optioned by a speculator from Dayton who never raised the capital for his housing development, but did persuade Tecumseh Township trustees to amend the area's building codes and permit construction of multi-unit dwellings.

Earl and Brandon were too busy to care. By tinkering and triage, they managed to coax fifty-one speakers, two projectors, and the marquee into a guise of functionality. They obtained rolls of tickets, cases of soda and kegs of beer. They tried to make a screen from billboard paper, but finally had to hire a Cincinnati theater supplier to erect and position the 35mm sheet.

Films proved easy to obtain. Brandon simply essayed a hadj to his second cousin, Louis "Capooch" Capagianelli, overseer of five mob-owned cinemas in Times Square and Harlem, who could supply pirated prints of whatever happened to be on hand. Few of them movies likely to be reviewed by Gene Shalitt or *Sneak Previews*, but all of them satisfying to Brandon's esthetics.

The issue of their labors, billed as the DMZ Drive-In, looked fairly pathetic, and pretty much like Earl Bittner's old place. Unpainted; cracked concrete; weeds. The junked cars stayed put. But to Earl and Brandon the site was transformed; and they officially opened on the last Tuesday in July with a triple feature of *Bloody Pit of Horror*, *Sugar Hill's Zombie Hit Men*, and *The Devil in Miss Jones*.

Earl's regulars refused to pay for parking in a lot they'd always used for free; they just drove around Brandon's frantically waving arms, until Earl dimly, gently explained the new order. Earl sputtered and pouted at Brandon's insistence that they sell refreshments, which Earl had fully intended to include in the admission price. The projectors broke often. Ticket-taking and food vending were haphazard. They didn't advertise, since they never knew what or whether Cousin Capooch would be shipping. The madding crowds never materialized; the gate fluctuated between two and ten cars a night. Brandon, who had moved into an abandoned van, scored no teen nooky.

Even so, *Meat-Cleaver Massacre* / *The Incredible Torture Show* / *Three on a Meathook* played, then *Barn of the Naked Dead* / *Ilsa, She-Wolf of the SS* / and *El Topo*; *Bloodeaters* / *Revenge of Monkey Fists* / *House of Whip-cord*; *Olga's Girls* / *Fists of Vengeance*, and *Let Me Die a Woman*. When they closed the season in October, the Zone had garnered gross receipts of nearly $3,000 . . . not counting expenses.

Brandon was ecstatic. He called other drive-in managers, pestering them for secrets; subscribed to trade papers; and dragged Earl to exhibitors' shows. Earl was stunned by his summer viewing: he'd never dreamt that certain events could *be*, let alone be captured on film; like any other convert, he'd beard strangers and proselytize, ". . . an' then *this* guy WRRRAAA and a bunch'a skinny Chin*ese* with pigtails WHAPWHAPWHAPWHAPWHAP an'he did this *jig* and th'*other* guy's head KA-*PLOMB!*", crudely miming rip-saws, psychokinetic explosions, and shaolin temple mixed crane/mantis kung. Earl was, for the first time in memory, genuinely enthused; and Brandon learned how much paperwork he had yet to start. All told, it could have been enough — enough knowledge, enough experience to have kept the Zone for a few seasons, another marginal Ohio enterprise staggering along on the edge of failure.

But that winter Brandon Pugnale attended a Famous Monsters of Filmland convention in Minneapolis, and returned to Leviticus with two inspirations.

The first was seen on a highway near the airport: a drive-in, the better to compete with mall cinemas, had tri-sected its parking lot and erected two more screens, enclosing an open-sided pyramid of film. Brandon promptly grasped the implications — more movies, more money, more fun.

The second inspiration followed Brandon to Ohio in a Winnebago crammed with cookware and cosmetics. She was 32, newly divorced, and had just changed her name to An'akist Verlaine.

Dissolving like a video space invader, Maharaj Ji's millenium self-destructed in a muddy scandal that seemed to involve too many wristwatches, too many Indian customs guards, too many stewardesses, too many hidden marriages, and one very jealous Mother of the Messiah, who unexpectedly declared that she had made a perfectly dreadful mistake: Maharaj Ji, she announced, was *not* God.

His little brother was.

By the time the mess was straightened out (if, indeed, it ever has been), most of the perpetually enlightened were drifting into neoconservative banking, Posse Comitatus, or Rajneeshpurim; some sat around, waiting to discover designer drugs.

But Chimoy Hanneesh, *né* James Hern Slavin, surfaced in Missouri renewed and recycled as Rev. J. Hern Sloane, pastor of the First Church of United Christian Life. Disdaining such old timey relics as a church and con-gregation, Rev. Sloane purchased weekly radio hours for his self-ordained, self-promoting ministry in the Wonderful News of Christ's Coming.

Which might be a terribly cynical way to describe acceptance of the eternal truth that cleansed a mortal soul in dramatic affirmation of faith — but them, Jim Slavin's vocation was suspect. He hawked indulgence.

SILVER SCREAM

All media evangelists spend much of their airtime hustling tithes and blessings. But Rev. Sloane bribed nursing home attendants to tune in his show, and slip him medically annotated patient lists, which inspired the texts of Jim Slavin's sermons.

"And in Springboro this beautiful morning, my heart is with all of our friends at the Elmbrook Home, over there, like Esther Hubbard . . . can ya'hear us this morning, Esther? Bless ya, how are ya', darlin'? Esther, dear sister, Jesus has a blessing He wants me to give ya'. The Lord GOD knows about the cancer, darlin'; He Whose love blesses all has witnessed to me about the cancer that's eatin' you alive, that's causing you such affliction. Well, Esther, it brings me pain to see you suffer, darlin' sister, and it brings GOD pain . . . GOD won't let ya die, dearest. GOD can't bear to see ya suffer; and GOD wants to bless your troubled heart." Rev. Sloane would explain that God could intercede if Esther obtained a beautiful and inspirational "Praying Hands" blessing (which 1X3″ card she should tuck beneath her pillow, thus letting Christ know whom to cure), which Esther would receive absolutely free upon receipt of her $75 offering. The more cards, the sooner God's arrival. Then on to Agnes Krienslach's arthritis and May-Belle Loteneau's paralysis.

Whether or not God approved, the terminally ill did. Jim Slavin had found his bandwagon: the market was bullish on Elmer Gantry. Bit time preachers raked in millions per week. Rev. Jim Jones was building an expensive South American retreat; Jim and Tammy Bakker sold salvation through eyeshadow; Ernest Ainsley one-upped psychics with over-the-air exorcisms; Billy James Hargis prophesized hellfire for sinners while he fucked the adolescent boys and girls of his travelling All-America choir; reruns of Leroy Jenkins collected offerings while the good parson himself was in a Georgia lock-up, convicted of complicity in an extortion and arson-for-profit ring that had caused a few deaths in some slums he owned. Prosperous, adored, tax exempt, and nearly beyond all legal accountability, the ministries were understandably thankful to God and the American Way.

As soon as he could afford to, Jim Slavin made the jump to cable.

Upon reaching age thirty, Mrs. Donald Simms Jr. discovered David Bowie, Darkover novels, and her sexual prime; she decided what she didn't want to be when she grew up was a Minnesota farmgirl turned Minnesota *hausfrau.* So, rather than get pregnant with Donald III, Mrs. Simms dyed, shaved and moussed her hair into a rainbow-spectrumed cockatoo crest, hung around Minneapolis clubs, and vanished on weekends to attend science fiction conventions.

PILGRIMS TO THE CATHEDRAL

Mr. Simms was displeased. Mrs. Simms soon found herself free to resume her maiden name of Ann Verlaine. She was 5'1", 92 lbs; she had charm, enthusiasm, a wicked basilisk glare, and ever-changing hair and make-up. She was an avant-garde chameleon with no concrete plans, just a dwindling divorce settlement, an r.v., and a powerful belief in flash. Ann became An'akist and was bracing herself to try Soho or L.A., when she met Brandon Pugnale.

Standing in the same convention registration line, they talked, touched, and almost instantly clung to each other without sleep for a week. They chattered all day, caroused all night, traded obscure rock tapes at dawn. Neither doubted it was It at first sight; both tried their best to live in each other's arms, glow in each other's eyes, kiss till their lips went numb. Their attraction was amazing, exhilarating, public, thrilling; it was absolutely, totally disgusting. Belying all pretense to their images of post-industrial cool, Brandon and An'akist cootchied enough to smother a Smurf or render a Care Bear bilious. No logic could explain the nouveau flashqueen's subsequent move to a parking lot in semi-rural Ohio. Suffice to say — Brandon spoke to her condition.

And she was the link, the fuel rod required for the Zone to achieve critical mass. A trinity of beliefs came together into self-sustaining reaction. A strange magic began to stir.

The magic was not apparent come springtime; but potholes were filled, fresh blacktop spread, parking lines and arrows painted along rows of leased speakers beneath a vast geometry of screens. Brandon and Earl built an expanded projection turret and acquired new used equipment. The ticket kiosk, bathrooms and pagoda gleamed with fresh paint and chrome. The snack bar actually passed Health Department inspection; an electric Dr. Pepper clock-menu listed variations on chili, popcorn, hot dogs, sweets, beer, and soft drinks plain or, for a buck-fifty premium, " + ". Earl was proud of his chile and moonshine and would part with neither: the corn liquor was, of course, against the law and there was no way around that save to dollop it under a code name. Distribution contracts were signed, and Cousin Capooch expanded the illicit library with filched pre-release directors' cuts of new and occasionally big-budget films. Brandon resprayed the faded ZONE graffito on the state route, and placed newspaper ads with the theater's new name. "Nine movies for the price of one in — *The Trilite Zone.*"

Each screen was usually reserved for its own specialty: Horror — Violence — and Sex. The opening gala featured *Eaten Alive / Zombie Flesh Eaters / Dawn of the Dead / Make Them Die Slowly / Baby Cart at River Styx / Twitch of the Death Nerve / Insatiable / Lucifer Rising / Shanty Tramp.* The 2000 car lot wasn't filled, but the first week's receipts outgrossed the entire previous summer's. The drive-in was suddenly suffused with an incense of viability.

SILVER SCREAM

Jubilation led to innovation: for the next few years An'akist, Brandon and Earl seemed able to take the business in any direction — every silly, gonzo, warped, drugged-out notion had its niche in the scheme of the Zone.

Ideas flowed from An'akist, who, pursuant to nothing would bounce as if goosed and cry, "OH! Y'know what we *could* do is?"; were caught by Brandon's "Yo! Wai'amintue wai'aminute, this could fucking be smooth, it's like 'it's real sick'. Sweet . . ." They'd hug each other, smooch, hold hands, tickle, giggle; and volley, spin, shape, kick the concept around while Earl stood by, shaking his head, muttering "What the hell's *that* shit . . .", happy to be involved.

God Told Me To / Mutations / Suspira . . .

An'akist piped punk and metal over the speakers before, between and sometimes during shows. The Not Ready for Airplay scores were like nothing broadcast in Mad River County including, over the years, Anthrax to Zott, Bitch, Bad Brains, Butthole Surfers, Shox Lumania, Afrika Bambaataa, Oingo Boingo, the Cramps, Screaming Hibiscus, Big Fat Hairy Pet Clams from Outer Space, the Dead Boys, the Voidoids, Mermaids on Heroin, SIC F*CKS, Throbbing Gristle, and Country Porn.

Dungeons of Horror / Nigger Lover / Mondo Magic . . .

An'akist hooked up a microphone to deliver color commentaries about the movies while they were shown; and started amateur theatrical contests, where audience volunteers improvised spontaneous redubbings of Filipino gore.

Do Me Evil / Dracula Sucks / Take It All . . .

An'akist felt sorry for all the poor couples forced to screw in Civics and Chevettes. She rented out sleeping bags and pup tents, then created a cordoned off intimacy section in a wedge between Sex and Violence, with flowerbeds, waterbeds, trampolines, a boxing ring — it came to be called the Fight-or-Fuck area . . . the Forf.

Toxic Zombies / Humanoids from the Deep / Children Shouldn't Play With Dead Things . . .

An'akist, challenged by *Rocky Horror*, got Brandon to sell make-up kits, vampire fangs, ghoul masks, water pistols; she ran costume contests.

Call Him Mr. Shatter / Night of the Bloody Apes / Satan's Sadists . . .

An'akist appropriated the Zone's borders for a vegetable garden, appointing Earl her serf. Earl groused until he bit into his first homegrown jalapenos and realised how their infusion would galvanize his chili. Henceforth the stuff would burn a patron's ass for days. The snack bar topped hot dogs with homemade relishes, mustards, and pickles.

Caged Heat! / Barbed Wire Dolls / Wanda the Wicked Warden . . .

An'akist booked a Columbus noise band to play Dead Kennedies covers, got Brandon to set up spotlights and a sound system, but forgot to tell Earl, who projected *Superninja and Drunk Masters* across the concert.

PILGRIMS TO THE CATHEDRAL

The result was so satisfying that An'akist brought in as many acts as she could find, from headbangers to glam gloom, performance art to gelatin wrestling, all of whom played simultaneously with the movies.

Breakfast at Manchester Morgue / The Honeymoon Killers / Slumber Party Massacre . . .

The Big Bang, however, was Earl Bittner's genius, his tribute to his faith. One crystalline –12° January night, Brandon and An'akist awoke in the Winnebago as a projector flooded a screen, the light echoing across the snow coated, ice-varnished lot. They roused in time to watch a power drill gore through an eye and turn into a striking rattlesnake that spat intestines over a headless cheerleader . . . they dressed, mufflered, dashed and climbed to the booth where Earl, face twisted into a lopsided grin, gleefully hiked a thumb toward the screen. He had, with ham-fingered patience, joined splices, trailers, and shots from duplicate prints into twenty minutes of nonstop trash climaxes — shock cuts, cum shots, head rolls, blow ups, boots, chops, thrusts, slashes, splats. By spring, Earl had assembled two more reels, and sluiced all three screens with a fireworks display as hypnotically searing to the eye and brain as Earl's chili was to the tongue and gut — a fest of f/x, a satiation of sleaze.

The Incredibly Strange Creatures Who Stopped Living and Became Mixed-up Zombies / Attack of the Killer Tomatoes / Andy Warhol's 3D Flesh for Frankenstein / Cannibal Holocaust / Pay Them in Blood / Ramrod / Talk Dirty to Me / Flesh Gordon / Star Whores . . .

Word of the Zone spread to midwestern campuses and air bases; meanwhile, graphic cheapies and big budget trash movies proliferated and grew more popular. Brandon subscribed to *Gore Gazette, Sleazoid Express* and *Splatter Times*; he and An'akist daydreamed about being the cutting edge of a cultural movement. Laughing, hugging, wrapped in each other, Brandon and An'akist were crazy-in-love. And Earl Bittner had found a family without leaving his home.

But beyond the underground, different forces propelled the social dynamic. Ohio was bashed by malaise, Iranian hostages, the collapse of smokestack industries; it slammed to a brief stop when a 21% prime interest rate collided with a 12% usury ceiling that made all loans illegal. Cleveland, International Harvester, and family farms went under; many thought the rest of the state would soon follow.

The same straits wracked the entire country, opening the portal to sweeping political change. Governor Ronald Reagan, formerly buried by the press as a superannuated sadsack with too-often repeated punch lines, snagged an interception and spiked one into the White House end zone: his tackles and offensive line were mystically transmogrified from knuckle-dragging fruitcakes and yahoos into respected mainstream conservatives and headline leaders of moral revivalism.

And the Reverend J. Hern Sloane was filmed shaking hands with Ron and hugging Nancy. The day after the election, he hired a toney Madison Avenue firm to create a high pressure opening credits sequence for his cable ministry. Less than six years after being a revolutionary Maoist dedicated to the violent extirpation of the capitalist bourgeoisie and American colonial-istic imperialist hegemony, Jim now emerged on screen preaching, pro-phesizing, shaking his head in sad judgement of sin, and setting down to a deep dish of apple pie amidst star spangled banners and unsung heroes dying on Freedom's Shores: the video suggested that the holy triune of Reagan, Sloane and Jesus marched, arms linked, to comfort and bless the needy of history's turning points, mixing hope with panic-peddling tirades against an endless series of buzzwords. Ratings sored. Cassettes were sold. More politicians shook his hand. Jim Slavin was joining the ranks of evangelic megastars.

However, local chickens were seeking roosts. Jim Slavin, in his nursing home scam days, had personally converted several well-heeled matrons to United Christian Life. Four had since divorced, and each sought to contrac-tualize her pentacostal passion. Rev. Sloane turned to the Good Book for guidance.

Not the bible.

The road atlas.

Meanwhile, Leviticus hired its first professional Village Manager. This was a major concession: Leviticus had never paid secular outsiders to attend civic matters. But the surging religious market had given rise to the career of Christian Management — people whose executive skills were turned to the service of the Word. Only two years older than Brandon Pugnale, Peter Everett LaMar had a business and a public management degree from Tufts, religious certification from two bible study colleges, and a resume citing Town Manager positions in Kansas and Wisconsin, as well as an Assistant City Manager stint in northern Michigan. Ev LaMar's credo might have been "The Good Lord loves a tough s.o.b."; and Leviticus was primed for that message. The village elected a more aggressive Council — realtors Buddy Roemer and Dorothea Twaits, loan officer and retired Air Force Major Orrick DeWine, pharmacist Abner L. Schlueuter, hog farmer Poole Neiderhous — and prepared for the challenge of the new decade.

Leviticus' most galling problem was the village's loss of status to its rival, Revelations, Ohio. The two communities, founded in the schism of an apocalyptic frontier church 250 years earlier, had always competed. Leviticus opened a bible college, Revelations' was large and better endowed; Revela-tions attracted a religious book publisher, Leviticus, a Christian FM radio station, Revelations' station had a bigger transmitter, Leviticus got an AM frequency. But now Leviticus' population was aging or inbred. Revelations scored a series of coups: recruiting a Christian software and gaming company, a cluster of Christian condominiums, a Christian direct-mail service. And, most public of all, Revelations opened a 16-hour-a-day Christian tv station, UHF Channel 59.

Leviticus was humiliated; Ev LaMar's specific charge was to catch up. LaMar authored a land development package combining condos, tennis courts, retirement housing, telecommunications relay and television broadcast studios connected to a church-reflection garden-revival complex, with room for a light industrial park, all to be built under an attractive bond and tax abatement plan. The best location was a 112 acre site: three adjacent and long unsold properties listed with Roemer Realty and Twaits Realty, but not actually within Village limits. Leviticus had no trouble extending its border via an annexation order. All LaMar needed was a buyer or investment syndicate.

That problem was solved by Bryce Magaw of Koogler-Magaw Construction: his nephew was an associate co-pastor for J. Hern Sloane.

An'akist Verlaine's crowning achievement was La Roofe, the inspiration that elevated the Trilite Zone from idiosyncratic grindhouse into the Cathedral of Sleaze. It was a magnet for Ohio's true decadent esthetes — the region's finest nouvelle cuisine and exploitation.

An'akist and Brandon had taken to throwing midnight champagne picnics: they'd climb onto the roof of the projection booth for poached duck breast with orange mayonnaisse, or crawfish — fettucine verdi salad, or hibachied pork sates, while waiting for Earl's Big Bangs to fill the screens.

Inevitably, An'akist said, "OH! Y'know what we *could* do is?"

The pagoda grew a gazebo.

The projection booth roof was tiled, railed, and enclosed with moveable plexi windows. Tables were adorned with damask, flowers, candles and speakers that could be tuned to any screen. Free mixers were chilled for a BYOB cocktail lounge, and, for voyeurs, Cousin Capooch liberated half a dozen 25¢ a minute stereo-telescopes from the prows of the Staten Island ferries.

Paying a table d'hote charge, patrons would scale ladders to La Roofe and sample An'akist's buffet fancy of the evening: from hors d'oeuvres, whether cognac-infused pate en croute, or avocado mousse with caviar; through entrees like boned quail in puff pastry, or beef mignonettes with tarragon-cornichon cream reduction, or pistachioed veal ballontine with

SILVER SCREAM

madeira sauce; such side dishes as wax beans chilled with fresh dill, or vermouth-steamed broccoli with horseradish mousseline sauce; to frozen raspberry-Chambord souffle with burgundy sauce, or triple-lime chiffon cheesecake, or chocolate-Grande Marnier divinity for dessert.

The diners were tu'penny lords of low-rent creation, clinking tulipes to the riot of sights around and below. One slumming regular, a grantless archaelogist turned mystery-bookstore owner, would pluck at her stud bracelets, twirl her champagne, and say to her guests as the Big Bang went off, *"That's* what I enjoy about this place — it's *everything* I used to adore about Bangkok and Beirut."

The Cathedral was ordained. In neon, striplights, moon and stars the acolytes came and the revels throbbed. Beneath *Videodrome / Eraserhead / Liquid Sky / Ms. 45 / Avenging Angel / Repo Man / Caligula / Sex, Drugs & Rock 'n Roll / Cafe Flesh*, dancers swirled and whirled, bikers postured and squared off in the rings, costumed monsters charged knights in tin-foil armor, country boys and women played tag with beer-filled balloons, and teens unselfconsciously scampered naked from the Forf, amid a carnival of creatures capering from darkness to dawn, seven nights a week, spring and hot summer and fall. It was a sculpted orison of lunacy, centered on three people who loved each other, loved the Zone, and believed in the architecture they had brought to life.

And that life acquired spirit.

Magic, amorphous and weirdly innocent, glowed.

Film buffs first noticed that all the movies were untouched by studios or distributors. Some of this was due to Cousin Capooch's unorthodox acquisitions, which might explain the return of never-before shown censored shots. But something else arranged the screening of films that had never been made: the marathon sixteen hour Jodoworski-Lynch collaboration of *Dune*; Alan Ormsby's direction of Paul Schrader's script for *Cat People* starring Nasti Kinski *and* David Bowie; David Cronenberg's *Ghost Story*; Roman Polanski's *The Shining*; Herschell Gordon Lewis' *Titus Andronicus*; and Ed Wood Jr.'s *Cleopatra*.

The magic grew into a playful prankster, a partying Puck. Sometimes bestial howls on screen were chorused from the woods; sometimes mummers were joined by dancers with too many arms and too few heads; sometimes cars bounced like hobby horses while unseen teeth nipped at bottoms or tentacles tripped passers-by.

And sometimes, during a Big Bang, *everyone* in the Forf experienced simultaneous orgasms powerful enough to ripple through the asphalt, tingling with a metal sigh up to La Roofe.

The Zone drained just enough ectoplasm from its celebrants to keep the scene from boiling over; the ground held vitality like a battery. On screen the effects seemed more convincing, the colored corn syrup more sanguine;

but on the lot, Earl's four commandments were never challenged. Fights never grew too brutal, wounds were never serious, groping never got threatening, cars were never broken into, money never stolen. And despite the Bacchanialian, seemingly lethal quantities and mixtures of inebriants poured down peoples' throats, no one ever drove away from the Zone smashed. The most determined substance abusers were always overpowered by a need to dance, screw or puke in time to get straight.

Even cleaning was easy. Every morning, the food, fluids and detritus vanished, as if scoured by pixies or sucked into the ground as offerings.

Earl, Brandon and An'akist were convinced the Zone was blessed.

Recognizing spiritual kinship, Ev LaMar and Jim Slavin liked each other on sight. Slavin needed only an introductory meeting to decide Leviticus was a place to do business and God's work. Rev. Sloane and the Village Council shared the deep camaraderie of those who stood to make each other millions.

The only fly in the soup was Minton Eggets, the new and very young chief of the village's four man police force. Eggets was pious and not too bright; a premature ejaculator of the law who'd bust the high school the day *before* a marijuana deal or openly follow one carload of teens while another boosted unlocked bicycles. And since annexation, Minton had been squirming for a chance to swoop down on the Zone.

"Reverend, don't you worry about *that pit,*" Minton blurted, vehemently disrupting a presentation on sewage and water line extensions and easements. "They won't trouble you *one bit,* Sir — they're a dozen ways illegal and I can clean out that nest like *that.* Like *that!*" He snapped his fingers. Slavin raised an eybrow, LaMar aimed a pointer at a wall map.

"There's a dirty moviehouse at that location," LaMar drawled, circling the hollow, "out of our jurisdiction until recently."

"Organized crime?" Slavin asked.

Ev snorted. "Hardly. An old drunk, some punk kid, and their girlfriend. There are numerous infractions we can cite them for; just a question of finding the most apropos timing."

"*Tomorrow!* I could have those so-and-sos on a rail *tomorrow,* Reverend —"

"Minton," Ev sighed, "I'm sure Reverend Sloane appreciates that, but — sometimes — when the victory against Satan is too easily won, some folks don't see it for the victory it is . . ."

Eggets wrinkled his nose, lost.

"Brother Minton," Jim murmured, "y'know, a few years ago my mother suffered from a cataract in her eye. She was in anguish; but neither doctors nor GOD would heal that eye until the cataract reached a size, 'ripened', a medical doctor would say. Well, friend, we prayed every day with all our hearts, and in time the Good Lord's blessing healed that dear lady and today she can see like a young girl. But GOD tells us that 'to all things comes there a season', Minton; sometimes that old cataract has to grow, the fever must run its course, and the Devil be given the rope with which GOD will scourge him." Or — even if the match is fixed, the crowd likes to see the champ bounce off the ropes before getting the pinfall. A carefully choreographed campaign would pay off in publicity, units sold, donations secured, investors committed; and Rev. J. Hern Sloane pulled higher ratings when he mixed the Word of Hope with the Witness of Dire Herald.

"Well . . . you just keep it in mind, Reverend — I can close'em down *like that!*" Snap.

Rev. Sloane smiled at Ev LaMar. "Perhaps you'd be kind enough to run me over to the site, tonight, so we can get a look at the problem . . ." Forestalling Minton's offer of a lift, Slavin raised a finger, "and we can finish discussing easements on the way."

"When the money starts flowing," Rev. Sloane said that evening, "your police chief's gonna be a little out of place." Cigar smoke whisked into the air conditioning of LaMar's Pontiac.

Ev shrugged. "There're a lot of Eggets around here, so as long as he wants the job, he'll keep it . . . but the situation should solve itself. Minton's got an ambition, you see. Wants to be Sheriff. Seems his daddy told him three County Sheriffs've gone up to the Statehouse or Congress, and Minton's sure he'll be the fourth. Of *course*, he wants to close his *only* big case a good fifteen months before the election . . . but with God's grace I think we can keep him from screwing up. Then he can spend the rest of his life running for the Legislature. And frankly, it *will* be a positive moral act to put this place out of business."

"But it doesn't violate your town smut ordinance?"

"*This* town," LaMar smiled, "has never needed one. We could pass a bill easily enough, but I'd rather not kick up some ACLU hornets' nest, when we can finesse the issue." He glanced over. "I imagine you're thinking, 'buncha hicks gettin' lathered over some place that shows *Debby Does Dallas*' . . ."

They turned down an overgrown tractor path running along the cornfields, and strolled to the edge of the hollow.

"Good location for an amphitheater," Sloane mentioned.

"Yessir, I'd noticed . . . it also connects the property quite nicely." LaMar handed Sloane a pair of binoculars. "Happy viewing."

"What the hell *is* that — a *cocktail lounge?*"

"And French restaurant, I hear. This place is a three-ring circus. Regular bona fide zoo."

PILGRIMS TO THE CATHEDRAL

Jim Slavin scanned twined legs stuck out of pup tents; aerobic dancers who bumped and ground to a band playing "Too Drunk to Fuck" while a group of jocks in college jackets sang "Bwana Dick"; in a boxing ring a Tae Kwan Do match was taking place; a tangible smog of body musk, perfume, weed and liquor swirled up the hollow. On two screens he could see a tree ripping off an actress' clothes, and a mohawked blond sticking his mailed fist through the windshield of an armored hotrod doing 200 mph. Eyes glued, Slavin threaded his way through cornstalks to get an open view of the occluded third screen.

He cleared the line of sight just as fourteen inches of Johnny Wadd Holmes torpedoed up Vanessa del Rio's trembling butt, and J. Hern had an epiphany. His soul swelled with a rising tide of wrath against the cankerous spectre arrayed in the pit below: the Zone was everything Ev LaMar had hinted at and more, a perfect dragon for a latter day St. George, a media vehicle rare beyond price.

Years had passed, but once again he would lead more than a flock; he would lead a Movement.

Slavin started to recall his old revolutionary tactics.

The construction of Christian Life Heights was announced in *The Levitious Weekly Witness*; and the drive-in's demise was fated.

More canny defenders might have seen the threat and angled for time, challenging annexation, demanding environmental impact and traffic studies, filing injunctions and appeals. Even so, red tape maneuvers could only have stalled for a graceful exit. The conflict was to be of the moral center *v.* the obscene fringe. Leviticus wanted Rev. Sloane — and didn't want the Zone.

But An'akist, Brandon and Earl had no scent of the wind; they were engrossed in plans for the coming season. They'd started new hobbies over the summer, which they naturally applied to the Zone. Brandon and An'akist refined the art of the multimedia Theme Night, while Earl found he liked attending auctions.

Earl's auctioneering was like automatic writing: he never knew when he'd speak up or raise his hand, never was quite sure what he was buying; but his choices were always great.

At his first auction, Earl bought a tractor trailer-load of processed food. The shipment was delivered while An'akist and Brandon were discussing one of their fascinations, the film festival. They stared at the mountain of junk food in dismayed shock for a minute: then An'akist cried "OH! Y'know what we *could* do is?", and created, on the spot, Retroroni.

SILVER SCREAM

It was the Zone event of the year. *Teenagers From Outer Space / Robot Monster / The Beast of Yucca Flats / The Beast that Killed Women / Mesa of Lost Women / Swamp Women / Truck Stop Woman / Angels' Wild Woman / Rebels on Wheels*, bracketed with vintage stage loops, Driver's Ed films, nudie volleyball shorts, and the worst '50s pop music they could scrounge. The snack bar served only bologna and oleo on Wonder White, Kool Ade and T-Bird; La Roofe featured shredded carrots in green jello, Franco-American-Velveeta melts, and tunafish-mushroom soup-potato chip casserole — all of which served as ammunition in a ten hour long food fight. The Jackson Pollack effect of pasta, cheese, wine and tomato sauce against the blacktop was outrageous.

Earl, urged to attend more auctions, amassed 300 picture tubes, 1000 cases of rolled pistol caps, 10,000 cut-out l.p.s, and a boxcar of canned novelties called Slime, Goo and Glop.

They had no idea they were the targets of a tv preacher's attacks, vilified coast-to-coast. They didn't feel the growing hostility in Leviticus because they never went into the village: a burg with no place for Brandon's leather had never tolerated An'akist radical hair and clothes. Unwarned, unarmed, they were blindsided by the assault that began in April, when opening night unexpectedly featured enraged pickets and voracious television coverage.

The result was drive-in auto-da-fe. The demonstrators were righteous, humorless and tearful to discover such filth in their back yards; their hair-raising yarns of brushes with depravity were lies — none of the protestors had ever patronised the Zone and many, in fact, lived outside Ohio — but, like all zealots, they believed themselves, which played well on the tube.

In contrast, Earl Bittner glared apoplectically, balled his fists, and tromped back and forth before the mob, hollering "What's *that* shit! What's *that* shit! What's *that* shit!"; Brandon, crowded by a cameraman, shoved back, yelling "Gedoutta here fuckin' asshole, y'fucking asshole get outta my face —" while An'akist looked struck and shellshocked, alternately shouting, "*What?* Get out! What are you *doing?* We didn't *do* anything? What do you want? *Get out!*", and breaking into tears before hecklers. On the news, profanities conspicuously excised, they seemed dangerous, deranged and drugged.

As bulldozers began to shape Christian Life Heights, the second front deployed. Although no brick had been laid, television eloquently portrayed the distress of young condo purchasing couples and helpless retirees, whose infants and/or golden years were suddenly menaced by perverts. Other churches eagerly joined the demonstrators; anti-porn activists, merely learning film titles, yearned to lynch anyone connected with the Zone: the land of the free had no place for deviants who showed *Bloodsucking Freaks, Lethal Injection, Hell's Orgy.*

PILGRIMS TO THE CATHEDRAL

No reporter noted that this threat to the local quality of life had been peacably operating for nearly a decade. Unmentioned were the deluge of vitriolic hate mail to the Zone, the death threats, the bomb scares. The ticket kiosk was knocked over and splintered. Bricks broke snack bar equipment. Molotov cocktails were thrown at the screens. Vandals swarmed down the unfenced hillsides, cut speaker wires, shrieked at patrons, tried to storm the projection booth . . . but on the evening news, the pickets stayed civil and off the lot.

Business plummeted through spring and early summer; An'akist, Brandon and Earl weathered the siege badly. They argued, bickered and found fault with each others' weaknesses as, in the crucible, the core of their love began to falter.

An'akist wanted to create a *cause celebre*. Had her pleas been planned, she might have enlisted Nat Hentoff and Bob Guccione, Stephen King and Joe Bob Briggs, Instead, she sent hand-scrawled appeals to people whom An'akist *wanted* to think sympathetic: David Letterman, David Lee Roth, Jaimie Lee Curtis, Sid Vicious, John Belushi, Elvira Mistress of the Dark. Some were inappropriate, some fictional, some deceased. None replied.

Brandon went to Cousin Capooch for muscle and was rebuffed; Louis Capagianelli wanted no territorial disputes nor grief from either New York or Ohio bosses. He kicked Brandon out of his office, ordering him never to reveal their kinship.

Earl Bittner sank into himself. He bought a shotgun, and divided his time between cleaning it, and compulsively stirring the chili tub.

Then, in the beginning of July, the furor quieted. The cameras were gone, the few pickets who returned each night seemed laughably ineffectual, and the Zone's summer crowds returned. It seemed that an astrological disjunction had ended and life could continue; which was what Jim Slavin and Ev LaMar intended.

Spirits perked up through Womens' Prison Night, the Staten Island Grade Z Film Festival, and I Night (*I Eat Your Skin / I Drink Your Blood / I Dismember Mama*) . . . the LPs were frisbeed during Smash UFOs Night . . . the caps set off during All Western Story Night . . . the tv tubes were built into Flyvision banks in La Roofe . . .

Brandon and An'akist regained enough confidence to prepare the First Annual H.G. Lewis Gorerama. They meant to rent fire hoses, pumps, and two huge tanks, one filled with crimson dyed Karo syrup, the other with Slime, Glop and Goo; and at intervals douse the crowd while showing a tri-screen glut of infamy by splatter's foremost auteur: *2000 Maniacs / Feast of Blood / A Taste of Blood / Color Me Blood Red / Something Weird / Gruesome Twosome / The Wizard of Gore / The Gore Gore Girls / She-Devils on Wheels*. It was to be the season finale in late October.

The hammer came down Labor Day weekend.

339

SILVER SCREAM

Minton Eggets finally got Ev LaMar's leave to raid the Zone. Earl, Brandon and An'akist were hauled to the Leviticus jail; but typically, Chief Eggets had forgotten to obtain search warrants and could only charge them with local misdemeanors.

As Ev LaMar expected. He felt no great desire to destroy Earl Bittner: he played to win, but thought a good executive should try to not let anyone walk away from the table humiliated. J. Hern Sloane had his ratings, Christian Life Heights its publicity, Minton Eggets would be elected Sheriff. So LaMar met the Zone's staff with an olive branch: Leviticus would, after the election, drop all charges and fines if the Zone showed only features "acceptable to the community". He doubted the drive-in could survive as a G-rated business, and had arranged for a front to offer a buy-out. Compromise, a face-saving gesture, fast cash and a one-way ticket out of town.

Unfortunately, LaMar assumed Earl was a tawdry schlockmeister, sly enough to know when the gravy train stopped. LaMar presumed Earl, Brandon and An'akist understood the Zone was just another lowly dive subject to the dictates of proper society. He simply failed to imagine that they could see the drive-in as a pride-worthy achievement, a work of art; failed to see in their refusal and anger conviction as deeply religious as his own. Finding them unreasonable, LaMar persuaded the state attorney general's office to prepare indictments and warrants, and unleashed Chief Eggets again.

The second raid came down at 1:15 a.m. on the third Saturday in September. Village, county, state police and federal agents seized the drive-in's financial records and film library, and arrested Earl Bittner. He was arraigned for: possession and sale of contraband alcohol; violation of liquor laws and licensing; federal racketeering in the theft, interstate transport and unlawful use of copyrighted films; tax evasion (from illicit gains to sale of the garden produce); pandering; and failure to maintain adequate insurance and performance permits. Film distributors, juvenile welfare officers, and various regulatory agencies filed complaints; and, covering all bases, the Zone's owner was cited for failure to pay residuals on the music piped through the speakers. The court appointed lawyer thought she'd be lucky to keep her inarticulate client out of prison through the initial appeals.

Most of the Zone's receipts had always gone to pay for new ideas and games; on a balance sheet, the drive-in had never been profitable. Even when Orrick DeWine agreed to float a small mortgage on the lot, three months passed before Earl made bail.

By then Brandon and An'akist were hurting each other.

After years of monogamy, An'akist had a two week fling resulting in yeast and bladder infections and a tubal pregnancy that required surgery. She felt guilty and unable to explain to Brandon why she couldn't be intimate; he, feeling rejected, haunted area bars, frantically failing to pick up women.

And their crucified spirits were no longer in sync; one prepared to fight for the Zone whenever the other was giving in.

PILGRIMS TO THE CATHEDRAL

An'akist wanted to stay and compromise. She decided they *were* all contemptible vermin as charged; and promoted the idea of a complete reform to showing PG films, while expanding the restaurant into a family dinner theater. Brandon knew Leviticus wouldn't accept them under any conditions. Privately he was afraid of even contemplating change; openly he wanted to sell the drive-in and start it intact, somewhere friendlier, in another state if need be.

Both positions were lost on Earl. Shaking his head dolefully and saying, "*may*-be I oughta. *May*-be I oughta," he seemed to agree with whomever was speaking, then he'd say "*may*-be I oughta. *May*-be I oughta" to no one and nothing at all. Earl kept his loaded shotgun in the booth, where he spent days at a time drinking – missed by the police, and splicing random scraps of film. He fixated on the coming season. Their distribution was cancelled and they had no money, but Earl insisted on opening the Zone. Word went out to regulars that, without license, liquor, food or features, they would run an all Big Bang night.

When Earl started the projectors, police arrived and arrested him for disturbing the peace.

Brandon and An'akist used the final receipts for bail. Earl Bittner came home and for the only time in over twelve years blew out the flame beneath his chili: then he turned all the snack bar's unlit gas jets on full, got a jug of +, and tried to drink himself to death. After a half gallon of 140° moonshine, Earl climbed to the booth, took his shotgun back to the gas flooded snack bar, and fired into the chili tub.

Breaking one of his own commandments.

The Zone's only phones were in the pagoda. By the time Brandon found a way to call the volunteer emergency squad, the building was beyond salvage.

In shock, facing burial arrangements, Brandon and An'akist fought that night in the cramped Winnebago. Each was almost unable to make sense of the other, as if they were screaming in different languages; only insults communicated clearly. Hysterical, frustrated, ironically trying to get through, Brandon backhanded An'akist. She shrieked, outraged, reflexively grabbed their cast-iron tea kettle and swung it against his skull, shearing open his scalp; Brandon staggered and blindly lashed back, punching her in the eye, then breaking her nose; she went into frenzy, his violence leaving her unaware of her own, and battered him repeatedly before Brandon got a door open and fell from the camper, fracturing his ankle. Heaving, thinking only of escape, An'akist gunned the engine and, leaving Brandon hobbling in her dust, leaving another broken commandment, pulled away from the Zone in fury, never to reconcile nor give nor accept apology.

The county, without funeral, disposed of Earl Bittner.

Then a paper surfaced, allegedly dated two days before Earl's death, selling his assets and mortgage to Miss Kathleen Daskalakis, town librarian and realtor Dorothea Twaits' spinster sister. The document's authenticity was irrelevant. Earl had died intestate, broke, and under multiple indictment, his only property owed to the bank. His death only expedited the inevitable.

Brandon tried to stay, camping in the Forf; but with no money and not so much as an abandoned car for shelter, he didn't even complain when Miss Daskalakis ordered him off her land, which she soon sold to Christian Life Heights.

Brandon headed East; An'akist, West. Had they stayed together, they might have found the strength to pursue new visions. An'akist wanted to open the next Chez Panisse, but had nobody to flame her ideas or help her put them into action; she wound up clerking at a hair salon. Brandon planned to recreate the Zone, but had nobody to spark his notions or challenge him to make them real; he wound up running a peepshow for Cousin Capooch. Apart, they were incomplete, dreams vanquished, they gradually collapsed into wounded routines of stagnant apathy, so shrunken that it might cause one to ponder whether the punishment was worth the crime of having dreamt at all.

Making peace with his Missouri divorcees, Rev. Sloane reconsidered the move to Ohio. The location of the planned new headquarters seemed, on reflection, impractical. Still, Jim Slavin recognized his Christian and realpolitick obligations: the development plan was an investment, years from completion; there was still profit to be accrued. The Witness Revival Amphitheatre, won so publicly, would have to be built and used for some time to come, which would demand still more fundraising.

So Jim Slavin announced a formal groundbreaking from Christian Life Heights, to be telecast from the site of the future arena.

On a Sunday morning in late October, a crew erected a control platform over the bare concrete where the pagoda's ashes had, like other debris, disappeared. They set up cameras, recorders, microphones, mixers; they set up projectors to turn the drive-in's screens into monitors. The Forf was covered with a grandstand for honored guests, the Inspiration Choir of Seattle, and the Dallas Sonnycalb Family Singers. Chairs were unfolded beside speaker poles; latecomers and the handicapped could see and hear from their cars.

PILGRIMS TO THE CATHEDRAL

The event drew nearly two thousand believers from eight states; most of them specially invited loyal contributors. When Rev. Sloane's helicopter landed, Ev LaMar and the Council were seated in the grandstand alongside contractors Bryce Magaw and Vernon Koogler, plus Chief Eggets, plus all their families. They were the ones responsible for the celebration and, in a way, this evening's events. The audience, though, were bible thumpers all, (Gretchen Bowers, Tod Critchlow, Christopher Dziedzic, Dewey Fouts, Harton Funderbeck, Lois Gilligan, Noyce Hunkeler, Sandy Kessler, Joyce Leonard, Carl Lofino, Jackson Mesarvey, Lilly Nonnemacher, Hiram Spruce, Constance Triftshauser, and Lyndon Upthegrove, plus dozens more) overly ardent right-wing couch potato pentacostals who had made the doctrinal error of placing their faith in Jim Slavin. This proved unforgiveable. It reduced them all from complex souls of intricate history, intrinsic sinfulness, innate worth . . .

Into cannon fodder.

The first salvo was fired at sundown.

The giant screens lit, filled with triplicate rippling American flags and the superimposed, smiling faces of the Rev. J. Hern Sloane and the President of the United States, then dissolved into the familiar, uplifting credit montage. The program director readied Camera #1 on the choir, #2 on the dignitaries, #3 on the podium. He cued the choirmaster.

When the choir stood, hands clasped, the ground heaved. Earth bellowed a thunderous lowering; a behemoth stretched in its unquiet lair. Jim Slavin pre-empted the chorus, taking up the microphone to offer prayers, and witness of reassurance.

Metal voices howled and sniggered. The cameras overrode their controls, killing the satellite feed and cutting to an enormous, extreme close shot of Sloane's face.

On all three screens his vast eyes were blinding red, without irises. Pus and lymph drained from festering boils on his cheeks, and from his open mouth spewed gouts of peppled diarrhea that booted from the screens to rain in real torrents on the crowd below.

Although Jim Slavin was prepared to bless the drive-in, it had not occured to him to perform the rite of exorcism; but then, exorcism wouldn't have helped.

The Zone was not possessed.

It was sacred.

It had been the venue for every weird picture, no matter how artistic, avant garde, vulgar or loathesome, ever filmed or dreamed of; and for that it had been revered. It had been consecrated, time and again, in blood and liquor, sweat and sperm. It had been the altar where scores were settled, gays turned out, and virgins deflowered in droves, until a communion of orgone, hormones and dark fantasy churned within the pyramid of screens.

It had been fed. It had been nurtured.

It had been magic. It had been believed.

It had an anima.

And that anima was being defiled.

The commandments had been shattered. Life had been sacrificed, love had been withdrawn. The acolytes had been shut out while an army of enemies stood in their place.

Neither malignant nor benign, the Zone reacted, defending itself with the weapons and tactics at its command. With the only knowledge and imagery it had ever learned.

Sleaze manifested as a quasi-sentient force.

Jim Slavin's demonic faces faded into a wash of salmon pink fleshtones, with dark purple slits at the centers. The slits flared and the circles of color retreated to reveal that the crowd was staring at dead center footage of a male erection. Hysterical moaning blared from the speakers; the phalluses lunged forward, mashing against the screens, which bulged under the impact, the metal struts warping. Carnal groans rose in volume as the thrusting accelerated. Bolts sheared and the screens rocked on their braces; immense reluctant hymens.

The organs drew back, throbbing, fully engorged, dribbling seminal fluid, shifted position, and slammed upward. Space between and above the screens flashed into nuclear light; a fireball arced over the Zone, paused, and settled back, congealing into a pulsing, vaginal pink dome of radiant plasm, a literal overturned fleshpot fraught with random lightnings. The strobing burlesque dazzle sent Tod Critchlow and Lois Gilligan into convulsive seizures as 2000 pole speakers burst into 2000 different songs.

Most of the crowd ran for exits or their cars and the blacktop rose in a circular ripple, fluid as water, plastic as a trampoline, firm as marble; the wave flung runners and cars in its swell, cracked open the helicopter, flowed harmlessly past the screens and expended itself with a crashing upward fillip that froze into a concave, twenty foot high wall surrounding the lot.

344

PILGRIMS TO THE CATHEDRAL

Tarmac bubbled into sudden gravy; spasming arthritic hands wrenched up out of the cement, clawing emptiness like midwinter groundhogs testing the air; apparently finding conditions to their liking, mutant cannibal corpses scrabbled through the concrete, littering the lot with scraped chunks of putrescent muscle. Evangelic ghouls, they shuffled toward the living, to win converts to the army of ambulatory rot.

The Big Bang —

— starts.

Kaleidoscopes of unsettling scenes swirl across the screens; but the action has shifted to audience participation.

Unaware that she's burst into flame, Sandy Kessler wonders why she can hear and smell her clothes, hair and nails scorch, see her arms and legs blistering into spitting coals that sear the air with shimmering mirages.

Ev LaMar spreads himself against the blacktop wall, seeking a weak spot; then he shrieks, his right hand crucified by a three inch long tenpenny nail. LaMar hears a sputter behind him; more spikes drill through his hand. He is grabbed by the shoulder, twisted around, and casually slammed against the wall. His tendons and wrist bones part loudly; his arm and pinioned hand fold together, neat as a carpenter's rule. LaMar slumps, sight blurring; through a teary haze he sees a button-eyed scarecrow in droolstained coveralls, carrying a pneumatic nailgun. And a toolbox.

Chief Eggets empties his revolver at dragon sized talons that stab through the top of the strobing pink dome. The talons withdraw, but Eggets, staring up, fails to notice the *kappa* at his feet. The Asian vampyr, a ropy turd-hued snake with a monkey's torso and chittering head, chews its way up Eggets' pants, its tiny hands using Minton's leg hairs as a ladder. The *kappa* penetrates anally, viciously, fangs sucking as they bite and little hands sinking filth-envenomed needle claws into his rectal flesh.

Joyce Leonard and Constance Triftshauser conceive immaculately and come to term within thirty seconds, their bellies splitting like the skins of overripe tomatoes, insufficiently elastic for their ballooning wombs. Their pelvises shatter and perineums tear as they fall to the ground in simultaneous labor.

Like spectral fungi, spongy phantom knobs sprout, unnoticed; the ghosts of the pagoda and ticket booth retumesce. They bob, squat and squishy; then, aroused, the kiosk springs to attention. The gazebo-pagoda twitches, elongates, fills and firms into place.

One moment the television crew perches on a raised open platform then they are in the Zone's projection booth as the pagoda reforms around

345

them, the tv electronics becoming the drive-in's old equipment and film library. the five men blink or shake their heads, aware first of the quiet; the howling below them shut out by thick glass and walls. Then that silence ceases as the projectors start, racheting and whirring, the vibrations rattling the shelves of movie cannisters. One can shakes loose, hits the floor, clanging, and cracks open, spraying the walls and ceiling with blood. The tin rolls to a stop, spouting a red fountain. More canisters reel from the wall, crash, blurt geysers; the projectors mask the sound of the door locking.

Kathleen Daskalakis feels slime on her temple and cheeks; she pats her head and retches — a mass of live worms is tangled in her hair. Miss Daskalakis tries to pull the nightcrawlers off. She discovers the worms aren't falling on her head; they're emerging *from* it.

Frantically ripping her scalp, Miss Daskalakis stumbles into Buddy Roemer, who is running from the roaring pursuit of cycle riding skeletons with jet-black bones and dayglo tattooed skulls.

The android has no eyes, no face at all, nor needs any. Its six spider-jointed arms have blades and axes in place of hands, while grappling cords swirl around its hips. It moves faster than the human mind can track, and it is programmed to collect. It has already collected Dewey Fouts, Gretchen Bowers, Christopher Dziedzic, Vernon Koogler and wife, and the Dallas Sonnycalb family. Their bodies lay where they have fallen, but their heads, dripping blood, sinus fluid and organs, float behind the collector like a swarm of obedient bumblebee do-bees, grimacing, grinning, and bobbing in the air.

Noyce Hunkeler, Carl Lofino, Lilly Nonnemacher, Hiran Spruance and Jackson Mesarvey race, panting, to the pagoda, praying for shelter. Each clambers over the snack bar counter and blacks out.

Poole Neiderhous dashes toward the resurrected ticket kiosk, aiming to scale the wall from its roof. Abruptly his path is blocked by a dwarfish, bearded, white robed old Chinese priest, and a seven foot tall Nubian clad in a leopard's hide, swinging a two-handed morningstar. Neiderhous stops. From the moment the services has been disrupted, Poole has been enraged. He deeply wants to hit something, smack someone around. The huge colored buck is too well armed, but the old gook looks frail and winded. Neiderhous has at least a hundred pound advantage. He bunches his fists and charges, hollering. The priest barely moves, but the heel of his hand brushes Neiderhous' face. Poole's jaw splashes from its hinges, plows through the side of his head and clatters to the ground, teeth scattering. His tongue, ripped clean from its roots, slides through the gap in his cheek.

Gibbering, Minton Eggets drops his pants, grabs the serpent tube hanging from his abdomen, and tries to yank the *kappa* out of him. The vampyr clenches its fangs and claws into Eggets' colon, feeding as it anchors itself. It reaches up into Eggets' intestines, shredding and sucking choice tidbits.

346

PILGRIMS TO THE CATHEDRAL

The Inspiration Choir is consumed by rutting fury; they grab each other, tumbling across the grandstand in an orgiastic mound of bodies. Every orifice is receptive and female, every extremity is virile and male. Each body joins to two, four, eight, ten more until identity and identification are lost in lust. Slots and tabs flow, glue, weld into undifferentiated tissue, five tons of cancer.

The director and sound engineer climb aboard tables, pounding the booth's windows with metal splicing blocks and movieolas; but the three assistants are standing, trying to force the door, when the bloodpool reaches the electric outlets. Lights explode; the booth fills with stenches of gasified hemoglobin and short-circuited flesh. In dusk the tide rises, bubbling from the floating film cans; the tables lift, corpses bumping into them. When the blood reaches a depth of five feet, fins briefly break the surface. Dozens of chitinous football sized claws with serrated pincers close on the corpses and pull them under the rippling flood.

The straw handyman braces LaMar's left hand steady against the wall, aims his nailgun, and fires stigmata into the palm; then he rivets Ev's feet to the ground. The worker stands back and contemplates his next shot, sighting artistically along his gloved thumb. The scarecrow chortles mouthlessly while he works, sounding quite like Disneyland's Goofy. Nodding amiably, he cross-stitches LaMar's knees, inner elbows, and groin.

Orrick DeWine watches his fingers stretch and twist into sharp unhuman daggers. He has always harbored a secret wish to become a wolf, a tiger, a merciless night hunter. Now his darkest desire is coming true. He quickly strips, paws shredding his clothes, and awaits a rush of unholy power.

The ancient priest knocks Poole Neiderhous to his knees, legs locked and paralyzed, tailbone destroyed. He barely feels the priest's fingers poke holes in his sternum, puncturing his lungs. The priest bows and the mace-wielding barbarian steps up, his crotch planted before Neiderhous' face. Poole feels an overwhelming need to fellate the black giant, then realizes with incredulous self-pity that, jawless, he can't. He looks up, pleading forgiveness, in time to see the iron ball swing down. His head pulps nicely for yards in all directions.

Carl Lofino awakens in a gargantuan chamber, its horizons fading into mist. Sticky pale shapes move in slow motion, forms against dimly lit waist-high blue gas jets. Lofino takes a step forward and his hand raps against a glass wall; Lofino discovers he is trapped in a jar the approximate size of an elevator cage. Pungent gravel crunches beneath his feet; Lofino reaches into it, finds he is standing on an inches-thick layer of spices. Savory aromas drift into his prison; Lofino turns to study two bubbling, steaming cauldrons. Doughy shapes stir one vat, filled with thick chili *con* pieces of Jackson Mesarvey and Hiram Spruance. The other, by the smell, holds gallons of boiling brined vinegar. Lofino whimpers as a half dozen dough-things pour

SILVER SCREAM

the boiling vinegar into his jar, which is then vacuum sealed and left to ferment, Lofino pickling within, still alive.

Joyce Leonard births a hoofed and goat headed mannequin; Constance Triftshauser, a flippered atrocity whose neck ends in sea urchin cilia surrounding a sucking maw. The infants scramble up their mothers' ravaged bodies, ripping blouses and bras to latch onto milk-laden breasts. The two women lie panting with exhaustion, nausea, and a chilling surge of maternal love. Then both gasp as fresh eggs are fertilized and their uteruses swell. Several hundred feet away, but in much the same way, Harton Funderberk and Bryce Magaw, too, are spawning tiny monsters.

Dorothea Twaits takes refuge in her Country Squire station wagon, where she unsuccessfully tries to raise help on her CB and car phone. The thing that crawls up the hood of her car is so alien that Dorothea, a stolid and unimaginative realtor, can't convince her mind to register its existence. A twenty-questions creature: torso like a globby cluster of smushed together liver balls; head a conical sampler of bruises and sores; droopy sensory clusters on stalks bounce aimlessly from the top of the cone while appendages, some like featherferns and some like four-sided cheese graters with sucker pads, strip and masticate the wagon's chrome trim. A thin, bubbling nozzle on the side of its head suddenly reminds Dorothea of the cappucino extension on her espresso maker. As she thinks that, a wart on the thing's head bursts; a ribbony tentacle unreels with hydraulic speed, smashes through the windshield and plucks out both of Dorothea's eyeballs, skewering them on barbed hooks that eject from its tip. The ribbon coils like highspeed footage of a bullfrog's tongue snagging a nymph fly, and pops Dorothea Twaits' sinew and nerve-trailing eyes into its wartlike wound. The action is so rapid that the thing gums and swallows before Mrs. Twaits realizes it had moved. She only notices when the first pain hits and blood squirts from her empty sockets. By then the tongue has come back for the rest of her face.

Buddy Roemer staggers and falls, circled by jeering dead bikers, the noise of their cycles deafening. Buddy wants to fight, but instead blubbers and begs, which incites the skeletons, who howl insults and pelt him with hot dog feces. As each bit of excrement strikes, it instantly turns to stone. Roemer is soon encased; he suffocates in petrified shit.

The scarecrow has Ev LaMar well secured. Chuckling and whistling, he takes some turpentine and a paint stripper from his toolbox, and commences renovations.

Something heavy and powerful crashes into the sound engineer's raft, flipping it; he screams as a rubbery limb wraps around his legs. The director's table is slivered by pincers attacking from the swirling blood; his back is pressing against the ceiling. Blood laps at his face.

The exquisite agony of Orrick DeWine's metamorphosis hits full force.

PILGRIMS TO THE CATHEDRAL

He writhes on the ground, pewling, as his skull pulls, cracks, reforms into a snout — a too long snout. His teeth — shrink. His sight dims, his limbs shorten into stubs, forcing his chest to the ground. His back hunches, spine and ribs prodding through his skin to blend into a segmented shell; the weight presses his bladder and he urinates on himself, his penis aimed at his belly.

Rock 'n roll whams in Abner L. Schlueuter's head, a hateful tinnitus ringing and Schlueuter is, against his will, dancing. Slam, hiphop, thrash. Invisible cavorters surround him, knocking him to the ground; when he falls, he is dragged back up, shoved back into motion. His hips, ankles, wrists are broken; his ribs, collarbone, cheekbones splinter, spearing and hemorrhaging him. He dances. An unseen reveler crashes into him and he falls, snapping his neck. Shards poke through his skin like ornaments. Abner bounces up again, dancing, dancing, long after he is pulverised into a flopping, spineless meat bag.

Chefs with white torques and gleaming knives serve a festive champagne buffet at La Roofe. "Tonight's appetiser," lisping waiters purr, "is a nice *carpaccio di Lilly Nonnemacher*, that's paper-thin slices of choice filet from the living breast of thigh, and tonight there's a lovely selection of freshly ground *Steak Tartare de Noyce Hunkeler*, or some nice variety cuts grilled *al dente*."

Kathleen Daskalakis rolls on the ground, ripping her flesh, smashing her head, slapping herself, wailing. All her body hair has turned into worms, wet, glistening, nipping and nibbling, wiggling from her pores; maggots drip from her eyelids and ears. All of them gnawing as they flail in her heart and breed in her brain.

Young girls with glowing eyes take Jim Slavin by the hand, lead him from Gehenna to a quiet place at the edge of the hollow, behind the screens. With dreamlike wonder, Slavin sees glimpses of ideals lost, goals unfulfilled, and the faces of women he wanted but never won. Bewildered and dizzy, he sits back against a tree, letting the girls untie his shoes. One child, perhaps nine years old, firmly holds his little finger. "Loves me . . ." she murmurs, and tugs the flesh and bone from the top joint of his finger, leaving nearly invisible filaments of nerve, "loves me not . . ." and pulls off the next joint, again leaving only raw ganglia, "loves me . . ." and finishes the finger, "loves me not . . ." and turns to his ring finger as the other girls shred his feet, hands, teeth like roses, leaving only thin wires of torment, all the while whispering "loves me loves me not . . ." their lilting voices badly dubbed, not matching their lip movement, "loves me not loves loves not loves loves me loves me . . ." His arms and legs fall away like old socks, muscles and bones easily removed; the children idly braid and swish the fragile threads that remain, negligently letting the ends trail in the dirt.

The scarecrow, approving his work, poly-urethanes Ev LaMar . . .

SILVER SCREAM

The grandstand collapses as the throbbing Inspiration malignancy bloats, stiffens in climax, and dissolves into a lake of scum and stray cells . . .

Lois Gilligan and Tod Critchlow dismember themselves but still convulse, flipping like beached fish, beaten by their own severed limbs . . .

The projection booth windows explode into bright cascading waterfalls of blood . . .

Hideous and helpless, Orrick DeWine — a half-human werearmadillo — waddles in circles . . .

Hiram Spruance's bodyfat glazes the top of the chili as Sandy Kessler stumbles into the kitchen; her flaming body ignites a grease fire that spreads through the pagoda . . .

Punched into puree, Abner L. Schlueuter's insides gush through his sieved holes . . .

Joyce Leonard and Constance Triftshauser slip into coma, their faces coated with sweat and spittle. Rows of multi-nippled breasts erupt along their ribs; teats too few to suckle the litters of hatchlings fighting to feed . . .

The *kappa* finishes Minton Eggets and crawls off in search of its next meal, leaving behind a parched dandruff of skin . . .

"Loves me me me loves not me not me . . ." Their cool soft fingers peel Slavin's torso and face, crack open his skull and chest and, working vertebra by vertebra, pull the rata through his loosened spine. Slavin remains alert and in pain beyond comprehension as the ultimate unanesthetized surgery proceeds, as the little girls free his nervous system from its home. They plait the ganglia into cats' cradles, slapping each other with the braided whisks while they giggle and whisper. They play catch with Jim Slavin's still conscious brain, the nerves soaring in a halo and running along the ground, until one toss goes wild and the brain snags on a tree branch. There they leave it, an abandoned kite, its tail of threads and snips of agony catching each stray breeze . . .

The Joe Bob totals: 651 head rolls; 5,083 lobbed limbs; 47 reamed — Enough.

Morals, if any, are difficult to discern. Certainly, most of the Zone's victims were comparative innocents who deserved neither death nor defilement, which suggests dynamic evil. But the magic was not deliberate nor wroth; merely reactive. When hundreds are killed by earthquakes, monsoons, famine, they are thought felled by acts of nature or Heaven, and are no less unfairly dead. No less unfair than Earl Bittner's destruction, Brandon's, An'akist's. Yet to conclude that even Jim Slavin's fate was judgement raises an uncomfortable notion, a question of faith.

SILVER SCREAM

It implies that the existence of sleaze is a proof to the existence of God. And that, if true, renders moral niceties even murkier. Still, the disappearance of a couple thousand followers of a televangelist, and of the minister, a county officer, a village government, caused private grief but no outcry. By the time police linked ten states' worth of missing persons reports, there were no clues. Rev. Sloane's parishioners delivered themselves to the next charming preacher who bought Sloane's airtime. Mad River County voters figured their sheriff had taken personal leave under cover of night, such events not being unheard of in Ohio. And the faithful of Leviticus, accustomed to denying reality, did so. Realtors, bankers, librarians, Councils and Managers are all societal by-products, disposable and easily replaced. Weeds soon covered Christian Life Heights and weather faded the graffito on the state route.

No angelic retribution was exacted against the Zone, unless being deprived of believers causes a temple pain. The spirit born in the Cathedral may have starved, dissipated of its own accord . . . or, as folk tales go, if it hasn't yet died, it's living there still.

Unless . . . unless it's grown restless. Hungering. Seeking love or a new party, in which case it might be flowing through the topsoil, unseen, inexorable and dreadful, creeping, creeping, sending out amoebic podia of sin and decadence . . . nearer . . . creeping nearer . . .

No. It was a strictly provincial phenomenon. The Zone was its womb, its shrine, its crypt. It would never escape from Mad River County.

But let this enter local lore: that there's some corner of a forlorn field that is for ever sleaze.

By false dawn the last cars and corpses were sinking into the subsiding tarmac: a few aerials; one hand frozen in a contorted rigor of supplication. The fleshdome evaporated in the gathering light, revealing that the screens canted at angles, most of the speakers were vandalised, and the pagoda snack bar-projection booth had again burned down during the night. Jim Slavin's brain hung on a hidden branch, suet for the squirrels.

By sunrise the evidence had vanished. The site of the old Buckeye was quiet, save for the crows and crickets of an Ohio Indian summer . . .

The ashy settling of charred timbers.

Rare, heartfelt subterranean screams.

And, of course, occasional chomping.

San Francisco — Yellow Springs

ENDSTICKS

SILVER SCREAM was born on Hallowe'en.

I was to meet Melissa Singer, my editor at Tor Books, for one of those "publisher lunches" of myth and legend. It was in the midst of a large conclave of writers, editors, publishers and readers, and things were hectic. By the time a waiter showed up to take drink orders, the sun was setting and our table numbered six. Company plastic is a writer magnet.

The glacially slow service of the restaurant staff afforded plenty of time for talk and idea bashing. Melissa was a fan of a bunch of short stories I'd written concerning the nasty things that *might* transpire in dark auditoriums, under the flicker of magic lanterns. She called it "cinema horror."

When editors are confronted by themes, extrapolation occurs. Chet Williamson suggested SILVER SCREAM as a title, and lo, and anthology was born amid knives, forks, dead meat and lots of alcohol. Everybody who crashed that lunch is in this book. Melissa pointed at me. "You edit it."

Thus was my fate — and yours — sealed.

From the jump, it was an experiment in terror. Literature has too goddamn many genres already, and fiction labeled *horror* is prejudged as often as music labeled *rock*. Come to think of it, horror *is* the rock 'n' roll of fiction — it strives to stay dangerous but when you look close there is a place for ballads and a place for speed thrash, and the last thing the neighborhood needs is more subdivision. I favor Rick McCammon's contention that "Horror writing is the fundamental literature of humanity . . . I'll stick to it until I find a kind of literature that speaks more strongly about the human condition. I don't think there is one."

Quite a few horror anthologies are too leashed by themes that invite trivial writing: It don't hafta be good, it just has to be about vampire low-riders. Some books spend too much time gloating over bad fiction by big names. Others are tinkered together by wanna-bes who neatly eliminate the need for their *own* writing to pass editorial muster by becoming the editor themselves.

SILVER SCREAM is a themed book, but that's the only conventional thing about it. To avoid hitting a single note repeatedly until a good migrane roosts, I tried to broaden so-called cinema horror past obvious haunted theatre stories, to include stuff about grindhouses, 3-for-1 fleapits, porn castles, werewolf circuit drive-ins, snuff films, peepshows, fly-by-night video rental shacks, has-been actors, never-was ingenues, Tinseltown burnouts, movie cults, immortal stars, film school dorks, media mutants and even that bastard 'lil bro, television . . . a wide variety of nightmares all predicated in some fashion on the cinema experience. Most stories are original to this volume; some aren't. It would be redundant to ask, say, Karl Wagner for a better cinema horror story than "More Sinned Against."

Still more terror was embodied in the prospect of playing editor to friends and peers; trying to blue-pencil, yet not deball, to push for clarity while leaving individual voice and style unsuffocated. Unless I could somehow better what I saw as the shortcomings of editors past, there was no reason to wear the hat, and I had a writer's responsibility to each author invited. F. Paul Wilson wrote back, "So you're gonna be one of those editors who really *edits*, ay?" And this bunch of writers was fabulously accommodating.

Which brings us to the dreaded Bio/Blurb.

Easy enough, if you lay out your contributors in the sort of statistical entry provided by every other book: Name, genetic info, cr lits and talkshow plug-o-rama . . . all of it dry as dead dogshit. More pigeonholing. I like everyone in this book too much to freeze-dry and serve them up to you like microwaved roadkill.

Here are the stats that matter: In SILVER SCREAM you'll find *New York Times* bestsellers and World Fantasy Award winners; people who also write novels, TV, scripts, music and people who have been consistently publishing short fiction for years (a helluva feat, in today's market) . . . plus a couple of first sales. The mix runs fifty-fifty between stories that feature paranormal stuff and those that do not. The range is broad and passionate enough to (I hope) permanently entomb more idiot subcategories like "magic realism," "dark fantasy" and "psychological horror" . . . whatever the hell *those* are.

Tappan King, editor of *Twilight Zone* Magazine, calls such work *contemporary fantasy*, which really isn't a bad way to delineate it for folks who watch *Entertainment Tonight,* provided you could get anybody to remember the primary definition of fantasy as "the free play of creative imagination."

For your pleasure, here is SILVER SCREAM's company of wolves.

*   *   *

ENDSTICKS

Richard Christian Matheson and I talk in the dead of night, sometimes running on until four in the morning. During one such phone marathon I suggested that if you lined up SILVER SCREAM's contributors according to height, facing west, the result would look remarkably like one of those charts depicting the evolution of *homo sapiens*, from typewriter monkey to bow-tied respectability. Naturally, Richard asked where he fit in on the chart. Why, in the *middle* section, sez me. The biggest section. The section double the size of any other.

The "cute writer" section. No other field boasts so many attractive and sartorial storytellers. Just so you'll know.

The only threesome who fit nowhere on the chart was that uncategorizable trio who could only be grouped if worthy stars were needed for an opera based on the midnight antics of Burke, Hare and Dr Knox. Imagine the libretto. The groupies.

Respectable, first.

Here comes the sort of in-depth reportage you all crave out there in Gossip-land, the answer to a question that still scorches hot in the hearts of those of good will and boundless nosiness. Yes, I am going to reveal to the world what the "F" in F. Paul Wilson stands for.

Francis.

He has the bookish look of a country parson about him; he also resembles newscaster Ted Koppel a bit. He prefers to be called Paul. Better yet, "Dr Wilson, sir" — but Paul looks like a practicing physician because he *is* one. Twist his arm and he'll confess to a secret delight in alligator farms, *As The World Turns* and the Peter Pan ride at Disney World. I was intimidated and unsure of how to approach him until I discovered we share the habit of xeroxing weird cartoons and clippings into stationary. He entered adolescence just in time to hear Alan Freed on live radio and buy EC Comics new. On Saturdays he'd sneak off to the Oritani Theatre in Hackensack to catch monster movies, then dash home to tune in more on *Shock Theatre* with Zacherley. When *King Kong* hit *Million Dollar Movie*, Paul watched it eleven times in one week. Today he can still lip-synch most of the dialogue. When I asked his three favorite horror films (anent SILVER SCREAM's central concern), he responded: "*The Exorcist, Alien* and *The Bride of Frankenstein*. The first because, like Blatty, I was raised Catholic and attended Georgetown; that movie followed me home and stayed for weeks. The second, because I came out of the theatre utterly drained. The third, because it's pure movie magic." And that soft spot for *Kong* persists.

Paul's "best dish in the culinary area is my special marinated charcoal-broiled butterflied leg of lamb," which sounds pornographically good. He is also the father of the next generation of perverted breakfast food for kids. Citing Frankenberry and Count Chocula, he posits: "Can you see it? A guy in a hockey mask with a bloody machete across his shoulder and a box of

SILVER SCREAM

cereal in his hand: *New vitamin-fotified JASONBERRY! Delicious little puffs of wheat in the shapes of eight different farm tools, with just the right touch of sugary red, Jasonberry-flavored coating on each delicious little point! JASONBERRY! Get it . . . before he gets you!"*

No doubt Paul is probably asked far too often to dispense medical advice for free. Wouldn't it be great if he could get some of the people you see at conventions to diet, stop smoking, and use soap once in a while?

If Paul is the first of this book's Three Musketeers of good social standing, Chet Williamson is the next. Whenever I see Chet I must fight this primal urge to show him my hall pass; he looks just like Mr Greene, my seventh grade geography teacher. We met for the first time at the SILVER SCREAM lunch, which was just "the lunch" until Chet thought up the title for this book. I'd thank him more if his agent hadn't been such a pain. Otherwise, our subsequent acquaintance has been fraught with such speculations as: "Could I do a story about a robot cat set on vengeance, called 'Return of the Neon Furball?'" Or: "Do we really *need* another horror novel set in the New York City subway system?" Or: "I think GRRRRRRRR was a lot more intense than having the cars go *ba-WOOMP, ba-WOOMP, ba-WOOMP* during the chicken run."

One of these days someone will make *you* edit a book, Chet. And I'll be waiting.

I asked the Question. "My three favorite whore movies, boy, what a bitch. After thinking long and hard, I came up with: *Psycho.* An indispensable film; the great grandaddy of 'em all. It scared the hell out of me when I was twelve (my parents were warped enough, god bless 'em, to take me). *King Kong* — maybe more fantasy than horror, but a great film nonetheless with some nice scary and gross moments, especially in the complete version. And *Carnival of Souls.* It is literally haunting, if more than a bit primitive, but dammit, it *works."*

Doug Winter confronts respectability as an attorney. And battles it as a writer. His faves are enumerated in his story. "Only true zealots are expected to know the American titles of the films given in Italian," he notes. "Then again, only true zealots are expected to *sit* through said films." I only missed two; I'm sure John Ford and Karl Wagner have seen them all, as you'll soon learn.

Doug has one of those William Devane faces that look boyish and cuddly from one angle and become evil and threatening with a shift of the light. No doubt this latent ability serves him well in the courtroom. His wit and impeccable comic timing can provide vast relief from the pain, pain, pain of one moribund panel after another at writer's conferences. The guy *mutates.* First his club tie gets replaced by an icky J.K. Potter T-shirt. Then he dons this pair of silly gold anodized goggles. Before you know it, he's slipped into his lizardy deejay mode to host an eve of moldies by such singing superstars as Lee Van Cleef and Otto Brandenburg (and only terminal hard-core zealots should know who the hell Otto Brandenburg was).

I got my SILVER SCREAM contract back from Doug with a scribbled rider attached to virtually each sentence. Nope, no surprise there. Of the films cited in "Splatter," he says, "I am a big fan of *City of the Walking Dead* — particularly when the zombies eat the *Solid Gold* dancers, and when Mel Ferrer repeats the line, 'Aim for the brain.'" We are both dedicated Tangerine Dream fans, and mention of Edgar Froese's electronic version of Tallis' "Mass for Four Voices" (done for the film of *The Keep*) got us into a heatedly anticipatory discussion of *Red Heat*, the German-backed sequel to the women-in-prison epic *Chained Heat*, starring Linda Blair and Sylvia Kristel . . . and featuring a score by Tangerine Dream. "That might be enticement enough," said Doug. "But just the thought of bimbos behind bars tends to get me running right to the rental outlets." One more "Splatter" point of interest: "Washington DC is not only the home of Ron and Nancy, poor misunderstood Jon Hinckley, endless marble structures, *The Exorcist*, Lynda Carter, the country's most dangerous airport, and not one goddamn baseball team . . . it is also the home of the lobotomy. Yes, it was here, in the Year of Our Lord Nineteen and Thirty-Six, that this jim-dandy procedure was invented."

Past Athos, Porthos and Aramis comes . . . well . . .

Dear Weird One: You are weird STOP a menace to society STOP your work must be suppressed STOP Ronald Reagan has declared war on you STOP . . .

So read Rick McCammon's first mailing to me. If the foregoing contributors are three of the most groomed, polite, normal-looking chaps an all-American woman could ever hope to bring home to mommy, then Mc-Cammon is like one of those lean, asthenic, homicidally cute varsity basket-ballers I used to hate because they made the jailbait cheerleaders so wet. Imp-eyed and dashing, he speaks softly, modestly, with the genteel purr of his Deep South roots. None of which belies the reality that he writes these *awful* horror stories in the dead of night. Once upon a time, he set his own birthday as the date of the end of the world.

Rick photographs well — in black tie, posed like a land baron on a Victorian highback, or braving the chill of an ancient Alabama cemetery. But I have a photo of him making a monster face, and another of him hoisting me off the ground. He's stronger than he looks. Like F. Paul Wilson, he jogs. He claims the highpoint of his college journalism career was interviewing Linda Lovelace during her porn heyday (she was wearing a transparent blouse). He once tried to crash the set of *Stay Hungry* by posing as a reporter from *Rolling Stone*. I discovered that we share roughly the same work hours — plowing into the predawn and waking up while most of the nine-to-five crowd is lurching to lunch. He is a simulation-gaming buff, which means I now have a place to send all those back issues of *Ares* Magazine.

Though his byline is Robert R., I call him Rick because only a boob would call him "Bobby," or worse, "Ricky" (and I've heard several dunces, all claiming to be good buddypals with McCammon, call him thuswise, unaware they are yanking their own blankets). John M. Ford likes to be called Mike even though the "M" stands for — he says — Milo. Ray Garton wants for everyone to call him Snorg the Omnipotent, but there you are. David J. Schow certainly wasn't the name *I* was born with. And Steve Boyett wants it known he's sick of know-nothings misspelling his name as "Stephen Boyette."

It's a lust, this need readers have to know chapter and verse. To answer such a profound sociological hunger, herewith find the SILVER SCREAM Middle Name Match-Up . . . just the thing to occupy yourself if you're stuck on a bumpy bus that disallows steady reading. Start now.

ROBERT BLOCH	Mason
STEVEN BOYETT	Alan
RAY GARTON	Rothbell
CHET WILLIAMSON	Scott
JOE LANSDALE	John
DOUG WINTER	Arthur
JAY SHECKLEY	Ralph
MICK GARRIS	Richard
CRAIG SPECTOR	Carlton
JOHN SKIPP	Albert
RAMSEY CAMPBELL	"The Hammer"

One of this is a trick question — actually the *first* name of a writer whose byline is made up of middle and last.

Upon asking Robert Bloch what his favored horror movies were, I prepared to hear a list of several hundred. "There are many I like for obscure or eclectic reasons," Bob said, "such as *Murder at the Zoo*, for Lionel Atwill's performance. But how about the Chaney *Phantom of the Opera*, and *Mad Love*, certainly. And what has to be one of the most subsequently plagiarized movies ever, *Diabolique*."

The tale of Bob's encounter with Lon Chaney as Erik is well known, but Bob was a movie buff even before that: "In fact, my first conscious

memory is of seeing Buster Keaton in *The Boat*, when I was five years old."
Flash-forward, and Bob found himself playing baseball with Keaton, in a
writers-vs.-actors game at Griffith Park, during a long strike by the Writers'
Guild that commenced almost as soon as Bob took up residence in Hollywood.

Born during the boom days of the silents and still one of their greatest
advocates, Bob is eminently qualified to write tales of Hollywood. During
the *Thriller* TV series, Boris Karloff was a frequent guest at the Bloch
household; during dinner there one evening, Karloff was introduced to Fritz
Lang, who told him, "We are the last of the dinosaurs." When Bob married
Ellie in 1964, their wedding cake was the gift of Joan Crawford.

Bob set out to chronicle old-time Hollywood from his unique and
encyclopedic perspective by beginning a trilogy of novels to be titled *Colossal, Amazing,* and *Stupendous,* after the hype seen on movie posters. The
ignoramuses at Pyramid Books published the first under the stupid title *The
Star Stalker,* behind a misleading cover intended to gull readers into thinking
this was yet another guide to the ways a scantily-clad vixen might be carved.
The Star Stalker concludes in 1931 as its protagonist, a screenwriter who got
his start in the silents, chucks the movie biz to open a used car lot (the
character also appears in Bloch's *Psycho II,* running a Studio City motel in
1982). The latter two volumes were to trace the writer's career through the
golden age of the talkies and the advent of television. While Bob still excels
in the mayhem department, some enterprising publisher should really slap
down the jack to insure that *Amazing* and *Stupendous* get rendered. "Now,
those are the books that *I'd* like to write," Bob says, and I do what he tells me,
because I have a book from him inscribed *From Your Illegitimate Uncle.*
Then again, Bob has a Bible that says *Autographed by the Author.*

Ramsey Campbell let me know that the moviehouse in his story was
derived from an old Liverpool cinema called the Hippodrome, now
demolished. "It was formerly a music hall; any number of corridors behind
the screen led to abandoned dressing-rooms and even a stable for horses.
Once, back in the early Sixties, I lost my way in those corridors while looking
for an exit, and 'The Show Goes On' eventually came from that experience."

Imitating Ramsey has become quite popular among today's horror
writers. I don't mean copping his writing style, I mean imitating Ramsey
himself — an expeience that must be seen live to be believed. Meanwhile,
the real Ramsey can list some of his favorite — or *favourite* — cinema horrors:
"*Vampyr,* for its unexcelled evocation of the supernatural; *Repulsion,* which
is the most terrifying horror film I've ever seen, and *Eraserhead,* which is the
most uncompromisingly nightmarish. If it was a question of which films to
live with on a desert island, I'd select *Vampyr* . . . even if I dared be alone
with the others, they'd be crowded out by Laurel and Hardy movies."

As I type this, Ramsey also let me know his next novel, *Ancient Images,* just so happens to involve "the dangerous search for a 'lost' horror movie." Which is a perfect transition to John M. Ford and Karl Edward Wagner, since both have committed in-depth research into movies not only lost, but never heard of. Mike explains it this way:

> "As all of us night owls know, the late tv movie is a truly essential part of Western culture, keeping alive art that would otherwise have been lost forever. I'll bet nobody went through the Library of Alexandria in the still watches, pulling the papyrus equivalents of *Dracula's Great Love* or *They Saved Hitler's Brain* off the shelf to save them from nocturnal papyrophages. Too late now, bunkies, the branch is closed, y'know? And there is more than cultural value involved here. Georges Méliès gave a bunch of his nitrate prints to the French government to make munitions during World War I, not only denying future generations the chance to see Méliès pioneering work but blowing up a lot of nice young guys who would otherwise have taken their girls to the movies and gotten a head start on those future generations. I like to think every time *Latitude Zero* or *Frankenstein vs. the Spac Monster* unreels on WPIX or WTBS, it's doing a little to keep the guns quiet.
>
> Here are a few of my late-night favorites, some you might have missed, or fallen asleep halfway through the credits; pictures that can turn your brain into thousands of julienne fries in seconds . . ."

Mike then plunges into scrutiny of such gems of Inoshiro Honda's *Poo-Bah vs. Earth* (the victim of a script switch from the libretto to Gilbert and Sullivan's *The Mikado* to *Pasta Beat from Planet X*), Fritz Lang's uncompleted *Metropolis of the Living Dead*, and similar classics filmed with the creative involvement of Umberto di Cannelloni, "one of the most deservedly forgotten figures in cinema history. Of the 1951 Edward D. Wood masterwork *Plumbers From Hell*, Mike writes:

> While having some plumbing work done on his house, Wood was seized with the cinematic possibilities of the situation and rushed to borrow a camera and some film stock. He then shot footage of the workmen (since identified by historians as the Ogurki Brothers, Vince and Bruno, who repaired plumbing for many of Hollywood's worst directors) until the raw stock was exhausted. While it was being processed, *auteur* Wood wrote a screen treatment involving extraterrestrial vampires who, to insure a steady supply of human blood, send their minions (the

Ogurki Bros) to build a pipeline from Earth to "the planet Mendocino in the Galaxy 555-2318" (making brilliant use of the sign on the side of the Ogurkis' truck). The plan is foiled when the scientist, Dr Tucker, completes work on his "Space Torpedo." Wood himself plays Tucker (as he played the transvestite hero of *Glen or Glenda?*), and his garage serves as the scientist's laboratory. He also dubbed the voices of the alien plumbers, apparently by speaking through a comb covered with tissue paper, and plays Tucker's fiancee, Norma Jean, in the famous Sink Trap scene. The two characters have no scenes together.

Note: In an apparent concession to censorship pressures, some prints of this film have been retitled. A hand, almost certainly Wood's own, holds a card bearing the letters *CK* in front of the *LL* on the original title board.

When not analyzing winners such as the little-known Ingmar Bergman/ Three Stooges collaboration *Three Wild Strawberries*, Mike corresponds via graph paper festooned with tiny calligraphy. "People have been known to get eight pages of this teensy little handwriting from me. Talk about horrors." As his three favorite films in real space-time, he picks *"The Haunting* for Best Old Fashioned, *Videodrome* for Best New Fashioned, and *Theatre of Blood* for Best Guilty Pleasure. I reserve the right to alter this list, every five minutes if necessary."

See? A perfect, quiet, unassuming Dr Knox for the opera, with Bob and Ramsey as Burke and Hare.

SILVER SCREAM permits me to cunningly turn the tables on an editor of mine, Karl Edward Wagner, by becoming an editor of his. Because Karl is such a civil and accommodating bear of a guy, this has been fun. Because Karl also resembles a Viking Biker from Hell, I want to keep to his good side. I paid him exactly what he paid me for my most recent reprint. Ah, balance!

Since I once wrote a bio declaring that Karl was "no relation to the composer, or the Austrian neurologist," I get to fix that now by saying yes, Karl is indeed related to *the* Richard Wagner. But they're no longer on speaking terms. Karl says that "'More Sinned Against' was written during the spring of 1984 for an anthology of original horror stories whose editor claimed to have read *In a Lonely Place* and who asked me for a story — no guidelines, just my interpretation of contemporary horror." The story was bounced, "with sincere regrets, on the fundamental grounds that the heroine had been able to profit from her ordeal with drugs and that this might tempt some young reader to experiment with drugs. Personally, I thought I was putting the exact opposite message across in the story, but no matter. And was it voodoo or was it drugs? A writer shouldn't have to tell a

SILVER SCREAM

reader anything. Or an editor." When I confirmed the story for SILVER SCREAM, Karl added, "It will distress (that editor) to see this immoral work further disseminated. He will pray for you."

For my money, Karl's *Year's Best Horror* series is the best regular horror anthology going. And just by coincidence, I ran across a letter from him, dated December, 1984, noting: "One of these days I'll edit an anthology exclusively of theatre stories . . ."

Karl is also a seasoned cineteratologist (thank Stanley Wiater for the term: "A student of the cinema of malforms, monsters and deviates") — as chronicled in a piece titled "Lost Turkeys of the Ether Waves."

". . . Talking about horror film is a cross between *Name That Tune* and telling spooky stories around a campfire . . . Somewhere out there, lost in the ozone or dusty bargain bins of cut-rate distributors, are hundreds of really obscure old movies — films that barely if ever and long ago if then managed to reach theatres, ignored even by Forrest J. Ackerman and unknown to modern fans. (They appear on cable) generally in the dead of night before dawn, when most births and deaths occur and wolves howl. This is when the Lost Turkeys return . . .

"*Plan 10 From Outer Space* (USA 1959). Seldom-seen Roger Corman film intended as a rip-off sequel to *Plan 9 From Outer Space*, but lacking that film's big budget and superior cast. However, it is a tidy little dud that can stand on its own foot, and its total-improvisation special effects approach was state-of-the-art for its day. The scene in which Touch Connors fights a 1957 DeSoto hubcap with his Zippo lighter cannot be forgotten.

"*The Eviscerating* (Canada 1982). A deranged child with telekinetic powers explodes body parts in slow motion of everyone in the cast. Its advertising teaser, 'The Movie That Makes YOU the victim!' won the *Consumer Reports* Truth in Advertising Award for 1982."

Of course there's more: *Night of the Leaping Dead* (a *Creature From the Black Lagoon* ripoff boasting live frogs tied to zombie costumes), *Curse of the Stoned Shriek* and *King Kong Excretes*. Thanks Karl.

When Mark Arnold was an editor, he went by the handle Mark Alan Arnold. When time came to pounce on "Pilgrims to the Cathedral," we microscoped every mote from the small ("WAITAMINUTE!" he typed at me. "*Fucker*! You *knew* that! You knew that . . . because . . . you quite properly corrected my capitalisation of AmeriKKKa, a rad-dementoid spelling that hasn't been used in over a decade!") to the tall. He unfurled such a passionate argument in favor of his story's prologue ("Here comes far

362

more analysis than the whole damned story, let alone one passage, merits.")
that I was totally bamboozled. Cornered. Snowballed. A virtual novelette, to
justify the novella. Damned sneaky, these editors . . .

Mark has spectacles and this incredible thundercloud of blondish hair.
We met once at Tor's offices, and again one fine drunken night at the Staten
Island eyrie of Tappan King (goddamn, another editor!). Soon afterward
Mark involved me in his "quasi-secret editing project," which sounds good
and mysterious. I'm new at this gig, he isn't, and he proved pretty adept at
the writer half of the push-pull. Like two other ex-deejays in this book,
Mark's voice is sonorous, resonant, bloody-near *chocolate.*

Diamond Ed Bryant is another of SILVER SCREAM's onetime DJ/
editors. He and I spent five or six years nodding at each other in corridors
before getting a chance to talk at length in Tucson, where we stowed at least
twenty-five breakfasts and allowed a lunatic to place balloons on our heads.
He was one of the earliest champions of my book on *The Outer Limits;* he
requested the "vacuum cleaner monster episode" and stayed up until three
ayem to see it. He dedicated a reading of his story "Mulchasaurus Rex" to
me because we dinosaur fans have gotta hang together, and now I must find
a way to dodge Steve Boyett's admonitions to do an anthology of dinosaur
stories. Ed sports a collection of berserk neckties — my favorite is the clear
plastic one embedded with enough bogus flies to clear the dinner tab for
thirteen. He possesses large, facile cowboy hands. A lady of our mutual
acquaintance once flattered him by saying, "Without touching me, he's the
most intimate man I've ever met." To which Ed later responded, "Maybe I
should use this as a blurb on my next book . . ."

As deejay he founded Wyoming's first-ever underground rock radio
show: "We were the first to broadcast the long version of the Doors' 'The
End.'" He says the single most disgusting thing he ever did involved a tub of
Vicks Vap-o-Rub, no specifics. Cinematically, he cherishes Pasolini's *Salo, or
the 120 Days of Sodom,* "certainly, for its sheer power to drive people
screaming from the theatre. *Alien* is one of the finest *sexual* horror movies
ever made. *Repulsion* scared the bejeezus out of me. Add *Rock and Roll
High School* to that list and you've pretty much represented my personality."
Never would I argue against the merits of *any* film highlighting rats that
explode when exposed to the Ramones.

Now it's time for the Ooze-It story, since it represents my sole practical
involvement with Clive Barker.

Got a midnight call from Craig Spector requesting a boxload of the
little devils; he'd scoured Manhattan and unearthed nary a one. For those
who toddled in late, an Ooze-It is a disgusting, crater-pocked, Basil Wolver-
ton-sorta plastic alien filled with mucilaginous crimson goo. Squeeze his
distended green belly and the (non-toxic) red glop percolates out through the
nose, eye, ear, and mouth holes to hang in cold, snotty stringers, generally

repelling everyone in the room. Tons of fun. I packed an emergency Ooze-It shipment off New York way principally because I knew one was destined to lend new relevance to Clive Barker's life. Later I saw him at an autograph event and he told me that he and Michael McDowell had used the tiny green guy to thoroughly upchuckify a coffeshop waitress . . . thereby changing *her* life, as well.

These horror writers. Such mad young wags.

Some say Clive resembles Paul McCartney; I can see it, but vote for a touch of Eric Idle as well. He's a furiously fast, intimidatingly intelligent talker, informed (like most in this book) by an unquenchable curiosity. He suffers fools politely and seems infuriatingly patient with even the dullest of dweebs — like the people who show up at autograph parties with a shopping bag-full of books for signing. While Clive talks with you, he'll scribble grotesque illustratons on napkins and suchlike (he did the cover paintings for the newer UK paperbacks of his *Books of Blood*). He read in English Lit and philosophy at university; today he collects pathology texts and attends autopsies as background for what he calls "god stories." Fact is, the sight of his own blood puts him away: "I'm squeamish. If I cut myself, I faint — *wham*, out. Gone. I've passed out in pictures (movies), okay?" As preferred cinema horrors his choices are strong: *Salo*, again, *Viva la Muerta*, and *Le Yeux sans Visage*: "One of the best horror movies ever made." Certainly one of his strangest experiences had to be running open auditions for the part of "a gay, tapdancing cartoon duck" for his play *The Secret Life of Cartoons*. Good quotation: "Subverting Christianity gets my vote any day of the week!"

For Clive, it is with deep regret I announce that the company that manufactures Ooze-Its has gone under. Last ones I saw had *quadrupled* in price. The refills are still around. Send them Clive's way; he's a quantity user.

It is quite fitting that Mick Garris delivered his SILVER SCREAM manuscript to me in a movie theatre on Hollywood Boulevard. The film was a preview of Clive Barker's *Hellraiser*. For more than a decade, Mick and I have been "doing lunch" here, and we have decided that if all other areas of endeavor fail us, we can still break and enter the history books for having invented the Universal Studios Tour Tram Dodge.

It's a fun game that can make anyone an instant celebrity. Now and then, Mick has an office on the lot. Once it was across from the three million dollar structure Universal put up for Steven Spielberg. MCA folks call it the bungalow. Others call it Taco Hell because it looks like a fast-food restaurant. The Universal tour trams buzz it all the time, packed with people dying to glimpse stars. They spy a gaffer, off lunch, wandering back to Stage Four, and assume he *must* be Michael J. Fox. Before tootling off to lunch, Mick and I would lie in wait for the tour tram, and when it passed Taco Hell we'd dash outside, averting our faces from tourist eyes with the classic gesture so many paparazzi know. I guarantee you our photographs are now enshrined in family collections all over the world. It's the cheapest form of immortality I know.

Never was I so happy to see Mick's goofy, congenial mug as the time he used his AmEx card to bail me out of jail. That makes us even for the time I loaned him money to buy food stamps; today his income has more pre-decimal zeros than will fit on the screen of my calculator. He showed me the Secret Way onto the Universal lot (there are several). Mick will tell you he got his start answering phones at Lucasfilm. Prior to that he sang in a band called Horsefeathers and ate a lot of rice. Today he is writer, producer, director, all for real. He knows the politics of moviemaking as keenly as he knows the frustrations of revisions-for-hire and deals that gobble up a year, then die in utero. Since he speaks the language, it's easy to assume he is a glib and superficial Hollywood bullshitter; I'm here to tell you that Mick, the founder of Nice Guy Productions (yeah, really), is one the most considerate, sharp, down-to-earth good guys left on the planet. Somebody should give him a merit badge. I won't tell you the grossest thing he ever did, because his mom would go ashen. He is the creator of Chicken a la Cronenberg, the movie terms "beat-off city" and "knifekill," and he does the best Alfred Hitchcock impersonation ever.

Once upon a different time, a woman Craig Spector had never seen before in his life wrapped him up in a steamy embrace, breathlessly asking how the hell he was, and it had been such a *looong* time, hug, smooch, squeeze. Naturally, she had mistaken Craig for Steve Boyett. This confusion of identity needs to be cleared up right here and now.

Craig is swarthy, swashbuckling, gypsy-like. Steve resembles one of those pale yet dashing British rockers . . . albeit one who has just realized his band has flown to a different airport. Craig is green-eyed and hirsute. Steve is clean-shaven and gray-eyed. If Craig shaved, he would not look like Steve. If Steve grew a beard, he'd look like a fifteen-year-old trying to grow a beard. If Craig shaved, he'd look like Tex Watson. He wears ear studs on one side; Steve, earrings on both sides. Steve can't get away with wearing Craig's fingerless gloves; Craig would look silly in the suspenders and bow ties Steve affects. If this still befuddles you, just look for the badge that reads YES I REALLY DRESS LIKE THIS and that'll let you know you're dealing with . . . uhh . . .

Perhaps confusable with Craig and/or Steve is Jay Sheckley, the only SILVER SCREAM contributor who submitted her measurements (36-24-36) and who complains that "just to see one basic dead body once, I had to crash Stanford and plead research." She admires oodles of scary stuff: the Murnau *Nosferatu* "for beauty alone;" camp grue like *Return of the Living Dead*; "bright creepies w/ desire" such as *The Stuff* and *Eraserhead*. For frightening as opposed to scary, she lists Jimmy Swaggart, Vanna White,

SILVER SCREAM

Divine and the recent articles about NutraSweet. Jay founded HubbyEnders ("to cut back"), has violent hair (which isn't as weird as it sounds), and keeps a wonderful pet parrot that shit on my sofa as soon as we were introduced.

Less likely to be mistaken for Steve and/or Craig is Little Johnny Skipp, horror's Number One Garbage Pail Kid, who waves a big hello from his end of the evolutionary chart, where he'll most likely be found wearing clothes held together with safety pins and duct tape. Want to know what Uncle Creepy looked like as a child? When John grows a beard, he also resembles Johnny Winter in his Jesus phase. His preferred toys are his plastic chainsaw, his Ooze-It, and his red baseball cap with the working clock that says LOVIN' TIME. He opens both sides of his cigarette pack. In public his name is usually followed by "and Craig Spector" since the two collaborate on words and music — in fact, I hope they get famous so my Arcade and John Terlazzo discs accrue value on the collector's market.

What better test of collaborators, said I, than to split them up and see which tenets of their bi-pack fictioneering settle into which camp. It's a mistake to try guessing, from their novels, who wrote what. From New York, John booked to the savage Pennsylvania outback "to unfrazz," where he drinks serious beer, makes novels and girl-babies, and watches television. John is the reason cable and videotape were invented. His favorite horror movies, therefore, equal whatever is in his tape stack at the moment. All the usual stuff everybody's friends collect. But press him into a corner and his choices are indeed considered: *Day of the Dead, Frances, Salvador* and *The Ruling Class.*

John says he's actually better-looking than Craig; he's just waiting for *People* Magazine to acknowledge this. "Not only that," he says, "but I have a bigger shoe size, given my height." And next year, Johnny gets to play editor . . . and bitch and carp about *my* story.

Chances are that by the time you read this, Steve Boyett will have regrown his hair. I shot a bunch of photos the night before he had it all chopped off; to this day he moons over the photos, bemoaning its loss. If you find any of it, please mail it back and mend his busted heart.

Like most weird habits, Steve's weirdest is superficially prosaic: He clips coupons. Wearing his bathrobe and his owl-sized eyeglasses (strictly contacts, in public), he snips coupons for "important stuff like M&Ms and gooshy kid crap you only find coupons for in the Sunday funnies." During the course of a *single* videocassette he'll consume an entire bag of Chips Ahoy and two pints of strawberry Haagen Dazs; then chug a quart of coffee, yell and wave his arms for forty-five minutes, then collapse into a sugar coma of near-suicidal malaise, spitting froggy croaks at any mortal who dares phone him while his systems are crashing.

Steve is one of the few men I know who has successfully attracted women by sitting at a bus stop and looking forlorn. Peter Gabriel changed his

366

life. He shoots a fair game of eight-ball, his William F. Buckley impersonation is good, and his banana-walnut-brown sugar pancakes are sumptuous.
He bestows presents and commemorates birthdays with style. Once a book
of his *that was never published* found its way onto a recommended-reading
list. There are two things he wants all his fans to know: He will never, ever
write a sequel to *Ariel* no matter how much you say you liked it. And he
hates your cat, no matter how much you say *he'll* like it. Leave him alone
with your kitty and he'll probably crack it like a whip. Meow.

Cultural Mulch Puppy and Lord of the Bastard Subculture, Craig
Spector (see Steve Boyett, above) loves wallowing in trendspeak, multiple
input, sensory overload, flash to the max and undiluted adrenaline. He
wants to be a rockstar when he grows up. But he ain't never gonna grow up,
nor will he ever be busted by the Style Gestapo. He argues with religious
fanatics in parks and is considering a career in televangelism. When he and
John Skipp worked for Educated & Dedicated Messengers in Manhattan,
John walked, Craig did it on roller skates. He talks with his mouth full. He
does dishes whenever you phone him. He enjoys meatless food and hitting
things. To him, music and novels are differentiated solely by the type of
keyboard required for composition. Since nobody else wants to claim the
title of First Novelist to Use a Word Processor from the Very Beginning,
Craig votes *yo*. Technology is his pal and Sweetouchnee Tea is his crank, his
drug of choice, the rocket fuel that will hyperburn him ever-closer to his goal
of Multimedia Stud. He's frenetic, he's totally nuclear, he's *in your face*. He
is, saints preserve us, the future. Stay tuned for the video.

Jay Sheckley just phoned to change all her favorite horror films to *The
Lost Boys*. Craig will approve — though he voted for *Threads*: "It was so
devastating that I had to take another hour and a half just to reassemble
myself. I found myself in a store, staring at cans of Pac Man Spaghetti-O's,
thinking that maybe I should stock up."

My solemn duty to the English language compels me to share with you
Joe Lansdale's warning about his own story: "This'un's a toughy. It'll knock
your dick in the dirt."

Joe no longer pilots a pickup truck; today he drives one of those roller
skate cars that, as James Crumley says, the Japanese have shamed America
into manufacturing. He holds forth from a jerkwater Texas hamlet called
Nacogdoches, where he just moved to the outskirts because it had become
too urban for him. He drawls. He can also sling some of the most brain-
damaged expression — colloquial and facial — that have ever made me shoot
fizzy drinks out my nose in public. It is impossible for me to see John Bloom
as Joe Bob Briggs, since I've had Lansdale's Huckleberry Hound mug cast in
that role from the git. Joe is hellaciously talented, a broad-spectrum writer
whose distinctive regional voice has matured into an arrestingly hardboiled
style, and it's about time the Western Writers of America gave him a Spur

SILVER SCREAM

Award. If Joe and I and Richard Christian Matheson took dinner, restaurant patrons would automatically assume that a noose-twiddling good ole boy and a crazed Satanist had abducted some nice young man from Woodland Hills and were doing vile things to his Gold Card.

Ray Garton looks like he needs a spanking. At least, that is what Mistress Chiffon told him during a "purely for research" visit to a North Hollywood B&D parlor. He is the only writer I know who is named after a disease. I can't tell you about that, though Ray, in his utterly convincing victim mode, will maintain that "my blood and urine has traveled to more places than *I* ever will." Catch him on the phone and he will relate a litany his week's horrors — tales of peculiar sightings and death threats, of being accosted or exploited, of mysterious portents. The new Lee Harvey Oswald sits in Ray's writing class. Once, while parked with a coed in the hills near Union Pacific College, he claims to have seen a lizard man scaling a sheer cliff. Soon afterward, a student at the college vanished. Or was found dismembered. Ray says the monster did it.

Ray is hopelessly smitten with junk culture and outrageous gestures. *Decolletage* makes him crazy. He was once struck slack-jawed by a woman he spotted in a credit card commercial, so he unearthed her number, phoned her machine in New York, and as a result dated her the very first time she visited LA. He adores horning in on radio talk shows, faithfully watches Oprah and Donahue, and his highest goal is to appear on the Letterman show. Chapel Records offered him a contract while he was still in high school: "They wanted me to *sing* for them." He once cast me as a murderer in a novel. "My favorite fright scene in any movie," he says, "is when John Wayne looks up in *The Greatest Story Ever Told* and says, 'Truly this man was the son of God.'" Ray's only 25 this year, with five novels in his wake already, so yeah — he's a hotshot long in advance of the "Jesus Age."

Which brings us back to that spy in the house of love, Richard Christian Matheson, brought to you at a cost of millions, after years of painstaking revision.

It is to our benefit that Richard — or "RC," a shortform that always prompts me to ask for a Moon Pie — laughed in the face of a high ticket career as a male model while still a teenager. Instead he has formented, initially, he says, as an "experiment," a fascinating writing style that seeks an ultimate concision — distilling phrases, simmering descriptions to their essence to yield a contemporary form of literary poetry much like punchy blank verse. Which is why, if you blink in this era of "fat books sell," Richard's output might evade your eye by its very brevity. Some of his best short stories are 400 words long. And he constantly returns to them, trimming, reducing, condensing, in search of sharpness. We spent ten minutes debating over whether a single word should be dropped from "Hell." One sentence took half an hour to re-evaluate. That is why it has taken his entire career, which spans hundreds of TV and movie scripts written just as tersely, to produce one thin book of his short fiction.

But short is in no wise trivial, and his focus is anything but casual. More like obsessive; you get the idea he really means it. As Joe Lansdale says, "The Devil is right behind Richard with a whip."

He writes songs; and says each of his stories was built to a specific tune. If you ask, he'll name the tune. "Hell"'s background music is obvious. "Sirens" was done with "Needle and the Damage Done" in mind. He's a drummer, and confers that importance of rhythm onto his fiction. He writes comedy, so his wit is quick, keen. His own laughter is robust. I get the impression that he is not surprised as much as he would like to be — by people, by events, by other lives.

When we're not knotting the phone lines with after-midnight discourse, sometimes we are aimlessly zipping up and down the Coast Highway in his Space Porsche, which contains more blinking console lights than the Millenium Falcon. It's all high-tech cellular phones and compact disc players and until Richard stopped smoking it was *all* covered in cigarette ashes. One of his fondest childhood aspirations was to have a "fly-vision" TV (like that mentioned in Mark Arnold's story) so he could watch all channels at once. He writes eleven movies at a time. He goes to sextuplet drive-ins and tilts his car mirrors to see several movies simultaneously. Again, he feels the need for speed. He probably watches videotapes on high-scan.

He rates two stories because double features are something I've never stopped liking.

(You can relax now, Richard. See? I didn't give away any of the Good Stuff.)

Voila — end credits. The storytellers whom this book was brought to you by. Plus a few others: Melissa Singer, for proposing the outrageous; Stan Wiater, for smoothing the bumpy road to Providence, and thanks to Tappan King, T.E.D. Klein, Alan Rodgers and Dave Silva, just because.

Nine thousand-plus words may be a world record for this sort of windy foma, but the people behind these words continue to enrich my life more than they may know, and besides, Bob Bloch encouraged my experimentation with the usually turgid "author piece."

Now go back and read the stories again.

— David J. Schow
September 1987.

This book is dedicated to
DAVID CRONENBERG
Long Live the New Flesh